Frances Milton Trollope, James H. Graff

Uncle Walter

Frances Milton Trollope, James H. Graff

Uncle Walter

ISBN/EAN: 9783743393165

Manufactured in Europe, USA, Canada, Australia, Japa

Cover: Foto ©Raphael Reischuk / pixelio.de

Manufactured and distributed by brebook publishing software (www.brebook.com)

Frances Milton Trollope, James H. Graff

Uncle Walter

MR. CHARLES LEVER'S WORKS.

Wit   hiz."

DAV   s.
ONE
THE
JAC
TOM
HAR
CHA
THE
THE
ROL
THE
THE

T   must,
like tl   find a
place   n pro-
ductions of fiction have gained a greater reputation for their writer:
few authors equal him in the humour and spirit of his delineation of
character, and none surpass him for lively descriptive power and never-
flagging story: and the whole Press of the United Kingdom has
lavished the highest encomiums upon his works.

CHAPMAN AND HALL, 193, Piccadilly, London.

CHARLES O'MALLEY, THE IRISH DRAGOON.

BY CHARLES LEVER.

TWO VOLS.

"The whole character of Mickey Free is indeed inimitable. We have no hesitation in affirming it to be the most perfect type of Irish humour that has ever been given to the world. It is perfectly sustained from first to last, and nothing in the conception of it is exaggerated or incongruous. Mickey Free is the Irish Sam Weller. He has, in fact, this advantage over Sam Weller, that he is the more thoroughly national and comprehensive type of the two. It is impossible but what this creation, which is in many respects the most felicitous of all Mr. Lever's creations, should live for ever **as a distinct** embodiment of national character."

ONE OF THEM.

BY CHARLES LEVER.

"The novels of Charles Lever, republished in a cheap form, must prove most acceptable to a very large portion of the readers of works of fiction. There is no modern writer who has thrown so much of genial mirth, such native humour, such a collection of humorous incidents, into his stories. There is a raciness in its humour that we look for in vain in the crowd of novel writers of the present day; and, combined with this native humour and ready wit, there are so many life-like sketches of character, so many touches of a master's hand, that one does not so much read of, as speak to and with, the leading characters to whom the reader is introduced."—*Observer*

CHAPMAN AND HALL, 193, Piccadilly, London.

UNCLE WALTER.

BY

MRS. TROLLOPE,

AUTHOR OF

"GERTRUDE," "YOUNG HEIRESS," "MRS. MATHEWS,"

ETC. ETC.

A NEW EDITION.

LONDON:

CHAPMAN AND HALL, 193, PICCADILLY.

UNCLE WALTER.

CHAPTER I.

'Twas a brilliant Sunday in the month of May, 184—; and the world of London was doing its best to look as like the festive time as its natural smoke-grimed complexion, and its respectable Sunday duties would permit. But both these circumstances were rather against the attempt. The glad brightness of the sun, it is true, almost contrived to gild the heavy masses of smoke which eternally overhang the metropolis of the world's workshop, and a large portion of its inhabitants were, it is also true, doing their best to enjoy the day, after the various fashions of their different ranks and classes.

That is to say, a pretty considerable majority of them were substituting occupations which they professed to believe sinful, for the duties which they professed to believe obligatory, but which they indisputably found disagreeable.

Among the more dignified and select classes of society it might indeed seem that very little could be gained by this bold emancipation from ecclesiastical restraint; for a dusty drive round the park seems, at least to the profane vulgar, not many degrees more agreeable than the dreamy imprisonment for longsome hours in a hot church, as prescribed by most

1

Anglican ministers. Nevertheless, the influence of the park, versus the pulpit, avails to ensure a sufficient number of lordly sabbath-breakers, to make it abundantly clear to the great unwashed, that their rulers were only humbugging them when they enacted Sabbath Observance Bills, and harangued against the wickedness of all popular Sunday recreations.

It was probably this not very unaccountable conviction, combined with the acknowledged sinfulness of human nature, which filled the streets, suburban tea-gardens, railway excursion trains, and all other haunts of plebeian pleasure with the teeming population; while, on the Sunday afternoon on which our narrative commences, many a metropolitan preacher was left in a degree of abandonment approaching that which reduced the Dean of St. Patrick's to the well-remembered formulary, "Dearly beloved Roger, the Scripture moveth you and me."

Indeed, on the particular Sunday in May of which we have been speaking, the streets of London presented in more than ordinary degree a variety of sights and sounds grievous to the eyes and ears of good churchmen, and legislative Sabbatarians; for it was the first Sunday of genial, bright May weather which the lagging spring of 184— had yet produced.

Thousands were thronging forth from their close, crowded homes, and dim alleys, to solace their toilsome lives with such pale pleasures as the law permits, or to indulge in those dearer stolen delights which the wisdom of our law-makers have rendered immoral, by pronouncing them illegal.

Great had been the disgust and indignation produced that day, by irreligious apple-women and rebellious news-vendors, on the well-regulated mind of the Reverend Henry Harrington, Doctor of Divinity, Warden of All Saints' College in the University of Oxford, Prebendary of the Cathedral Church of Glastonbury, and Rector of a large and wealthy parish at the west end of the metropolis. Very great and very fervent had been his indignation, as he was returning home with his family in their carriage after the exemplary discharge of their morning duties.

For many weeks past had the worthy Dr. Harrington been engaged in a vigorous attempt to put down, overcome, and annihilate these particularly scandalous offences against religion and decorum, within the bounds of his own parish; but the inefficiency of the law, or the supine apathy of the secular arm which should have enforced its provisions, had ill seconded his laudable endeavours; and apples and newspapers were still sold under his very nose every Sunday, to his great and very painful irritation.

The outrage thus offered to his professional feelings had tinged the usually placid temper of this excellent divine with a slight exacerbation, which in some sort spoiled his enjoyment of the neat little hot luncheon which awaited his return from the morning service, though it was as usual invitingly spread, and as usual in a peculiarly snug room of that peculiarly comfortably residence, which called the Rector of St. Martin's in the West its master.

This room indeed was a most enviable sanctum: but we must now take the liberty of following him to its privacy.

Enough has already been said to convince the reader that the Warden of All Saints was what the world very justly calls, and considers, a fortunate man; yet the entire catalogue of good things that had fallen to his share has not yet been rehearsed; and while he is employed in taking off his beautifully starched bands, washing his white hands, and pouring a little eau de Cologne on his delicate cambric handkerchief before addressing himself to the refreshment just placed upon his table, we will give a brief sketch of Dr. Harrington's past history, and present social position.

His father, the Rev. John Harrington, had held the family living of Stanton Parva; which was a snug piece of preferment, worth about seven hundred a-year, with a population under two hundred, the said population being wholly composed of the household of Stanton Hall, the ancestral seat of the Harringtons, and of the tenants and labourers on their property.

Although this Rev. John Harrington, who held the living, was some five years younger than his brother Walter, who held the estate, the Rector was the father of a couple of sons, some ten or twelve years old, before the squire was married, and it can hardly be supposed that the congratulations from the Rectory to the Hall, when this event at length took place, where wholly unmixed with a feeling of disappointment.

The Rector, excusably enough perhaps under the circumstances of the case, had lived up to the extent of his income, and now there were two boys to be educated, who had to make their way in the world.

However, the Squire was a good brother, and lent a helping hand, and the two boys were sent to one of those provincial schools whose merit is more to be found in the scholarships and fellowships, which the local partialities of pious founders have indefeasibly established in our universities, than in the particularly brilliant educational powers attributed to the management of them.

It seems strange that these worthy founders and benefactors should have been so ignorant, or careless, of the inevitable fact, that by such bequests they were for the most part providing a very powerfully operative premium on idleness and dunce-hood. But thus it is. The notions which are self-evident to every school-boy in one generation, were in a previous age truths too recondite to be discovered by the wisdom of sages.

In the case before us, however, the good things provided by the founder of All Saints' College for the natives of the hundred of Whippleshaw who should be educated on the foundation of Frambury school and proceed thence to All Saints in the University of Oxford, failed to produce the mischief alluded to. Of Walter Harrington, indeed, the Rev. Theophilus Porsonby could make nothing at all; but of Henry, his younger brother (whom we left washing his hands, while his butler was waiting for the bell that should summon his luncheon), he made, despite her assured fellowship, an excellent scholar.

And it must be admitted, moreover, that this latter result was extremely creditable to the scholarly tastes and habits of Dr. Porsonby, for nothing but a genuine love for learning could have induced him to take any trouble in the matter, the mastership of Frambury school being richly endowed by the same munificent founder who had built the venerable halls of All Saints.

The master was indeed bound by the statutes to teach Latin, Greek, and chanting, to all such poor students born in a certain district, as should present themselves; but in the course of ages it came to pass, that very few of the inhabitants of the hundred of Whippleshaw cared to be taught Latin, Greek, and chanting, so that the richly paid mastership of Frambury school became by degrees very like a sinecure; and would no doubt have become so quite, had it not been for the bribe held out to students in the shape of the scholarships.

Dr. Porsonby had just sent off his own son brim full of "Adam's Antiquities," and Greek plays, to enjoy the bounties of the pious founder; and had literally no recipient for the overflowing treasures of his erudition, when the two Harrington boys were sent to him.

It is quite clear that the most palmy state and most perfect beau-ideal of a richly endowed school must be to have no pupils at all, as evidently as it is that of an unendowed school to have the greatest number possible ; so that the labour bestowed by the good Doctor on the education of Walter and Henry Harrington, can be regarded in no other light than as a true labour of love.

The first half-yearly report, sent home with the two boys from Frambury to Stanton Parva at the holidays, informed their father that Walter had been a little unruly, and not a little idle ; but that his brother Henry was a model of application, and manifested dispositions of the highest promise.

The subsequent half-year brought with them further bulletins of exactly similar import, till, in the year which made Walter fourteen and Henry thirteen, Dr. Porsonby wrote to Mr. Harrington, explicitly declaring that he feared it was but too clear that his eldest son was wholly averse to intellectual pursuits, his utmost efforts having proved unavailing in leading him to perceive in "Virgil" higher beauties than were to be found iu "Robinson Crusoe," which in truth was the only book that he ever seemed to open willingly. He had brought with him, from home, as it appeared, a copy of that idle work, which had unfortunately had the effect of withdrawing his mind from all useful studies to a most lamentable degree. The learned gentleman added, that he could not but take that occasion to remark how very pernicious it was to permit lads to obtain any access to modern literature during the precious years of youth, which ought to be devoted to laying on the solid rock of classical learning, the foundation of a truly liberal education.

On other points, however, the Doctor seemed quite ready to avow that Master Walter Harrington was not a bad boy ; far from it indeed, for he manifested many amiable qualities, and was a particular favourite with Mrs. Porsonby. Nevertheless, he added, he could not but feel that he should fail in his duty if he omitted to inform Mr. Harrington, that he saw no probability that his eldest son would achieve any satisfactory success in the noble career that had been marked out for him.

Of the younger boy, Dr. Porsonby had the satisfaction

of reporting very differently. The only book that had
ever been found in the hands of Harrington, junior, beside
the immortal master-pieces of Greece and Rome, was a little
work that contained detailed information respecting all the
scholarships and fellowships in the University of Oxford, their
value, and the conditions and methods of election to them.

His progress in his studies had been most satisfactory; and
if it pleased God, said the Doctor in conclusion, that he should
succeed during the ensuing half-year in imbuing the young
gentleman's mind with the spirit of Aristophanes, as
thoroughly as he had grounded him in that of the great
tragedian, he doubted not that he would live to be a comfort
to his family, and an honour to his country.

Now it so happened, that much about the time when this
discouraging report of his eldest son reached the Rev. Mr.
Harrington, the Squire's lady at the Hall had presented her
husband with a fine boy; thus definitively cutting off any
lingering hope the younger brother might have still suffered
to lurk in his heart, that his own son might inherit the acres
which had been so long attached to his race. It also happened much about the same time, that a cousin of the family
was on a visit to the Hall, who had just returned from
Australia, and was about to proceed thither again. He had
originally gone out with about two thousand pounds, together
with a fine stock of health, energy, and industry. All these
talents had increased and multiplied. He was now the owner
of some thirty thousand sheep, and the father of a large
family. He was an intelligent, bright, laughing-eyed, broad-
shouldered man of five-and-forty, and an excellent good
fellow. He and the young Walter became great friends,
and soon fell into the habit of taking long rambles together
over the surrounding country. The intelligence which had
remained so perversely closed to the beauties of Horace, and
the merits of Greek metres, seemed to kindle and expand
readily enough as the boy listened to Cousin George's accounts
of the stirring life he had been leading in the Bush, and the
varied incidents of a settler's struggle with the elements of
nature, on a soil not yet subjugated to the uses of civilized
man.

At length, and nearly on the eve of Mr. George Harrington's departure for Sydney, he proposed to Walter's father
to take the boy with him to that young world where no man
endowed with health, courage, and intelligence can be a

burden to his fellows, and there to put him in a fair way
to find his own path in the world, in a manner that should be
more congenial to his nature than the learned career in which
he had so signally failed.

Walter himself was delighted with the proposal much
beyond his power of expressing the strength of his approval.

To cross the ocean, to see new countries where there were
primeval forests and real wild men, and never to hear mention
of prosody more, appeared to him an exuberance of good-
fortune almost beyond the bounds of credibility.

To the worthy Rector, who was just then very sadly at a
loss as to what he should do with a stalwart boy of fourteen,
over whose indocile mind all the culture of the Rev. Theophilus Ponsonby had passed bootless as water over a duck's
back, the offer was far too good, and too commodious to be
rejected.

And so, despite some natural reluctance on the part of poor
Mrs. Harrington, whose motherly love had been in no degree
diminished by her Walter's short-comings in the career of a
scholar, it was speedily determined that the offer of Cousin
George should be accepted with all thankfulness.

Cousin George was not one of those that let the grass grow
under their feet, and but little time was suffered to elapse
after the offer had been made and accepted, before he started
with his young friend for his home at the antipodes. And
thus Walter Harrington, with many blessings from father and
mother, and a present of five hundred pounds from his uncle,
the Squire, had a second start offered him in the race of
life.

With what success he pursued it we cannot now inquire,
for it could only be done at the cost of keeping his learned
brother a most unconscionably long time waiting for his
luncheon. We must, however, hereafter take time to say a
few words concerning that learned brother's subsequent
fortunes. But this is a topic, the discussion of which we
would wait for patiently, especially as nothing can be stated
concerning it but what must be altogether pleasant for him to
hear.

CHAPTER II.

THE course along the railroad in which Henry Harrington had been appointed to run, by the regulations of the sage founder of All Saints, was perfectly smooth and uninterrupted.

From being a scholar on the foundation of Frambury he became in due course a scholar at All Saints. From a scholar of that magnificent institution he became by the natural operation of time, and a regular consumption of "commons," a fellow of the same.

And here he might have stopped. Thus far the mere fact of being a native of Whippleshaw Hundred, and a pupil at Frambury Grammar School, would have advanced him; but for his further advancement he was altogether indebted to his own abilities and qualifications.

Without the dignified propriety of demeanour, and courteous suavity of address, for which he was distinguished, he never would have attained the position in which we find him.

Nor could this have sufficed alone to make him what he was. Neither his dignity nor his courtesy would have been so rewarded, had not their effect been aided by that profound far-sighted and ever-present perception of the side on which his bread would ultimately be found to be buttered, which, in the opinion of the majority of mankind, constitutes virtue. Without all this he never would have been Warden of All Saints, Prebendary of Glastonbury, or Rector of St. Martin's in the West.

When chosen Warden of All Saints by the votes of the majority of the fellows, the Rev. Henry Harrington was in his fortieth year. But regular habits, ease both of body and mind, a daily "constitutional," and daily dinner eaten,

"Untaxed, untroubled, under
The portrait of the pious founder,"

joined to a naturally well-formed frame, and good constitution, made him still a young and very comely-looking man.

Regular and well-shaped, though rather heavy features, coal-black hair, eye-brows and eyes, a clear healthy-looking complexion, and a stature of six feet without his shoes, were gifts which, joined to a generally placid and easy temper, rendered the Rev Mr. Harrington a very popular man at this period of his life in more circles than that of the common room at All Saints.

It was about the same time, and just previous to his election to the headship of his college, that he had been called to Stanton Parva by the sudden death of his father, an event which put him into possession of the family living; for the Squire of the family for the time being, had no second son to present to it.

So the fortunate Henry was presented to the living, and about the same time to a lady, who within a month or two afterwards became his wife. This was no other than the Lady Augusta Withers, third daughter of the Earl of Bentley. The match was promoted and approved by all the members of both families, so the world could not but consider the union as a highly proper one. The world did so consider it, and poured in congratulations and cards accordingly; and none but envious old maids, sulky bachelors, and others of the small fungus tribe, whose conduct must appear detestable to all well-constituted minds, were sufficiently illiberal to speculate whether the reverend gentleman would have thrown himself and his fellowship at the feet of the Lady Augusta, if it had not chanced that his Oxford letters brought him news that the Warden was given over, and that he felt himself pretty sure of succeeding him.

Neither, perhaps, might the Lady Augusta's heart, and her father's unqualified approbation of the connection have been so readily obtained (if we may believe such envious gossipings) had not the indiscreet "Peerage" of those days made patent to all the world that her graceful Ladyship had attained her thirty-fifth year. Such suggestions are really odious! But in spite of them, the parties were joined together in very holy wedlock; and it would be well if as much could be truly said of half the *soi-disant* holy wedlocks which the world witnesses.

Their married life passed smoothly and prosperously; successive pieces of preferment had made the Warden a wealthy man, and his aristocratic marriage had greatly assisted him in obtaining such a standing in the fashionable world as suited his own tastes and propensities, as well as those of his high-born partner.

Their union had been blessed with three children. Henry, the eldest, was now eight-and-twenty; James, the second son, who was in holy orders, was twenty-five; and their sister Catherine had just completed her nineteenth year. This clerical son James, was now rector of the family living of Stanton Parva, his father having resigned in his favour.

Now the reader is in possession of all the particulars of the history and present position of the Rev. Dr. Harrington, which it is needful for him to be acquainted with at this period of our story. If the uniformity of all this prosperity was, as may well be supposed, not altogether unchequered by annoyances and vexations less apparent to the world in general than his brilliant success had been, it is probable that the reader may discover them, as well as the sources from whence they sprung, in the course of that more intimate acquaintance with his family to which it is our purpose to introduce him.

And now it is high time that the exhausted dignitary should be supplied with the refreshment, which his morning's exertions have made so necessary to him.

"Send Hutchinson to me," said the Doctor to the footman, who was putting his appetizing little repast on his study-table; and as he spoke he sank into the morocco easy-chair which had been just wheeled to the said table with the air of a man extenuated with fatigue.

He had preached that morning, and was to do so again in the afternoon; and it is probable enough, as the day was warm, and he, though a fine well-preserved old man, was of rather a full habit of body, that he did feel the need of a little stimulus.

For the Doctor was now seventy. The once abundant black hair, though nearly as plentiful as ever, was perfectly white; the florid complexion, though still clear, had become of a deeper hue than the consulting physician of an insurance-office would have approved; the full rich tone of his voice, though still mellow and powerful, had been rendered some-what thick by years and good living, and the burly propor-tions of his person, which were well carried off by his six feet of stature, though they did exceed sixteen stone, rested on supporters which, to judge by his outline of them as shown by the close-fitting long black gaiters, might be warranted to carry any weight.

Add to these particulars an abundant double chin reposing on a still more abundant cushion of soft cambric, a still bright eye and a large good-humoured mouth, still very tolerably well filled with stout teeth, and you will have a very fair notion of the Warden of All Saints in his seventieth year.

Hutchinson was a contemporary of the Warden's, had risen through the various grades of College service from scout to common-room man, and now filled the easy and dignified post of butler and confidential servant, to which he had been promoted at the time of the Doctor's election to the headship.

He was a long bony dry old man, as tall as his master, but very much less stout, with a knowing shrewd expression of features, and a nose into which many successive pipes of common-room port-wine had contributed to infuse a bright shade of ruddy hue, which gradually deepening in intensity became a glowing purple at its extremity.

Hutchinson loved his master much, and venerated him more, for in his order of ideas the most important and most venerable spot upon the earth's surface was Oxford, and the most important and greatest man in Oxford was the Warden of All Saints. Oxford was the central sun of Hutchinson's cosmogony, London England, the world were but greater or less outflying planets which revolved round it.

Such was the respectable functionary who now presented himself at the door of the Doctor's study.

"Hutchinson," said the Doctor, in a languid voice, "I won't take any sherry to-day; let me have a glass of the twenty-two India Madeira. I really am worn out."

"Of course, Sir! of course! These great crowded London churches is fit for nothing but a strong young curate to preach in. I hope, Sir, you are not a-going to preach again this afternoon?"

"I must, Hutchinson! I must," returned the Doctor; "the world expects it of me."

"The world ought to be taught," returned Hutchinson, doggedly, "that the properest place for the Warden of All Saints to preach in is All Saints' College chapel; and if he takes to a London parish for the good of the church, it is as much as they can expect of him to read the Commandments and the Gospel at the altar now and then. That's what I say."

"Well, Hutchinson, bring the Madeira, and reach me that bundle of sermons from my writing-table."

The Doctor helped himself to some pulled turkey from a covered silver dish that stood before him, added a few delicate green peas to it from another silver dish, and proceeded while eating to look over the pile of sermons he had referred to, in order to select one for his afternoon's discourse.

They were the first-fruits of the Doctor's ecclesiastical labours, having been written by him during the early years of his incumbency of Stanton Parva, and preached to the two hundred rustics which formed his congregation there.

The Doctor had a great objection to clergymen preaching sermons which were not their own composition. To do so, he argued, was to abandon all attempt at supplying the peculiar teaching which every different congregation required according to its circumstances and condition.

On the present occasion, he felt desirous of touching severely on those street desecrations of the Sabbath, which had given him such offence on his way home from the morning service. So he selected one which had been written at a time when the country around Stanton Parva had been infested by Swing riots and incendiary fires. The text had been taken from the 7th verse of the 28th chapter of the Book of Proverbs: "Whoso keepeth the law is a wise son, but he that is a companion of a riotous man shameth his father."

This text was evidently admirably adapted to the case of the apple-women. So the sermon required only a few alterations, here and there, to render it exactly what was needed for the peculiar teaching required at that especial juncture by the parish of St. Martin's in the West.

Thus, in the following passage, a few words only were required to be changed. In the Stanton Parva discourse it had stood written: "Nor in our own neighbourhood, my brethren, have there been wanting signs and portentous warnings, which speak trumpet-tongued to every thoughtful and pious mind, of the especial dangers of these latter days! Dangerous doctrines are abroad, and we read them translated into deeds of lawless violence and terror, in things that are passing round us."

The latter phrases were, he thought, perhaps a trifle too strong for the apple-women, but a stroke of the Doctor's pen

rapidly changed them into the softened epithets of "lawless
indecency" and "alarming impiety." Then followed:
"Hideous anarchy has invaded our peaceful *villages*"
(which was altered to *streets*, "and no man can any
longer feel that his *life and property* are secure" (altered to
church and religion)

Towards the close of the discourse, an entirely new
passage was inserted to complete its perfect adaptation to the
occasion. It ran thus:—

"But painful, my brethren, grievously painful to every
thinking mind as are all these evidences of the prelude of a
subversive and irreligious spirit among our people, there is no
one symptom which so irresistibly proves that the insidious
poison of revolutionary doctrines have spread among the
masses of the population, as the shameless, the revolting
practice of openly desecrating the Sabbath and defying the
police, by carrying on a traffic demoralizing alike to purchaser
and vendor in the public streets. For what guilt can be
worse than his who seeks to make a profit of the wickedness
of that portion of the community whose tender years lay
them most open to insidious temptation? And is it not an
additional aggravation, which deepens indignation into horror,
and nurtures disgust into loathing, when the sex of the
tempter is that in which every pure feeling, and every holy
instinct should lead to the shedding of tears over the loss of
the young soul thus lured to destruction?"

The Doctor was getting rapidly into the highest regions of
the pathetic, and was polishing off a peroration, in the construction of which he had got a little hampered between "sin
against the Holy Ghost," and overt rebellion against the
police, when he was admonished by a silvery sound from the
little time-piece on the chimney, that it was already half-past
two o'clock.

So he was obliged to draw his pen through the straggling
members of the unfinished sentence, and to give up a very
forcible parallel which he had intended to draw between the
first apple which caused the universal fall of man, and those
later specimens of the same ill-starred fruit, which were every
Sunday causing the still deeper fall of so many of the children
of men.

He hastily poured out a second glass of Madeira, rose with
a sigh from his easy chair, and ringing for the footman, sent
him to ask the Lady Augusta whether she intended to go to

church, or whether her Ladyship needed the carriage else-where.

The answer which was speedily brought back, stated that her Ladyship did not feel equal to attending church a second time that day, and that she should be glad of the carriage at half-past four, which would just give time for it to bring him back from church.

The good Doctor had feared that he might very possibly have had to make that journey on foot. The distance, indeed, was not above a couple of hundred yards, so it was not on the score of bodily fatigue that he disliked the walk, but he did not think it seemly, he said, that when lawyers, bankers, and merchants, were taken up at the church door in their own carriages, that a dignified representative of the ecclesiastical hierarchy should be seen to wend his way among them on foot. God knew that he cared as little as most men for the pomps and vanities of life, but it was impossible not to feel that the Church must lose station and influence if her aristocracy were not placed on a level with that of other professions. Different tasks were assigned by Providence to different labourers in the Lord's vineyards; it was the duty of some to carry the precepts and consolations of religion to the poor and lowly, and it was well that the Church should be provided with ministers whose social position did not place them at too great an elevation above that of their flocks. On him had been imposed the surely more onerous task of making the glad tidings of salvation acceptable to the great ones of the earth, and it behoved him to take his station on the vantage-ground of a distinguished social position accordingly.

These were the considerations which made it agreeable to him to have a handsome, well-appointed equipage waiting at the church door to take him home after the service.

So to this message from her Ladyship he graciously answered: "Tell your mistress that I will take care to be in time," and then turning to the handsome glass over the chimney, he was in the very act of tying on his bands, when a gentle knock was heard at his study door.

"Come in, Kate, my dear!" said the Doctor, for he knew beyond the possibility of mistake, that the modest little tap came from no other fingers than those of his young daughter. "But say what you have to say in half a minute," he added, as she opened the door, "for that is all the time I have to spare before starting for church."

"My errand may be easily packed into that short space, papa," returned the young lady, "for I only came to bring you this letter, which was given to mamma by mistake when we returned from church this morning; and to say that if Mr. White and Mr. Caldwell are to dine here to-day, she thinks it would be less insufferably dull if you were to ask the Miss Wigginsvilles to come in the evening. You will be sure, you know, to see some of them at church."

"Oh!—a letter from my brother Walter, I see," said the Doctor, taking it from his daughter's hand. "That will keep very well till to-morrow morning. Yes, my dear, if I should see either of the spinsters, tell your mother, that I will ask them," and so saying the old gentleman bustled off to church, and Kate returned up stairs to report the result of her embassy, and then to retire to her room to make her carriage toilet in preparation for her drive to the park with her mother.

CHAPTER III.

THE reader has had a peep at the Doctor in his *sanctum sanctorum*, in the snug little study which was situated behind the dining-room in his house, No. 5, in one of those quiet aristocratic streets immediately to the east of Park Lane. We will call it Vale Street for the purpose of our tale.

It will probably be now expected that we should present the Lady Augusta Harrington to him; and this, I believe, would be doing things in the proper order, and it cannot be denied that etiquette ought to have great weight in all things appertaining to No. 5, Vale Street; but, nevertheless, I cannot resist the temptation which the course of the narrative seems to offer, of introducing my favourite Kate, while the Warden is in church putting down apple-vending Sabbath-breakers, and Lady Augusta is in the drawing-room, with her friend Lady de Paddington, who had dropped in after morning church for the advantage of enjoying a little quiet chat with her.

Having described her reverend papa's *sanctum sanctorum*, we will now describe hers. It was two stories nearer the sky than that of the Doctor, and was situated over the back drawing-room—nay, her special premises extended also over the boudoir which stretched beyond the said back drawing-room—and an excellent bed-room and dressing-room might have been made out of the apartment thus situated; but Kate had arranged her little territory otherwise. The small room over the boudoir contented her both for bed-room and dressing-room, and thus the really handsome-sized room over the second drawing-room, was available for securing the dear delight of an independent sitting-room, *all her own*.

This much-prized retreat, furnished according to her own fancy, stored with her own properties, and sacred to her own employments and pursuits, Kate styled her "cell," in con-tradistinction to her reverend father's "study," and her lady mother's "boudoir." Shall we indulge ourselves with a glance at the plenishing of Kate's "cell," while she has gone to put on her bonnet? Much may be divined, as any naturalist can tell us, respecting any creature from a minute and intelligent examination of its *habitat*.

Kate's domain was most fortunately situated, for an opposite break in the buildings of Park Lane opened to her high windows a full view of the park, and of the noble woods of Kensington beyond it. This view was Kate's great joy and pride, and she was at this time intent upon a grand scheme of getting her windows cut down to the floor, and having a little conservatory constructed, balcony-wise, outside them.

There were difficulties in the way of this project: not arising from the expense, for Kate was in the happy position of having wherewithal to gratify her tastes, without making any inroads on the large, but quite sufficiently bespoken income of her father; for a maiden aunt of his, who had died at an advanced age some six years before, had left her the whole of her snug little fortune of seven hundred a-year, the trustees of which paid fifty pounds on each quarter day into her own fair hands, and an equal sum into those of the Doctor, for her maintenance. So the cost of the much longed-for con-servatory did not present much difficulty, for the reasonable Mr. Banbury, of Lincoln's Inn, Kate's acting trustee, made no objection to supplying, from Kate's accumulated savings, the needful funds.

But the Doctor had fears for the solidity of his excellent house, and doubts how far its walls might be safely trusted to bear such an additional burthen, as must be occasioned by the picturesque excrescence projected by his daughter. The Doctor was very subject to fears for the stability of constituted things, and being with good reason exceedingly well contented with the world as it is, he was strongly attached to the wisdom which counsels to "let well alone."

In this difficulty, Kate built considerable hope on the assistance of the Mr. Caldwell who has been mentioned as having been invited to dinner on that day; for the said Mr. Caldwell, though not an architect, but an officer in the Engineers, was a man of science, and though a young man, was one whose opinions on such a question, as well as on most others, was certain of being listened to with attention.

Katherine had already contrived that he should be consulted on the subject, and his visit on the present occasion was for the especial purpose of talking over some of the plans that had been already suggested for indulging her fancy, without endangering her cautious father's property; could she obtain an opinion favourable to her scheme from so high an authority, she felt tolerably certain that she should be able to overcome all parental objections to it.

Between the windows and the fire-place of this dearly beloved apartment stood a grand pianoforte, which had been Kate's first important purchase, and had absorbed the greater portion of her first year's allowance; but it was her favourite boast that it was a finer instrument than the one in the drawing-room.

The opposite side of the room, which was unbroken by either door or window, was occupied in its whole extent by a range of shelves, whose contents, as the most cursory glance at them would show, were culled from most of the modern languages of Europe. There were the poets of almost all nations, the leading histories of many, and of their novels and romances not a few; and, moreover, there might be found, if we had time to examine the shelves closely, more decided evidences as to the owner's growing tastes and opinions, in the miscellaneous mass of occasional literature—books evidently not bought to form a library, but to read at once, on the spur of the occasion.

Among these, there were, it may be feared, some few which

2

the Doctor would have been more surprised than pleased to
find there, had it ever entered his head to visit his daughter's
book-shelves, and examine their contents.

As for the Lady Augusta, she exercised a most conscientious, scrupulous, and vigilant control over her
daughter's wardrobe and toilette, but it never occurred
to her to open a volume in Kate's room, any more than in
her own. Once, indeed, she remarked upon the rapidly
increasing accumulation of volumes.

"Really, my dear Kate," she said, "if you add many more
books to your collection, you will make your library out of
proportion to the rest of the furniture in your pretty room.
But you are right, I believe, in thinking it very much the
fashion at present to have quantities of books about one ; one
really sees them lying about now almost everywhere; and I
greatly approve your taste, my dear, in your selection. For
the most part they harmonize admirably together. Those
white and gold, in particular, are exceedingly elegant,"
which latter phrase very satisfactorily developed her Ladyship's meaning when she talked of an harmonious selection in
a library, which, without this explanation, might have had
something obscure in it.

On the side of the room opposite the windows was a little
easel, commodiously placed to receive the light duly from
the left, and on it an unfinished drawing in water-colours, of a
part of the interior of St. Peter's, while the original from
which it was in process of being copied, was supported on a
little desk, which stood on a table crowded with all the most
improved appliances for the art.

Beside the door of entrance was a second book-case, small,
but deep-shelved, containing a variety of works on the fine
arts, with a small collection of fine engravings on the lower
shelves, while the upper ones were occupied by a goodly range
of music, both vocal and instrumental.

On the table which stood before her sofa was lying a
copy of Mr. Ruskin's "Seven Lamps," and Froud's
"Nemesis of Faith," the latter open, and with its leaves
turned downwards on the table, as having recently left the
reader's hand.

And now what shall we say of the mistress of the room
thus imperfectly described ?

We must, I suppose, endeavour to give our readers some
notion of her "bodily presentment." As to her inward self.

our history will be little worth if, in the course of it, we fail in making it manifest.

Let the reader then imagine a light slenderly-formed figure, somewhat falling short of what is authoritatively pronounced to be the model height of woman; but her beautiful proportions gave a grace and charm to her carriage and movements, which more than atoned for the want of commanding stature. Her fair broad forehead was well set off by wavy braids of rich brown hair. Her eyes were brown too—dark brown—and were beautifully softened in their surpassing brightness by a deep fringe of dark silken lashes.

The well-defined eyebrows were almost straight; but there was a mobility in them which sometimes gave a look of decision, and sometimes of *mutinerie*. It was not a regularly beautiful face. Perhaps no features so rich in expression, so stamped with intelligence, and with ready capacities for expressing sympathy with every genial mood of mind ever were regularly and perfectly beautiful. Witness the incontestable insipidity of Raphael's Madonnas. But to those whose hearts are to be fascinated only by something more rare and more ethereal than mere beauty of feature, Kate Harrington was infinitely more attractive than any mere faultless animal organization could have made her.

The chiselling of her features was delicate, and of that sharpness which so much heightens in a youthful face that *espièglerie* which our language has no adequate term to express. But if a certain amount of what perhaps comes nearest in homely Saxon phrase—if a little *devilry* might be read in the eyes, all sweet affections and soft sympathies dimpled round the mouth; and the influence of her frank, clear, silvery voice and bright child-like smile, won kind thoughts and admiring words, even from the least genially-minded of those who knew her.

Nothing could be more becoming to a face and figure like hers than the admirably fitting dress and mantle of pale lilac silk in which we now present her to our readers; and the almost Quakerish simplicity of her snow-white chip-bonnet was prettily relieved by the sprays of hedge-roses which clustered under it round her sweet face.

Thus equipped, and perfectly ready to step into the carriage at a moment's notice, Kate came forth from her little bedroom, and resumed the volume she had been reading.

2—2

CHAPTER IV.

The Doctor having performed his afternoon duty, and returned punctually at the time stipulated, the Lady Augusta proceeded to perform hers.

Kate was summoned from her retreat to join her mother in the drawing-room, when one rapid glance from that excellent mother's practised eye sufficed to assure her that her fair daughter's toilet was irreproachable, and then they rolled away together to perform their joint duty in the park.

Duty? Yes, duty is the word, for in her inmost heart Lady Augusta considered it to be so, and she would have scouted the notion that she went there every Sunday for her pleasure. Could it, in truth, be a pleasure, even to her? It could scarcely be so described, although the want of it would have been an annoyance and a misfortune, and the hours so occupied would have been felt to be painfully long and listless without it.

But its greatest zest most certainly arose from considering it as an important duty duly performed. For so necessary to happiness is the feeling of having something to do, and the consciousness of doing it, that the very idlest people fancy they have an immensity of necessary business to get through, and never awaken to the knowledge of the dismal fact that their whole lives are spent in doing nothing. This admirable propensity to useful activity is the gift of nature; the counteracting habit is the fruit of education. Query: What is the degree of moral responsibility attached to this species of training?

But in Lady Augusta Harrington's case, this drive in the park was very easily brought under the general head of "duty to her daughter." It was part of the great and important duty of presenting Miss Harrington to the world, in a manner and style befitting the grand-daughter of the Earl of Bentley, a phrase which that nobleman's daughter was very filially prone to use.

But though Lady Augusta was thus absolutely bound to undergo the labour of park-duty, it does not follow that we are bound to share it with her. Of course the drive afforded the usual amount of such occupation as is found in exclaiming: " Ah ! there is so and so." " Did you see Lady This ?" " Was that my Lord T'other ?" And sometimes there was a lively variety of remarks such as : " Look at that horrid Miss Puddingthwaite and her odious britska ! She has got another new lining, Kate ! she has upon my honour ! Rose colour this time !"

" Well, mamma," was Kate's answer, " I am sure I shall be very glad to see Miss Puddingthwaite *couleur de rose.*"

" Ah ! my love," rejoined her mother, who occasionally thought it was right to be a little sentimental and pathetic, " ah ! my love, to you everything appears *couleur de rose!* But to me ——"

And she would on this occasion have probably gone on for her daughter's moral instruction to quote " the rose that hides the thorn" from Solomon, and might have bid her remember how beautifully Haynes Bailey observes that " all flesh was grass," had not Kate suddenly interrupted her by exclaiming :—

" Why, mamma, there is Lord Brandling walking arm-in-arm with Mr. Caldwell ! I thought Lord Brandling was at Rome. He must have just returned again. I shall be so glad to see him !"

" Yes ; he is just come back. Lady de Paddington told me so this morning," returned her mother. " But just look, Kate, what a lovely horse young Filchingham is riding ! I never saw him look so well !"

And so the dull drive went on; but happily came at last to a conclusion, as even drives in Hyde Park must do, be they never so tedious. And then the ladies returned to dress for dinner.

The party at the table was increased to six, by the presence of Mr. Harrington, the Doctor's eldest son, who, though residing in London, did not avail himself of the paternal roof as his domicile ; nor indeed did the family in Vale Street see as much of him as the good Doctor would have wished ; for though very far from being a severe father, either in theory or practice, and by no means wishing to have the decorous routine and tranquil comfort of his home disturbed by the somewhat incompatible habits and associations of his son, the Doctor felt sometimes a little uneasy respecting the sort of life this son was leading; and though his own path lay in so wholly contrary a direction, that he in truth knew exceedingly little respecting the young man's whereabouts and occupations, certain reports had occasionally reached him, which led him to fear that more particular inquiries were not likely to lead to any satisfactory result.

The other guests, in addition to the usual family party of the Doctor, his wife and daughter, were, as we have mentioned, Mr. Caldwell, and Mr. White, the Doctor's curate.

It was past seven, and for some minutes the Doctor had been sitting with his hands folded before him, and his eyes turned upwards to the ceiling, the very picture of martyred resignation. Mr. Caldwell was showing Miss Harrington some drawings which he had brought with him, and Mr. White was cudgelling his unhappy brains in the hope of finding something proper and appropriate to say to her Ladyship.

How far Mr. Caldwell might have shared in the general gladness when his artistic *tête-à-tête* with Miss Harrington was brought to a sudden stop, we will not pretend to say; neither is it necessary to describe Kate's degree of sympathy in the general feeling, but certain it is, that the rest of the party were infinitely relieved by the entrance of Henry Harrington at twenty minutes past seven.

The Doctor, who was nearly as angry as it was possible for him to be with any being above the rank and station of an undergraduate, could not help saying, rather stiffly :—

"When you do condescend to dine with us, Henry, I wish that you would also condescend to dine at our hour. You have kept us waiting nearly half an hour."

And then Mr. White gave his arm to her Ladyship, Mr. Caldwell to Kate, and the Doctor and his son followed them down to the dining-room.

"I did not see you at church this morning, Henry," said the Doctor, after he had swallowed a plateful of very restorative soup; adding, as he pushed the sherry towards his son, "some little indisposition, I suppose?"

For the worthy Doctor asked nothing but a decent excuse on such occasions, and like all worshippers of decorum, deemed a decent lie far preferable upon such a point to a less decorous truth.

"Never was better, my dear Sir," returned the young man, filling himself a bumper, and nodding to his father as he tossed it off. "But I must say, I am rather astonished you should wish to peril my religion by attending service at St. Martin's."

"Hallo! Mr. White," cried the Rector to the curate, with the same sort of good-humour Lord Eldon might have done, had some pet of a grandchild set about to impugn his law, "here's Henry going to bring a charge of heretical teaching against us."

"Indeed, Sir," pursued Henry, gravely, "I fear it amounts to no less. For I am assured by James, St. James of Stanton, as I call him, that nothing is so bad for the salvation as living in one parish, and going to church in another. He says that the thing is thoroughly recognised as a fact now."

"Pooh, pooh, Sir!" quoth the Doctor, on whose heavy brow a cloud now really lowered; for the *high* tendencies of his son James were a source of great annoyance to him, and very highly offensive to his feelings and prejudices, in many ways and for many reasons. "James might occupy himself far better than in spreading such dangerous doctrines, which he has picked up from innovators who will do the Church more harm than their boasted learning will do it good; and you might do better than make such a graceless use of them."

"Nay, Sir," persisted the scapegrace, with a wicked glance at his sister, who was sitting on the other side of the table; to which glance Kate only replied by a demure compression of her lips, and an almost imperceptible shake of the head, "nay, Sir, I protest I was about to ask your advice on a point which James's teaching has rendered very embarrassing to me. You see, I spend most of the day at my club, and have all letters and cards addressed to me there. But unfortunately the lodging at which I sleep is in the next parish. Now which is my parish church?"

"Pooh, pooh, Sir!" again ejaculated the Doctor, with something very like a growl, "I request that I may hear no more of this stuff."

"But I assure you, Sir," persisted his incorrigible son, who seemed determined to spoil his father's dinner and torment him with an indigestion, "I do really assure you that the question is one which deserves examination. For just observe, Sir. James tells me that the priest of my parish is the pastor and master specially appointed by providence to teach me; that I must hear the Church and listen to the Church, and that no other does or can represent the Church to me. But the most curiously unfortunate fact of the matter is, that Providence has provided that 'the truth' taught to parishioners of the parish in which my club is situated differs very much, and is, indeed, in many respects quite contradictory to 'the truth' taught to the inhabitants of that in which my lodging happens to be. And I thought, Sir, that perhaps you might be able to explain to me how it is, that the obedience which I am so anxious to render to the Church, may oblige me to change the whole fabric of my religious convictions in consequence of my changing my lodging. Certainly," he added, with an air of profound meditation, "nothing can appear more puzzling in all the inscrutable ways of Providence than that the divinely appointed teaching of the Church shall prescribe to the faithful the doctrine of prevenient grace, perhaps, in Mary'bone, baptismal regeneration in Bloomsbury, election and reprobation in Pall Mall, and the operative efficacy of absolution in Piccadilly."

"Said I not well, Sir," broke forth the Doctor, addressing Mr. White, with an explosion of voice, deep-toned, and sonorous, "said I not well, when I told you the other day that our lot had been cast on evil times? What mischief may we not expect when laymen, whose presumption is equalled only by their ignorance, meddle with questions which even the Fathers of the Church ought only to approach, and that with deep awe and cautious forbearance. Of a truth, may we say that, 'Fools rush in where angels fear to tread.' But this, Sir, comes of the presumptuous folly of self-sufficient young men, who must needs proclaim themselves to be better and wiser than their fathers, and who, by seeking to introduce changes in a fabric which has been hallowed by the veneration of ages, have caused schism and perilous questionings to creep in, where before were unity and peace. Eh, Mr. White?"

"Dangerous indeed, Sir," replied Mr. White, in a doleful tone; which probably appeared to him as safe a reply as he could make under the circumstances.

"So then, if I understand you rightly, Sir," pursued Henry Harrington, still addressing his father without taking any heed of gentle Mr. White's contribution to the conversation, "what you would recommend to us of the laity, is to eat, drink, and pay our tithes, and trouble our heads no further in the matter."

"The tone you take, Sir, precludes the possibility of my conversing with you on the subject," retorted the Doctor, in his most magnificent and Johnsonian manner.

"Have you any news from Glastonbury, Mr. White?"

Mr. White hailed this diversion with infinite alacrity. He had no taste for theological disputes, especially when his venerated superiors in the Church were so apt to take different sides, as seemed to be the case at that unfortunate moment; whereas on the subject of news from Glastonbury, he felt very considerable interest; for Mr. White, who had been educated as a Bible-clerk on the foundation of All Saints, and had from the connection so formed become the Warden's curate on his London preferment, was exceedingly anxious to obtain by the same interest a minor canonry in the Cathedral of Glastonbury. It was a position which would suit him much better than the curacy of St. Martin's in all respects.

He hated London, and its inhabitants, and its clerical duties. With the rich and noble of his parishioners he felt himself *génée*, ill at ease, and never for a moment free from an awkward feeling of restraint; while the ways, and habits, and troubles of the London poor were of a class for which he had neither comprehension nor sympathy; and to deal with them judicially, required an amount of experience and worldly wisdom which he did not possess.

He might have acquitted himself very respectably of such duties as visiting a rheumatic old dame in a country cottage, or investigating the claims of a distressed labourer to out-door relief; but he was altogether at sea among the more complicated requirements of the London poor.

Moreover, he was musical, and had a fine voice; an advantage displayed to great advantage in the situation of minor canon. In short, the duties which would be required of him in the chair of Glastonbury, were precisely such as he was conscious he could perform with pleasure and credit both to himself and the Cathedral.

His tastes and habits, good man, were altogether countrified and rural; many excellent qualities of heart, and some of head into the bargain perhaps, had the Rev. Jonas White; and the worst thing, I believe, that his worst enemy could say of him was, that perhaps he was a little addicted to

poaching, and a trifle fonder of taking a part in a glee, or a
bowl, after he had heard the chimes at midnight, than quite
became his cloth.

But then, as to the fact of his wearing that cloth, was it
the fault of poor Jonas White that his father, being a chaplain
in the University, had destined him for the clerical profession
from the cradle upwards? that he had obtained the promise
of a Bible-clerkship for him before he could go alone? or that
the only educational preparation for the sacred calling had
been, the giving him clearly to understand that he was to get
his bread in the Church?

Yet had Jonas White been intended for a bricklayer, his
spiritual breeding might have been much the same. The
result of this was, that Jonas entertained a very truly conscientious conviction, that he was admirably performing his
duty in that state of life to which it had pleased God to call
him, by not getting rusticated as a Bible-clerk, by not getting
plucked as a candidate for a degree, by duly passing his
examination for Holy Orders, and by labouring away diligently at marrying, baptising, and burying the parishioners
of St. Martin's in the West, as Curate.

The Doctor, therefore, touched on a very interesting topic
to Mr. White when he asked about the latest news from
Glastonbury. Old Mr. Jackson the Precentor was supposed
to have at length sung his last anthem, and Mr. Jackson was
by far the oldest of the cathedral clergy at Glastonbury,
where he had been Precentor for nearly half a century, and
was now dying at eighty-seven, after having been the glory
of the choir for the first twenty years of his incumbency, and
its destruction for the last seventeen.

"I got a letter this morning, Sir," said the well-pleased
Mr. White, in reply to his Rector's question respecting news
from Glastonbury. "I believe poor old Jackson is going, Sir.
I am told that he cannot last many days longer."

"Well, White, I'll be as good as my promise, and do all I
can for you. But you must not be too sanguine. There's the
Dean, you know, and he perhaps ——"

"I happen to know, Sir," returned the Curate, rather
eagerly, "that I am so fortunate as to have had my musical
abilities, such as they are, favourably mentioned to the Dean,
and that he has written to a friend at Oxford to inquire
respecting my voice. Dr. Barringham, I am told, takes great
interest in the choir, and is very anxious to make it once

again all it is said to have been in poor Jackson's younger days."

"Well, in that case," replied the Doctor, "I think we shall have a very good chance; for Dr. Blanchard will go with the Dean, of course, and I think I can count on the support of my old friend Tarleford. Well, White! I am sure I wish you all success, though it will involve the necessity of my looking out for a new curate."

While this conversation had been passing between the Doctor and the gentlemen near him, Lady Augusta, Kate, and Mr. Caldwell, had been engaged in a discussion on the causes of the lamentably low state of architectural art at the present day in England. The conversation had commenced by Kate making a vehement attack on the unfortunate National Gallery, which, truth to say, was rather like "kicking one who had no friends," but Kate had a theory of her own on the subject of a building for the exhibition of pictures, and the subject was a favourite one with her.

This had led to a general view of the deplorable number of fine opportunities, which had recently in London only served to produce disgraceful failures in our architectural attempts.

The splendid exception of the "Palace of Westminster," as our parliamentary chambers are rather affectedly called, was, however, not forgotten, and had all justice done it; but for the rest, but little mercy was shown. Mr. Caldwell had ventured to throw out a suggestion that the real root of the evil must be looked for in the defective education, and consequent unenlightened judgment and bad taste of our upper and middle classes generally, rather than in any epidemic of incapacity on the part of our architects.

This audacious heresy had "called up" Lady Augusta, who, in the first place, really could not see what the education of the upper classes could have to do with the matter at all; and in the next place had "always understood that no more liberal and perfect education *could* be given than that afforded by our public schools and universities."

This latter subject was an ocean too vast and too deep to be plunged into with such a fellow-swimmer as the Lady Augusta, with the slightest hope of reaching a sure footing on any shore; so Mr. Caldwell contented himself with observing generally to her Ladyship, that he thought the practical architects of the present day had many difficulties to contend against.

"They are," said he, "more apt than they should be to make the rules of Art, which ought to be as eternal as the laws of Nature, bend and yield before the caprices of a patron's taste; and if they cannot please the said patrons with what is good, they condescend to content him with what they know to be bad."

"But we have been talking chiefly of public buildings, Mr. Caldwell," observed Kate.

"And it is especially with regard to public buildings that the deficient education I have mentioned operates most fatally," said Mr. Caldwell. "What we want is not so much a general diffusion of taste, or even a knowledge of artistic principles, as of serious appreciation of the moral and political influence of art, especially of architectural art, on the fortunes and civilization of a nation. Members of executive committees, and gentlemen of the House of Commons cannot be got to understand what wide-spread and self-propagating mischief they are doing by extinguishing the sense of beauty in the minds of the people, and making those 'sermons in stones' which the great edifices of a nation are eternally preaching, lessons of ugliness, vulgarity and meanness."

"Well, I protest," exclaimed Lady Augusta, shrugging her shoulders, and elevating her eyebrows, "I do not see what architecture can have to do with politics."

"A vast majority of the collective wisdom of the nation agrees with your Ladyship," replied Mr. Caldwell, smiling. "It would be unfair not to confess it."

The ladies now rose to leave the room; the Doctor filled and drank a second bumper of port, and then, pushing the bottle towards Mr. Caldwell, threw himself back in his arm-chair for the enjoyment of a short nap, and soon gave very convincing evidence of having found the blessing he sought, by a regular series of deep-toned snores.

CHAPTER V.

"I say, old fellow," said Henry Harrington to Mr. White, "shan't you find it rather difficult to make it all right down at Glastonbury? What with the governor here, and old Barrington, I think you'll be puzzled. The governor is quite one of the old sort as St. James of Stanton calls them, but the Dean, I am told, is pretty considerable 'high.' Perhaps it comes from keeping him too long without a bishopric. What d'ye think about it? How shall you manage to be all things to all men? to all prebendal men, I mean, down at Glastonbury? Eh!"

"By minding my own business, which I take to be singing," returned White. "If I sing in tune, my doctrine will neither be found too high nor too low, I believe; and as long as I have got a good tenor, I shall have no fault found with my way."

"Well, I hope it may answer," returned Henry, "and that I may live to hear you give them 'Glorious Apollo' as well at Glastonbury, when sober, as I have heard you give it to us in the common-room at All Saints when a small matter the reverse."

"For shame, Harrington. Hush! There's your father waking," said the Curate, looking frightened.

"Not he, friend Jonas. I say, Caldwell, are you and the governor going to talk architecture and politics all the evening? For if so, I think I shall take myself off. That is if I knew what on earth to do with myself. Surely there never was any incentive to suicide like a Sunday evening in London!"

"Come, gentlemen," said the Doctor, aroused by the vehemence of his son's accents, "come, let us go and get a cup of coffee in the drawing-room. I daresay our three Graces, or Muses, if that title may be thought to suit them better, have arrived by this time."

"What, Sir? you do not mean that you receive the noble race of Wigginsville in your humble halls to-night?" cried Henry, in an accent of affected delight. "Come, come, things are looking brighter—there will be better fun than I bargained for. But perhaps by this time I ought to say De-Von-Fitz-Mac-ap-Wiggonsville in speaking of these noble products of heraldic art? But I can't help thinking that, if I had been called in as Garter King of Arms, to operate on the plebeian patronymic of Wiggins, I should have refined it into Wyggynnes. There is very great aristocratic virtue in a *y*, especially if pronounced long, and a veritable Norman savour about a double *n*, finished off with an *e*. Methinks Fitzwyggynnesville would have been highly effective, imposing alike to ear and eye, and must have consigned the worthy distiller deceased, and his objectional appellation, to merited oblivion for evermore."

The Doctor half smiled, but shook his head, and held up his fore-finger very reprovingly.

"But, Sir," persisted his graceless son, "if you must make a mythological triad of these high-born spinsters, allow me to suggest the Fates as more calculated to convey a just idea of Miss Hannah, Miss Mary Jane, and Miss Jemima Wigginsville, than either Graces or Muses."

"Be quiet, Harry, I won't have the good souls laughed at," said the Doctor, leading the way up the stairs. "There are worse people, I assure you, than the Miss Wigginsvilles, in many ways."

"Quite true, Sir," rejoined his son, with a profound sigh; "but scarcely any more variously ridiculous, I should think."

"Well, well, you are incorrigible! But at any rate I must beg and entreat that if quiz them you must, you will not do it so as to run any risk of giving them pain."

"Would not hurt a hair of their heads for the world, Sir! I doubt though, if dear Miss Hannah has any to hurt," replied his son. "But I will tell you," he added, "what I will do to please them, if you will allow me. I'll send Robert with a note to my old acquaintance, Mr. Garble, and ask him to come here to tea. If that is not self-sacrifice and devotion in the service of your *protégées*, I don't know what you would call so."

"I am not particularly fond of Mr. Garble myself, Henry," returned his father. "But, however, as the three spinsters certainly are, you have my full permission to get him if you can."

Despite his friendship for the Misses Wigginsville, the good
Doctor was not sorry to hear any aid suggested which might
remove from himself the fatigue of entertaining them.

So the note to Mr. Garble was really written and dispatched; and this being done, the well-satisfied gentlemen
entered the drawing-room, which they found occupied by half
a dozen ladies, for besides Lady Augusta and Miss Harrington,
there were the three Miss Wigginsvilles and another lady
whom it is now necessary to present to the reader.

Indeed, as she is a member of the Doctor's family, she
ought to have been mentioned before. But having been
absent all day at a short distance from London, with friends
with whom she had been passing the Sunday for the purpose
of attending a favourite preacher, she has not been exactly
within our reach.

It is the Lady Juliana Witherby of whom we are speaking, the younger and unmarried sister of Lady Augusta
Harrington.

For many years past she had been an inmate of the
Doctor's family, and now, having dined with her suburban
friend Mrs. Larraby, " between the services," she had
returned home in time to take her evening coffee in her
sister's drawing-room.

This home in Dr. Harrington's family was not altogether a
happy one; yet, perhaps, under the circumstances, it was less
the contrary than might have been expected; for in the first
place it was a home accorded by charity, as Lady Juliana's
pitiful little fortune would scarcely have sufficed to procure
her decent food and lodging; and somehow or other, this
charity did not seem to be of the species which blesses both
the giver and receiver, In fact, poor Lady Juliana was,
in different ways, disagreeable to every member of the
Doctor's household.

To that dignified and orthodox divine himself, her propensity to run about after popular preachers, and all the
other amusements of *dilettante* religion, was particularly
distasteful.

Yet, to do the Warden justice, he was far from being
unkind to his sister-in-law, and he was much too gentleman-
like and generous ever to have felt the maintenance of the
poor soul as any burthen in a pecuniary point of view, and if
his tolerance of her offending religious crotchets was somewhat too evidently tinged with contemptuous superiority, it

must be remembered that they assailed all his prejudices in their tenderest point.

To poor Kate she was certainly an unmitigated bore, and perennial source of annoyance; for it unfortunately happened that all Kate did, said, thought, read, painted, or sung was, in the opinion of her aunt, so thoroughly saturated with the abounding original sin of her nature, as to make it her spinster Ladyship's imperative duty to be continually entering one never-ending still-beginning protest against the whole tenor of her niece's life.

Kate returned this very unpleasant solicitude for her spiritual welfare by an equally incessant, and much more effectual care, for her aunt's temporal comforts; and really never attempted any resistance, except on one cardinal point, namely, the sacred preservation of her cell from all intrusion. And truly, without this magna charta of her rights and privileges, Kate's life would hardly have been worth having under the same roof with the Lady Juliana.

It was, however, to Lady Augusta that her sister's residence under the Doctor's roof gave, perhaps, the most pungent annoyance. At all events, it was Lady Augusta's temper that suffered most from the petty troubles produced by Lady Juliana's whims and ways, and it was assuredly she who most punctually repaid them by making the offender suffer in her turn.

There were, in truth, many causes why the two sisters were not well calculated to live amicably together.

Lady Juliana had in her day been a beauty. Lady Augusta never had. Hence, in two narrow, ill-regulated minds, innumerable jealousies, heart-burnings, and mutual dislikes had sprung up from their earliest years.

A marriage, which it had once appeared probable that Lady Juliana would have contracted, had been broken off under circumstances calculated to throw a certain degree of shade over the noble family of Witherby, and this was an offence which it was not in Lady Augusta's nature to forgive.

And then in matters of daily life, wherein Lady Augusta found that her position in society, and her duty as a mother, required her occasionally to act in a manner not altogher accordant with the strict rules of religion, Lady Juliana was for ever near her, protesting by conduct, by look, and by insinuation, most provokingly against all such offences.

So that, from one cause or another, there was always a sort

of semi-subdued acrimony and mutual irritation between the two sisters. They were, moreover, very essentially unlike in mind as well as in person.

Lady Augusta was rather short, and though not fat, was decidedly *embonpoint*. The most remarkable feature in her face was an immense Roman nose, which imparted a sort of hawk-like expression to her face. A sharp, bright eye, high cheek-bones, a somewhat large, but very well-formed mouth, and a broad square chin, gave indications of energy, firmness, and strength of will, at the expense of everything like softness or gentleness of character.

Her sole pretension to beauty of any kind had consisted in remarkably well-formed feet and hands, and of these graceful appendages her Ladyship was still proud at sixty.

To irreproachably elegant manners, a tolerable knowledge of the small world in which she had moved, calling it, and believing it, the great world, and to a fair share of common sense, it must be confessed that Lady Augusta added that deep-seated vulgarity of mind which is the inevitable product of a life spent in looking up to that on which we ought to look down; reverencing that which deserves no reverence, mistaking small things, and small people, for great things, and great people, and in contracting all thoughts and all feelings within the narrow circle of a paltry, yet arbitrary conventionalism.

Lady Juliana was ten years younger than her sister, and had never quite lost the habit acquired in early life, of looking up to her with a certain amount of respect and fear. She was herself a remarkably elegant looking woman; tall, and was perhaps somewhat too thin, but she still retained, both in form and feature, considerable traces of her former beauty. She had a fair pale forehead of that peculiar form, which though high, is so narrow as to impart no indication of intellect; a large pale-blue eye, a clear and delicate complexion, and that delicately small conformation of the lower part of the face which, though in youth it may be termed pretty, is an unfailing index of weakness of character.

In disposition she would have been better, had she been happier. This approaches perhaps a little to the dictum of the critic, who pronounced that the picture would have been better if the painter had taken more pains with it. And of which of us may not the same be said? But truly, in the case of poor Lady Juliana, it might be declared that

3

all her bad qualities arose from her false position in the world.

She was a blighted plant. All her life had been a mistake. Nature had certainly intended her to suckle fools, and not to have anything to chronicle.

Had she married in her own station, and produced a few noble little creatures in her own likeness to suckle, it would have brought out all the gentleness, tenderness, and love of her soft nature; and who knows whether, as a mother, that soft weak nature might not have been strengthened into a capability of self-sacrifice and devotion? As it was, poor soul! there was no active good in her at all, and continual discomfort and discontent, together with vexations and vain regrets, engendered but too much active ill in the shape of acerbity, irritation, and uncharitableness. In a word, all that mixed result of *ennui*, peevishness, and disappointment, which the self-deluded lady consoled herself by calling "her religious feelings."

Lady Juliana was reclining, when the gentlemen entered, in an elegant attitude, on a *chaise longue* on one side of the fire; for, May as it was, and a lovely May-day as it had been, luxurious Londoners still welcomed the cheerful aspect of a fire in the evening. A little table stood at her elbow, beside which sat Miss Mary Jane Wigginsville, the youngest of the three spinster sisters. These two ladies were in very close, and apparently very interesting conversation across the little table, the diminutive dimensions of which permitted their *tête-à-tête* to be perfectly confidential.

Miss Mary Jane Wigginsville had not fully attained the completion of her thirtieth year, but she was very near having done so; and like all other unwedded ladies, she felt it to be an important era. Small and very delicate features, large light-coloured eyes, an oval face, a beautiful complexion, and a very abundant decoration of long and almost flaxen ringlets, gave to this *cadette* of the house of Wigginsville very fair claims in the eyes of many to be considered as a very pretty woman.

There was considerable congeniality of tastes and pursuits between these two ladies; and although their tempers were widely different—for there was not an atom of either sour or bitter in the disposition of Miss Mary Jane—they were very intimate.

On the opposite side of the fire-place, Lady Augusta was

sitting in a deep *bergère*, in which she had fallen asleep over a meditation on the best means of securing the presence of the Duchess of Benlomond at a large party which she shortly intended to give.

Miss Jemina Wigginsville, who was five years older than Miss Mary Jane, and very like her, save that these five years had left their disagreeable traces on her once beautiful complexion, turning delicate pink to dingy red, was seated with Kate at a large round table in the centre of the room, where they were turning over picture-books, and chattering away at a great rate.

We must now introduce Miss Hannah Wigginsville to the reader, or more properly speaking, Miss Wigginsville, *par excellence.*

This lady was the daughter of the late Mr. Wigginsville, by his first wife; his marriage with the mother of the before-named two ladies having been contracted much later in life, and after he had retired from business. There was probably not less than twenty years difference between the age of the eldest Miss Wigginsville and that of her youngest sister, for Miss Hannah must certainly have been fifty years old at the time of which we are now speaking. Not that any uncertainty on the point can have arisen from any wish on her part to conceal her age; for Miss Hannah would not have given a farthing for the power of mystifying the whole world upon the subject. For though she was not, perhaps, quite without pretension, of more kinds than one, she was by no means one of those unlucky females who consider juvenility as the greatest of blessings while present, and the most indispensable of fictions when past.

On the contrary, Miss Hannah, with her tall large bulky person, her short scratchy "front," her large massive forehead, and her never-absent spectacles, would utterly have scorned any soft impeachment of the kind.

She was now sitting exactly in front of the fire, with one knee crossed in somewhat masculine fashion over the other, and reading the *Quarterly Review,* which she had coaxed Kate to fetch for her from her father's study. Such was the manner in which the ladies of the party were distributed when the four gentlemen from the dining-room made their appearance among them.

CHAPTER VI.

THE entrance of the gentlemen, of course, made a complete revolution in the arrangement of the whole party.

Lady Augusta waked, opened her eyes, stared at them all, and asked whether it were not getting rather late. The other ladies all moved a little, more or less, and looked as if they were holding themselves in readiness to form themselves into new groups if required to do so.

The Doctor, after taking his coffee, placed himself in a chair, before the round table, saying: "Now then, Caldwell, let us have a look at your drawings." Whereupon Kate, and Miss Jemima, being already seated at the same table, naturally joined themselves to the Doctor and Mr. Caldwell, apparently for the purpose of enjoying a renewed exhibition of the young engineer's very admirable drawings.

Henry Harrington drew a chair to the side of Miss Hannah, with whom he knew himself to be a sort of a favourite, though he was always quizzing her, and "drawing her out," as he called it.

But the real fact was, that in the frequent sharp encounters of their wits, Miss Hannah had a tolerably comfortable conviction that she had no reason to consider herself the vanquished, victimized, or most bequizzed party, but rather the contrary; and, perhaps, Miss Hannah was not altogether wrong.

In this state of affairs, Mr. White, unfortunate young man! saw himself in imminent danger of having again to expose himself to all the horrors of a *tête-à-tête* with the awful Lady Augusta; for Lady Juliana and Miss Mary Jane seemed evidently determined to continue their conversation apart. Anything, he thought, was better than this, so, although he knew that Lady Juliana had a particular dislike to him, and that he was sure to meet with something disagreeable by addressing her, he bravely marched up to the two serious ladies, and with all the boldness of desperation, commenced the conversation by asking Lady Juliana where she had been passing her Sunday.

"I was permitted the great privilege of passing it at Highworth, Mr. White," replied her Ladyship, "where, as I have just been remarking to Miss Wigginsville, the sheep never have to leave the fold in search of food, Mr. White." The latter part of her speech being added with a dry stiffness which was meant to convey a crushing reproof.

Poor White, whose very narrow and uniform path in life had led him quite away from those social latitudes in which the language now used by Lady Juliana was current, and who, moreover, was really as simple and single-minded as a child, replied, with much enthusiasm :—

"Ah, Lady Juliana! if you feel it a privilege to get out of the smoke, think what it would be to me! I, you know, who have been panting here from week's end to week's end, without ever smelling country air! But I did not know that the system of feeding which you and Miss Wigginsville have been discussing had been tried in that part of the country. I have heard of it in Lincolnshire, but had no idea that anything of the kind had been tried near London."

And hereupon Miss Mary Jane permitted herself the worldliness of a very modified half-suppressed titter, which, however, she brought into proper keeping as to time, place, and her companions, by letting it glide imperceptibly into a sigh, while a very seraphic upcast glance of her large blue eyes served the double purpose of exhibiting them to the sinner as he stood looking down at her, and at the same time manifesting a due sense of the enormity of his sinfulness.

"What *can* you mean, Mr. White?" demanded her Ladyship, with more of hauteur, however, than of anger; for there was something soothing and agreeable to her feelings in the mental attitude of looking down upon the "outer court" sinner, from the conscious elevation of her own godliness. "What can you mean, Sir? And what system do you allude to?"

"I beg pardon, your Ladyship," said poor Jonas, beginning to perceive that he had made some great mistake, and for what he knew, poor man! might, perhaps, have fallen into some grievous sin against good-breeding or etiquette. "I beg pardon, I am sure. You must excuse me, but I thought that you and Miss Mary Jane had been speaking of the system of turnip feeding."

Poor little Mary Jane was again obliged to stifle a worldly

titter with a deep and very godly sigh. And then she ventured to say :—

"The manna of the word, Mr. White, and not turnips, was the food Lady Juliana was alluding to."

"Ah, Sir!" ejaculated Lady Juliana, after relieving her wounded feelings by a very awful groan; "ah, Sir! The faithful shepherd ——"

And here her Ladyship went off into a metaphorical pastoral about good shepherds, and bad shepherds, and wolves, and sheep, and sheep-dogs, and sheep-folds, all very fine, and very spiritual, but at too great length to make it safe to follow her.

"I say, White," interrupted Henry Harrington, from the other side of the hearth-rug, whence he had been talking with his friend, Miss Hannah. "Have you seen a pamphlet which Miss Wigginsville here has been telling me about? She says it is entitled 'The utility of our Cathedral Chapters, considered on the true principles of supply and demand.' The name of the author it seems is Mr. Ricardo Macmalthus, and she says that she hears it has made a great sensation at Manchester and Glasgow. Have you heard of it, White?"

"No, Sir; never heard of it," said White, suddenly turning round, and inexpressibly relieved by being thus released from Lady Juliana and her fold. "But I really think it a very important and proper view of the subject, and I should say," he added, thoughtfully, and as if pronouncing the result of a well-weighed calculation, "I should say it would take three times the number of minor-canonries that there are, to supply the demand for them satisfactorily."

Miss Hannah and Henry Harrington burst into a laugh at this somewhat exclusively professional mode of viewing the matter; and the spectacled spinster, who was a great political economist, undertook to explain the subject to him.

"Why really, Sir," said she, "I think you are likely enough to be right, if indeed you do not fall short in your estimate. But I suspect Macmalthus was thinking more of what might be the demand for canons, than for canonries."

"I am afraid we are broaching what the Governor would call very dangerous doctrines, eh, White?" said young Harrington.

"I don't exactly understand what is meant by a demand for canons," replied poor White, simply. "But the Church prays for a due supply of them, you know, included of course

in the general prayer read at the University, for a due supply
of men fitted to serve God in Church and State."

The announcement of Mr. Garble at this moment
fortunately put a stop to the conversation, before the
"Governor" had become aware of the sort of ordeal which
his worthy curate was likely to be submitted to by his very
graceless first-born, and his rather partially privileged guest,
Miss Hannah; for had he been aware of it, he must have felt,
to use that phrase so dear to tender consciences, that he owed
it to himself to have testified his very decided disapprobation
of them both.

CHAPTER VII.

MR. JAMES GARBLE, attorney-at-law, was a little under-
sized, slight-made, half starved-looking figure, with a narrow
face, having a sharp nose, and a cautious, cunning-looking
mouth, the whole visage being attenuated and rat-like, but lit
up by a pair of very bright piercing black eyes. He had,
moreover, very brilliantly white teeth, and showed them
often. But his smile was not a pleasing one; it was neither
frank nor joyous.

Yet though all this can hardly be said to constitute an
engaging individuality, few persons cast their eyes upon
Mr. James Garble once, without being tempted by some feeling or other to take a second look. Was it that his high,
well-developed forehead imparted to this otherwise mean face,
that impress of intellect which never fails to command some
degree of instinctive and involuntary observance?

As he saluted, one after the other, most of those assembled
in the Doctor's drawing-room, there was nothing objectionable in his bearing or manner, unless, indeed, it were a tinge of
that extra and studied politeness which occasionally marks
the consciousness of being among persons felt to be of superior
station.

He was no favourite of the Doctor's, though it would be

difficult to say why he was not; unless, indeed, a sort of
mutual antipathy may be supposed to have been generated by
the excessive contrast of their respective persons; and this
was certainly such as to place them at the opposite extremes
of the species "homo." The Doctor must have weighed a
good sixteen stone; Mr. Garble certainly not above eight.
The Doctor's great sonorous voice resembled the small treble
of the attorney considerably less than that of a mastiff does
the sharp yelping of a lap-dog; and it really seemed strange
that the huge square ruddy visage of the one, should belong
to a being of the same species as the keen sallow features of
the other.

"Good evening, Mr. Garble," said the Doctor, putting out
his right hand to him over his shoulder, as he sat with his
left holding the drawing he was examining.

"Good evening, Sir," replied the other in a tone of much
less indifference, and receiving the hand thus placed within
his reach with something of a reverential air. And then
glancing at the drawings which were occupying the reverend
gentleman's attention, he added, after the pause of a moment:
"What indefatigable mental powers you must possess, Dr.
Harrington! After the great fatigues of such a day as this, it
is really extraordinary that you should feel sufficient energy
to occupy yourself with works of art!'"

Mr. Caldwell glanced towards the attorney's face, thinking
for a moment that he was venturing to banter the reverend
dignitary; but he read nothing there but deep admiration and
reverence.

Having administered this little bit of adulation to the
Doctor, Mr. Garble glided noiselessly across the room, bowing
low to the chair in which Lady Augusta was again sleeping,
to the little table beside which Lady Juliana and Miss Mary
Jane were still talking, with every appearance of earnestness.

Here he ventured to draw a chair and seat himself, and
then to enter into conversation with them both in a *sotto voce*
style of confidential intimacy, which plainly indicated that
there was some sort of tie between the trio beyond that which
existed between the little attorney and any other individuals
of the party. That such a tie existed is quite certain, and its
strength will be readily understood, when it is stated that it
was furnished by the community of their religious feelings.
For Mr. Garble was one of the elect, having been fortunate
enough to have had a "call."

We might perhaps safely leave the reader to form his own notions respecting Mr. Garble and his call, but on the whole, we prefer making no mystery about the matter, and, therefore, state at once the plain truth, namely, that Miss Mary Jane Wigginsville had been made the means of grace to the regenerated attorney.

It was perfectly well known to all men whom it might concern, and to many whom it might not, that the late Mr. Wigginsville, *ci-devant* Wiggins, had left above a hundred thousand pounds to his daughters, and accordingly, the three ladies resided in the aristocratic neighbourhood of St. Martin's in a style that might well indicate the possession of three or four thousand a-year. A handsome house, a handsome equipage, a good deal of society, a costly style of dress, at least in the juniors, and a yearly autumnal excursion to some fashionable watering-place, showed plainly enough that their expenditure could not fall far short of that income. But beyond this, nothing was known among their friends and neighbours about their pecuniary concerns.

They had migrated from the far east upon the death of their father, and had found little or no difficulty in forming a very agreeable set of acquaintances among the western tribes, in whose precincts they had ventured to settle themselves.

Mr. Garble was one of the individuals whose interest and friendly feelings they had the most rapidly awakened among their new acquaintance; and he, as well as some few others, had thought it best to settle all doubts and fears concerning their respectability, by at once ascertaining the real state of the case from the best authority. The unerring archives of Doctor's Commons were applied to, and sundry monies were pocketed by the functionaries thereof in return for the indubitable information that Joseph Wigginsville, &c. &c. &c., bequeathed all the property of which he died possessed, consisting of a dwelling-house, situated so and so, together with whatever amount of monies in the three per cent. consols which might belong to him at the time of his decease, to his three daughters, Hannah, Jemima, and Mary Jane, in equal portions.

This will was dated only five days before the old gentleman's death, so there could be no doubt or mistake about the matter.

The very marked difference in the character of the three ladies made this little investigation peculiarly necessary in the

ease of any Cœlebs in search of a dowered wife; for the style
of wooing adopted for the entanglement of Miss Hannah's
affections would have been altogether inefficacious when
brought to bear upon the feelings of the scientific Miss
Jemima; while the deepest devotion to every "ology" and
"ism" under the sun, would have been worse than thrown
away upon Miss Mary Jane. It may easily be supposed that
the three well-to-do sisters were not left to waste their sweetness, and that of their handsome income, upon the desert air of
a solitude unpeopled with pretenders to the honour of their
alliance. They were not among the number of fair ones left
to sing, "Nobody coming to marry me, nobody coming to
woo!" Many came to woo, and to marry also, if they could
manage it.

But every suiter found it absolutely necessary to single out
at once from the group the object of his intended adorations.
Each sportsman had to mark his bird. It would by no means
do to take the chances which might arise from blazing away
at the whole covey at once; nor was there the remotest
possibility that one head might by mere luck be bagged when
another was shot at.

The three ladies really lived together in very perfect
sisterly harmony and good understanding with each other;
but, nevertheless, each very decidedly took her own course,
and followed her own line across the thoroughfare of life.
Moreover, they each kept a hobby of their own, and they all
rode hard.

And thus it naturally came to pass, that each lady had her
own set of attendants, adherents, admirers, and hangers-on.

All were received, however, with equal hospitality and
politeness at the frequent evening _réunions_ which took place in
the Wigginsville drawing-rooms; not but what it was perfectly
well known amongst them for whose sake individually the
most assiduous guests made their appearance there. In fact
there was no more risk that the "following" of one sister
should be confounded with, or mistaken for the "following"
of another, than that a blunder should be made between the
birds of the air, the beasts of the field, and the fishes of the
sea.

It had become necessary, therefore, for our friend Mr. Garble,
at an early period of his acquaintance with these interesting
ladies, to make up his mind as to the most promising mode of
turning this acquaintance to account. He speedily felt the

necessity of submitting to the general rule thus enforced upon all the friends of the house of Wigginsville, and it had been a matter of much deep consideration with him under which of the three banners he should enrol himself.

He would for several reasons very greatly have preferred leaving the question for some time open. But this he soon found would be impossible ; and so, after very earnest though but short deliberation, he became "serious" and displayed himself openly as a Mary-Janite. This choice, though of necessity made rapidly, was grounded on very solid considerations. In the first place, the assumption of the "serious" colour might not improbably prove a good speculation in a professional point of view, for it was a notorious fact that the leading attorney in that particular neigbourhood was a decided Tractarian, and there was certainly at that moment, a very good opening for a "serious" practitioner. It was a notorious fact also, that in these days high church families employ high church butchers and bakers, and that low church families employ low church butchers and bakers, and it could not be doubted that both parties were likely to select their legal advisers upon the same system.

This was, as of course it ought to have been, a very strong argument in favour of displaying himself to the eyes of all men either high or low.

And another reason for his deciding upon immediately becoming "serious," was the much greater facility of preparing himself for it, than he should find in getting up the necessary stock of talk in either of the departments of worldly wisdom to which the two elder sisters had devoted themselves. He felt, in short, that it would be easier for him to become a saint, according to the rites and ceremonies enjoined by Miss Mary Jane and her friends, than a deeply read political economist of Miss Hannah's school, or a natural philosopher with Miss Jemima. Moreover, his natural sagacity led him to suspect that the heart of the youngest lady was by its nature more easily impressionable than the hearts of her sisters. Besides all this, we must do him the justice to admit, that he did certainly remember and allow some weight to the consideration that Miss Mary Jane was not only the youngest and best-looking of the three, but that she really was very pretty, while her sisters were as certainly not pretty at all.

So that in truth the wooing of Mr. Garble, though entered

upon in a decidedly business-like spirit, was not altogether a disagreeable business.

On the present occasion, however, it had to be carried on almost entirely by looks, and amatory sighs; for although Lady Juliana would not have objected to any amount of pious *double entendre* about love, and the spirit which constitutes the flirtation of the elect, and to which "serious" phraseology so happily lends itself, she would not have tolerated, despite her fifty years, that the whole of such heavenly-minded tenderness of feeling should have been appropriated entirely by Miss Mary Jane.

The clever little attorney, therefore, in order to turn the present opportunity to the best profit, was obliged to divide his soft and piously-worded cajoleries as dexterously as he could between his two gentle listeners, and trust to the language of the eyes, and all the other eloquent little asides with which mankind are all, more or less, familiar, in order to make the younger lady understand how exclusively the meaning of every tender sound he uttered, was for her.

Before long, however, the appearance of the tea equipage broke up the different coteries into which the party had divided themselves. Lady Augusta roused herself, and taking her place at the tea-table, said to her husband :—

"Well, my dear, what did your brother say to you in the letter I sent down to you by Kate this morning?"

The Doctor started.

"Upon my word," he exclaimed, "I had entirely forgotten it! The fact is, that at the moment you sent it to me this morning, I was on the very point of starting for church. I had no time to look at it then, and, to say the truth, I have never thought of it since. Kate, my love, be so kind as to bring it to me from my study. You will find it on the mantel-piece."

Kate vanished, and re-appeared again in a wonderfully short space of time, and quietly glided back to her place as soon as she had put the forgotten letter in her father's hand; but if she flattered herself that the conversation which had been interrupted by her leaving the room was to be resumed upon her return to it, she was disappointed; for the thoughts of all present were speedily turned into a new current, and that so effectually as to render the recurrence to any former theme quite impossible.

CHAPTER VIII.

SCARCELY had the Doctor perused half a dozen lines of his letter before he exclaimed :—

"God bless me, Lady Augusta ! It is indeed fortunate that you recalled this letter to my recollection. Why, Walter has returned to England, my dear ! He must be in London now ; and as far as I can make out will, in all probability, be here this evening. What in the world are we to do ?"

"Do, Doctor Harrington ? Of course we can do nothing at this time of night," replied Lady Augusta, with very unmistakable manifestations of not being particularly delighted at this sudden invasion of her dominions. "Do you really suppose that your brother can expect to find us prepared to receive him for the night at such very short notice as he has thought proper to give us ? Even if his letter had not been so unluckily forgotten all these hours, it would have been strangely abrupt. I really think it is impossible !"

"My dear Lady Augusta !" replied the worthy divine, with sundry symptoms of uneasiness, "I fear there is no doubt about the matter. Just hear, my dear, what he says in his letter," and then he read as follows :—

"MY DEAR HARRY,

"I reached Liverpool this morning, and I am now going to the Museum, which I am told contains some specimens which I particularly wish to examine. I purpose leaving this place to-morrow by a train which they say will reach London by nine p.m. I have neglected to keep a note of your London address, and, therefore, enclose this to my friend and agent, Thackley, of Threadneedle Street, who will forward it to your residence without delay. You will doubtless be surprised at my unlooked-for return to Europe—but more of this when we meet, which I hope will be in time for going to roost Sunday night.

"Your affectionate brother,
"WALTER HARRINGTON."

" Decidedly there is no mistake about the matter," said young Harrington; "and if he has not jumped out of the railway-carriage, *en route* in pursuit of some butterfly or tom-tit, which by all I can learn of my venerable uncle and his habits, is not unlikely; but, if he escape the temptation, it appears to me highly probable that I may have the advantage of making his personal acquaintance in a minute or two."

" In truth, Harry," said the Doctor, pulling out his watch, " it is just about time for him to be here."

" Well, I must say, that I think it would have been kinder, to use no other word," said Lady Augusta, "if Mr. Harrington had either given us a rather longer notice of his approach, or had taken up his quarters for one night, at least, at an hotel."

" It would surely have been more decent too," murmured Lady Juliana, with freezing propriety, "not to have broken the Sabbath by this evidently unnecessary journey, even if Mr. Harrington be so unhappy as not to be influenced by any higher motive."

" There's a carriage at the door," cried young Harrington. " It brings our long-lost relative, I am quite sure."

In another instant, the deep sonorous baying of a large hound, as it seemed, was heard reverberating through the entire house, and almost shaking the walls with the unwonted echo. A few more minutes, and a heavy tread was heard on the stairs, and the door of the drawing-room was opened for the admitance of Mr. Walter Harrington.

The unsatisfactory termination of the Rev. Dr. Ponsonby's attempts to make a scholar of Walter Harrington, and the subsequent departure of the boy for Australia at the age of fourteen, is probably still fresh in the recollection of the reader. From that period to the summer in which our narrative commences, and which witnessed the completion of his seventy-first year, Walter Harrington had never been in England, nor indeed in Europe, save once. Yet all these years had not been passed by him as a sheep-farmer in Australia.

Circumstances had occurred in the interval which had very materially altered the position of the young emigrant, and that, too, while he was still far from being an old man. About twenty years after his departure for the Antipodes, his young cousin, the heir of the family estate, sickened and died.

His uncle, who had never had a second child, and was then an old man, did not very long survive his son, and Walter succeeded to the property, his own father having died about two years before.

It might have been expected, that the thriving Australian sheep-farmer, now that he had become one of the landed aristocracy of the old country, and owner of some thousands per annum, would have hastened to take his place among the fortunate few of the old world.

But this, however generally expected by his connections in England, did not take place, nor would it have taken place even if the inheritance had fallen to him earlier, for it would have been nearly impossible at any period of his life, that Walter Harrington could have settled down into a quiet, stay-at-home country gentleman.

The same restless activity and imaginative excitability which had impelled him as a boy to range the fields, when he should have been seated at his desk, impelled him still to range the fields; and the Robinson Crusoe infection which he had received in boyhood had never been eradicated.

Not that the accquisition of his inheritance was in any degree unwelcome or indifferent to him, for it enabled him to extend his wanderings unchecked over almost every part of Earth's surface, and these wanderings had formed his occupation, and the history of his life for the last thirty years.

Immediately upon hearing that the well-remembered woods and meadows of Stanton had become his own, he disposed of his flocks and wider extent of acres amid the virgin forests of the new world, and hurried home to have one look at the well-remembered scenes, and to arrange the business necessarily arising out of this acquisition of property; and this done, he started on a course of wide-world travel, the wanderings of which now brought him once again to his native land.

It must not, however, be inferred from this statement that his years had literally been spent like those of the Wandering Jew, in perpetual change of place without ever resting for two nights together in the same spot. He could not have been the same man he was, had this been so.

Walter Harrington had found time and opportunity amidst the immense variety of scenes he had passed through, to read much, and to think and examine more; but his studies had all been of the kind which the natural bent of his mind dictated, and referred almost wholly to those external aspects of Nature, which his widely-extended acquaintance with her had made especially interesting to him.

He had become a profound, as well as an enthusiastic botanist and zoologist. Entomology and ornithology were perhaps his favourite pages in the great encyclopedia of Nature, and as an active cultivator of those departments of science, he was well known to the learned societies both of London and Paris, though personally a stranger in both; and the name of Walter Harrington ranked among their most valuable corresponding members.

Of pretty nearly any other knowledge he was almost as ignorant as a child, and of all sorts of etiquette, convention-alities, habits of acting, and modes of thinking, which make up civilized social life, he was more ignorant than most children.

That noble largeness of mind, however, and that peculiar directness and singleness in every intellectual operation, which always results from conversing with Nature, more than with Man, was especially his.

Deeply rooted also in the foundations of his mind was a pervading sentiment of that true and sublime piety, and that heartfelt adoration of the Creator, which is sure to spring from the same source. His readings in the great book of Nature, which all nations and all creeds of men must admit to contain an indisputable revelation of the laws and the will of God, had taught him that *good*, physical and moral, is the normal condition of all that He has created, and that *evil* is the abnormal condition of the same; and he had faith unbounded in the ultimate godlike destiny of the immortal soul.

The tone of mind and feeling which had thus become habitual in the old naturalist, produced in him a most large and abounding charity towards all the follies, faults, and frailties of humanity; for his genuine *bonâ-fide* persuasion, that no sin or error, great or small, can by possibility escape its accurately measured quantum of painful consequences, caused him habitually, and almost involuntarily, to comtemplate the erring with pity rather than with anger.

But if it be desirable that the reader should really become acquainted with the moral and intellectual peculiarities of Mr. Walter Harrington, it may be better to leave them to develop themselves in the course of the narrative, lest any further attempt at psychological portraiture of him should cause our song to become a sermon.

So we will now direct our attention to the lighter matters of his outward man, as he appeared when, at the age of seventy-one, he arrived at the house of his brother, the Warden.

He was about six feet in height, being a trifle taller than his younger brother, and was probably also a heavier man than the Doctor, although much thinner : for his breadth of shoulders was immense, and the limbs and whole frame-work of the man were in proportion.

The face, and all the features in it, were large also, but totally free from everything like heaviness. A noble massive forehead, high, broad, and square, surmounted it. Large, bushy, black eyebrows sheltered a pair of finely opened large blue eyes, bright with intelligence, and laughing with joyous frankness.

The large mouth was filled with a magnificent set of teeth, almost in as good repair as they had been half a century ago. His complexion was deeply tanned, by long exposure to the sun and wind of many a clime, to a fine ruddy brown, and though not free from wrinkles, showed that clear purity of skin, which more perhaps than any other peculiarity, indicates well-preserved health.

But the greatest peculiarity of Mr. Walter Harrington's appearance was his hair. Abundant as that of his brother, he wore it very much longer, so long, indeed, that it fell in huge wavy locks almost upon his shoulders ; but unlike the Doctor's which was silvery, the original black was only mingled with a sufficient quantity of white to produce the general appearance of a very dark iron-grey.

He was still as upright as an arrow, and trod, though not quite so lightly, yet still with almost as much vigour and alertness as he had ever done, and very decidedly with more than half the Londoners of forty displayed.

His voice was of the same sonorous quality as that of the Warden, but entirely free from the thick huskiness which the burly fatness of the portly divine had imparted to his. The sort of pompous slowness of delivery, too, which well enough became the position and character of the ecclesiastical dignitary, was changed in the case of the elder brother for a jovial frankness of manner which was irresistible, and which

4

sufficed to atone to most persons, even in the most refined society, for the rather startling body of sound which was apt to issue from the capacious chest of the magnificent old man.

In a word, Walter Harrington, in his seventy-first year, was one of the finest old men ever seen, notwithstanding the peculiarities of his dress, which, in one or two respects, was certainly not exactly such as old gentlemen of seventy, with several thousands a-year, are in the habit of wearing in this country.

A huge pair of leggings, made of dark pepper and salt cloth, and fitting tightly from ankle to knee, encased his mighty lower limbs; while his body was clothed with a sort of frock of the same material, bound round the waist with a girdle of leather some six inches broad, to which were attached a variety of pockets and pouches, of different size and various construction.

Over the collar of this frock, which buttoned close round the throat, fell a deep shirt-collar of very white and fine linen; while a strangely incongruous look of dandyism was produced by broad wristbands of the same material, turned back over the sleeves of the frock which buttoned closely at the wrists.

The same Brummel-like appreciation for "fine linen, and plenty of it," showed itself also on his broad chest, where the frock opened, permitting this under garment to be visible, almost to his girdle. A very broad-brimmed, low-crowned hat upon his head completed his costume.

The sensations of the party assembled in Doctor Harrington's drawing-room were very various when, after a moment spent in expectation, the door was flung back against the wall, and this long-lost relative made his appearance, closely followed by an enormous and very handsome dog of the huge Labrador breed.

One stride brought him to the spot where his brother was standing.

The reverend dignitary's soft white hand was grasped in the huge iron palm of the wanderer, and the tea-things rung upon the table with the reverberations of the cordial, "Harry, my boy! how are you?" with which he greeted this astonished and almost stunned brother, while his left hand and arm administered to the startled divine something between an embrace and a slap on the back.

The Doctor sank into a chair which stood near the table, as soon as he could fairly disengage himself from his brother's circling arm, and for a minute or two was utterly unable to speak from violent coughing, and positive want of breath. As soon as he possibly could, however, he said, while he leaned with his elbow on the table, and the water streamed from his eyes :—

"My dear brother!—ugh!—ugh!—ugh! This is very dangerous doctrine—ugh!—ugh!—ugh!—very dangerous practice, I mean! I am most happy to see you—ah!—ah!—ah! But I never was so strong as you, you know, Walter; and to say the truth, my habits have not fitted me for such violent . . pastimes," he added, after vainly seeking some more appropriate term.

"Ah! you gentlemen of England who live at home at ease ——" returned his brother, looking round him; but what he might have said further remains unknown, for his friend and follower Faust, as he called his noble dog, was causing as much sensation in another part of the room, as his master had done, and of a somewhat similar kind. On their first entering the room, Faust had gravely and far more quietly than his noisy master, proceeded to make a detailed and careful investigation of all the circumstances of the new world to which he found himself introduced. He had received, with dignified self-possession, the salutation of "fine fellow!" from Kate, nor had he shrunk from rather a cordial caress from Mr. Caldwell. He had solemnly sniffed round the chair from which Lady Augusta had risen to welcome her brother-in-law, and had silently received a pat on the head both from Henry Harrington and Miss Hannah.

So far all was well; but unfortunately, his onward march brought him to the group consisting of Lady Juliana, Miss Mary Jane, and Mr. Garble, and here his investigations assumed a more active and accurate character. The Lady Juliana was the only one of the party who still kept her seat, not deeming it necessary to incur the fatigue of rising from it, till it should come to her turn to receive the greetings of her brother-in-law.

Now, whether it were that the abundantly pomatumed and perfumed ringlets of the noble spinster had attracted the attention of Faust, or whether her reclining attitude had excited his curiosity to discover whether she were asleep or dead, it is impossible to say; but certain it is, that the huge

beast suddenly, yet very deliberately, raised himself on his
hind legs, and, placing his fore-paws on the lady's uncovered
shoulders, set about diligently examining with his nose every
part of her *coiffure*.

It must be owned that the attack was an alarming one for
an elderly London lady; for the enormous weight of the dog
did, really, and without any affectation at all, nearly overset
her backwards. Nevertheless, it certainly was not necessary,
nor very reasonable, that it should call forth the rapid succession of crescendo screams that were now uttered by her
Ladyship.

An immediate exclamation of "Faust, Sir, come to heel!"
shouted by his master in the tone and key that had been
wont to make the primeval forests ring, instantly caused the
obedient animal to withdraw himself, and crouch at his
master's feet.

But the mischief to the lady's nervous system was not so
easily repaired. It was, indeed, some time before the united
assiduities of the other ladies assembled round her, were able
definitively to ward off the alternate threatenings of hysterics
and fainting fits; but when, at length, she was sufficiently
restored to composure to permit anger to take the place of
terror, she turned her eyes on the huge offender with no very
gentle or forgiving look.

Mr. Harrington, who certainly at first had been rather
inclined to laugh at the assault his favourite had committed,
now stood in utter astonishment at the effect it had produced;
but when, at length, there appeared to be a possibility of
speaking to the terrified and offended lady, he approached her,
saying, that had he not well known the dog to be as gentle as
a lamb, he should not have brought him into the house, and
that she need not be under the slightest alarm in case a similar
accident should occur again.

"Occur again, Sir!" cried the outraged lady, with a
strongly accentuated expression of indignant astonishment,
"I trust, Sir, that you will not dream of further tempting
Providence by suffering the creature to live. Surely, after
the merciful escape I have had—and I pray God most
fervently that I may recognise, as I ought, with due thankfulness the special mercy shown therein!—surely, Sir, you
will not tempt Providence any further? Surely you will
think it right to have the dangerous beast shot immediately?"

"*Shot*, Madam!" returned the old man, with a sudden

and rather portentous contraction of his bushy black eyebrows.
But, immediately recovering his look of open-hearted good
humour, he added: "Pooh, pooh! you are joking. No, we
won't shoot Faust, but he shall undergo a punishment
almost as terrible; he shall be turned out of the room, and sit
without daring to move on the staircase."

And so saying, he opened the door, and announced his
sentence to the obedient beast, who forthwith obeyed with an
air of unmistakable penitence, and consciousness of disgrace.
But despite this atonement, those of the party who best knew
the Lady Juliana, felt no doubt respecting the nature of her
feelings, both towards the dog and his master.

The three Miss Wigginsvilles now discreetly arose and took
their leave; Mr. Garble, too, jumped up, as in duty bound, to
lead them to their carriage, and also made his parting bow.
And then Mr. Caldwell, having promised Kate to call in the
morning to examine the site of her proposed conservatory, and
pronounce his opinion of the practicability of her scheme, also
took his leave, and the family party were left to themselves.

CHAPTER IX.

Then came all the hospitable inquiries from Lady Augusta
and the Doctor as to what the traveller would have to eat,
together with a *sotto voce* discussion as to what might be in
the house, &c.; and her Ladyship was again a little startled
by hearing her guest, when pressed to say what sort of
refreshment he would prefer, reply:—

"Anything, my dear sister—anything you will. Give me
a broiled turkey, if you like it."

The good gentleman had quite forgotten that turkeys do
not run about London streets as they do about the homesteads
on the other side of the Atlantic, and was perfectly ignorant
that the *improvisé* supper he had selected as the easiest and
simplest in the whole bill of fare known to him, was, under
the existing circumstances, rather an *exigeant* one.

The lady was, in fact, obliged to confess that she feared there was no such thing as a turkey in the house, and, being Sunday, it was impossible to get one.

Then followed a discussion concerning the best arrangements that could be made about a bed for him, and very civil regrets were expressed on the part of her Ladyship that the shortness of the notice precluded the possibility of her doing all she could wish for his accommodation; and again her nerves were doomed to endure a shock that made her inwardly shudder from head to foot, by a proposal from the hardy old traveller that he should have "a shake-down in the room they were in."

"Merciful Heaven! a shake-down for an old man and his dog in her amber satin drawing-room! Must not the being be an absolute savage who could propose it?"

Such assuredly was her thoughts; but all she said was, gently, though with a slight touch of despair in her accent, "that she trusted they might think of some plan more convenient than that."

A short muttered conversation then followed between Kate and her mother, which ended by the young lady's saying, with a pretty mixture of frankness and timidity, that if her uncle would accept a bed in a very tiny bed-room it would be a great pleasure to her, as she herself could sleep perfectly well on the large sofa which stood in her mother's dressing-room.

Uncle Walter of course protested against any such arrangement; but Kate persisted so earnestly, and the sincerity of her wish that he should accept her offer was so evident, that he yielded, and so the matter was arranged; and then Kate led him off, while his supper was being prepared, to show him his quarters, and herself do the honours of her own little territory.

This was in truth a labour of love, for Kate was rather proud of her dominions; and somehow or other, she already felt that she should take more pleasure in showing her books, and her music, and her drawings, and all her other treasures, to this great, rough, stranger uncle, than to all the rest of her kinsfolk and acquaintance.

There is no way of accounting for this, save by the mysterious doctrine of sympathy.

It was but little that Kate knew, or had ever heard, of her uncle, for it was very little that any of her family could tell her about him. The one fact, that he was known to the scientific world as a great traveller and naturalist, comprised pretty nearly all she knew concerning him; yet certain it is, that before they returned to the drawing-room, Kate and her uncle were very fast friends.

Moreover, she had actually confided to him the great conservatory project, into which he entered, heart and soul; and she told him, moreover, that Mr. Caldwell was coming to-morrow to pronounce his opinion on the feasibility of the construction. And she mentioned, too, that this Mr. Caldwell was an officer in the Engineers, and reckoned by everyone to be particular clever, and quite a man of science. And then she added, that he was also considered by everybody, she believed, as extremely agreeable. Nor was the eccentric old uncle blind to the fact that his beautiful niece looked more beautiful still, as she said all this, and that the delicate colour in her cheeks became perceptibly heightened.

The *genus* young lady was a branch of zoology which the old bachelor had enjoyed very few opportunities of studying. But he noted these phenomena in his mind.

The *habitat* of the pretty creature he was studying afforded him great interest and satisfaction, for, to say the truth, Kate's cell appeared to him the only part of the house he had seen, which promised any of the comforts of existence. Not only were there books, music, and drawing materials, but there were also indications of their being used.

In the drawing-room the pianoforte was closed, and no sign, in the shape of music-books, that it was ever open. Not a book of any kind was to be seen there, save that one number of the *Quarterly*, which Miss Hannah had, with her usual audacity, contrived to extract from the Doctor's study.

But here, on the contrary, all that he saw seemed for use, and in use; so that Kate and her uncle returned to the drawing-room, as I have already stated, fast friends.

"I have been telling Kate," said Mr. Harrington, as he re-entered the drawing-room, "that I shall really be ashamed of myself for appropriating what appears to be evidently the best quarters in the house; but she won't listen to me, and so I suppose I must submit."

"Upon my word, Walter," said the Doctor, looking at him, "I think that anyone would take you to be twenty years my junior, instead of being my senior. But care and grave responsibilities will tell; and an over-laboured brain," he added, shaking his head with a sigh of resignation, "will bleach the hair that covers it."

"And learning, too, Harry! You know," returned Walter, while his eyes laughed gaily, "all the learning they crammed into you, must, I am very sure, help a good deal in making a man old before his time. You remember, Harry, don't you? how stedfastly I refused to swallow poor old Ponsonby's doses of Greek."

"In truth, the sword sometimes will wear out the scabbard, Walter," rejoined the Doctor. "Incessant mental labour of all kinds cannot be expected to leave the body at seventy, in such a state of health and perfect preservation as it is evident you enjoy. It is only one more instance of the domination of mind over matter."

And the Doctor said this very solemnly, with his fat husky voice, as he crossed his hands resignedly upon his rotund stomach.

"True, brother," returned the elder Harrington, in a very grave tone, but with a merry twinkle in his eye; "but you must take as much care of yourself as you can. And, by the way, what hours do you keep, Harry? when do you go to bed?"

"Oh! we are early people, we generally get to bed by midnight; and Hutchinson always brings me my hot water at nine; for the breakfast is punctually on the table at ten."

"That's what you call early, is it?" said the other, with genuine surprise. "If I don't get my first draught of morning air within half an hour after the sun gets up, it never seems to me to be fresh enough. And what do you do with hot water, Harry, at that time in the morning?"

"Do with it?" returned the Doctor, staring at him, "why wash and shave, to be sure. What do you do?"

"Why I jump into the coldest bath I can get," returned the senior, laughing.

"What, in winter?" said the shivering Doctor, aghast.

"Winter and summer, seed-time and harvest, every morning of my life if I can possibly manage it," said Walter, finishing his supper as he spoke, by tossing off a tumbler of water.

"You have taken no wine, brother," said the Doctor. "You will find that sherry excellent."

"I have not the least doubt of it, Harry; but I never

drink wine," was the reply. "Do you use it much?" added
Walter, glancing at the Warden's rubicund visage.

"But little," replied the reverend gentleman, gravely.
"I very seldom take above a glass, or at most two, at
luncheon, and very rarely exceed a pint at dinner."

"Well," returned the senior, after the pause of a moment,
"to tell you the truth, Harry, I rather wonder that the
scabbard has lasted so well, if that is the treatment you give
it. But now before going to bed I must beg your indulgence,
Lady Augusta, for a companion of my journey, who is not
quite so hardy as I am, and who cannot do without the luxury
of a fire at night."

"My dear brother, I had no idea that you had anyone with
you," cried the Doctor, rather uneasily. "I fear that we
have not the means of accommodating any——"

"Oh! she will share my room," returned the elder
brother, laughing; "or if not, she will do capitally well in
Kate's cell, if she has only a fire in the room—that's the
great point."

"Some wretched Indian woman!" thought the Doctor,
greatly shocked, and equally embarrassed and surprised at this
utter disregard of decency; and he was meditating in very
awkward silence how best to point out to him the impossi-
bility of his consenting to receive such an inmate, when
Walter added:—

"I should like to show her to you. I'll have her brought
up here;" and before his brother could interfere to prevent
his purpose, he had opened the door, and ran down stairs into
the hall.

The Doctor and the Doctor's wife looked at each other in
dismay; and young Harrington and Kate looked at each
other and laughed; while Lady Juliana sat muttering that
she was not the least surprised, and that nothing better could
be expected from one who travelled on a Sunday, when
Mr. Harrington re-entered, followed by a couple of men-
servants, carrying a large deal box about four feet square,
which by the old gentleman's direction they placed on the
floor.

The party round him exchanged glances, expressive both of
astonishment and dismay, but waited in perfect silence for
what was to follow, Mr. Harrington the while occupying
himself busily in preparing to open the case.

"I was determined that you should be the first to see her,"

said he, affectionately; "and she will be presented to-morrow, I hope."

"Presented! Brother Walter," cried the agitated Doctor, "what *are* you talking about? and what *do* you mean? and what can this great box have to do with the person you were speaking about?"

"Ha, ha, ha, ha!" laughed Walter, who had by this time unloosed the fastenings of the case. "This box, Harry, is for the present the residence of the *person* I have been speaking about. And the person herself," he added, raising the lid as he spoke, with an air of the utmost pride and satisfaction, "the person herself is no less, as I flatter myself, than the most magnificent boa-constrictor ever brought alive to this country."

It would be difficult to describe the various symptoms of terror and surprise which this announcement produced among most of the persons present.

The Doctor, who had been standing close beside his brother, retreated four or five paces, with a more rapid and much less dignified step than usual, exclaiming:—

"God bless my soul! Is the reptile safely secured, brother Walter? Surely it is not desirable to introduce animals of so formidable a species into—into—the privacy of domestic life! It is very dangerous doet . . . . that is, I mean to say, a very dangerous beast."

Lady Augusta and her sister had rushed to the furtherest corner of the room, and were screaming together, "Shut the box! shut the box!" in tones that indicated approaching hysterics.

Young Harrington had advanced to his uncle's side, and was gazing with interest on the apparently slumbering monster; while Kate, with her hand on her brother's arm, and half shrinking behind him, was timidly venturing to gratify her curiosity also.

Mr. Harrington, after striving in vain to persuade the two elder ladies to come and look at the animal, by assuring them that it was in a perfectly torpid state, closed the box, and informed them, to their no small relief, that he had brought it to England as a present to the Regent's Park Zoological Gardens, and that he intended to send it thither on the morrow; and then it was very satisfactorily arranged that it should be conveyed to Kate's cell for the night, and that a fire should be lighted there for its especial accommodation and comfort. The family party then separated for the night, but not before Lady Juliana had observed, that she felt she owed it to herself to say that, "it was in her judgment a vain and sinful tempting of the Lord, to feed and cherish animals which He had selected as the fitting form of incarnation for the eternal enemy of man, and a wicked disobedience and rebellion to preserve and cherish a creature whose head he had been positively commanded to crush."

~~~~~~~~~~

CHAPTER X.

WE must perforce follow the Doctor and Lady Augusta to their own apartment, for it was there that a conversation took place between them, too important to our story to be omitted. It was the lady who began it, which she did by addressing her husband by a title which she now rarely used, except when she was not well pleased.

"Well, Mr. Warden!" said she, "what is your opinion of this newly-found brother, who is come back upon us like the prodigal son?"

"My dear love!" quoth the Doctor, "the parable, since you have referred to it, is assuredly intended to teach us what example to follow, and what to avoid. I trust we shall be ready to behave as did the prodigal's father, and not as his brother. More especially, Lady Augusta, as in this case, the lost sheep has not spent all he had in riotous living—or otherwise, but very much the contrary."

"Come, come, Mr. Warden, let us leave texts and parables to their proper place, if you please, and endeavour to consider the important matter before us with common sense if we can," said Lady Augusta, which meant, in plain English, and divested of the ordinary decencies of expression, "Let us, in the consideration of this matter, be guided wholly and solely by motives of the most sordid kind; let us throw out of sight altogether, all thoughts of duty, kindness, or brotherly affection, and look entirely at our own interests—our interests of the meanest and lowest sort." And yet how unfeignedly shocked would that pattern of propriety, the Doctor, or his superlatively correct lady have been, if this species of conference had been openly and nakedly proposed by the one to the other.

But the worshippers of decency and propriety never do look at their own thoughts naked. Indeed, for the most part, their thoughts can scarcely be said to be born naked, but rather to spring from the mind ready clothed with a becoming and presentable vesture of decorous semblance, and with the decent and becoming veil of proper phraseology.

The Doctor replied accordingly to his respected partner's harangue, and earnestly assured her that his wish was to consider the subject on the soundest and broadest principles of common sense; and he proceeded at once to give proof of docile obedience, by observing that his brother must now be in possession of at least four thousand a-year, and probably of a very considerable sum of ready money besides; for it was well known that he had never spent above half his income since he succeeded to the estate; "and even of that annual expenditure, he tells me," said the Doctor, with a tinge of pitying contempt in his manner, "that a few hundreds only have supplied all his personal wants, while full fifteen hundred a-year have gone in the purchase and transport of specimens for his museum."

"Specimens! specimens of what, in the name of Heaven?" cried Lady Augusta, with a vivid appreciation of the value of fifteen hundred a-year.

"How should I know," returned the Doctor, with the dignified contempt which he invariably felt for everything of which he was ignorant. "Sticks, and stones, and trash of all sorts—birds, beasts, and reptiles, dead or alive! I have no doubt that horrid monster he has been so inconsiderate as to bring home with him, has cost him more than a hundred pounds."

"Gracious Heaven!" cried her Ladyship, "is it not dreadful to think that a man capable of such preposterous absurdity, should have the uncontrolled disposition of four thousand a-year! I am sure many a statute of lunacy has been taken out on less cogent grounds."

"Walter *is* eccentric, lamentably eccentric!" replied the Doctor; and then, he added, with a touch of the pompous tone, and regular and piston-like rise and fall of voice which constituted his pulpit manner, "There never was a more striking instance of the fatal results arising from the neglect of a regular education, than is exhibited in the deplorable wreck of his mind—and intellect."

"The property is entailed, of course?" said Lady Augusta, interrogatively.

"No, my dear Lady Augusta, it is not. The entail was cut off by my poor uncle and his son, who died very shortly afterwards. Walter has the entire and unrestricted possession of the property, and may sell the whole to-morrow, if he should think fit."

"Gracious Heaven!" again ejaculated her Ladyship, "I wonder that I should have never informed myself of all this before! But, in truth, I felt certain that our poor dear Henry was heir to the estate as a matter of course. And so, as a matter of course, he would be, entail or no entail, if Mr. Harrington were a different sort of man; or, in short, if he were in a condition to be considered as of sound mind, which, to say the truth, I cannot consider a man to be, who is likely to defraud his natural heir for the sake of selling his estate, and sinking the entire produce in the purchase of snakes! I don't know what you may think of it, Mr. Warden, but I am very decidedly of opinion that the Lord Chancellor's opinion would be found to agree with mine."

The Doctor shook his head very mournfully, but it might be doubtful whether it was because he differed from his lady, or agreed with her.

"The very fact of his bringing that most awful and abominable serpent into my drawing-room," she continued, after pausing for a moment to shudder as the fearful outrage recurred to her; "this very fact alone, the mere statement of his having brought a boa constrictor into the drawing-room of Lady Augusta Harrington, would go far towards convincing a jury of his insanity."

The Doctor listened to her very attentively, and then replied:—

"Absurd as my poor brother's notions appear to us, my dear, and monstrous as they must appear to every man of enlarged mind, and regularly finished education, I do not think that his perversity of intellect amounts to what the law calls lunacy. Moreover, it is a deplorable fact, my dear Lady Augusta, that there exist large bodies of men deeply infected with various forms of very analagous mania."

This opinion was delivered in the Doctor's most dogma-
tizing and impressive manner; but after a short pause, he
added, in a less magnificent tone of voice :—

"However, despite his follies, my dear, I must own that
Walter has shown himself a good and kind brother on more
than one occasion; and I cannot but think that he will
eventually make such a disposition of his property as we shall
all think right and becoming. But this, my dear Augusta,
you must be sensible, is but one part of the question."

"Of course," replied her intelligent Ladyship; "and
though, for dear Henry's sake, it may eventually be considered as the most important, it is not the most pressing
subject for immediate consideration."

"You allude, my love, to the probability that my brother
may wish to reside with us?" said the Doctor.

"I allude, Mr. Warden, to the four thousand a-year which
this half-crazed brother has to dispose of, whether he live
with us or elsewhere, and which he has evidently no more
need of, and no more idea what to do with, than that great
monster of a dog he has brought with him."

"It would be a great thing for him to reside under our
roof, Lady Augusta," said the Doctor, in a meditative and
rather melancholy tone. "He must, my dear, be in sad want
of guidance and assistance of all sorts—even to the enjoyment
of the natural and most ordinary comforts of life, of which he
seems almost to be wholly ignorant."

The words of very decent, well-behaved people, like the
Doctor, often require translating into plain English, in order
to be fully intelligible even to their own hearts.

Thus the real thought which the Doctor's last words ought
to have expressed was: "It would be a great thing for *us*
if my brother Walter could be persuaded to live with us, and
pay us a handsome sum from his abundant income for board
and lodging." Nay, if the exact idea is to be completely
rendered, the recollection that the Brother Walter took no
wine must not be omitted.

Lady Augusta, however, who was a finished mistress of
decorum in all its branches, including, of course, the use and
ready comprehension of its phraseology, was at no loss to
understand the Doctor's full meaning; she understood it
perfectly well.

The key to this language is simply putting words indicative
of the generous, the noble, and the great, in order to express

thoughts shabby, dirty, and little. It is a figure of speech which furnishes immense resources; and it may almost be said, that in the present state of society, *decency* could scarcely exist without it.

And Lady Augusta replied accordingly,—

"It would, indeed, my dear Doctor, be everything for the poor lonely man! And the thought does honour to your goodness of heart, Henry! But there are many objections— many things to be considered. It must be admitted, I know, that a brother has great claims! and God forbid that I should put any difficulty in the way, from any consideration for my own comfort."

"My dearest Lady Augusta," replied her husband, with a tone and look of deep admiration, "you are ever ready at the call of duty House-rent is enormously high in this neighbourhood. I daresay now that it would appear almost incredible to poor Walter, that we should pay eight hundred a-year for this house."

"The expenses of housekeeping, too, at the West-end of London," rejoined Lady Augusta, "would doubtless appear to his almost savage nature absolutely preposterous. I daresay, poor man, that he did not mean to ask for anything out of the usual way, when he told me to give him a turkey for his supper to-night; and turkeys costing, as our last did, twenty-five shillings!"

"If my brother's tastes and habits should be found to require that our moderate housekeeping should be modelled on a more expensive plan than heretofore, which certainly, from the circumstance you mention, does not seem altogether improbable," said the Doctor, "if such should really be the case, my dear, it would not be right, I think, to make our home distasteful to him by denying him comforts which he has such ample means of commanding."

"Perhaps not," replied Lady Augusta, with an air of lenient indulgence towards the sybarite tastes attributed to Walter on the strength of the turkey supper hypothesis. "Perhaps it *would* be too much to expect that an old, self-indulged bachelor, possessed of such a fine income, should content himself with such frugal housekeeping as ours; for, Heaven knows, I am often obliged to be careful. But it will be absolutely necessary, Doctor, *remember*, should any arrangement of the kind be proposed, that this difference as to expenditure should be borne in mind."

"Unquestionably!" was the only word uttered in reply; but it was spoken in the Doctor's most decisive manner, and Lady Augusta was so perfectly well satisfied by it, that early peas, house lamb, and *pêtè gras*, were mentally set down to Walter's account as necessaries that he would consider indispensable, and must pay for accordingly. And then her active mind passed on rapidly to another item in the account, and to this she alluded in her own peculiarly decorous manner:—

"A brother, my dear Doctor," said she, in a tone both gentle and affectionate, "a brother has great claims, immense claims; and God forbid, as I said before, that I should stand in the way of your doing a brother's duty. No, not for the world would I be guilty of this; but the bringing any inmate into such a family as ours is a very serious thing, Dr. Harrington, and ought to be very maturely considered in every point of view. Now, there is one consideration, and I should not be doing my duty if I did not confess it, which may tend to render your brother an objectionable member of our family circle. I allude to our daughter, Dr. Harrington. Kate is young, and extremely impressionable; and I leave you to judge whether the manners of savage life; such—in short, as we know must necessarily be those of Mr. Harrington—are exactly the model on which you would desire to see your daughter's fashioned?"

The Doctor, in his secret heart, knew perfectly well that this high-sounding objection was not intended to be insuperable, but was only brought forward as an item in the bill to be charged and paid for; so he very gently replied:—

"It is, as you most justly observe, my dear, a matter of great importance, and one that demands mature deliberation; yet I cannot but flatter myself, Lady Augusta, that this danger may be met, and conquered, by a little increased vigilance on your part; and from this labour, fatiguing as it may be, I know you will not shrink. Nevertheless, I own that I certainly do think that the necessity of imposing all this additional trouble upon you, ought to be taken into consideration when we are fixing the amount which my wealthy brother ought to contribute to the expenses of our family establishment. This would be but common sense and common justice."

"I knew you would agree with me, dear Doctor," replied her Ladyship, well pleased with the deceit drapery with which he had so readily covered up her not very gracious suggestion; and, after the pause of a few seconds, she added, in an accent of the most perfect conjugal confidence: "Well then, taking all things into consideration, what sum do you think it would be right to name? We had better make up our minds on this point at once, my dear Henry; for if your brother has any idea of the kind, it is highly probable that he will mention the subject to-morrow, and it is quite as well we should have mutually made up our minds upon the subject beforehand. Indeed, even if he should not touch upon the matter at all, you will probably think that it would be no more than brotherly affection demands, if you were, unsolicited, to propose this truly kind arrangement to him. In any case, however, it is highly desirable that you should be prepared. Our greatest difficulty will be about a sitting-room for him. I suppose it will be necessary to give him one of some sort or other? I am afraid it would be very inconvenient to give up your study. Do you think you could manage without it?"

"My dear Lady Augusta, it is wholly impossible—altogether out of the question—not to be thought of for a moment! I would far rather give up London, and divide the year between Oxford and Glastonbury."

This hint was sufficient, as the sympathising feelings of the Doctor led him to anticipate would be the case, and Lady Augusta made no further allusion to the sacred accommodation he so dearly valued.

"There would be no difficulty," she resumed, "in getting Kate to relinquish her rooms, but I am afraid, from a few words which I overheard to-night, from her uncle, that he would object to any such proposal."

"My dear Lady Augusta," said the Doctor, eagerly, "now you mention Kate's room, I remember Walter expatiated upon the great pleasure and advantage arising from her windows commanding such a fine view of the Park. Now it is obvious, I presume, for I have never been in that part of the house myself, that the view must be finer still from the room above. Surely, my dear, the two rooms over Kate's bed-room and sitting-room would accommodate Walter very satisfactorily? With his extraordinary activity, too, it must be quite delightful to him to ascend so many stairs. It is a law of nature, a well-known law of nature, Lady Augusta, that all creatures delight in exercising the faculties which they possess in the greatest perfection."

5

"In that case," replied Lady Augusta, looking extremely well-pleased, "in that case, Doctor Harrington, all the servants must *at once* be instructed that those apartments are no longer to be called the back attics. The housekeeper has hitherto slept in one of them, and the other has been used as a lumber-room. Briggs must now share my maid's-room, and the lumber-room must immediately be cleared out. The two rooms will then, indeed, form a most desirable apartment. Indeed, considering the purity of the air, the beauty of the view, and the very much greater quiet and tranquillity which they must possess, they may very fairly, I think, be considered as the best and pleasantest quarters in the house."

"And even if they are so, my dear love," rejoined the Doctor, with an air of almost angelic benignity, "even if they are so, I should still be well pleased that they should be given up to my brother. His means are amply sufficient to justify his being allowed to occupy the best part of whatever house he may reside in. And it will be a great pleasure to me, in any conversation I may have with Walter on the subject, to point out to him the desirable features in the rooms which we are so fortunately able to offer him."

"I am sure it will! I am quite sure of it!" replied her Ladyship, approvingly. "But now, my dear, let us return to the important question—always bearing in mind the heavy expenses which it is clear, even from the cursory examination of the subject that we have now given it, that we must incur in making your brother as comfortable as we would wish him to be, and not altogether losing sight of what is due to ourselves, and our children—what sum per annum, Dr. Harrington, do you think it would be right to propose to him?"

Up to this point the conversation had proceeded briskly enough, but this was the heart of the matter, and it was a knotty heart, and the Doctor paused long ere he replied to it, so long, indeed, that his impatient consort hastened his deliberations by exclaiming:—

"Well, Mr. Warden! have you gone to sleep? or do you mean to keep me all night, waiting for your reply?"

Thus strangely urged, the worthy dignitary, who, far from forgetting this part of the subject, had in truth been concentrating the whole power of his mind upon it, at length made up his mind to speak as follows:—

"I am of opinion, Lady Augusta, that it would be very greatly for my brother's advantage to purchase all that a residence under my roof—and yours, Lady Augusta—would give him, for the annual payment of one thousand pounds. I am sure we could not do it for less in justice to ourselves."

Lady Augusta was disappointed. She had in her own mind determined upon trying for half as much again. So she returned to the charge by very emphatically exclaiming:—

"No, Mr. Warden! no! that will not do. It is all very well, and very natural for you to feel generously disposed towards your brother, but you ought not to exercise your generosity at the expense of justice to your own family. You *must* know, perfectly well, that a thousand a-year will *not* pay for choice rooms in a house of eight hundred a-year; a table of the most costly, and probably troublesome kind, great fatigue, great care, great anxiety, and responsibility, and the use of a carriage. Besides, Sir, use your common sense for a moment, and tell me, if you please, what is your bachelor brother to do with the remaining three thousand a-year? Squander it, Mr. Warden! squander it in an unprincipled manner, in purchasing absolutely useless trash. Is this right, Sir? Ought we to permit such shocking, such sinful waste of money, if we can in any way prevent it? No, Mr. Warden! most assuredly we ought not. I think," she continued, in a gentler tone, after taking a few minutes to recover herself from the shock which the Doctor's shabby little estimate had caused her, "I think, that with my careful management, I might be able to make fifteen hundred a-year suffice—but certainly not a shilling less, certainly not. In justice to myself and my three children, I could not attempt it."

"I have not the least doubt that you are perfectly right, my dear Lady Augusta," replied the Doctor, very docilely; "not the least shadow of doubt. You understand such matters much better than I do. I am only afraid that Walter, who is of course more ignorant of all these things than even I am, I am only afraid that he might think fifteen hundred a-year rather high for board and lodging; and that it might not occur to him to make any allowance for ——" here the Doctor hesitated a little, "for—those other considerations, which it is absolutely necessary to take into the account."

"Upon my word, I will not suppose anything so absurd, Dr. Harrington," said the bolder-spirited lady. "If your brother," she continued, "is really so completely ignorant of the modes and customs of civilized society as to be unconscious of the fact, he must, by some means or other, be made to comprehend, that mere food and lodging do *not* include all the requirements and expenses of a gentleman in London. But I cannot think," she added, after meditating in silence for a minute or two, "I cannot think that a man who is capable of paying above a hundred pounds for a hideous, venomous snake, is likely to care much whether he pays a little more or a little less for anything."

And herein Lady Augusta made a nearer approach to speaking the thoughts of her heart than she had yet done. Her hopes of obtaining a handsome addition to her husband's already handsome income, were chiefly based on the conviction that her brother-in-law was too "savage" to know or to care much about the value or the use of money.

"Well, my dear love," resumed the Doctor, "I defer entirely, as I said, to your better judgment; and whenever the subject comes to be spoken of, I shall tell Walter that for fifteen hundred a-year he may have in this house all the comforts and blessings of a family, and a home. But that for a smaller sum, it would be impossible for me, without injuring my own children, to receive him."

"The latter alternative to be, of course, touched on *only* in case he object to the sum named," said Lady Augusta.

"Of course, my dear, of course," was the reply.

And then this admirable couple turned each on their respective pillow, and sunk into that sweet sleep which those blessed by the approval of their own consciences—and a good digestion—are sure to enjoy after the fatigues of a well-spent day.

    *   *   *   *   *

And now before closing this chapter, we will relieve the anxious reader's mind, by communicating at once the result of the important proposition which had been decided on in the preceding conversation.

Walter, as his thoughtful relatives had anticipated, did not let the morrow pass without adverting to his future plans.

It was in the Doctor's study, and immediately after breakfast, that the conversation between the brothers took place. The proposal that the elder should find a home in the house of the younger came from Walter, who went on to talk of his brother's children, and of their being all that he had to care

for in the world; and he said how much he had been charmed
with all he had seen of his niece Kate, and how needful it
was to happiness to have something to love, especially when
one felt old age coming on. All which were sentiments
highly praiseworthy, and pleasant to hear from a wealthy
bachelor-brother. But still there was no opening afforded by
which the Doctor could enter upon the £. s. d. part of
the subject.

He began to get embarrassed and fidgety; and at last, as
Walter did not appear to be getting at all nearer to this
important portion of the question, he desperately determined
to dash at it boldly, by saying:—

"Ah, brother! would to Heaven, it were in my power to
offer you all the blessings you have been speaking of as freely
as I would wish to do it."

"My dear Harry," cried the simple Walter, "is there any
objection in the way? I am heartily sorry for it."

"There is no objection, my dear Walter, but such as
arises, alas! from my restricted means, and the terribly large
expenses incidental to my position."

"But this would surely be amended, dear Harry, and not
aggravated by our uniting our means together," returned
Walter. "My expenses are small, and my wants few and
simple."

The Doctor was cruelly puzzled by this little speech. The
first clause of it seemed to intimate a possibility, that Walter's
notions of contributing to the family expenses far exceeded in
liberality all he had ever dared to hope for. But then, the
latter part of it seemed to indicate a valuation of what he was
to receive, which would fall far short of what he and his
admirable helpmate hoped to maintain.

After a short pause given to a hasty and nervous calculation
on the probabilities, he decided that in any case it would be
best to come to the point at once, and he replied:—

"You are, as ever, all generosity and kindness, my dear
Walter, and your truly brotherly proposition emboldens me to
say frankly, that I think, by careful management, and by the
help of Lady Augusta's admirable economy, all those blessings
of which you have been speaking might, without injury to my
own family, be secured to you for fifteen hundred a-year;
including, you know," he added, hastily, as if anxious to
modify the effect of his proposal, "always including the use
of a carriage."

"Well, my dear fellow, so be it," cried Walter, cordially. "And I shall truly rejoice," he added, "if the arrangement is any assistance to you in defraying the heavy expenses you speak of."

"Heavy indeed, my dear brother," returned the Warden, with a sigh. "Ah, Walter!" he added, "you don't know all that the world expects from a man in my position."

And so it was definitively settled, to the satisfaction of all parties, that Walter should have board, lodgings, family ties, and something to love in his declining years, including the use of a carriage, for fifteen hundred pounds per annum, paid quarterly.

~~~~~~~~~~~~

CHAPTER XI.

THE important arrangement which has been recorded in the last chapter, caused Lady Augusta to postpone the great party, which has been already alluded to, for a week or two. She had originally intended that it should come off about the end of May, but the little revolution in family arrangements which the arrival of Mr. Harrington had occasioned, made it convenient to postpone the ball, and the 25th of June had ultimately been fixed on for it, which day was now near at hand.

For although not a day had passed since Walter's arrival, unmarked by some circumstance connected with his initiation into civilized society, well worthy to have engaged the attention of such small chroniclers as ourselves, we are compelled to pass them in silence, in order to leave time and space for what is to follow; and we must, therefore, hasten over the events which have befallen our *dramatis personæ* in the interval, at a hard gallop.

Walter had already seen much which had appeared to him to be fully as astonishing as anything that his widely extended travels had shown him; and the curious interest and very great surprise and *puzzlement* which many of the

aspects of civilized life afforded him, were increased in no
slight degree by an inveterate habit, very difficult to be
broken through when once contracted, of believing everything
that was told him.

Lady Augusta had done her best to make her brother-in-
law a little more presentable, as she called it, and her well-
meant efforts had taken the form of sundry earnest lecturings
upon certain points in his conduct and bearing, which Walter
thought infinitesimally small in their significance; and which
soon caused him to assign to his sister-in-law a place in his
mind, next door to that still occupied by his recollections of
Mrs. Ponsonby, whose unceasing warfare against the dirty
shoes and rumpled shirt-collars of his naughty-boyhood still
lived in his memory.

He considered Lady Juliana as a very curious but rather
incomprehensible animal. There was no great chance,
certainly, that there would ever be any great sympathy
between them, and in truth, the pious spinster already hated
the "Godless savage," as she called him, with a very zealous
hatred. But it is true, also, that he had given her considerable cause to do so, and there really was great reason
to fear that the poor lady's life would become a burthen to
her, in consequence of Mr. Harrington's residence in the
family, for causes of very vehement offence were perpetually
occurring.

Sometimes when Lady Juliana would heave a sigh, or
breathe forth a groan, such as are considered in all civilized
society to express reprobation of the wickedness of those
around, or of compunction for the sins of the whole world in
general, Walter Harrington would earnestly ask, " what ailed
her?" and that, too, in a tone of such truly genuine
solicitude, as made it difficult for any bystander to hear it
without a smile. And, moreover, the extreme amusement
which every such occurrence evidently afforded the unregenerate Kate, occasioned Lady Juliana the disagreeable
sensation of extreme and intense provocation.

Moreover, the offending wanderer was always, and for ever,
in such detestably high spirits, and with so provoking an
appearance of happiness, that not even her secret conviction
of his eternal perdition, appeared sufficient to soothe the
irritation of spirits which his joyous hilarity produced—for
did not his rude health seem to defer to an almost indefinite
distance this just requital for all he made her suffer?

Once, indeed, matters threatened to become still worse
between them, for she almost succeeded in really offending
the old gentleman.

It happened that Walter had, one Sunday afternoon, proposed to the ladies that they should accompany him to the
Zoological Gardens, and Lady Augusta and Kate had readily
accepted the invitation, to the great scandal and indignation
of Lady Juliana, whose feelings were so vehemently excited
by it, that she turned to her sister, and said, with great
animation :—

"Mr. Harrington, *as an Atheist*, acts with perfect con-
sistency in breaking the Sabbath ; but I do hope, Augusta,
that you ——"

A sudden and very unusual flush had spread over the
face of Walter Harrington.

"*What* do you say ?" exclaimed he, with an intonation
that made all present start. "But it would be very silly,"
he added, in quite a different tone, "it would be very silly to
be angry about it. Ladies should not use Greek words,
which, doubtless, they do not understand."

"You must pardon me, Mr. Harrington," replied the
irritated lady, with an intensity of bitterness, which she took
no great pains to conceal, "you must pardon me, if I do not
plead guilty to the excess of ignorance which you are pleased
to attribute to me. An Atheist, Mr. Harrington, is one who,
as the Scripture awfully describes it, lives without God in the
world—unhappily, we see but too many such around us'"

"And may I ask you, Lady Juliana, upon what grounds
you have come to the conclusion that I, and those you class
with me, live, as it is phrased, without God in the world?"
And now Walter Harrington spoke gently and calmly

"I have but to answer in the words of holy writ, Sir'
'By their fruits ye shall know them,'" replied the lady, with
awful emphasis, and a most lofty air of superiority. "And
how can it be supposed, Sir," she added, very solemnly,
"that those who break God's commandments can have the
fear of Him before their eyes?"

"Perhaps, Lady Juliana," replied the old man, with a
mild and solemn thoughtfulness, that rendered his venerable
physiognomy the *beau idéal* of a pious patriarch, "perhaps
many such may have that perfect love of God in their hearts,
which we are told casteth out fear. But let me suggest to
you, my good lady, that it is unreasonable, as well as un-

charitable, to conclude that those do not recognise God who conceive of Him differently from yourself."

It must, of course, be scarcely necessary to mention, that Lady Juliana considered it now more clearly proved than ever that Mr. Harrington *was* an Atheist, and that her conscience very much applauded her for hating him more than ever, accordingly

The gentleman on his part, however, began very seriously to nourish an opinion that her Ladyship was a little, or perhaps not a little, insane upon such subjects. And, perhaps, he was right; although her insanity did not reach the point at which it was likely to be recognised as such by the world in general.

How arbitrary are the distinctions, and how narrow the divisions of our phraseology! The world would have denied that the mind of Lady Juliana was in a state to deserve the appellation of *insane*, but a large portion of it would have admitted that it was *unsound*. Walter did not sufficiently recognise this difference between tweedledum and tweedledee; yet it lawfully divides the inmates of a madhouse from those who put them there.

Meanwhile, a very strong and fast friendship had sprung up between Kate and her uncle. There had been a mutual tendency towards liking each other on the first evening of their acquaintance, and this had ripened into a warm and firm affection, with a rapidity which could have been consistent with enduring solidity only in the case of natures as wholly guileless, open, and unreserved, as those both of the uncle and niece. It is curious to observe how quickly and spontaneously natures which deserve to be trusted, trust, when they encounter beings as single-hearted as themselves. Kate, though she was a good and very affectionate daughter, and had never in her life dreamed of mistrusting her father in any way, yet felt conscious that somehow or other she could a thousand times more readily have confided the inmost secrets of her heart to her Uncle Walter than to her father, or to her mother either.

And what heart is there, however innocent, however guileless, but has its secret?

It was fortunate that this confidential feeling existed between the uncle and niece, because Walter was a person from whom it was very difficult to hide any secret in which his heart took an interest. The secret which reconciled the

seeming contradictions of Lady Augusta's burning desire to
have the Duchess of Benlomond at her ball, with the constantly disparaging way in which she spoke of that noble
star of fashion, might have rested securely impenetrable by
Walter to the end of time; and yet there were other secrets
which some persons might think quite as much beyond the
sphere of an old bachelor, which it would have been very
difficult to conceal from him.

Not, indeed, that the noble-hearted old man had the
remotest thought of prying into the secrets of anyone, for he
would most scrupulously have looked to the left, had anyone
told him that if he looked to the right he might see what the
parties concerned desired to conceal from him. But he was
slow to suppose that anybody wanted to conceal anything;
nevertheless, the habits of more than half a century, spent in
observation of all that was presented to his reasoning
faculties, had given an acuteness to his observing powers,
which enabled him to understand much which might have
passed unnoted, or remained unintelligible to less practised
faculties.

And thus it had come to pass that Uncle Walter was very
considerably more aware than his niece Kate herself, that she
was rapidly learning to consider Mr. Caldwell as so very
admirable a person, that pretty nearly all the world beside
was absolutely naught in comparison. He knew that young
ladies from about seventeen, to—not all his acute observations
had enabled him to assign the other limit to the period—but
he knew that ladies from seventeen upwards, were liable to
this sort of vehemence in their feelings and opinions, and like
a dutiful disciple of Nature, he accepted the fact as incontrovertible. It next became a question with him, whether
he should turn his acute perspicacity to account by communicating his discovery to the young lady herself, or
whether he should do no such thing, but suffer matters to
take their own course. After some consideration, he decided
on the latter plan.

All he had seen of Mr. Caldwell, inclined him to think
highly of him; but his interest in Kate, and her welfare, did
not permit him to remain satisfied with so slight an acquaintance, and the active old man had taken measures to obtain
further and more particular information. The more he
learned concerning him, the more inclined he became to
hope that the attachment would prove to be mutual; and

accordingly, he decided in his own mind that if Mr. Caldwell and Kate chanced, or chose to fall in love with each
other, there was no just cause or impediment why they should
not be joined together.

Between young Harrington and his uncle there was also
a sort of friendship, and a certain degree of mutual liking.
There was a fresh sincerity, and very genuine dislike to
falsity, cant, and humbug in them both; and this very soon
operated as an attraction and tie between them. But the
same quality had produced different effects on the two
natures, or rather, perhaps, the effects varied because they
had been called into action under widely different circumstances.

The younger man had passed the last half-dozen years of
his life in the fashionable world of London and Paris, and the
averseness to *seeming* which has been mentioned as a promi-
nent feature in his character, had generated in him a bitterly
sarcastic spirit which was far from producing a healthy or
fruitful condition of mind.

The truthful simplicity of the old naturalist, on the contrary, was that of a man who has hardly ever made acquaintance with falsehood, who knows nothing of it, nay, disbelieves
in its existence except as a rare monstrosity.

There was ever in young Henry Harrington's mind, and
in his manners, too, a something of harshness, and a tone
of sneering which grated painfully against the warmer
sympathies, and more genial temperament of his uncle;
while, on the other hand, the simplicity and worldly
ignorance of the senior frequently produced something very
like contempt from the worldly wisdom of the far more
narrow-minded junior.

Both, however, were very strongly persuaded that the
other would have been a very noble fellow, had he but
enjoyed the good fortune of living the life, and passing
through the training which he himself had done. Such an
opinion as this, is far on the road towards mutual esteem.

With all the three Wigginsville sisters, Walter had
become, more or less, an intimate and valued acquaintance.
Miss Mary Jane did not, indeed, venture to display too much
cordiality towards him in the Vale Street drawing-room, and
in the presence of her valued friend the Lady Juliana, for she
was perfectly aware that her regenerated Ladyship had pronounced him to be a brand given over to the burning, and

considered him as neither more nor less than pitch, which could not be meddled with without defilement. At the Wigginsville tea-table, however, at which Walter had several times been a guest, the gentleness of the fair devotee's nature was permitted to mitigate the severity of her theology, and she suffered herself to hope that the call, which she confessed, with a sigh, had been lamentably long delayed, would come at last.

Miss Hannah's really sound sense and goodness of heart constituted a natural bond of alliance between her and Mr. Harrington, which, to say the truth, was not a little strengthened by the trifling eccentricities, and small rebellions against society in the matters of bibs and tuckers, coat-lappets and hats, of which both were wont to be guilty.

As to Miss Jemima, she very naturally considered this new acquaintance to be clearly marked out by his attainments, pursuits, and high reputation in the scientific world, as one of her especial subjects and admirers; while, on the other hand, the venerable philosopher was fully aware that he owed to her particular *penchants* and habitual associations, the pleasure of frequently meeting in the Wigginsville drawing-room many persons distinguished in various scientific pursuits, with whose names and reputation he was perfectly familiar.

If to all this we add, that Mr. Garbel had been briskly pushing on the siege he was laying before Miss Mary Jane's gentle heart, the reader will be able to enter with us on the next scenes of our drama with a clear comprehension of the position of the *dramatis personæ.*

CHAPTER XII.

As volcanic eruptions, earthquakes, and other such great convulsions of nature, are generally heralded by portentous heavings, thunderings, and rushing of mighty winds, so did the Doctor's house in Vale Street show for many days manifest signs and warnings of the coming eruption of festivity, so long projected by Lady Augusta.

This fated 25th of June fell on a Wednesday, and it was now the preceding Monday. Already the first floor of the house presented the appearance of the main-deck of a ship of war prepared for action.

The unhappy Doctor—happy enough, indeed, in the prospect of the splendour which was to be the result, but most unhappy amid the agonies and convulsions of preparation—the miserable Doctor kept himself hid and sheltered, as far as was possible, in the sacred retreat of his study. But even *that* was to be invaded on the morrow, for it was there that the family must live, and—deplorable profanation!—it was there that on the great day itself such miserable morsels as they might obtain by way of dinner, must be eaten! the handsome dining-room having to be surrendered into the hands of Gunter and his myrmidons. Moreover, this sacred scene of sacred study was to become the receptacle of cloaks and shawls throughout the livelong night!

Walter, whose rooms might on this occasion, with some show of truth be, indeed, called the most desirable part of the house, inasmuch as, in their lofty tranquillity, they were far above the tumult and the din, Walter wandered about the transformed mansion greatly astonished and inexpressibly perplexed; observing everything, but comprehending nothing.

On one occasion he ventured to ask Lady Juliana, who was superintending the tying up of flowers into garlands, why the comfortable chairs had all been removed from the drawing-rooms, and those very disagreeable and ugly-looking benches ranged round the room?

"I am seeing these garlands constructed at my sister's urgent request, Mr. Harrington," she replied. "But these

are pomps and vanities which I do not willingly meddle
with. You had better ask Lady Augusta."

"*Vanities!* These miserable little mimicries of seats are
indeed a vain delusion for all who would rest upon them;
but I should not think, Lady Juliana, that the severest
anchorite that ever lived could call them *pomps*. They
appear to me worthy of a penitential cell."

"How hardly shall the things appertaining to the spirit be
understood by such as are under the dominion of the flesh!"
returned Lady Juliana, with a groan. "But I assure you,
Sir," she added, "that I am not sufficiently of the world to
explain its ways to you."

Lady Juliana was one of the tolerably large class who profess to think, and probably do think, that *fêtes*, and finery, as
well as most other pretty and agreeable things, can only be
enjoyed at the risk of eternal burning hereafter, a bargain
which with great prudence and good sense they decline
making.

And in this respect, at least, the position of Lady Juliana
in her sister's family was a fortunate one, for the *ci-devant*
beauty might there enjoy the pomps and vanities which she
had been early taught to love, at the expense of her sister's
soul, and that of the Doctor, on the very easy condition of
entering, in her own person, an occasional protest against
their worldly-minded enjoyments.

It is curious to see how easily professing believers in the
doctrine of eternal punishment for the sins committed during
our present state of existence, make up their minds to believe
that all those nearest and dearest to them (if they choose to
differ in religious doctrine, or religious practice) will not only
perish everlastingly, but will be subjected during countless
ages to the most torturing agonies that their organization can
be made to endure.

Both Romanists, and Calvinists gravely proclaim that such
is their belief; but if it be so, it is really difficult to comprehend how they can look forward to such a destiny for those
they love, with the philosophical composure that we witness.

The Romanist, indeed, has the consolation of believing that,
if he can but contrive to raise money enough to pay for masses
for those who have died in their sins and their unbelief, they
may still have a chance, or rather a certainty, of escaping;
but the adherents to the Lady Juliana's much more terrific
creed permit themselves no such soothing alternative, and it

is, therefore, really astonishing to see with what unflinching courage they contemplate the awful result, of which they declare themselves sure, beyond the possibility of mistake.

Walter, whose curiosity respecting the comfortless benches, was perfectly genuine, and still perfectly unsatisfied, ventured to attack Lady Augusta herself on the subject in the very midst of her cares and manifold anxieties.

"Lord, Mr. Harrington!" was her impatient reply, "it is to make room to be sure. I hope," she added, with conscious pride, "that there will not be standing-room, even on the stairs. I have more than three hundred on my list."

"But surely, in that case, my dear sister, your friends will find themselves very uncomfortable, especially in this hot weather. Would it not have been more hospitable to have named a whole week instead of one day, and have let them come in comfortably, forty or fifty at a time?"

"Fiddlesticks! Friends and hospitality indeed! Do you really suppose now, Mr. Harrington, that I care one quarter of a straw for all these people? Not I, Sir, believe me. But you do not understand these matters, my good Walter. Friends and hospitality are all very well in the country, but they have very little to do with a London cram."

It was not a very easy matter, however, to enable Walter Harrington to bring his barbarous mind to take in the fact that the coming solemnity owed its origin in no respect and in no degree to any feelings of kindness, hospitality or friendship whatever, but wholly and solely for vanity and ostentation, stimulated, however, by the hope that every penny expended would be repaid by a *quid pro quo* of some sort or other.

This, indeed, might be said with equal justice of all the parties given by Lady Augusta, and all the other ladies of her class; but this identical party had a special and more than usually important end in view, and one that it is necessary we should explain to the reader. The said reader already knows that Lady Augusta Harrington had a daughter; and as this fair daughter had attained the witching period of eighteen years of age, it was become, of course, the first object of her mother's life to obtain a good marriage for her. That her beautiful Katherine should marry *well*, was at this period decidedly the most anxious wish of her mother's heart. There is no need to explain what Lady Augusta meant when she talked of Kate's marrying well, for the phrase is too generally

understood to bear the sense which her Ladyship assigned to
it, for any explanation to be necessary.

How this great object of securing a *good* marriage for Kate
was to be forwarded by her mother's cramming all her
acquaintance into a space too small to hold them, would have
furnished another puzzle for Walter, as difficult to solve as
the substitution of hard benches for soft chairs; but this
needs no explanation to those who are initiated into the
mysteries of the fashionable world. And Heaven forbid that
we should do any of our readers the cruel wrong of supposing
that they are not of the number.

But in thus brilliantly filling her rooms on this particular
occasion, Lady Augusta had an especial object.

The London season of this year had witnessed the first
introduction of the young and immensely wealthy Lord
Goldstable to the perils and delights of our magnificent
metropolis. This fortunate youth, who had just reached the
conclusion of a long minority, was the only son of a long-
descended Scotch Earl; a strange sort of man, half-philo-
sopher, half-misanthrope, and, as some of his neighbours
declared, very nearly whole madman; some proof of which
was furnished by the fact that in dying, he left his little
motherless son to the sole management of an old bachelor
acquaintance and neighbour, a recluse whom nobody knew,
and nobody cared to know.

A tutor had been provided for him, who remained with him
till within a few months of his coming of age, when the poor
man died, leaving the young Earl and his old guardian to a
rarely-broken *tête-à-tête*.

By the especial request of the late Earl, this very faithful
old guardian had taken up his residence in the wide old
Scotch castle, in which his friend had lived and died. This
castle had a noble lake near it, so the young Earl had learned
to manage a boat, sails and all; he could moreover swim like
an otter, and row like a Thames waterman. Game of all
kinds abounded in the woods, so Lord Goldstable had learned
to be a capital good shot, and he could hunt, too, and leap
anything.

In addition to all this, he had learned to read, write, and
was tolerably well acquainted with the initiatory parts of
arithmetic; but he stopped short at the rule-of-three.

Moreover, from the age of ten to sixteen, he had been constantly attended once a-week by a dancing-master, who drove

himself over from a town at the distance of ten miles from the Castle, to perform this service.

That the tutor, who was an "Oxford scholar," had duly gone through the ordinary routine of instilling as much Greek and Latin into his pupil as he could contrive to make him imbibe, is not to be doubted, for the tutor was a very honest, worthy man; but he died in consequence of a fever caught during a long and stormy passage across the lake, before his pupil had made any very great progress in classical erudition.

The only relation the young man had in the world who moved in the circle denominated "the great world," was old Lady de Paddington, who has been already mentioned as the intimate friend of Lady Augusta Harrington. For some time before Lord Goldstable had obtained the age of twenty-one, and for some time before Kate had obtained the age of eighteen, it had occurred to these very intimate friends that the great-nephew of the one would make an excellent match for the daughter of the other, and many had been the pleasant half-hours they had spent together in laying plans for bringing them together in such a manner as to ensure the young man's falling in love with Kate, before he could have an opportunity of falling in love with anybody else.

Kate Harrington, in truth, was so very pretty a creature that it really seemed almost as certain to Lady de Paddington as to the proud mother herself, that it would be only necessary to let the young man see Kate once, looking as they had both seen her look in the brilliant atmosphere of a ball-room, in order to enchant his eyes, win his heart, and obtain the offer of his hand.

It was obviously certain, however, that dozens of other mothers, and most of them of higher position than Lady Augusta, would be equally anxious for the honour of becoming his mother-in-law, and, therefore, both the plotting ladies felt that priority in "the start" might be everything.

Lord Goldstable had been just turned out from the bag of his minority, a fact perfectly well-known to all studious mothers possessing "The Peerage," and was expected to give the town a very fine run. By the invaluable assistance of the great-aunt, an assistance *bien entendu* to be paid for by sundry grateful and convenient little attentions, Lady Augusta had been enabled to dart upon him the very moment his nose had become visible, and by the skilful management of Lady de

Paddington the "honour of his company" at Lady Augusta's
ball had been secured, before he had entered as a guest into
any house in the metropolis save her own. Whether such a
manœuvre might be within the limits of fair sport, or whether
it might be stigmatized as poaching we must leave to the jury
of mothers to decide.

Lord Goldstable was, as we have said, very rich, and he
certainly was, moreover, very silly. His riches amounted to
eighty thousand a-year, and the accumulations of a long
minority. The amount of his silliness cannot be stated with
equal accuracy, but it was very great, and we shall probably
not be far wrong, if we estimate it as being as much above
the ordinary average, as his wealth was. But despite
his silliness, it would be cruel not to feel some degree
of interest for him. Reared in deep seclusion, ignorant
of almost all things, and especially so of the world and
its ways, shy, diffident, and awkward, the unfortunate
lad was turned out to run for his life as best he might,
through the hungry pack of scamps and blacklegs, both noble
and ignoble, plotting mammas and fascinating daughters,
rogues, libertines, and leeches of all sorts. And to these
tribes, as to all others, their natural prey is appointed, and in
sufficient quantity. But hares have their swiftness, bulls
their horns, and horses their hoofs, as the Grecian poet
remarks; and rarely indeed does it happen that any animal is
delivered over to his natural enemies in so wholly defenceless
a condition as was that helpless young peer. With such an
auxiliary as his great-aunt, and only near connection, it must
be evident to all that Lady Augusta Harrington started with
very great advantages. It so chanced that she had it in her
power to be often of very essential service to the high-born,
but far from wealthy old lady, who almost appeared to have
the right of disposal of the helpless young peer: the right of
presentation, we may fairly say, to that rich and eligible piece
of preferment amounting to eighty thousand a-year, with a
capital mansion, and very light duty.

And thus it came to pass that the contracting parties, Lady
de Paddington, to wit, and Lady Augusta, had determined
and arranged that the first London ball-room which his young
Lordship entered should be that of the last mentioned lady.

This having been decided between them, the preparations
for this important _fête_ were commenced immediately not,
however, till Lady Augusta had performed that first and most

precious duty of a good wife, namely, the taking her husband into her confidence.

The Doctor had already heard Lady de Paddington speak repeatedly of her great-nephew, with all the tender interest which such a rich great-nephew was likely to inspire in such a poor great-aunt—for Lady de Paddington was really, for a person of high rank, very poor; but he had never himself felt any particular interest about the young man, till Lady Augusta opened all her maternal heart to him on the subject.

The Doctor listened to her with deep attention, and replied, very solemnly, after she had completed the statement of her hopes and her wishes:—

"A great thing, indeed, my dear! Such a marriage would, in truth, be an immense thing. Dear child! she would do honour to such a splendid position, Lady Augusta. It really is all that my fondest ambition could wish for my darling Kate; and I must say, Lady Augusta, that your management of the whole affair does you the highest honour. Pray, my dear love, let nothing be spared to make this *fête* all that it ought to be with such an object before us. Upon such an occasion, expense becomes a very secondary consideration."

"I confess that I do flatter myself that the thing has been conducted with some skill," returned Lady Augusta. "But what will not a mother's affection for her child accomplish?"

"Eighty thousand a-year, I think you said, Lady Augusta, and the savings of a very long minority! God bless my soul!" ejaculated the meditative Doctor. "Did you hear anything of parliamentary influence, my dear? But, of course, a man with such a fortune *must* have influence; and I know that when Dr. Halchard got his mitre, I was spoken of very favourably in high quarters. You remember my having preached once.—Well, well! God's will be done!"

With this pious feeling beaming in every feature, the excellent divine settled himself down into his arm-chair, to indulge in a little comfortable castle-building, while his more active consort proceeded to seek an interview with her daughter, for the purpose of forwarding the hatching of the chickens which she left the Doctor counting.

CHAPTER XIII.

"My dear Kate," said Lady Augusta, seating herself in the arm-chair, which occupied one side of the fire-place in Kate's own sacred room, and motioning her daughter, at the same time, to place herself on the sofa opposite, "my dear Kate, there are two or three important words which, busy as I am at this moment, I am very anxious to say to you. So listen to me, my dear, with you best attention."

"I will indeed, mamma," replied the unconscious Kate.

"You are well aware, my dear Kate," resumed the anxious mother, "how earnest and how unceasing have been the endeavours of your father and myself to give you every advantage which our position would admit of; but ——"

"I am indeed, dear mamma," interrupted Kate; "and I am so truly sensible of all I owe you, that I would do anything and everything in my power to testify it; but, unfortunately, it is now very near the end of the quarter, mamma, and I am afraid ——"

Kate had fallen into an error, as people who have the hasty and bad habit of interrupting are very apt to do. But the fact was, that Lady Augusta had so frequently prefaced little demands on her fair daughter's purse by a precisely similar exordium, that Kate had taken it for granted that the sequel was to be the same. But her lady-mother now interrupted her in her turn, and proceeded with some asperity of manner to express herself as follows,—

"I really am at a loss to guess, child, what it is you mean about quarters. If you would have had the good-breeding to permit me to finish what I was saying, you would have found out that it had nothing whatever to do with quarter-day. Let me beg of you, at present, if you please, to listen to me with sufficient attention to prevent your making any more such extraordinary and very ridiculous blunders."

The penitent Kate begged pardon very earnestly for her stupidity, and declared herself ready to listen with the greatest attention.

"I consider you, Kate, at this particular moment, in the very act, as I may say, of beginning life."

Kate felt rather puzzled, but she had promised not to interrupt again, and, therefore, looked with an air of innocent ignorance into her mother's face, but said nothing.

"What I mean," said Lady Augusta, in reply to this look, "is, that as you were only presented this year, I consider your real life, properly so called, to be just begun. The ball which we are now about to give is entirely for the purpose, Katherine, of letting you be seen to advantage. You are, I am sadly afraid, still younger in mind than in years, at least, upon some subjects of the very first and greatest importance; yet still I think you cannot be so very childish as not to know, that the first duty of a mother, who has before her the anxious and important task of marrying a daughter, is to take every possible means of securing this object."

"Mamma!" exclaimed Kate, trying to laugh, and to look as if she hoped that her mother was laughing, too.

"This is no subject for jesting, Kate," returned her mother, solemnly, "and your father would be very deeply shocked if he could believe for a moment that you could speak, or even look jestingly on such a theme. But let me go on, and I trust that your good sense will enable you to feel that it is no jesting matter that I am now speaking of. This season, Kate—this London season, I mean—will be rendered peculiarly interesting to all persons in the higher classes of society, by the introduction among them, for the first time, of one of the most distinguished young noblemen in Europe. I am speaking, my dear, of the young Lord Goldstable. He has just attained his majority, Kate, and I believe our ball will be the first large assembly of the fashionable world at which he has ever appeared. Now, listen to me with attention, my dear, that you may properly appreciate the nature of the position in which we are placed, and be prepared to act accordingly. Lord Goldstable has eighty thousand a-year, Kate, beside a vast amount of ready money. He has been educated in strict privacy, and has hitherto seen nothing whatever of the world; so that simple tastes, and virtue, and everything of that sort, so very desirable, you know, in a husband, my dear Kate, is in this particular instance perfectly assured, and, in fact, a matter of absolute certainty. He has, as yet (except his great-aunt, Lady de Paddington), no friends, nor even acquaintances in London, and naturally, of

course, you know, he is very shy; but this must give such a
charming freshness of mind and manner, as every one of right
feeling must be delighted with. Now I happen to know,
Kate, that this admirable young nobleman has heard of you
in a manner that has very strongly impressed him in your
favour; and, in short, I have every reason to think it
extremely likely that he will propose to you, Katherine; and
if this most happy chance should befall you, my dear love,
I surely need hardly tell you that your acceptance of him will
make your excellent father and myself the very happiest
parents in the world."

"Oh, mamma! mamma!" ejaculated Kate, with something
very like a groan. But in the next moment she felt again
inclined to laugh, so truly comic did this specimen of maternal
partiality appear to her.

❊   ❊   ❊   ❊   ❊

But her Ladyship said no more than the truth, when she
stated that the young Lord Goldstable had been already
strongly prejudiced in favour of Kate; but the means taken
for impressing his simple Lordship thus favourably, had,
indeed, been rather stronger, and more direct in their nature,
than Lady Augusta deemed it expedient to avow to her
daughter.

The poor unfledged recluse was, in fact, most painfully
anxious about his *début* in fashionable life. He had notions
rather vague, yet pretty strong, too, concerning the con-
spicuous place which he was destined to fill in the world, but
these notions were painfully blended with an indistinct sort of
consciousness of his own unfitness for the career before him.

In him the fear of ridicule—as is generally the case in
weak minds—was so extreme, as almost to amount to agony,
and the clever Lady de Paddington had pitched on this point
of character whereon to rest the fulcrum of her lever.

She had represented to him that she fortunately had it in
her power to present him to the family of a young lady
who was the present reigning beauty of the town, the
admired of all admirers, for whose hand nearly all the leading
unmarried nobles of Englands were competitors. She informed him also that this lovely creature has hitherto refused
all the splendid offers which had been made to her, for an
unconquerable dislike to the bold, confident, and greatly
sophisticated manners of the fashionable town-bred men of the
present day. She also recounted in the most easy and

pleasant manner possible, that she had mentioned him as a
near relation, for whom she felt the most affectionate interest,
to the young lady's family; and that when the lovely
daughter heard her say that the life of her amiable young
nephew had been hitherto passed wholly in the country, she
had exclaimed with great enthusiam :—

"Well, then, once in my life, I have a chance of seeing
someone that I shall really like."

The young man listened to all this with a heightened
colour, and with such a look of interest and curiosity, that
the skilful negotiator was tempted to proceed.

"Sweet pretty creature!" she exclaimed. "I do assure
you, my dear Goldstable, that I would have given a great deal
at that moment if you could only have looked at her, for I
really don't think that any man could have looked at her
with indifference as she said this. There was something
so beautifully innocent, yet so sweetly animated in her
countenance, that, if you are not in love already, my dear
nephew, she must, I think, have captivated you."

"But why should you wish for that, aunt?" returned the
blushing young nobleman, laughing. "I don't think it's
very likely that I should have a chance, when all the
handsomest fellows in London have been refused."

"Well, Edward," pursued the clever old lady, with an
admirable air of simple sincerity, "I am not much surprised
at your laughing at me, because, as you have never seen this
lovely, gentle, admirable girl, you can have no notion of what
she is, or of the perfectly good reasons I have for wishing
what I certainly do wish, my dear nephew—namely, that you
shall have the happiness and the honour of carrying her off
from all competitors. You have no idea, Edward, how everything, and everybody is canvassed in the fashionable world!
Great people, you know, have no business to occupy them,
and I suppose that is the reason why they occupy themselves
so much about the affairs of other people ; and the consequence
of this is, that no new person can make his or her appearance
in this said fasionable world without being talked over in
every drawing-room. Now there is yourself for instance, my
dear Edward, you would hardly believe how much you have
been talked of already."

"Of me, my dear aunt? How is it possible that anyone
can talk of me? I don't know anybody in London."

"That makes no difference whatever, or rather it causes

you to be still more talked of than if you were known," replied the old lady. "That you are *personally* a stranger in the circles of fashion is quite certain, but that by no means impedes your being talked of. You have a Viscount's coronet on your head, my dear nephew, and, moreover, it is well-known that your income is large, and that your minority was long; neither is it any secret, my dear, that your education has been a very singular one, and that you have been brought up in very strict retirement. The natural consequence of which is, of course, that there is a strong propensity among our gay nobles, both male and female, to suppose that you will be found excessively shy; and I rather suspect that some of these gay young lordlings enjoy not a little the idea of being able to throw you into the background, notwithstanding your title and your noble estate."

"Then I am sure it is a great folly in me to come to London at all, aunt," he replied; "and, to tell you the truth, I do not think it was very wise, or very kind of you, to urge my doing so in the way you have done. If you had not told me to come, I should have put off all that bore about taking my seat, for I don't know how long."

"And it was for that very reason, Edward, that I was so very anxious that you should come at once. Nevertheless, my dear nephew, I do not think I should have had courage to urge your doing so in the manner I have done, had I not clearly seen my way before me, and felt very sure that instead of having the mortification of seeing you puzzled, I might have the extremely great pleasure of seeing you quiz everybody."

"And pray, how is that to be managed, aunt?" returned the sensitive rustic, very eagerly. "Prove your words in this respect, and I will thank you heartily, for it is just exactly the thing I should best like."

"And it is very natural that you should like it, Edward. All men like it, and more particularly, I believe, all young men. The way, my dear boy, is very easy. I have told you that all the fine fashionable men about town have absolutely lost, not only their hearts, but their heads, from their admiration of my beautiful young friend Kate Harrington. Had I seen any chance of her being persuaded to accept any one of the splendid offers that were made her, I most assuredly would have done nothing to prevent it, for I should have considered the doing so as nothing short of a sin; but when, on the contrary, I saw her weeping day after day, because her parents were displeased at her so perseveringly refusing all the proposals that were made to her, my heart ached for her, and I determined to make her tell me why it was that she continued to act in a manner which evidently rendered her unhappy, as well as her parents. Dear child! She really is an angel, Edward! I am sure I shall never forget her answer."

"But what was her answer?" demanded the young man. "May I not hear it?"

"Yes, my dear," replied the old lady, after the meditation of a moment. "I really do not see that there can be any harm in telling you what she said; her answer was this: 'My dear Lady de Paddington,' she said, 'I would do anything in the world to please my dear father and mother that I did not think *wicked* But I do assure you, that it would be very wicked in me to marry any one of the young noblemen that have proposed to me, for in the very bottom of my heart I hate them all! What other girls seem to admire,' she continued, 'I positively detest. I cannot bear their conceited air of fashionable assurance. I would rather die an old maid ten thousand times!'"

"What did you say in reply?" said Lord Goldstable, opening his eyes very wide, and looking greatly interested.

"I only said, very quietly," returned Lady de Paddington, "'Well, Kate dear, if you are resolved to die an old maid you must, so I do not see the use of teazing you any more about marrying.'

"'It can be of no use, indeed, Lady de Paddington, as long as I am asked to marry such men as have had their heads turned by being worshipped by all the ladies in London. I hate such men! and I think it very hard that they cannot be contented to marry some of the young beauties who all seem dying for them, instead of tormenting me. But I cannot help thinking sometimes,' she added, 'that I am very unlucky, for if any young man who was not spoiled by London conceit were to fall in love with me, I feel almost sure that I should fall in love with him.' This it was, Edward, that made me so urge your coming to London, and it is this which makes me so anxious that you should see this celebrated beauty. If you admire her as much as I think you will—and on this point I have little doubt—your London career will, indeed, open most brilliantly. Propose to her at

once, my dear Edward, and instead of being stared at and
quizzed by all the conceited puppies who have vainly sought
her hand, you will burst upon the town at once as the winner
in the hottest race that has been run for years!"

The shaft was well aimed, and so keenly pointed, that the
noble mark was pierced to the centre as soon as hit.

Poor Lord Goldstable poured out his silly soul in gratitude
to the scheming old lady; and it was decided that he should
be presented to Kate Harrington on the night of Lady
Augusta's ball, which was to take place on the following
night; and that if he then found that he admired her as much
as he expected to do, his proposals should be made with as
little delay as possible.

All this was, of course, duly and accurately reported to
Lady Augusta; and far as was our simple-minded Kate from
filling, or having dreamed of filling, the place in the public
eye which Lady de Paddington had assigned to her, her
mother judged, and correctly enough perhaps, that she
possessed abundantly sufficient charm, both of person and
manner, to sustain the part that had been allotted to her,
before more critical and experienced eyes than those of Lord
Goldstable.

＊   ＊   ＊   ＊   ＊

Lady Augusta's interview with her daughter was very
skilfully brought to a conclusion, by her Ladyship's hastily
starting up and declaring that one of Weippert's men was
waiting for her, that the exact place for the orchestra might
be finally arranged; and Katherine, to do her justice, very
soon forgot the nonsense her mamma had been talking, by the
simple process of remembering that all mammas were said to
fancy that gentlemen were ready to fall in love with their
daughters.

CHAPTER XIV.

The important evening of Wednesday, 25th June, at
length arrived, and found the house and family in Vale
Street duly prepared for the great occasion. The first floor
was as brilliant as a profusion of wax-lights, and a profusion
of flowers could make it; the supper, which was to be served
at two, a.m., had been prepared in Gunter's very best style;
the music was excellent; and anyone unaccustomed to such
things, might really have supposed that they were going to
enjoy themselves exceedingly, if they had taken a review of
the preparations before the arrival of the actors who were
destined to fill the scene.

Our readers, however, are, of course, not so rustically
ignorant, and so wholly unaccustomed to fashionable parties,
as to suppose anything so preposterously ridiculous, and so
utterly unlike the truth. *They* know, unless indeed they are
absolutely and altogether nobodies, how much, and how little,
of real enjoyment is to be hoped for, when space enough for
one hundred is to be occupied by three.

The Doctor had petitioned hard for a whist-table in the
boudoir beyond the second drawing-room, but this had been
very properly and prudently refused by the judicious Lady
Augusta. This charming little third drawing-room, this
"sweet boudoir," was destined for a far different purpose;
nor was there a pretty woman in the room, or a pretty man
either, who would not have been ready to declare that placing
a card-table in it would have been absolute profanation.

A profusion of the most beautiful hot-house flowers, in
gorgeous perfection of bloom, were grouped whimsically, but
very gracefully, about the entrance, so as at the first glance to
suggest the idea that no ingress to it was intended; but these
enticing obstacles were speedily discovered not to be invincible,
and once passed, something like a fairy bower was found
within.

Experienced mammas will readily understand me, when I
say that such a spot is of as much important use to their
operations, as a landing-net to an angler.

The door had been removed from its hinges, but its place was admirably well supplied by the graceful folds of a floating curtain of delicate muslin, the drooping festoons of which, mingling with the boughs of the plants beneath, rendered the retreat within almost as effectually hidden from passing eyes, as if it really had not been open to all who deemed it proper to penetrate its verdant recesses.

The other rooms were, as we have said, very brilliantly lighted; but here one alabaster lamp alone hung from the ceiling, and shed a delicately tempered light, which bore about the same proportion to the glare of the drawing-rooms, as that of the pale moon does to the lustre of the garish sun.

In the centre of this pretty trap, was—not a morsel of toasted cheese, but a bewitching little table with a set of chess-men upon it, and with a small sofa behind it, and a large arm-chair in front; moreover, there lay beside the chess-board a small portfolio of drawings. Playing chess, and looking at drawings, are by no means among the least important, or the least useful occupations, that can be found to vary the monotony of waiting.

Having been very officially and effectually warned off from the boudoir, together with his whist-table, the doctor had proposed to establish himself and it in Kate's cell; and to this arrangement she had very willingly consented, having, however, very carefully taken precautions before the great day arrived, so to stow away her secret treasures of all sorts, as to permit the profane vulgar to approach the sacred precincts without danger.

In the midst of all these busy preparations for worldly, and, therefore, undeniably sinful, amusement, it must not be doubted that Lady Juliana suffered various great and grievous pangs; but she assured herself, as well as everyone else who would listen to her, that it was her duty as a Christian, to submit herself meekly to the yoke which she had been appointed to bear; moreover, she also felt it her duty, in return for her sister's hospitality in affording her a home which she could not very conveniently have afforded to herself, to comply with her taste and wishes in respect to her attire, and she, therefore, appeared on this great occasion dressed in the most becoming manner, and in the extreme of the reigning mode; and having thus in all things meekly resigned herself to the doing her duty in that state of life to which it had pleased God to call her, she proposed to watch

with a scrutinizing eye, all the little insects that were about
to play around her, unconscious of their doom, and mark them
all sliding down into the deep gulf of eternal perdition, with
that fervent species of holy satisfaction which must naturally
arise from the delightful consciousness that she was not "of
them." Her friend and faithful ally, Miss Mary Jane
Wigginsville, was quite ready, and even eager to confess, that
she certainly did not think balls "consistent," but professed
the most amiable and flattering willingness to be guided in
her conduct on the present occasion, wholly by Lady Juliana's
high principle and excellent judgment; and after a long and
edifying conversation which they held together on the subject,
she became persuaded that if it were not her own fault she
might convert the abomination into a blessing, for she might
place herself near her devout and noble friend, and listen to
the pious and eloquent outpourings of her spirit as she uttered
those solemn predictions of the wrath to come, with which
she never failed to be inspired whenever she saw people who
appeared to be enjoying themselves.

Henry Harrington had undertaken to constitute himself his
Uncle Walter's *cicerone* for the night. He was too much
blasé to find much pleasure and amusement in a ball, or, at
least, in such a ball as his lady-mother was likely to give
under the reverent roof of his respected father; but he
thought that very considerable entertainment might be found
in listening to his fresh-minded old uncle's remarks, and in
listening to all the questioning he anticipated from him concerning all he heard and saw; for Walter's curiosity concerning the whole process was evidently excited in no common
degree.

Lady Augusta meanwhile, though a slight shade of care
rested on her brow, was still herself, and like a consummate
general on the eve of an important action, felt that she could
depend upon her own resources, and was confident of success,
though at the same time anxious and vigilant to neglect
nothing that might contribute to it.

The first carriage is heard! This is always a nervous
moment, when it suggests the question, "Is everything
ready?" But, most fortunately, Lady Augusta had given
orders ten minutes before, that the candles should be lighted:
the rooms, therefore, were not in total darkness, although
considerably less than half that operation had been as yet
achieved.

"I will bet a thousand pounds that it is now, as always, that detestable Miss Puddingthwaite," exclaimed Lady Augusta, "who is here half an hour before anybody else! She does it on purpose, in the hope of catching us with the servants and ladders in the room, and the candles not half lighted!"

"Why should she wish that?" asked Walter, determined to lose no opportunity of informing himself of everything connected with the details of the curious ceremony which was about to take place, the whole of which appeared to him unintelligible, and mysterious in no common degree.

"Why?" returned Lady Augusta, in a tone of considerable acrimony, and with a shrug which she intended should be very expressive, but which in no degree assisted the comprehension of Walter. "Why?" she repeated, bitterly, "because she knows perfectly well that her doing so will plague us! Nobody, I believe, likes to be caught in the very act of preparation at all better than I do, and she is not at all likely to forget that the lighting two or three hundred candles before it is necessary, is what nobody in their senses would choose to do if they could help it. I know perfectly well now, and always, that she does it on purpose to plague me!"

"Then why ask so very spiteful and odious a person to your house?" said the investigating Walter.

"Miss Puddingthwaite goes everywhere," was the reply, and it was uttered in an accent which plainly expressed, that the information it conveyed was not of a nature to leave any doubt as to its authority.

The puzzled Walter stared at her, and as he had deliberately given himself up upon this occasion to the study of the new scene and the new people about him, he would probably have proceeded further with his inquiries had not his sister-in-law stopped him by an expressive sign, and by whispering almost in his ear the words, "Hush! she is here!"

And Miss Puddingthwaite it certainly was. Lady Augusta's long experience and intimate knowledge of the spinster's ways had not deceived her. She stepped most cordially towards her, however, and holding out both her hands, cried, in most affectionate accents:—

"How *very* kind this is of you, my dear Miss Puddingthwaite! We were just saying that we hoped you would come early! It is so friendly!"

"I was sure you would say so," replied the smiling persecutor, casting round her a sharp scrutinizing glance. "I certainly do like to see the rooms everywhere before the crowd comes, and you know you must let me go on in my own way, and look at everything. What a magnificent show of flowers! But isn't it a pity when one thinks how soon they will begin to look faded? for, of course, we all know that not quite all the blossoms we see, grow on the stems which they now decorate so cleverly. However, you certainly beat Lady Mary Compton in your exotics, my dear! By the way, I happened to be with her this very morning when the gardener's bill for her last *fête* came in; and it was no trifle I assure you!" she added, directing a sharp glance towards the Doctor, for the amiable creature thought it by no means improbable that Lady Augusta had been exceeding the limits prescribed to her, and that she might produce a somewhat uncomfortable feeling in the minds both of the husband and wife by this statement of costs. Lady Augusta, however, answered, very quietly:—

"Yes, indeed, these things are shamefully dear, like most other luxuries; it is impossible to do things liberally without paying for it. But you know, my dear Miss Puddingthwaite, that I am a very prudent person, and I limited Jackson to forty pounds."

"Many of the specimens here are cultivated with great difficulty in this country," said Walter; this subject being probably the only one concerning the preparations for the evening upon which he could have hazarded an opinion.

But his having made this remark caused Lady Augusta to say: "My brother-in-law, Miss Puddingthwaite. Mr. Harrington is a recent accession to our circle." Miss Puddingthwaite immediately honoured the old gentleman with a sharp look of observation, and a low sweeping courtesy, after which she prepared herself to pursue her voyage of discovery round the rooms.

"Well done, Lady Augusta," she exclaimed, after contemplating for a moment the metamorphosed boudoir; "how beautifully you have arranged that little back drawing-room. I do declare it is perfectly charming! such a Paphian bower! is it not? But I can't help thinking, my dear friends—I know you will excuse me for making the remark—that it is not quite impossible that ill-natured people might hint something rather saucy and disagreeable, in the way of quizzing I

mean, on the perfect—seclusion—I suppose we must call it of
this delicious retreat. One might almost fancy that it had
been arranged for the express purpose of favouring a tender
tête-à-tête. He, he, he! You must forgive me for laughing
at my own ridiculous idea. But all joking apart, you know
the real fact is, that there are some people so abominably
censorious and ill-natured, that I should not be in the least
degree surprised, if disagreeable observations *were* to be made
about it. If I were you, Lady Augusta, I really think I
should be inclined to remove those pretty delicate curtains,
or, at least, I would loop them up a little higher." And
Miss Puddingthwaite gently extended her long arm, and
raised the drooping drapery as she spoke.

"Indeed! do you really think so?" returned Lady
Augusta, with an aspect so indifferent and so immovable, that
Miss Puddingthwaite must have been tempted to wish herself
at home again, enjoying the luxury of her own sofa for
another hour or so; nor were the words of her philosophical
hostess at all more satisfactory than her looks, for she only
added, in the very gentlest tone imaginable: "Do you really
think so? Gliddon's people put them up as you see them,
and they have a very general reputation for understanding
this sort of thing. They are thought, I believe, to know
what is graceful and pretty better than anybody, so I think
we had better let them alone. And as to the dangers and
difficulties of the retreat, everbody must judge for themselves."

While this conversation had been going on in the second
drawing-room, Walter, who had withdrawn himself from the
group in which it had taken place, was receiving his first
lesson from his nephew, Henry, in the first and finest apartment of the suite.

"Now then, Henry," said he, "you must begin your
duties by explaining to me, first, why this Miss Puddingthwaite, being so very disagreeable a person as she seems to
be, should be invited at all anywhere, and still more why she
should, as your mother says, be invited everywhere? And,
secondly, why her being invited everywhere else, is any
reason for your mother inviting her here, notwithstanding the
strong feeling of dislike with which it is evident she has
inspired her? Both these points seem to me to be full of
mystery. But I presume that, notwithstanding all that is so
highly objectionable in her character and disposition, she

must, nevertheless, possess some marked talent, or some noble trait of heart, or intellect, sufficiently valuable to overbalance all that has been stated against her ? "

"One answer, oh, most methodical investigator, may reply to both your questions," returned Henry. "All Miss Puddingthwaite's acquaintance dislike her as much as my mother does ! and all invite her for the same reason, namely, because all the rest do. To the best of my knowledge and belief, she has no good quality either of heart or head to recommend her ; *but* she goes everywhere, and there is no one of whom this is said, who could by possibility find the very slightest difficulty in going anywhere. You must be pleased to understand, oh, most unsophisticated uncle, that all the denizens of this our mighty Babylon are ever and always engaged in a vehement twofold struggle, consisting on the one hand of a constant effort to get pulled up into the social level just above them by a sort of moral clinging to the skirts of their superiors in the great hierarchy, and on the other by an equally increasing endeavour to shake off, and kick down, those who from below are striving to cling to them. All this is very hard work, and requires an immensity of patient persevering exertion ; but it is really wonderful to see the unwearying courage with which this ceaseless labour is pursued ! If the same principle of our nature could by any accident be set to work upon learning to fly, depend upon it you would speedily see the whole atmosphere crowded by ladies and gentlemen, meandering between earth and the blue expanse of heaven. Such ardour and perseverance must succeed in the long run, let it aim at what object it will. But to return to our Miss Puddingthwaite. It so happens that she has, and is perfectly well know to have, a particularly tight hold of the skirts of the Duchess of Benlomond, and my good mother, therefore, clings with an equally tenacious grasp to her skirts. In such a struggle as this, it is evident that if we *seem* to fail, we fail ; and if Miss Puddingthwaite were not here to-night, it would be deemed a certain symptom that the star of the house of Harrington was sinking, which would be seen, noted, and perhaps triumphantly hailed by some of our most particular friends."

"Our name stands in the list of the knights who fought and conquered at Cressy," said Walter, laughing, "but I do not remember that of Puddingthwaite either there or in any similar chronicle."

7

"There be many among us, good uncle," replied the nephew, "who in our millocratic philosophy have deemed it 'wisest, discreetest, best,' to discard altogether the old-fashioned pride of ancestry. Ancestry, Uncle Walter, will not enable a man to give a good ball, or even a good dinner. It is possible, certainly, that a man who traces his pedigree to the Conquest, *may* be admitted into the charmed circle of fashion, but most assuredly he will seek to enter it in vain, if he have no claims which entitle him to a more substantial and younger-born sort of sympathy."

"Really?" said Walter, with the air of one who meditates upon a proposition that is new to him; and after a minute so spent, he added: "Well, perhaps it is more reasonable that it should be so; but it is an innovation, Harry."

It was evident that Walter's education was going on very prosperously, but it was interrupted ever and anon by the arrival of more guests. We shall not trouble the reader with the bead-roll of them. There were, of course, the usual proportion of wits and fools, of beauties and frights, of quizzers and quizzed—in short, the usual proportion of the usual types; for the social world may always be ranged under a few strongly marked classes, each cast in its own mould, for very rarely, indeed, do we meet with an individual who has a mould to himself; and when we do, we shall find that the world looks on him as a monstrosity, and generally treats him as the herd, full of the pasture, does the solitary stricken deer.

   *   *   *   *   *

Lord Goldstable was among the early arrivals. Of course, he appeared with his great-aunt, Lady de Paddington, and was duly presented by her to every individual of the Harrington family. His arrival caused no little sensation among such of the company as were already assembled, for no sooner had his name been pronounced, than he was at once recognised as the newly-emancipated minor whose great possessions had for some time past been canvassed and estimated by all the mammas, a good many of the daughters, and not a few of the gay young sons, who constituted the "fashionable world," of the present season.

The poor golden calf himself, whom all these various devotees were zealously preparing to worship, was very far, indeed, from being in a state of enjoyment. He was a tall gawky lad, with large heavy features, which though not particularly ill-formed, were utterly devoid of all intellectual expression, or any such degree of animation as might redeem their heaviness. His complexion was ruddy and betokened abounding health, his eyes bashful and dull-looking, and his straight hair of a light straw colour.

The poor boy's face became positively purple as he advanced up the room to the group of which Lady Augusta was the centre, and every feature, every limb, and every movement gave token of shyness and embarrassment. Poor fellow! he would at that moment have thankfully given a large slice out of his wide-spread acres could his so doing have enabled him to look, and to feel, like any one of the gay and graceful young men whom he saw around him. The only redeeming peculiarity of his appearance, which was a look of unmistakable good-humour, could not avail him now, for he looked and felt infinitely more disposed to cry than to laugh.

Kate's reception of him was admirable, and such as nothing but a large share of good sense could have enabled her to achieve under the existing circumstances; for most assuredly, if it had been Lady Augusta's object to make her daughter look and feel annoyed and awkward, upon seeing him, instead of graceful and gracious, she could have done nothing more likely to produce such a result than what she had done.

But our quiet Kate appeared not to be in any degree affected by it. The very keenest eye—and there were several very keen eyes fixed upon her—could not detect the slightest shade of greater or of less *empressement*, of greater or of less courtesy, than the occasion called for.

Had she, indeed, never heard of the awkward and painfully shy young man before, she would very probably have been induced by his evident suffering to take some pains to put him at his ease, by at once entering into conversation with him. But this she did not do. Her mother's harangue concerning him was too fresh in her memory to permit it, and this omission was the sole effect as yet produced by it. But if Kate did not converse with him, her mother did; for passing her arm under that of her dear friend, Lady de Paddington, she led her, accompanied, of course, by her young nephew, to the second drawing-room, and thence into the sweet dimly-lighted retreat afforded by the boudoir. And here for a few moments the young novice almost enjoyed himself, for he cordially agreed in the opinion expressed by his great-aunt that it certainly was the very prettiest thing in the world. Moreover, he had the satisfaction of hearing the sound of his own voice again, for the easy, amiable questionings of Lady Augusta, as to what he had seen in London, and how he liked it, made the effort of replying to her, wonderfully more easy than he could have believed possible before their conversation began.

Lady de Paddington, perceiving that her *protégé* was getting on admirably well, ventured to leave him for a few minutes, that she might indulge herself by a short tour round the rooms, chiefly for the purpose of turning the heads of all the mothers and daughters she met, by making them comprehend that the first match of the season had been brought to the identical ball-room where they now found themselves *by her*, that she should be delighted to introduce this darling nephew to them, &c., &c. And then perceiving in the most satisfactory manner that she had made herself of immense consequence to them all, and that dinners and opera boxes would be speedily at her feet, she suddenly bustled back to the boudoir, declaring that her dear Edward would think she had forsaken him.

She found her friend Lady Augusta still busily engaged in convincing Lord Goldstable that he was the most lucky fellow in the world, for having made acquaintance so early in his career with such a very kind and charming person as Lady Augusta Harrington; for she had already given him to understand that, in consequence of the tender friendship existing between his admirable Aunt de Paddington and herself, she felt the truest interest for *him*, and that she hoped and trusted that whenever he had an hour to spare he would bestow it upon them. *An hour to spare!* He who had not the very slightest idea what he was to do with himself during all the multitude of hours that he was going to pass in London! Certainly, Lady Augusta Harrington was the most delightful woman he had ever seen in his life; and if the beautiful daughter was but as kind to him as the mother, it should not be his fault if he did not give the go-by to all the young fellows in London, and carry her off as his bride.

He had very fully arrived at this conclusion, when his aunt, Lady de Paddington, re-entered the boudoir. The two ladies interchanged one rapid glance; it was very rapid, yet it said, plainly, "All goes well," on the part of Lady

Augusta, which the answering glance said as distinctly, assisted by a very slight movement of the head, "Go then, and leave me with him."

Need it be said that Lady Augusta took the hint?

"Now then, dear Edward, tell me what you think of a London ball-room?" said Lady de Paddington, gaily. "Can you deny that there is something enchanting in the whole scene?"

"It is all beautiful, aunt!" eagerly responded the young man. "It is almost midnight, I believe, yet I will be hanged if I don't think it is lighter than mid-day."

"And the splendid dresses, Edward, and the beautiful women? I flatter myself that you are not conscious of any feeling like disappointment."

"Not I, indeed, Aunt de Paddington. But I can tell you that the girl you called Miss Harrington is the handsomest of them all. She is for all the world like what one sees in a picture. I don't at all wonder at what you told me, about all the young fellows wanting to marry her."

"It will be your own fault, Edward, if any young man succeeds in that quarter except yourself. Just remember all I told you about her dislike to all young puppies. But hark! they are beginning to play a waltz. Come directly, and ask her to dance. As you are the stranger, and the man of greatest consequence in the room, it is absolutely necessary that she should open the ball with you. Come with me directly, Edward. There she is!"

Not one word of all his aunt had told him respecting Miss Harrington had escaped his memory; and it was, therefore, with a stouter heart than he had himself dared to hope for, that he now approached her, and said in a much steadier voice than might have been expected :—

"Aunt de Paddington says, Miss Harrington, that you and I ought to dance the first waltz together. Will you, please?"

"I would have done so with pleasure, my Lord," she replied, good-humouredly, "but that I am engaged."

"Dear me!" returned the young peer, looking considerably disappointed, "I wonder what we had better do, then? I will go and ask her, shall I?" And away he went to consult his instructress on this unforeseen emergency.

Kate, meanwhile, stood up to dance with Mr. Caldwell, the young barrister, and her doing so was in fulfilment of an engagement of some days' standing.

It had by this time become sufficiently clear, both to the
gentleman and lady, as well as to Uncle Walter, that the
moments they spent together were far sweeter than any other
moments in their lives. The young man, indeed, had very
stoutly made up his mind to attempt, without further delay,
to secure a continuance of these delightful moments for life;
and it would be inconsistent with the veracity of her historian
to pretend that no idea of the same sort had ever presented
itself to Kate. In truth, Kate knew perfectly well, or to
speak more correctly, she believed, without any mixture of
doubt, that she was beloved; nor did she make any attempt
to conceal from herself that the love she had inspired was
reflected back again from her own heart, and that nothing
less than the breaking of that heart could destroy the image
impressed upon it. Kate was very young, and very young
people are generally sanguine in the view they take of the
future; had she been a few years older, her imagination
might not have passed so rapidly, or so easily, over the
impediments which were pretty sure to intervene between her
and her hopes.

As to the young man himself, though he was a good ten
years her senior, he was, to say the least of it, fully as
sanguine as her hopeful self in his contemplation of the future.
But his hopefulness was of a totally different kind. Perhaps
he knew, even better than Kate herself, how utterly her
mother, and it might be her reverend father, too, would
scorn, and how resolutely they would reject, such an offer as
he could make her. But the conviction of all this did not
discourage him. Frederick Caldwell was, in many respects, a
singular young man; and the view which he took of the
probable result of the step he was resolved to take, was more
influenced by his own character than by the apparent
circumstances of the case.

He felt quite certain, and his opinion on this point was
perfectly correct, that he should not, or could not, have fallen
in love with Kate had she in any particular, or in any degree,
inherited the intellectual peculiarities, or the social views and
opinions, of her parents.

The beauty of the young girl had certainly appeared to him
of a peculiarly captivating character, but this would never
have sufficed to induce him to seek her as a wife. But it had
chanced that they had more than once fallen into conversation together in a strain not quite so common-place as he had

usually found to prevail among the young and lovely of his female acquaintance; and the opinions he contrived to elicit from her, were for the most part so exceedingly unlike what he probably expected from the daughter of the Warden of All Saints, and the Lady Augusta his wife, that he was caught almost as much by the feeling of surprise as of admiration.

One of the earliest thoughts suggested to him by the closely observant study which he bestowed upon her character, was that such a creature as Kate Harrington would never permit herself to be wooed, and won, by any man whose chief claim to her favour consisted either in rank or in riches. He was himself a gentleman by birth and education; and though his fortune was not such as to justify his feeling himself independent of the profession which the father he had so recently lost had chosen for him, it was sufficient to make him feel very nearly indifferent to the fact, that the young lady he loved was comparatively rich.

Never for an instant did the idea occur to him that her being so would influence her reception of his proposal; and as to the opposition which, as a matter of course, he knew would arise from the evident vanity and ambition of her parents, he looked at it certainly without alarm, and almost with indifference; for who, knowing Kate as he knew her, could believe that she would permit herself to be the victim of such opinions, or yield to any authority which would seek to enforce them?

As yet, however, he had not proposed to her, but Kate, as we have said, was pretty certain that he would; and the nonsense which her mother had talked about Lord Goldstable, was most assuredly not remembered by her as being sufficiently important to increase any difficulties she might have to encounter, when she declared it to be her intention to accept his hand.

But neither the gravity of this her fixed determination, nor any doubts or fears respecting its effect upon her family, could prevent her enjoying the happiness of the passing hour; for was she not dancing to sweet music? and was not the man she loved her partner? And she yielded herself to the influence of these circumstances, according to the ancient and immemorial custom of eighteen.

Before this first dance was over, Lord Brandling, a College friend and companion of Mr. Caldwell's, had engaged her for the ensuing quadrille, so that a second application from poor Lord Goldstable proved as unsuccessful as the first. But on this subject his aunt had in the interval given him a useful hint, by which he immediately profited, for when refused for the next dance, he boldly begged to be accepted for the one after; and this was accorded to him.

Lady de Paddington had meantime found a moment to ask Lady Augusta hurriedly, what was the meaning of the strange mischance which had occurred? and what her daughter could be thinking of? Lady Augusta declared herself, and with very perfect sincerity, to be excessively angry.

"It is impossible to understand it," she exclaimed, "but I will speak to her instantly." And she drew near her beautiful daughter accordingly, and said, in an angry and hurried whisper:—

"Good Heaven! why are you not dancing with him? What are you dreaming of?"

"Do you mean Lord Goldstable, mamma?" replied Kate, quietly. "I am going to dance the next dance with him."

"And take care, if you please, that I see no levity of any kind!" again whispered her mother. "Your whole life may depend upon this evening. For goodness sake be careful!" And so saying, the anxious mother and the gracious hostess glided away to a distant part of the room, leaving Kate to finish her dance with Lord Brandling; but this time the poor girl thought more of the difficulties before her, and vastly less of what she was doing, than before this first change of partners had taken place. But on the second change, which made the blushing Lord Goldstable her partner, she really exerted herself to be agreeable, for she was full of good-natured consideration for his evident shyness; and so well did these efforts succeed, that before the dance was ended, the poor boy began to feel that his excellent great-aunt was quite right, and that the very best thing he could do would be to marry Miss Harrington directly.

The unaffected good-humour and quiet simplicity of her manner, had in truth made him feel completely at his ease, and so perfectly happy and comfortable, that he was quite ready to declare a fine London ball-room to be the most agreeable place in the world, and falling in love there the most agreeable, as well as the most natural occupation.

Nevertheless, he discreetly determined that he would not be *too* much in a hurry, and, therefore, very deliberately decided that he should postpone the making an offer of marriage to the charming young lady, so skilfully and so kindly selected for him, till the next quadrille, for which he engaged her as soon as she had given him to understand that the next dance was a polka, for his Lordship did not "polk" (the last May Fair supplement to "Johnson's Dictionary," if we be correctly informed, contains this verb), and, therefore, his rival, his perfectly unconscious rival, Mr. Caldwell, had the advantage of being her partner during the intervening dance. Now this trifling delay caused, as it turned out, an important change in the aspect of Kate Harrington's affairs; and it furnishes an important lesson to all young men at present entering upon life, by showing the immense importance that may, and probably must, attach to their learning to *polk*.

At the conclusion of the quadrille a pause ensued in the dancing, occasioned by the entrance of half a dozen ice-trays, which had to win their by no means easy way round the ball-room.

"The whist-table is in your cell, Miss Harrington, is it not?" said Mr. Caldwell. "Shall we pay your father a visit? The crowd here, just now, is perfectly overpowering."

"It will, indeed, be a great relief to get into a cooler atmosphere," replied Kate; and they made their way accordingly through the ice-eaters who had established themselves on the staircase, and succeeded, though not without some little difficulty, in getting to the card-room.

Here they found eight very comfortable looking ladies and gentlemen, so quietly amusing themselves at whist, that they really looked as if they intended to exhibit the strongest possible contrast to the scene below, to all such as might seek refuge there from the brilliant suffocation of the ballroom.

Kate paused behind the chair of her father, for a moment; but that moment was a critical one, for the fate of the rubber depended upon the odd trick, for which the parties were in the very act of struggling.

"Well, papa, how goes the game?" said Kate.

"Lost! if you come and talk to me, my dear," replied the Doctor. "Pray go away," he added, very gravely.

Whereupon his daughter, who really felt shocked and penitent at having been guilty of so ill-timed an intrusion, took advantage of the open window, which led to her recently completed conservatory, and stepped out into the midst of her own roses and geraniums. And it so happened, that before she stepped in again she had accepted Mr. Caldwell as her affianced husband, just as her father exclamed, in a voice of triumph, the important word, " Won."

Miss Harrington danced the next quadrille, according to promise, with Lord Goldstable. They spoke but little during the dance, for Kate was rather absent, and her noble partner was screwing his courage to the sticking place, and considering how best to word the proposal, which he had determined to make the moment he had led her to a seat. Nor did he, even when this tremendous moment arrived, shrink from his purpose.

" Miss Harrington," said he, placing himself beside her in a corner, which was fortunately at that moment perfectly unoccupied, " my aunt, Lady de Paddington, Miss Harrington, who knows London well, and all the people in it, I believe, my aunt tells me that my having such a large fortune, and a coronet, too, you know, would be enough to make all the pretty girls in it quite ready to marry me. I am quite sure you won't say yes to me for that reason, because you are, and must be, so very much above anything of the kind—but yet I hope and trust you won't say no. Do be so very good as to accept me, will you? It would make me so very happy! And I should love you so very much ; and we should be so very happy together. Do say yes, will you?"

The astonishment of Kate, at this unexpected address, was so great, as positively to deprive her for the moment of all power to answer it. And then indignation, or something like it, succeeded to surprise, and her complexion, which had been considerably paler than usual but a moment before, became flushed, and her eyes flashed, too. But before she could turn their angry glances full upon the offender, she became so conscious of the absurdity of her own situation and of his, that if she had looked at him at all, she would very probably have committed the extreme impropriety of laughing.

The feelings which led to this were not, however, likely to last long ; she felt that however ludicrous his mode of wooing her might be, it must very gravely and very effectually be put an end to ; and the anger of her indignant mother then came before her with so much distinctness, that the drollery of the business was very speedily forgotten.

Lord Goldstable meanwhile stood beside her twitching the tips of his gloves, and shifting from one foot to the other in an agony of uncertainty as to what was to be done or said next. At length, however, Kate turned gravely but gently towards him, and said :—

" Your opinion of me is very flattering, my Lord, but believe me, you will spare both yourself and me pain, if you will say no more upon the subject."

Her voice betrayed agitation, which the young man immediately perceived, and that with very considerable satisfaction, for he thought to himself that it was as clear as daylight that they both felt just the same. It was, therefore, with renewed spirit that he replied :—

" Not say any more upon the subject? How can you say such a thing? But you can't think it, I am sure of that. Not say anything, indeed! Oh! Miss Harrington, I don't think I shall ever be able to talk about anything else! No, then, I know I shan't, so it's no good to expect it. And then they say—that is, *she* says—that it is the very best thing in the world for me to do. Come, now, do say yes! But, at any rate, don't say no!—Silence you know!—Eh! Miss Harrington? Well, then, only just say that you will dance with me again after the next polka. How I do wish I could dance the polka." And as he said this he turned suddenly towards her, and attempted to take her hand.

She rose suddenly for the purpose of leaving him, for at that moment she felt she had no power of bringing this most absurd scene to a conclusion in any other way.

"Oh, dear! oh, dear!" he cried, "you are not going away, are you? Pray don't, Miss Harrington! I am not going, you know, to think that you are in love with me *now*, I don't expect such a thing. But, indeed, indeed I'll do everything you like : and, upon my honour, I'll make you quite comfortable and—and—all right now, isn't it?"

At this moment a rapid step approached, and on looking up, Kate saw Mr. Caldwell standing close to her. She instantly passed her arm under his and walked away, flattering herself that the reception she had given to the young rustic's strange attempt at love-making, was such as would effectually prevent his renewing it.

CHAPTER XV.

L<small>ADY</small> DE P<small>ADDINGTON</small>'s first care on learning from her
hopeful *protégé* that he had actually "popped the question,"
as he gracefully expressed himself, and that "though the
young lady had not said *yes*, she had certainly not said *no*,"
was to assure him that he ought to feel extremely flattered
and perfectly satisfied with this, for that no reasonable young
man, let him be whom he would, could expect more under
the circumstances.

"I don't mean to blame you, Edward," she continued,
very affectionately, "quite the contrary, I assure you; but
you certainly were *rather* hasty, you know, and her not refusing you outright, is quite proof sufficient that she means to
accept you—therefore, on the whole, I am rather glad that
you lost no time about it. But I certainly did not expect
that you would be quite so much in a hurry. I thought that
you might begin to be a little particular, perhaps, and that
at supper you might have *hinted* that you were charmed with
her more than you had ever been with anybody. But I had
no notion, my dear boy, that you would absolutely propose
before the end of the second dance."

"*Hinted!*" exclaimed the youth, in an accent indicative of
something very like contempt. "Why, didn't you tell me,
aunt, that all the finest young fellows in London were
after her? Much good I should have done by *hinting*,
shouldn't I?"

This lively sally was received with a gracious nod, and
an approving smile, by the scheming aunt, who forthwith
hurried off to report progress to Lady Augusta.

"And what did Kate say? What answer did she give
him?" returned Lady Augusta, colouring with sudden
emotion. "He has been determined to lose no time, at
all events," she added.

"Thanks to my priming," returned Lady de Paddington,
laughing. "Just look round at all the bright young eyes,
and at all the motherly glances directed towards him, and

then say whether I was not right when I resolved that no time should be lost?"

"Oh! perfectly right! most perfectly right," was Lady Augusta's grateful rejoinder. "But I should like to know how Kate received it," she added. "We can scarcely expect that she should manifest an equally sudden attachment, you know; not that I shall permit any shilly-shally nonsense on her part; nor would her father permit it either. It will all end as it ought to do. You may depend on *us* for that. But she must have been a good deal surprised, I think."

"That is just what I said to Edward," replied her friend; "but, though he did not tell me, in reply, exactly her very words, he seemed to be perfectly contented with them. He only stated, in a general way, that he had *not* been refused; and that he had given her to understand, when somebody came up and interrupted them, that he considered everything was right between them."

"Of course, after what I said to her," returned Lady Augusta, "there could be no danger of her offering any serious opposition; but girls will be girls, you know; and they don't always like to let things of this kind be settled too easily. However, I will no more quarrel with our bride for being *trop facile*, than he will quarrel with her for being *trop belle*. Everything is just as it ought to be, dearest Lady Paddington; and depend upon it, I shall never forget the friendly feelings you have manifested on this occasion. Kate shall be a good niece to you; I will take care of that."

And then the ladies parted, "that they might not," as Lady de Paddington said, "be suspected of plotting together."

Lady Augusta, perfectly satisfied by what she had already heard, nodded her approval of this discreet separation, and then stepped forward among her guests with a prouder eye, and a prouder step, than before; for the news she had heard was glorious news, and the value she put upon it was not small; it might be, perhaps, a little beyond what it was worth.

Meanwhile, the affairs of another pair of mortals were, to all appearance, progressing towards their desired termination. By means of Henry Harrington's good-nature, and habitual indifference to everything like right honourable etiquette, Mr. Garble, the young attorney, who has been already presented to the reader, received a card of invitation to this

splendid and every way important ball, and he and pretty
Miss Mary Jane Wigginsville employed nearly the whole
evening in "taking sweet counsel together."

It was in vain that the Lady Juliana made not the slightest
effort to conceal her profound disgust and indignation thereat,
for the holy flirtation had gone a great deal too far to be
checked by any harmless, although vehement opposition. It
was in vain that her moody Ladyship had the courage to
utter, very audibly, the words, "low worldling," to her sister,
the Lady Augusta, as they passed together within hearing of
the tender pair. It touched them not, or, at any rate, it
seemed not to touch them. And yet the epithets, alas! both
epithets, were merited.

To the censure conveyed by the painful epithet *low*, he was
decidedly obnoxious; for not only was he a special attorney,
but no one had ever heard any reference made to the fact of
his having had a father; and as to the charge of his being a
worldling, we have strong reasons for suspecting the circumstances of his second birth to be quite as doubtful and unsatisfactory as those of his first.

Nevertheless, pretty little Miss Mary Jane found the
attorney's sweet counsel too pleasant to be sacrificed, even
to her habitual reverence for her noble friend's title or her
godliness. It was very plainly evident, indeed, that Miss
Mary Jane nourished the hope that they might "walk
together in the house of God as friends"—nay, it might be,
perhaps, as something more!

It really seemed fated that this very remarkable evening
should be to her, as well as to Kate Harrington, the most
memorable she had ever passed; for, before the end of it,
Mr. Garble found courage, notwithstanding the dazzling
station of the friends by whom she was surrounded, to
ascertain distinctly what might be his chance of obtaining a
comfortable provision for life through the agency of her fair
hand and tender heart.

Nevertheless, although Mr. Garble was not a man
generally troubled by nervous weakness, he deferred the
decisive question till the genial hour of supper.

Seated close beside her, while the eyes and thoughts of
those around were occupied by other things, he felt that he
might speak and she might hear what could not so safely be
pronounced at any other time. Not that the hours preceding
supper were idly spent by him; far from it. He was, indeed,

but a novice in the peculiar phraseology of godly love-
making; but some few holy phrases were familiar to him,
and he felt certain that he should be able to introduce them
to great advantage. Before we give any specimen of the skill
with which this was achieved, it may be as well to mention
that the eloquence of Mr. Garble had on all subjects one
marked peculiarity, namely, that of constantly removing the
letter h from the beginning of every word where it usually
appeared, and atoning for the theft by scrupulously prefixing
it to every word where it did not.

"Oh, dearest Miss Mary Jane!" he murmured, "if it were
the Lord's blessed will those lips could eal the cart those
heyes are wounded, and that only by letting judgment go for
the plaintiff. Grant me my suit, Miss Mary Jane, and this
will be the appiest our of my life!"

"Oh, Mr. Garble!" was the only reply Miss Mary Jane
could articulate.

"Surely, it would be for the glory of eaven," he resumed,
"that two serious carts should hexecute a bond and covenant
on ymen's halter!" softly whispered the attorney.

"A holy love is, indeed, a blessed thing," returned the
gentle lady, with a sigh; "but, oh, Mr. Garbel, this carnal
scene is not a place to speak of such a subject."

"But only tell me that my hanxious cart may ope," he
replied, in the very tenderest of whispers; "only promise
that you will consult the Lord in his good time. Let me take
a *rule nisi*. Oh, dearest Miss Mary Jane, grant me a *rule
nisi!*"

Miss Mary Jane returned a look by no means calculated to
generate any feeling of despair; and then she suffered the
ardent little man to take her hand furtively beneath the
sheltering table-cloth, and press it in his own.

After this it would be surely unjust to accuse Mr. Garble
of presumption, even though he did lay down to rest that
night without feeling the poisoned horror of despair rankling
in his heart.

    ❉   ❋   ❋   ❋   ❋

Let it not be supposed that the hour of supper had arrived,
without Lord Goldstable's having been presented to sundry
thoughtful mothers and pretty daughters, none of whom were
inclined to neglect this fortunate opportunity of entering
themselves for the "great Goldstable stakes." It was, of
course, to Lady de Paddington that all petitions for an intro-

duction were addressed, and these petitions it was, in most cases, of course, impossible to refuse ; but true as steel to her purpose of bestowing this great prize on the daughter of her devoted friend, Lady Augusta, she invariably accompanied every introduction by the following words, whispered in the ear where it was most important they should be registered : " Only fancy ! so very young as he looks, that he should be engaged already."

This was certainly, under the circumstances, the best and most easy course to take, and it promptly and effectually nipped many young hopes in the bud, or, in other words, it served to warn trespassers off the preserves, and that, too, in a manner which could not be called otherwise than civil.

Nevertheless, there was one enterprizing individual whose steadfast purpose was not to be checked by any such gentle means ; nay, the startled Lady de Paddington was soon made to understand that, not even a point-blank refusal, though uttered in the most direct and unmitigated manner, could avail her.

But this individual was of a species known to be by far the most dangerous. extant. Not the loveliest and most designing daughter, nor the shrewdest and most intriguing mother, could be compared to her, for this individual was a widow !— young, lovely, intriguing, designing, shrewd—and a widow ! But this widow is by far too important a personage to be introduced at the end of a chapter.

CHAPTER XVI.

MRS. FITZJAMES, so was this beauteous young widow called, was a lady who would never have been found at the house of Lady Augusta and Doctor Harrington by their own good will ; but she had been brought thither by a very free and easy person, and one whom they neither chose to offend, namely, the identical Miss Puddingthwaite, who has already been introduced to the reader.

It is not exactly correct, however, to say that she was *brought* thither by this accommodating and *passe par-tout* lady, for not even the temptation of showing herself at so brilliant a party as that now given by Lady Augusta Harrington, could have induced Mrs. Fitzjames to have made a toilet so hurried as would have been required, to enable her to accompany that reconnoitring lady, at the early hour at which she had chosen to make her appearance there. Nay, even if the elaborate business of dressing could *par impossible* have been got through in time, yet still Mrs. Fitzjames would not have accompanied her at that hour, for she knew too well what she should lose by it.

A very well-dressed, and very beautiful young woman cannot be seen under any circumstances without creating a certain degree of attention, admiration, and curiosity ; but far different is the degree in which these desirable effects are produced, if she be first looked at when weary of waiting in a half-filled room, instead of being for the first time seen to make her slow and graceful entry through an admiring crowd, whose eager glances both excite, and account for, that pretty fascinating expression which hovers between coquetry and embarrassment.

It was *thus* that Mrs. Fitzjames chose to make her *entrée* into every ball-room, and it was thus she made her *entrée* now into that of Lady Augusta Harrington.

The maiden name of Mrs. Fitzjames was Barlow. She was the daughter of a broken-down, but very gentlemanlike and handsome-looking, Colonel Barlow, who, having sold his commission, as well as nearly everything else which he could convert into ready money, had systematically taken to living upon his wits just about the time that his daughter had completed her seventeenth year.

The poor girl's mother had, at this time, been several years dead, but it was only upon the death of her maternal grandmother that she had been handed over to her precious father for protection. It is highly probable that this protection would have been altogether refused, had the young lady been as plain as she was strikingly the reverse ; but no sooner had her admiring father looking at her after the interval of about seven years, than he decided that he would himself take the charge of her.

What his projects were concerning her, may be doubtful ; they might be no worse than having for their object the

selling her as a wife to the first man, old or young, handsome
or ugly, worthy or worthless, who was rich enough to bid for
her; but the ruined gambler had a run of ill-luck, which
settled the matter at once.   A certain Major-General
Fitzjames happened to win of him a sum considerably
larger than he was able to raise, whereupon his unfortunate daughter's fair hand was generously accepted as
payment in full for the debt, without entering very scrupulously into the question of whether the blooming Sophia
were willing or not.

But even had the parties considered this branch of the
subject as being of any real importance, it is probable the
result would have been the same; for the blooming Sophia
was already extremely disgusted with her papa's style of
housekeeping, which consisted of eternal scoldings because she
spent too much, and eternal complainings because his luxuries
were too few.   And so, without the shadow of a principle to
keep her right, and every species of inclination to go wrong,
the beautiful girl of seventeen became the dashing bride of the
débauché of forty-seven, and took up her residence in a smart-
looking lodging, *au troisième*, on the Boulevard des Italiens at
Paris.

Her father, however, very soon changed his quarters from
Paris to New Orleans, and his daughter never heard of him
more.

She lived with her gay husband for about a dozen gay,
though not particularly respectable, years, and was then left,
considerably improved in beauty, and considerably deteriorated
in character, with the pension of a General's widow, and a
good many gay trinkets.

She might certainly have lived much better on her pension
in Paris than in London; but Mrs. Fitzjames was not without
ambition, and as yet she had not felt any of the illness that
attends it.   Miss Puddingthwaite was her father's first cousin,
nay, it had once been rumoured that there had been some
passages of love between them; but, be this as it may, it is
certain that when the stikingly lovely and very stylish-looking
Mrs. General Fitzjames claimed kindred with her in all the
modest elegance of black and grey, Miss Puddingthwaite
received her very graciously, and speedily determined to
extend to her a little of the influence, which she had contrived, from various lucky accidents, to have acquired in the
fashionable world.

Nevertheless, this much-needed assistance was not bestowed without some mixture of interested calculation on the part of the bestower, for Miss Puddingthwaite, although from many fortunate accidents she had obtained a footing in very high society, was by no means unmindful that such a face, figure, and general appearance as those of her cousin, Mrs. General Fitzjames, might often be useful to her.

In short, the claims of her Parisian cousin to her friendship were welcomed, rather than repelled; and having once determined upon this line of conduct, Miss Puddingthwaite was not a person to be turned out of her path by anyone. She had, therefore, upon this occasion, as well as upon many others where *large* parties were given, asked and obtained, a card of invitation for her cousin; and in this way, the beautiful Mrs. General Fitzjames was already beginning to be talked of as one of the loveliest women in London in many drawing-rooms; and it may be that, in more than one club-room, these speculations upon her beauty were accompanied by less flattering speculations respecting her character.

Her husband had been dead about two years at the time our narrative falls in with her at the house of Dr. Harrington, and she was now thirty-one years old. But not a shadow of diminution had as yet fallen upon her beauty; on the contrary, she was decidedly more captivating now than she had been at the time of her marriage. An extremely beautiful woman, while under five-and-twenty, is apt to show her consciousness of the power which she never can altogether resist; and though many may be ready to declare that this *naïve* vanity becomes her, it is, neverthelesss, pretty certain that she may employ her power with more assured success, when she has learnt to conceal the youthful consciousness that she possesses it.

At any rate, Mrs. General Fitzjames was unquestionably more passionately admired now than she had ever been at any former period of her life, and she was fully aware of this, and also very fully determined to profit by it. In one word, she was as fully entitled to be called a dangerous woman as any to whom the phrase was ever applied. She was in figure tall, and decidedly more slight and fragile in appearance than plump; nevertheless, she possessed in an eminent degree that peculiar feline grace of movement, and natural picturesqueness of attitude which is never found to accompany any form of bony angularity. Her hands and feet were models of delicate

8—2

symmetry—the long lithe throat which sprung proudly from
her skilfully half-dropped shoulders, rescued the whole figure
from any charge of insignificance ; and the small Greek-shaped
head, wreathed with the luxuriant tresses of her dark brown
hair, though not, perhaps, formed to excite the adoration of
Messieurs Spurzheim and Gall, would have assuredly received
due worship from Titian or Correggio.

But the face—yet why should we say but ?—the face was
beautiful, decidedly, undeniably beautiful. It had beauty of
outline, beauty of feature, and beauty of colouring ; but those
who were gifted with the power of looking at her, without
falling in love at first sight, might see on it occasional
shadows of meaning which were certainly not lovely.

Her dark eyes were bright and sparkling, in truth, they
almost glittered with the brilliancy of foil ; but the small,
bright red mouth, with its rapid and often recurring smiles,
was frequently at variance, as it were, with the expression of
those glittering eyes ; and this, to a keen observer, imparted a
character of insincerity to the whole countenance.

Mrs. Fitzjames, however, laughed musically ; talked
fluently, wittily, and occasionally without much restraint ;
she, moreover, danced like a fairy, sang like a nightingale,
and was, in fact, what all fast-young men call, in their vulgar
jargon, " a splendid creature."

With all these gifts and graces, and with the countenance
of Miss Puddingthwaite, and of one or two aristocratic connections of her husband, she had contrived, without much
difficulty, to obtain a certain footing in a certain set, consisting principally of that section of the fashionable world, whose
mode of life and conduct would be " really too bad for anything," if they were *not* members of the fashionable world.

Now, the beautiful Mrs. Fitzjames was quite aware that
she was an extremely lucky lady in finding herself so placed,
and she was very fully determined not to waste the brief
space of time, during which she might still hope to obtain a
permanent position in the brilliant set, who seemed to be so
very good-natured to her ; in a word, she felt that this was
her time, or none, to open for herself " the world, her
oyster," and in such a sort, too, as to make her independent
of all its caprices for the entire term of her natural life.

Such was the lady who appeared suddenly before the eyes
of Lord Goldstable, just after Kate had withdrawn herself
from his sight.

Mrs. Fitzjames had already made herself acquainted with all the *most interesting* particulars concerning him; and having learnt these, she looked at him. She looked at him, indeed, very attentively; and most certainly there was no want of "speculation in the eyes that she did look withal." She addressed herself to Lady de Paddington, and requested that she would do her the favour of introducing her young nephew to her. To this request she received a positive refusal, upon the pretence that Lord Goldstable was so shy, that it was painful to him to be introduced to strangers. But Mrs. Fitzjames was not likely to be so easily defeated. Of course, she uttered no word of remonstrance, but, bowing slightly, and smiling rather more slightly still, she passed on. Lady de Paddington walked on likewise, and immediately left the ball-room in search of Lady Augusta, being eager to tell her of the dangerous request which had been made, and also the ready wit with which she had refused it.

Mrs. Fitzjames watched her as she left the room, and then gently and gracefully drew near to the young man, and having caught his eye, she looked at him, timidly, yet smilingly, for a moment, and then said :—

"Lord Goldstable, you have no recollection of me, I daresay?"

"Recollection, Ma'am? no, Ma'am, I can't say I have; I'm afraid not!" said Lord Goldstable, colouring violently.

"Nay," she replied, with a smile of irresistible sweetness, "I am not the least surprised to hear you say so: it is so very natural that you should have forgotten me! But I remember well having seen you, I won't say how many years ago, in Scotland. Our fathers, Lord Goldstable, were great friends at that time; but when my poor dear father settled abroad, his Scotch friends saw no more of him. I do not see, however, why we should not renew our old acquaintance. My name now is Mrs. Fitzjames, but you never heard of me by that name, I daresay. However, you must have heard of me, I think, as Sophia Barlow."

Lord Goldstable heard that name now for the first time, and it would have been equally new to his noble father, had he been there to hear it now; nor had the beautiful Sophia ever been at any period of her existence within some hundred miles of the "land of cakes." But what did that signify?

The notion, however, of meeting an old friend, though an unremembered one, was very pleasant to the shy youth; so colouring up to the roots of his pale hair, partly from embarrassment, and partly from pleasure, he stammered out:—

"I'm sure you are very kind, Ma'am. I daresay I might, if I was to try to recollect—I'm sure I don't know ——"

And there he stopped. But the more fluent lady relieved his embarrassment by continuing, with gay and smiling rapidity:—

"Well then, now we must be very great friends; I am sure we ought, dear Lord Goldstable, for many reasons. We ought to be friends, because our fathers were friends before us; and I think, too, we ought to be friends, because we both seem to be strangers in this immense crowd."

"Indeed, yes, Ma'am," said Lord Goldstable, looking at her more steadily, and thinking, as he did so, how *very, very* beautiful she was.

"Oh, don't say Ma'am," she replied, with a still kinder smile; "it sounds so very formal. Your dear father always used to call me Sophia. I was but a baby then, to be sure, but yet the idea of it is pleasant to one who has so few friends as I have now. I am so perfectly a stranger here, Lord Goldstable, that the name of an old friend goes to my very heart."

"Dear me," returned Lord Goldstable, "I should think that everybody in the world must be your friends—and I did not suppose that anyone could be a stranger here, excepting myself."

"Alas! no one can be so completely a stranger as I am," she replied, and with a movement that seemed most perfectly natural in so old an acquaintance, she passed her beautiful white arm under his.

"You have lost your father," she resumed, as they slowly walked on together, "and so have I, dear friend; but I have lost my poor husband, too! It is true he was as old, or, I believe, rather older, than my dear papa, and, therefore, I was never, you know, what people call *in love* with him, but he was always very kind and good to me. I used to call him, my dear old Robin Grey. Do you know the song of 'Old Robin Grey,' Lord Goldstable?"

"Oh yes, I know that to be sure; that is a real old Scotch song, you know."

"Well, then, if you will come and call upon me to-morrow, I will sing it to you," said she, kindly, "and then

we really shall be like old friends. Will you come, dear
Edward?"

"Yes, that I will," replied the greatly delighted youth,
giving a friendly pressure to the fair arm which rested on his.
"How good-natured it is of you to call me by my name.
How did you know that my name was Edward?"

"Because I remembered it, old friend," she unblushingly
replied.

And, in truth, she did remember it, and the recollection
served her well. She had read, not only his name and age in
the peerage, but the names of all his race, and of all their
mansions, and she knew them as well by heart as she did the
christian appellation which she now so dexterously ventured
to give him.

For the arrival of the youthful nobleman, in London, was
by far too interesting a fact to be long a secret to any whom
it might concern, even to the far-away gossipings of many
who might live and die without beholding him; and that the
piercing intellect of Miss Puddingthwaite should have speedily
acquired all the information it was possible for her to obtain
concerning him, was truly a matter of course. In addition,
however, to all that her patronising cousin could tell her on
the subject, Mrs. Fitzjames had the good sense to seek for all
the solid information that the peerage could give her, and this
enabled her, with the most easy and graceful assurance, to
carry on her "old friend" fable, without the slightest fear of
making any important blunder.

As to Lord Goldstable himself, he was speedily becoming a
new man under the happy influences of this cleverly-imagined
old friendship; he was not only rapidly recovering the power
of speech, but was every instant becoming more thoroughly
aware of the value of his eyes. He not only totally forgot all
that his aunt had said to him about Miss Harrington, but all
and everything which he had so lately spoken to that young
lady in consequence of it.

From having felt so painfully overpowered by the newness
of everything around him, that he would almost have given
one of his fingers to have found himself fairly rid of it all,
and snugly tucked up in his bed; he suddenly began to fancy
that he had never been so happy before in the whole course of
his life, and that there was no danger of his ever feeling shy
again, so that he could but keep out of the way of all stiff,
formal people, and always keep near such a dear, delightful,

beautiful old friend as he now felt gently leaning upon his arm.

" Well, to be sure," he exclaimed, in a tone of the most innocent and heartfelt satisfaction, "nothing was ever further from my thoughts when I came in here, than that I should meet an old friend. It is such an unaccountable piece of good-luck, that I feel as if I could never be thankful enough for it. And now I think we ought to begin and tell one another everything that has happened to us since we used to play together in Scotland. Where did you go to school? Or did you have a governess at home, in the same way that I had a tutor ?"

"Did you never go to school, dear Edward?" returned the lady, bending forward, and looking innocently up in his face. "Now that is another odd resemblance between us, for I never went to school either. My poor dear papa undertook the care of my education entirely himself."

"Only think of that now," cried the delighted Lord Gold-stable, who really began to fancy that he must have known her in some previous state of existence, because, as he told her, he had felt so delightfully free from shyness with her from the very first.

And then, before they began dancing together, which, of course, they had agreed to do, Mrs. Fitzjames declared that she was perishing for want of a little change of air and refreshment, and that he must take her down stairs to the supper-room.

The delighted boy, whose shyness seemed completely banished, leaving nothing but the very happiest hilarity in its place, agreed to the proposal by a declaration that it was exactly the thing he should like best in the world; and accordingly they set off together arm-in-arm, he carrying her bouquet in his right hand, while she playfully threw her lace scarf over his left, upon which arm her own delicate hand still rested.

Just as they reached the door leading out upon the stair-case, they found themselves exactly in front of Lady de Paddington, who had placed herself near it for the sake of imbibing a little fresher air than the ball-room afforded.

Mrs. Fitzjames was not quite a novice, but was, on the contrary, fully aware of all the disagreeable feelings which were likely to agitate the breast of the dowager, upon per-ceiving how little she had gained by refusing the introduction she had asked for, and, to say the truth, she enjoyed this little vengeance exceedingly

Lord Goldstable's first notion on seeing her, was that he must, of course, immediately introduce to her the charming old friend whom he had had the great good-luck to stumble upon; but the skilful Sophia whispered close, very close to his ear, " Not now ! "

And then, drawing him on immediately before the old lady, in order to pass through the door, she said, in accents very distinctly audible :—

" Tell me, dear Edward, who is that old lady you came with ? "

" Hush ! " whispered Lord Goldstable, " she will hear you ! " But that was all he said, and they passed down the stairs closely linked together, and without taking any further notice of the frowning great-aunt. Lady de Paddington felt as if she must sink on the floor, and really looked very much as if she were about to be visited by a fit of apoplexy. No words are strong enough to describe her astonishment and indignation. When asked for the introduction she had so unceremoniously refused, she had soothed herself with the complacent feeling of being wide-awake, muttering to herself, as she turned away from the beautiful but disappointed petitioner :—

" Introduce him to her ! A very likely thing, of all the women in London ! It would be as good as throwing up the game at once ! "

Yet, now, what had this refusal availed her ? Had it not just sufficed to prove that she had no efficient power either to grant or to refuse ? For three miserable moments and a half she remained on the spot where they had left her, as if paralyzed ; but then she recovered herself sufficiently to call to our friend Mr. White, who was at no great distance, and in a very coaxing accent, said to him :—

" Do, dear Mr. White, have the great kindness to find out my nephew, Lord Goldstable, for me. I think he is gone into the supper-room. Will you, my dear Sir, be so extremely good as to tell him from me, that I suddenly feel myself extremely unwell, and that it is absolutely necessary that I should go home immediately. Say *immediately*, absolutely this very moment, my good Sir, and that I am only waiting for him."

Mr. White, after delaying for a moment to profess his pro-

found regret at the nature of the message he was commissioned
to carry, darted down the stairs with headlong speed to perform his errand. It was the first occupation of any kind that
he had had that evening, and he felt it to be quite a
blessing.

He had to return, however, not with Lord Goldstable, but
with Lord Goldstable's answer, which he distinctly delivered
in these words:—

"Lord Goldstable desired me to tell your Ladyship, that he
is exceedingly sorry to hear of your Ladyship's indisposition;
but that you need not trouble yourself about waiting for him,
for that he was not near ready to go yet, and that the carriage
of a very old friend of his would set him down when the ball
was over."

This most alarmingly independent reply was a severe and
most unexpected blow to Lord Goldstable's great-aunt; but
she felt that, for the moment, at least, all interference and all
remonstrance must be vain; but not choosing that the detestable Mrs. Fitzjames should have the triumph of witnessing
her discomfiture, she persevered in her intention of going
home, soothing her wounded feelings as well as she might, by
meditating upon the very spirited and decisive line of conduct
she should pursue on the morrow.

Meanwhile, Mrs. Fitzjames, who understood the meaning
of Lady de Paddington's embassy a good deal better than the
unsuspicious individual to whom it was addressed, was not
idle; nor was she slow in deciding upon the line of conduct
which it would be best for her to pursue under the circumstances.

A short interval of silence followed the dismissal of Lady de
Paddington's messenger; and then the beautiful dark eyes of
Mrs. Fitzjames were timidly and almost tenderly raised to the
face of Lord Goldstable.

"My dear Edward," she then said, while a sigh agitated
the delicate lace which shaded, without concealing, her
bosom. "My dear Edward, do you know, that though I felt
so very happy a few moments ago, I have now some very
miserable thoughts tormenting me?"

"What about?" said Lord Goldstable, pressing her pretty
arm very lovingly. "I won't let you have any disagreeable
thoughts. Tell me, what is it? What is the matter?"

"Yes, I will tell you!" she replied, in an accent of
affectionate confidence. "My mind is tormented about that

great-aunt of yours, that stern-looking Lady de Paddington. It has always been a name of ill omen to me, and now, if, in addition to all the rest, she should be the means of prejudicing your mind against me, it would be dreadful indeed! I do think it would break my heart!"

Lord Goldstable was, of course, greatly delighted, but he was greatly puzzled too.

"Prejudice me against you?" he repeated, looking at her very lovingly. "Why should she prejudice me against you? And what else is it that she has already done to vex you? Do tell me all about it; you may depend upon it, Sophia, that I shall take your part?"

Sophia thanked him by again pressing the arm she held, and then said:—

"Can I trust you with the confidence you ask for? Yet, alas! whom should I trust, if not the oldest friend, or rather the earliest friend I ever had? The son of my poor father's faithful friend ought to be my faithful friend also, and I will, and *do* believe that you will prove so. But you must promise me, dear Edward, you must solemnly and faithfully promise me, that no syllable of what I am going to say to you shall ever pass your lips. Nay, you must not let any allusion to it escape you. It would, believe me, be doing me a cruel, in fact, an irreparable injury."

Of course "dear Edward" vowed the required vow, and that, too, with very hearty energy, and a very sincere intention of keeping it.

"Now, then, listen to me," resumed the fair deceiver, "and I will tell you all! A singular accident brought to my father's knowledge, the disgraceful fact, that Lady de Paddington had been *unfaithful to her husband!* and there were some unfortunate circumstances connected with the affair, which rendered it absolutely incumbent upon my poor dear father, who was the very soul of honour, to communicate to the unfortunate Lord de Paddington the fact of his dishonour! He did so, Edward, and the undying hatred of that most wicked woman to my poor father, and to me, his unoffending child, has been the result. There is nothing, Edward, no, nothing, that she would not either do or say to injure me, and I foresee, but too plainly, that she will forbid all further intercourse between us."

"Forbid! Goodness gracious, my dear Sophia, what a fool you must take me for! *She* forbid our intercourse? By

Jove, that is a good joke! If it is to come to *that*, I can promise her wicked old Ladyship that I shall clear off, and get out of her house in double quick time. Perhaps she may not remember that I am twenty-one—but I do!"

"Not for worlds would I be the cause of any disagreement between you, and any friend you valued. Oh, not for worlds!" vehemently exclaimed the lady. "Only promise me that you will not listen to any of the infamous falsehoods that I know she is continually inventing against me—only promise me this, and I shall be satisfied. Oh no! I do not wish you to quarrel with her, or with anyone else in the whole world, on my account. Only do not let her deprive me of your friendship! I am so very much a stranger in England, and have so few friends, that the loss of one so very long known to me, would be a cruel blow!"

And here a delicately embroidered handkerchief was pressed to eyes, which Lord Goldstable believed, at the very bottom of his heart, to be the most beautiful in the world.

It was not very likely, therefore, that he should refuse to give the promise required of him; on the contrary, he gave it again and again, and moreover, he swore by Jove, and with sundry other mighty oaths, that Lady de Paddington would soon find that he was not quite "raw enough to swallow all the gammon she chose to poke down his throat."

And so they parted, but not before Mrs. Fitzjames had given her valued friend the number of her lodging in Jermyn Street.

CHAPTER XVII.

ON the morning following this important ball, both Lady Augusta Harrington and her new ally, Lady de Paddington, awoke with the consciousness of having a great deal of important business before them.

The latter felt that it would be absolutely necessary that before the day was over she should confer at length with the former; but she had another interview before her quite as important, and still more immediately necessary—namely, the one she intended to hold with her great-nephew at the breakfast-table.

Lady Augusta, too, felt that it would be absolutely necessary that she should see Lady de Paddington before the day was over; but she, too, felt also that she had business to do that was more pressing still—namely, the reporting progress to the Doctor, and then entering upon the very decisive conversation which it was her purpose to hold with Kate.

The Dowager Lady de Paddington inhabited a stately, but grim and melancholy-looking house in Charles Street, St. James's Square. The mansion was a world too wide for her Ladyship's dowager establishment and moderate jointure; but she inhabited it rent-free: for it was her son's property, and he was abroad.

It may easily be supposed that a very stingy and not very rich old dowager did not make so great an innovation on the habits of herself, and her small household, as must, of course, follow upon Lord Goldstable's visit to her, without the hope, or rather the certainty, of obtaining a satisfactory *quid pro quo* for it.

This branch of the subject was very far from being indifferent to her; but the notion which she had taken into her head, that this arrangement might, must, and certainly would give her great influence on the important point of disposing of his hand and coronet in marriage, was, in her estimation, of much greater importance still. But in order not to be defrauded of her just and reasonable expectations in both matters, it was, as she was already become fully aware, absolutely necessary that she should bestir herself.

She might, perhaps, after so late a party, have preferred the dowager indulgence of taking her breakfast in bed; but if she did that, Lord Goldstable might be up and out before she left her room; and thus, a very important move in the game she had to play would be lost. By ten o'clock, therefore, she was at the breakfast-table, with her great-nephew sitting opposite to her.

After the morning salutations had been exchanged, and the question of "Tea or coffee?" answered, she began her operations.

"Well, Edward," said she, smilingly, "I have to congratulate you, on having made a most favourable impression on the whole of the Harrington family. I told you, if you remember, that I was sure your shyness would not injure you in that quarter; and it is quite evident that I was right. You will, indeed, be a very fortunate, as well as a greatly envied man, when you have made that charming Katherine Harrington your wife."

"Good gracious, Lady de Paddington! What chance is there that I should ever make her my wife?" replied Lord Goldstable, very gaily. "Did I not tell you last night, that though she did not say *no*, when I asked her, she most certainly did not say *yes*?"

"What you told me last night, my dear Edward, was in every respect calculated to set my heart at rest upon this very important subject. No young lady in the world, brought up in the dignified and proper manner that Miss Harrington has been, could possibly, on first listening to such a proposition as you last night made her, do more than give token of acceptance by modest and maidenly silence. I know the world better than you can yet do, my dear Edward, and I do assure you that it was quite impossible her acceptance could be more properly expressed."

His young Lordship, on hearing this, looked greatly more surprised than delighted.

"Well now, Aunt de Paddington," he replied, with considerable augmentation of colour, "that certainly does seem very comical to me. At any rate, I must think a little more about it, if you please, before I make up my mind. I felt so frightened just at first, last night, that I hardly knew what I said."

"Unfortunately, Edward, it is not at all likely that other people will be equally forgetful. I happen to know that the sweet girl has already confessed to her mother, that she had never liked anyone so much before in all her life; and yet, because she did not show herself to be as indelicately bold as she is the reverse, you seem inclined to change your mind, and forsake her. What would be thought of any young lady who, when a gentleman proposed to her, should answer: 'Yes, if you please, Sir—much obliged to you?'"

Lord Goldstable laughed heartily at this, with considerably more gaiety of heart than his great-aunt quite approved upon the present occasion.

"My words were not spoken as a jest, Edward," she

resumed, "but to make you feel how greatly you wrong Miss Harrington, when you attribute to her the levity of having refused your offer of marriage, when it was so perfectly her intention to accept it."

"Well, aunt, we shall see bye and bye how it will all turn out," replied the youth, presenting his coffee-cup to be replenished, with so very gay and happy a countenance, that her Ladyship became very seriously alarmed at the little effect her words seemed to have upon him. She, therefore, after filling the said coffee-cup, returned to the charge.

"Believe me, Edward," said she, with great solemnity, "that you have totally deceived yourself, if you have really taken it into your head to believe that it was the intention of Miss Harrington to refuse you ; on the contrary, I can assure you, that if you should now unfortunately fancy that you no longer wished to marry her, you would find it very difficult to shake off the engagement. Her father, mother, uncle, aunt, and brother, all look upon your marriage with her as, perfectly settled ; and, you may depend upon it, they would call upon you to explain this very extraordinary change of purpose on your part, in a manner that you might find exceedingly disagreeable."

"Do you mean, aunt, that some of the ladies and gentlemen belonging to her would be wanting to fight me?" said he ; and the light-hearted lad, who was thinking what good fun it would be to tell his old friend Sophia the whole story, again laughed heartily.

This strong symptom of gay indifference, considerably alarmed the old lady ; for not only did it prove that his promising love-fit for Miss Harrington was already passed and over, but that he had in no degree the fear of her indignation, or that of her family before his eyes. Still, however, she cheered her spirits by remembering, that there was the unlimited fund of the poor boy's profound ignorance to draw upon, and she showed not the least sign of being disconcerted as she replied :—

"It is very evident, my dear Edward, that you do not understand these things. Not only would the young lady's family, and society in general, consider that you were bound in honour not to recede from the proposal which, according to your own statement, you made to her last night, but even by the law of the land you would be considered guilty of breach of promise of marriage ; the consequences of which would, I

fear, be considerably more serious than you are aware of.
Depend upon it, Edward, that after what passed last night,
you may have an action brought against you for breach of
promise of marriage."

"No! you don't mean that?" said he, with a look of dismay, which she did not at all like; for though it proved that
her statement was believed, it proved also that he had neither
intention or inclination to fulfil this imaginary engagement.

"Not mean it, Edward!" she repeated, with great
solemnity; "indeed, indeed, I do! Did you not offer to
marry her?"

"I said to her the nonsense that I told you of last night,"
replied the young man, in an accent which was by no means
either gay or good-humoured.

"And did she say, in reply, that she would not accept your
hand?" demanded Lady de Paddington.

"She did not say exactly that, but she walked off without
saying anything," he replied.

"Then it is my duty to tell you, Edward, that what has
passed is amply sufficient to make her family consider you as
her accepted lover and affianced husband. But why all this
idle discussion, Edward, in order to prove that you cannot,
even if you would, escape being the happiest and the most
envied man in London? Do not let us waste any more time
so foolishly. It is particularly foolish to do so just now,
because there is another subject upon which I wish to speak
to you very seriously. Tell me, how did that very objectionable, I must say plainly, that very improper person,
get introduced to you, with whom you went home last
night?"

"Do you mean Mrs. Fitzjames, aunt?" replied the young
man, looking steadily in her face.

"Yes, Edward, I certainly do!" she replied, with great
solemnity.

"Mrs. Fitzjames is an old friend of mine—Lady de
Paddington; and I never give up an old friend," returned
the youth, very evidently intending to be dogged and
resolute.

"What do you mean, my dear Edward? How can she be
an old friend, when she applied to me last night for an introduction to you?" replied the old lady, adding, in an under-
tone: "which I, very properly, refused."

"She did *that*, because it was such a monstrous long time

since she had seen me; and very natural, too!" he replied, snappishly.

"I should exceedingly like to know how she got to Dr. Harrington's," muttered his aunt, seemingly in soliloquy. "Really people ought to be more careful who they ask to their houses."

"I can ask her how she got there, if you like it," returned his Lordship, now evidently prepared for open rebellion, "for I am going to call on her directly after breakfast."

"I do most sincerely hope and trust that you will do no such thing!" exclaimed her venerable Ladyship, who was becoming every moment more seriously alarmed. "If you were a few years older, my dear Edward, it would be more easy to make you aware of that abominable woman's real position and character. And then I am quite sure you would no longer feel any wish to continue your acquaintance with her."

"I am quite old enough, Aunt Paddington, to know that she is the most beautiful, and in every way the most charming woman I ever saw. So don't let us talk any more about it, if you please, Lady de Paddington, because it would be of no use, for it is quite clear we should not agree; and it is as well to tell you at once, that say what you will about her, I am quite determined not to give up the acquaintance of so very charming a person."

This was the young gentleman's sturdy reply, and it was uttered in a tone that showed him to be very sincerely in earnest.

Lady de Paddington saw at once that any further opposition at this moment could only make matters worse; so, after the interval of a moment, she replied:—

"Well, Lord Goldstable, a wilful man will have his way, we all know that; and I am the less anxious on the subject, because I know that it is impossible that many weeks, or even many days, can pass away, without your finding out that I am right, and then you will wish that you had been guided by me in this matter. However, I am truly thankful to know that you are affianced as fast as the laws of the land, and the laws of honour, too, can make you, to so every way admirable a young lady as Miss Harrington. On that point, thank Heaven! you are safe. And this is a great blessing, Edward, for it is impossible to say to what lamentable absurdity that

9

infamous and designing woman might not lead you. I am thankful now that you lost no time about it, for this most desirable engagement renders you perfectly safe."

And with these words, her Ladyship left the breakfast-room to the young man and his reflections.

He lost not many minutes, however, in meditating on the lecture he had received. On the subject of his engagement with Miss Harrington, indeed, he felt considerably puzzled; but as yet he was not sufficiently in love with her brilliant rival, to make him feel any very great horror at the idea of being engaged to be married to Kate. He had not as yet quite forgotten the sweet voice, and the sweet smile, with which she had addressed him, and which had awakened in his breast the first gleam of hope that he might some day or other like dancing in a ball-room very much.

But still, though not very unhappy about this engagement, he was a good deal puzzled. He had read in the newspapers about ladies bringing actions against gentlemen for breach of promise of marriage, and he thought he should not like to have such a thing happen to him at all, and the idea of it gave him a decided qualm. But then, on the other hand, something which very strongly resembled instinct, created a feeling of doubt in his mind as to the probability of Miss Harrington's doing anything of the kind, even if she really were very much in love with him, on account of his not being so conceited, as all the other young gentlemen of her acquaintance were.

In short, he did not very well know what he thought, or what he ought to think, on the subject; and it was in this frame of mind that he set forth on his expedition to Jermyn Street, whither we should have much pleasure in accompanying him, were it not absolutely necessary that we should attend at a conference in Vale Street, between the Doctor and his lady, preparatory to the important conversation which Lady Augusta purposed holding with her daughter immediately afterwards.

CHAPTER XVIII.

THE total dislocation of all his usual habits caused by the ball and its attendant miseries, joined to the operation of three or four glasses of champagne and a supper of lobster salad, had, in some degree, exacerbated the usually placid temper of the excellent divine, and caused him to reply to his lady's amiable salutation, by growling forth his conviction, that if the necessities of a London season often entailed such persecutions and sufferings as those occasioned by the entertainment of last night, Oxford would be a far preferable residence during the spring.

"Perhaps it would, my dear," replied Lady Augusta, meekly, for she was an admirable proficient in the *suaviter in modo* system, "but at present," she continued, with a sort of tender smile, "I want to speak to you on much more important matters. You have not as yet, I presume, heard from Kate what passed between herself and Lord Goldstable, last night?"

"No, I have heard nothing, Lady Augusta. You mean that he asked her to dance, I suppose?" quoth the Doctor, surlily.

"No, Dr. Harrington," she replied, with solemnity, "that is not what I mean. I am come here to inform you that Lord Goldstable has asked her to marry him."

"Good Heavens, Lady Augusta! what is it you say? You cannot mean it seriously: it is impossible!"

Lady Augusta only smiled and nodded her head in reply.

"What!" resumed the electrified Doctor, "the first time of seeing her?" But after meditating, with a look of exceeding benignity, for a minute or two, he added, with a shrug: "Well! so much the better, my dear. So much the less trouble, you know, in balls and parties, and all follies of that sort. And it is all positively settled then? Pretty, dear Kate! She is a lucky girl, Lady Augusta, and I congratulate you also, my dear, with all my heart."

"The offer has certainly been made, Dr. Harrington,"

9—3

resumed the lady, gravely, "and I will not deny that this is a subject of congratulation; nevertheless, we must not be too hasty in supposing that the marriage is absolutely settled. You have yet to learn what your daughter's sentiments may be."

"Gracious Heaven, Lady Augusta! why do you talk such nonsense?" cried the dismayed Doctor, while a very apoplectic flush impurpled his face, "you do not mean to tell me that there is any chance of her refusing his offer? Refuse eighty thousand a-year, with large accumulations in the funds and ministerial interest! It is quite impossible! It is utterly incredible, Lady Augusta! What on earth could have put such an idea into your head?"

"The real fact is, Dr. Harrington, that Kate, on receiving the proposal, walked away without saying a single word, I believe. At least, that is all I can make out from Lady de Paddington's account; and her authority, of course, is her nephew."

"Mere shyness! Mere childish shyness! Where is Lord Goldstable? I wish to speak to him myself. The error must be remedied immediately. I am confident that his Lordship will not take offence at the silly shyness of so young a girl. On the contrary, I should think he would like her the better for it. She is a mere child, Lady Augusta, a mere child!"

And here the Doctor, whose emotion had caused him to rise from his chair, was compelled by difficulty of breathing to resume it.

Lady Augusta, who had not forgotten that he had threatened to make her pass the London seasons at Oxford, was malicious enough to remain silent.

"Am I to understand by your silence, Madam," thundered the Doctor, "that your Ladyship acquiesces in this preposterous absurdity, and very evident mistake?"

"Why what would you have me do, my dear Doctor?" returned his wife, with very provoking meekness and resignation.

"Do, Madam! I would have his Lordship made aware, that, whatever movement might have been dictated by the shy young girl's agitated feelings at the first hearing his flattering, but very sudden declaration, she never had any idea of indicating a refusal by it. And, moreover, he should be given very clearly to understand, that her family accept his very flattering offer with gratitude."

"That has been already done, Dr. Harrington, with the exception of the *gratitude*, which I did not think it necessary to mention," replied her Ladyship, with something like a noble sneer.

"Well, well, Lady Augusta, very well," growled the Doctor, partly in manifestation of standing corrected, and partly in token of being in some degree satisfied.

"Does nothing else occur to you, as proper to be done under the circumstances?" rejoined the lady, with something of reproof in her tone.

"Assuredly it would be desirable to ascertain that his Lordship's sentiments remain unchanged."

"And about Kate's sentiments, Dr. Harrington?" returned Lady Augusta, very quietly, but throwing a glance full of meaning at the Doctor's face.

That illuminated and illuminating beacon, instantly indicated an enormous change in the moral attitude of his spirit. In speaking of "his Lordship's sentiments," there was all the intense reverence of tone and manner, with which *such* members of the Church are apt to mention all members of the House of Lords. But now it was with a bent brow and a fiercely raised voice, that he said :—

"My daughter's sentiments, Lady Augusta, are, it is to be presumed, in no way discordant or contradictory to those of her parents; or the Christian teaching which it has pleased Providence to provide for her, has been of little avail. I beg, if you please, that I may not hear of any folly or wickedness on Kate's part, in this very important affair : none of the silly speeches of a child, under such circumstances, ought to be attended to, or repeated."

Lady Augusta perfectly well understood this to mean, that any trouble, or difficulty, or disagreeables of any kind, which the task of coercing Kate's inclinations might entail, should be borne wholly by her mother, and in no degree by her reverend father. But this she did not intend should be the case. She, therefore, replied :—

"Would it not be better, Dr. Harrington, that you should hear, from her own lips, what her feelings are upon this subject? I have not myself spoken to her at all, since Lady de Paddington announced to me that the offer had been actually made."

"No, Lady Augusta, I decidedly think that it would not be better," replied the Doctor, very authoritatively, "she might be too much overawed by the presence of her father, to

have the power of speaking her sentiments freely. It is a
mother's duty, Lady Augusta, to be the counsellor in matters
of this sort." And the last words were spoken with a very
striking degree of moral dignity.

"Well, Dr. Harrington, so be it, then," replied his
obedient wife, "I will see Kate, and hear from her what
she may wish to say upon the subject, and what explanation
she may choose to give of her having ran off in so extraordinary a manner. But I warn you beforehand, Mr.
Warden, that it will probably be necessary for you to exert a
father's authority in this matter. Lord Goldstable has been
assured, by his excellent aunt, that her conduct was entirely
the result of girlish folly and bashfulness, and that it meant
nothing in the least degree approaching a rejection. So far
all is well; but I will own to you that, from what I heard
last night, I think there may be reason to fear, that Kate has
much worse nonsense in her thoughts than any which can be
characterized as mere girlish shyness. If this should prove to
be the case, is it your pleasure that she should be permitted to
follow the dictates of her own whim, or of her own *heart*, as
she would be sure to call it?"

"Lady Augusta," replied the exemplary divine, in a tone
in which indignation and surprise seemed to contend for
mastery, "it is exceedingly vexatious, and I must add, that it
is not consistent with your usually admirable sense of
decorum, to put such a question to me, or even to conceive
such an hypothesis. Is it *my pleasure* that my daughter
should be permitted to throw herself away, without a saving
hand stretched out to save her? Gracious Heaven! what
a question! *No*, Lady Augusta, it is *not* my pleasure, and so
both you and the young lady shall find, if—if you should find
it necessary, as I trust you will not, ever to allude again to so
very disgraceful a supposition."

"That is quite sufficient, my dear Doctor," returned her
Ladyship, with two or three significant little nods; "now
that I am in possession of your views on the subject, I doubt
not that we shall be able to act together in a way that
may enable us to settle this very important business as it
ought to be settled. Kate is a very good girl, and though
she might, like other young things of her age, be guilty of
folly, I believe her to be incapable of disobeying her parents.
I will now go to her, and I will not trouble you again unless
it should be absolutely necessary."

And so saying, the excellent mother walked up stairs to her boudoir, and immediately dispatched a note to Kate, intimating that she was to come to her there.

The poor terrified girl was expecting the summons, and instantly obeyed it.

She found her lady-mother radiant in smiles, and with every outward appearance of being in the happiest state of spirits imaginable.

"Well, Kate," she began, "I know you have great news to tell me. But your news is no news, my dear, for I heard all about it last night from our excellent friend, Lady de Paddington. I have just been telling your father, my dear child, that all my brightest hopes have been more than realized, by Lord Goldstable having proposed to you last night. He is, I need hardly tell you, my dear Kate, as much delighted with the tidings as I am myself, and most sincerely do we both congratulate you. You have a high destiny before you, my dear child, and you will, I am certain, wear your honours gracefully and well. Both your good father and myself, are confident that you will be everything that you ought to be in the very exalted station which awaits you. But what is it, my love, that your too devoted lover has got into his head about your having left him, before he could express one-half of all the happiness he felt? Did you really forsake him so very cruelly, Kate? However, it was not very difficult to guess how the matter really stood, and that you made your escape, in order to prevent his raptures from attracting too much attention. And, upon my word, I cannot blame you for this—and so I told Lady de Paddington: and I flatter myself I have set everything right. You will soon give him a little more usage *du monde*, Kate. Meanwhile, I have guarded against all mistakes, and the happy young peer considers your engagement as indissoluble as it is delightful."

"My dear mother," murmured the agitated Kate, blushing and turning pale with rather alarming rapidity, "my dearest mother, I am deeply grieved that you should have been led into such an error! I neither am, nor ever can be, engaged to Lord Goldstable; and there was no mistake in his supposing that I left him so abruptly, in order that he might at once understand that it was not my intention to listen to him. Had the manner of his proposal been less abrupt, mamma, the manner of my rejection would have been so likewise."

These words were spoken with the utmost gentleness, but

with a good deal of firmness also, and there was a short pause after she had ceased speaking, as if the adversary was preparing for an effective attack.

"Let us understand one another clearly, Kate," said Lady Augusta, at length, speaking in a low quiet tone, that seemed to express both wisdom and gentleness, "let us understand one another. Young ladies often talk a great deal of very pretty bashful nonsense about taking time, and not knowing their own hearts, and so forth; and all this does very well, and may be excusable, perhaps, when they are discussing such a subject with their young friends and companions. But with a mother, Kate, the case is wholly different. In speaking to your mother, and especially on the present occasion, when speaking of a match which is decidedly the most brilliant that can by possibility be offered to you, such childish folly is sadly out of place, and we must have no more of it. This is a business of very serious importance, not only to yourself personally, but to every member of your family, and as such, if you please, we will now speak of it. Lord Goldstable offers you his hand in marriage—he offers you his coronet and eighty thousand a-year. Am I to understand, that you wish to reject this offer?"

"Yes, mamma," replied Kate, very firmly and distinctly, "yes, mamma, I do wish to reject it; and I do and must reject it."

"Very well, Kate. Now listen to me," returned Lady Augusta, with a cold, quiet firmness in her manner, that had more of stedfast determination than gentleness in it. "Such perversity, and such unnatural disobedience as you now exhibit, might justify my withdrawing my care and affection from you altogether, by permitting you to rush unchecked on your own destruction. But it is not my nature so to treat a child, to whom from its birth I have used nothing but affection and gentleness. No, Kate, I will not so abandon you to the fate you deserve. You *will* marry Lord Goldstable: it is best that I should at once tell you so. In talking of rejecting him, you speak with equal ignorance and presumption. You are a minor, an infant in the eye of the law, and, therefore, most fortunately! you have no power, either to reject or to accept any such proposal, without the consent of your parents. If your own good sense is not sufficient to convince you that your father and mother must be the best judges of what is best for you; if, unhappily, your sense of religious duty is not sufficient to induce you to yield obedience to your parents, it is fortunate that the law of the land provides a remedy Our glorious constitution has not left the well-being of families, and of society in general, to the judgment of wrong-headed children like yourself. Now retire to your room, think over what I have said, and remember that we consider you, and that you must immediately learn to consider yourself, as the affianced wife of Lord Goldstable."

Kate rose from her seat, and leaning on the table with both her hands—for she was trembling in every limb—she said, in a low voice, "It is absolutely necessary before I go, mamma, to confess to you another fact, which makes it impossible that any law should compel me to be Lord Goldstable's wife:—I am affianced to another, mamma; and I was so at the time Lord Goldstable proposed to me."

"What words are you saying?" cried Lady Augusta, vehemently. But immediately resuming her former cold and quiet tone, she said, with a bitter sneer, "And is it your purpose to favour me, by communicating the name of the gentleman?"

"It is Mr. Caldwell, mamma," faltered Kate, almost inaudibly.

"Infamous! It is too bad to be possible! It is absolutely infamous!" cried Lady Augusta, in a tone considerably more vehement than ladylike. "For you, poor silly child," she added, "I can almost pity you, for you must have been most basely beguiled into this disgraceful conduct. But in what words can I describe the conduct of the villain, who has thus beguiled you? *He* knew, if you did not, that a child of tender years can give no promise of marriage without the sanction of her parents. And well, too, did he know that your parents would never consent to such an alliance."

"Speak to my Uncle Walter on the subject, dear mamma," said Kate, gently. "I do not believe that he thinks Mr. Caldwell's alliance would be objectionable."

"Your Uncle Walter? It is he, is it? But no, I will not believe anything so very disgraceful! Yes, I will speak to your Uncle Walter on the subject. And now, once more, I tell you to retire to your room. But do not let your meditations there deceive you. You are *not* to become the wife of a man, who has got to work for the means of existence. But you *are* to become the wife of a highly descended young nobleman, with an income of eighty thousand a-year. A

cruel alternative! Is it not?" and as she spoke, the Lady
Augusta waved her daughter from her presence with a degree
of dignified scorn, which was intended to be overpowering.

But poor Kate saw it not. She did not wait to hear her
dismissal again repeated, but crept to her cell, and shut
herself up therein, with no very hopeful or happy feelings.

~~~~~~~~~~~~~~~~~~~

CHAPTER XIX.

WE left our poor Kate, at the conclusion of the last
chapter, frightened and alone, to do battle, as best she might,
with the first great misfortune of her life. As far, indeed,
as threatening her with the hand and coronet of Lord Goldstable was concerned, the whole thing appeared to her
deliberate judgment to be too monstrous, too absurd, to
justify any very serious alarm about the consequences.

Had there been no Mr. Caldwell in the case, she would
probably have very soon recovered her tranquillity; for with
all her young ignorance, she was fully aware that the laws of
the land would be quite as effectual to prevent a forced
marriage as an imprudent one; and though the idea of
opposing both father and mother with such resolute firmness,
as must oblige them to abandon their hopes of making her a
peeress was very painful, she still felt that she *could* do it—
that she *ought* to do it—and that it would be done.

But she was far less sanguine as to the result of her
attachment to Mr. Caldwell; for even if he would consent to
wait patiently till she was of age, she did not feel so sure of
being right in marrying in direct contradiction to the wishes
of her parents, as in refusing to marry in direct contradiction
to her own.

The more she thought about it, the more she doubted, and,
as a matter of course, the more miserable she became. Long
did she sit with her aching head resting on her hand, and her
unconscious eyes fixed upon one particular star in her carpet
without advancing a single inch one way or the other; for

neither did she teach herself to feel that it would be at all possible to live without Mr. Caldwell, nor yet that she should ever have sufficient strength of disobedience to marry him in opposition to the will of her father and mother.

In the very midst of this melancholy and well nigh hopeless musing, a bright thought suggested itself to her, which came like a gleam of sunshine to her heart : "She would go to her Uncle Walter, and tell him everything !"

The interval between the thought and the deed, was no longer than was needed to climb the attic stairs which led to her uncle's little sitting-room, and after one moment's pause at the door to collect her scattered thoughts, and recover her breath, she gave the usual little knock by which she was accustomed to give notice of her approach.

"Come in, Kate !—come in, my child ! I know your knock, Kate, and your step, too," were the words which greeted her from within.

She entered, and found the old man busily engaged with his eye at the magnifyer, and his hand at the object-glass of his microscope, while a large manuscript volume lay open on his desk, ready to receive his observations.

"You are just in time, Kate, to note down for me the particulars of my examination ; so take that pen, my dear, and scribble away from my dictation."

As he said this, the old gentleman's steady eye and hand were still employed with the business he was upon ; but the very first sound of Kate's voice, as she answered him, at once arrested his attention, and caused the microscope to be instantly laid aside. And then poor Kate began to feel timid and embarrassed. The conversation which she had determined to have with her uncle, seemed much more difficult to begin now, than it had done before she mounted the stairs ; and it was with rather a faltering voice and frightened manner that she began to explain her errand, while her uncle led her to a chair, and placed himself in another by its side, still retaining the hand he had taken in his own.

"I came, Uncle Walter," she began, "I came to you, because I thought that you would kindly listen to me while I told you something that has happened, which has pained and frightened me very much."

"Come, come, darling, look up at me ! It is nothing very bad, I daresay," said Walter, smiling cheerily, as he bent his head to look into her downcast eyes. " But whatever it be, Kate, scruple not to speak to me with entire confidence ; and whatever your trouble be, I daresay that, between us, we shall find out a remedy."

" Dear uncle ! I know I may count on your kindness ; but I know also that it is very possible you may think me too resolute, and too self-willed, if I tell you everything."

" It certainly may seem likely enough, Kate, to you, and to everybody, that no two creatures could be found more widely sundered than an old forest-bred barbarian, past seventy, and a blooming young London lady, in her teens. Yet, nevertheless, Kate, I have a pleasant sort of notion that there are some points of sympathy between us."

" It was something of the same sort of feeling, I believe, Uncle Walter, which prompted me to run up stairs to you in my trouble," said Kate ; " and this trouble is no light one, dear uncle ; and I don't see very clearly how you or anyone else can help me."

" Tell me what it is, my dear, at any rate. And if I cannot help, I may try at least to comfort you under it. Speak then, dear child, and tell me all about it."

" Yes, I will tell you everything," she replied.

" Last night at the party, Uncle Walter, there was a young nobleman called Lord Goldstable. In the very strangest and most sudden manner in the world, he told me that he wished me to marry him."

" Impertinent scoundrel !" muttered Walter Harrington. " Do you think he was tipsy, my dear Kate ?"

" Oh ! dear no, Uncle Walter, not at all. Strange as it seems, I believe he spoke quite seriously ; and his aunt, Lady de Paddington, and my mother, too, I believe, knew what he intended to do. At least, mamma has spoken of it to me, as if she did not think it strange at all—and she wants me very much to accept him."

" How long have you and your mother known him, Kate ?" inquired Walter.

" We never saw him before last night, Uncle Walter," she replied. " He is a perfect stranger to us all."

" And what answer did you make to this presumptuous gentleman, my dear," said her uncle.

" Indeed, Uncle Walter, I don't think I said anything ; but instead of speaking, I walked away from him directly."

" Well, Kate, and I really know not that you could have

done anything better. Perhaps it was the least objectionable way of giving him to understand, that you do not wish to have anything more to do with him. It certainly was rather a startling adventure, Kate; but I do not see why it should make you look so unhappy."

"I should not look unhappy, Uncle Walter, if that were all. But I have a great deal more to tell you! Mamma says that I *ought* to marry him, and that I *must* marry him," rejoined Kate, mournfully.

"And from what motive does she wish you to marry this perfect stranger, my dear child?" said the old man, looking at her anxiously. "Are his parents among your mother's particular friends?"

"No, Uncle Walter," replied Kate, blushing violently. "But mamma thinks it a great advantage to be so rich as he is."

Something like a groan burst from the broad chest of the old man, and for a moment, his singularly benign aspect was changed to a look of great anger, but this lasted but a moment only.

"One may live long, Kate, and study nature through a microscope daily," he added, with a smile, as he pointed to the instrument on the table, "and yet we must be contented to pass off into a higher sphere, without being able to comprehend one half of the phenomena, either physical or moral, which surround us in this. But do not let us quarrel with this glorious portion or creation of that account, my dear child. If you and I were more intimately acquainted with the philosophy of mind, and all the puzzling series of causes and effects by which all minds are actuated, I daresay we should be more disposed to laugh than to cry at what now appears so terrible to us."

Kate listened to him very meekly, but not much as if she was likely to find consolation from his speculations; and despite all her efforts to prevent it, her eyes were full of tears.

"My dearest," he exclaimed, "do not let me see you so overcome by discovering that all people do not feel and think alike;" and then added, laughing: "Fear not, sweet wench! They shall not touch thee, Kate! I'll buckler thee against a million!"

"Then to you, and your influence, I will trust myself, my dearest uncle," replied the comforted girl, with a smile that spoke hope and confidence. "And yet," she resumed, while a warm blush mantled her cheek, and a look of sorrow again took possession of her features, "and yet I have hardly a right to say that either—for—you do not know all—you do not know that my mother has said that Mr. Caldwell—you do not know that she has declared that I *shall* marry Lord Goldstable! And how can I deny that she is right, when she tells me that it is *my duty to obey her?*"

"Obey!" shouted the old man, in a tone which Kate feared would convey to the whole household the subject of their conversation. "Obey! You do not, I presume, mean me to understand that your parents, either one or the other, would lay on you as a parental command, the injunction to marry a man whom your own feelings did not prompt you to marry? You cannot mean to say, my dear, that they have the slightest wish of the sort? Kate Harrington, I neither do nor will believe anything so shocking and preposterous!"

Another knock was at this moment heard at the door of the attic study of Mr. Harrington; and this was immediately followed by the entrance of Henry.

"What! Kate here!" he said; "I fear, from the looks of you both, that I have interrupted a very interesting *tête-à-tête*. I came, uncle, to propose to you a visit to the Esquimaux family, exhibiting at the Egyptian Hall. But there must be something stranger than they are, here; for Kate looks melancholy, and Uncle Walter angry. And this must betoken something very extraordinary. I hope Kate has not been doing anything very naughty, has she, uncle?"

"What she has done, Henry, is this. She has suspected her father and mother of intending an infamous atrocity," replied Walter.

"What awfully strong expressions, uncle!" returned Henry, "we do not believe in infamous atrocities now-a-days, in polite society. What is your account of the matter, my little Kate?"

"I am shocked, Henry, to have appeared to Uncle Walter to make such an accusation; but, perhaps, Henry, I may seem less blameable to him, if you should agree with me in thinking that my fears are not quite unreasonable."

"In Heaven's name what is that you are looking and speaking so solemnly about? Tell me what has happened,

Kate?" said her brother, gravely, and with every appearance
of real interest.

"This it is, Henry," she replied. "Mamma has just told
me that she wishes me to marry a man whom I have never
seen but once, and whom I never want to see again; and I
was telling my uncle of my distress at finding myself obliged
to make such a marriage, or else of disobeying the command
of my parents. But Uncle Walter thinks it wicked and
absurd in me, to suppose that any such obedience could be
required of me."

"I am afraid," replied Henry, with a touch of his usual
sardonic gravity. "I am afraid that my uncle is not sufficiently acquainted with the habits and customs of the
gr-r-r-and monde, to judge very accurately what they may be
expected to do, or not to do. We are very highly civilized,
Sir, in this part of the world."

"Am I to understand, then, Henry, that you, too, are of
opinion that it is the wish of your father and mother to
coerce the affections of their daughter, in order to give them
an opportunity of selling her?"

"My dear uncle! what very shocking words you use,"
cried the young cynic. "I declare," he continued, affectedly
casting down his handsome eyes, "that it seems to me to be
positively indecent to speak of such things. There is no
refinement, no delicacy in your language, Uncle Walter, so
that it is almost unintelligible to polite organizations."

"Harry! Harry!" returned the old man, shaking his
head, "this is no subject for jesting. Tell me plainly, boy,
is it your opinion that my brother and his wife could be
guilty of this enormity?"

"If it be so, Uncle Harrington," replied the young man,
more gravely, "I do assure you that they would be doing
nothing out of the usual course." And then resuming his
former tone, which was but too natural to him, he added,
"It is, I assure you, usual, and, doubtless, altogether proper,
that parents should advise their children, especially their
daughters, on a subject of such great importance; having, *of course*, their happiness solely in view. And it is
generally found, I believe, that those daughters who decline
taking such advice, very frequently find the paternal roof
rather a disagreeable shelter afterwards. Indeed, in some
instances, I believe, their young lives become rather a burden
to them than otherwise."

"Alas! alas! If this be true, it is worse than madness!" groaned Walter. "First to cherish and foster every feeling of delicacy, and then ——"

"Nay, *halte là!*" interrupted Henry, "for now, at least, you are doing our social system injustice. My sister Kate's education may have been somewhat neglected in this respect, but as a general rule, I must protest that the young ladies intended for the market, are carefully and admirably trained to prepare them for it. I can assure you, uncle, that our practice in that respect puts the method of the Constantinople dealers to shame. There, the fair ones, we are told, do shrink painfully from the exhibition made of them, and evidently dislike the *trotting out.* But with the superior methods of training for our market, the pretty creatures are fully as anxious for the sale, as the seller."

"Oh, Henry!" broke in poor Kate, who for some minutes had been sitting with her face buried in her hands; "for my sake do not say such dreadful things! and in that jesting manner, too!"

"My dear Kate," returned her brother, "I really am very sorry for it, but, unfortunately, it is often the case in this world, that truths sound much more terrible than the falsehoods we are in the habit of uttering, instead of them. But that is not my fault."

"What then, Harry, is your conception of the duty of a young female in such a case as that of which you have been speaking?" demanded Walter.

"I have always been taught, uncle," replied the young man, demurely, and exactly with the air of a child saying its catechism, "I have always been taught that marriage is a holy state instituted for the better securing of a handsome establishment and equipage, and that it is the bounden duty of a well-principled young lady to obey her parents, and keep these objects steadily in view in forming a matrimonal connection."

"And what becomes of her affections?" demanded the old gentleman.

"My dear uncle," replied the nephew, "we find it much more consistent with propriety to ignore all such secondary considerations. Any examination and investigation of that part of the subject would lead at once to objectionable topics, and infallibly suggest what my father would call very dangerous doctrine."

Having quietly listened to this speech, Walter Harrington crossed the room to the chair in which Kate was sitting, at two strides, and laying his large hand upon her shoulder, he said :—

"Now then, my niece, hear my doctrine, dangerous it may be, to some of the framework of the blundering and corrupt social system under which you appear to be living, but it may prove, Kate, a very ark of safety to the pure of heart. I cannot be mistaken, my dear child, in thinking that I perceive in you such instincts as to what is right, as fairly to suggest the hope and expectation that you will not wilfully do what is wrong. And be assured of this, Kate—for it is as true as that the sun shines in the firmament—that no law, no sanction, no duty, authority, or any consideration whatever, can justify or excuse a woman for giving herself to any man whom she does not love. The doing so, my child, is an outrage against nature, and the God of nature. It is, perhaps, the worst and most mischievous departure from nature's law that can be committed by a young and hitherto innocent female, and it is accordingly followed by the heaviest retribution. An union formed wholly from the dictates of passion is a grievous error; it is a wrong and disloyalty done to the higher portion of our nature ; and it is an error which, I believe, rarely escapes its merited result of disappointment, sorrow, and suffering. But she who has accepted knowingly and consciously an unloved husband, has inflicted on her soul a stain from which recovery can hardly be hoped ; for she has crushed out and destroyed in her heart all nature's promptings, and this can never be done with impunity. But if, in addition to this ill-judged self-sacrifice, the motive be the very basest possible, if gold be the bait, if the transaction be one of absolute and literal sale, I should not choose to use in your hearing any language adequate to express the depth of its infamy, or the frightful nature of its results."

The old man paused, and looked at Kate, as if he feared that he were treating her too roughly ; and, in truth, the tears were trickling between her fingers as she hid her face behind the hand which rested on the table. Walter took a turn or two across the little room in silence, and then, turning to Henry, he said, in a lower tone :—

"Is it not inconceivable, Henry, that the same society which thinks no language strong enough to upbraid the degraded creature who sells herself, when the price paid is to

10

save her from starvation, should smile upon and approve the
very same act, when not the necessaries, but the luxuries of
life are the legalized payment? Not to mention that, in the
latter case, the additional impiety is incurred of invoking the
sanction of religion upon the sacrilegious atrocity?"

"The feelings of society on the subject *are* rather anomalous,
it must be owned," replied the more civilized nephew, with
his usual coldness, "but really I don't see how it would hold
together at all, if many people were to insist upon describing
its doings in such very plain language as yours. If you do
not conceal your opinions, my dear Sir, you will be voted the
most troublesome, improper, indecent, and, above all, the
most dangerous person going. Ay, Uncle Walter, dangerous
is the proper word; for who is there who has married a
daughter, or, especially, who is hoping to marry a daughter,
for title, estate, opera-box, or any other such natural consideration, but would listen to you with equal fear and
aversion?"

"Have I then said anything that is not true?" asked the
venerable philosopher, "nay, have I even said anything con-
trovertible, or even very profound? Is not what I have
uttered, truth of the very simplest kind?"

"No doubt, uncle, no doubt," replied Henry, smiling.
"But permit me to tell you," he added, "that you appear to
me to be altogether incapable of appreciating the enormous
value of cant. It is quite a vulgar error to suppose that the
principal or most valuable effect of cant is to deceive
others. This is very far from being the case. Those
born and bred under its influence, not only speak, but
think cant; and it is quite certain that they must do so in
order to speak it well. It is like a foreign language. To
speak French well, you must think in French. In fact, it is
this alone that makes our actual system of society possible.
All crooked paths are made to look straight, and the rough
places not only plain, but very particularly smooth. By the
aid of its omnipotent eloquence, all the infamies committed
among us are concealed even from the actors in them; and if
the said actors do not appear absolutely holy, they, at all
events, appear perfectly decent. Trust me, Uncle Walter,
you will be held as an unwelcome intruder into this part of
the terraqueous globe, if you persist in rudely tearing down
the delicate and graceful veil which cant throws over us.
Respectable people will, for the most part, be quite ready to

declare that your language is that of a very dangerous libertine."

Kate had risen from her chair during the latter part of this tirade of Henry's; and she now approached her uncle, and taking his extended hands in both hers, she said:

"You have certainly spoken much, dear uncle, that it was very terrible to hear; but you have, at least, made me feel that the course before me is a clear one. I think you have taught me to know real right from real wrong, more clearly than I ever did before. God bless you, dear uncle, and me, too; and give me strength to act as I ought, let me suffer what I may!"

"God bless you, my own Kate!" returned the old man, fervently. "I still hope that means may be found to make the right path no very painful one. We shall see."

And so saying, he led her to the door, her brother following her, for he wished to learn from herself the exact state of affairs as they now stood between her mother and herself; and he listened to her painful narrative with more sorrow than surprise.

CHAPTER XX.

WE must now follow Lord Goldstable in his visit to Jermyn Street. It would probably have been evident, to anyone more versed in such matters than was our noble young Scotchman, that his visit was expected by the charming widow. The indications of this consisted of small matters; but even those would have been perfectly intelligible to an experienced eye.

He was immediately shown into a very prettily arranged, but rather small back drawing-room, in which he found Mrs. Fitzjames reclining on a couch, in one of those elegant morning attires which such ladies know how to make more bewitching than the most splendid dress that ever graced a ball-room; and Lord Goldstable accordingly thought her ten

times more lovely than he had thought her the night
before.

In truth, it would be difficult for anyone to imagine a
greater perfection of coquetry, or a prettier material on
which to exhibit it, than was now displayed by Mrs.
Fitzjames.

She had many a year yet to pass, ere she reached that fatal
period when candle-light is more favourable to the complexion, and to the eyes also, than the more truth-telling
light of day. Nor was it even necessary, as yet, for her to
make any skilful arrangement, in order to produce a *demi-
jour* when she expected a morning visitor.

The white muslin lace-bedecked *peignoir*, from beneath
which her exquisitely-shaped feet *chaussés* to perfection, and
crossed over each other at the ankles, peeped forth, could not,
it is true, display as fully as the dress of the preceding
evening the ivory shoulders, or the beautifully-formed bust;
but it admitted of being so arranged as to afford a partial view.
And if the single white camelia of the night before, had
shown to greater advantage the glossy tresses of her dark-
brown hair, there was something, perhaps, more bewitching
still in the pretty composition of ribbon and lace which called
itself a cap.

In one fair hand she held a book, with a slender finger
between the pages of the "Loves of the Angels." It might,
or it might not, attract the attention, and assist the talk of
the expected visitor. But at any rate it had not been selected
at random. Yet it would be doing wrong to the widow's dis-
criminating good sense, did I omit to observe that had her
expected visitor been a dozen years older, the subject of her
studies would have been differently selected.

"Ah, Lord Goldstable!" she exclaimed, with very con-
spicuous delight, the moment he appeared. "This is, indeed,
kind of you." And then holding out her hand to him,
without changing her recumbent position, she added, "I
am really ashamed to receive you thus. I know that I ought
to have been dressed long ago. But the ball of last night,
delightful as it was, fatigued me. I do not stand the late
hours of London very well. I always look like a witch the
next morning. Do you like these very late hours?"

"I don't think I should, much in a general way; but I was
pleased enough to be up last night, after I met you," replied
his gallant lordship.

"Ah! that strange—that most unexpected meeting!" she exclaimed, clasping her white hands, and raising her beautiful eyes heavenward. "I can give you no idea of the pleasure it gave me! And then it was so delightful a change for me! Such a relief from the misery of finding myself among utter strangers! I should as soon have thought of meeting the sun in that strange ball-room as an old friend. I do assure you, Lord Goldstable, that I don't think I should forget that meeting if I were to live a hundred years!"

"Don't call me Lord Goldstable! Call me Edward, as you did last night; I like it so much better," said the youth, charmed out of all his shyness, and with a secret conviction at his heart, that he had never seen a really beautiful woman till he met his charming old friend Mrs. Fitzjames.

"Do you really choose that I should always call you Edward?" said she, with a smile of quite indescribable sweetness. "At any rate, it must only be when we are alone, you know, or else people who did not know anything about the intimacy of our fathers would think it very odd. And, moreover, if I call you Edward, I shall insist upon it that you should call me Sophia. Will you?"

"Won't I!" returned the delighted boy. "But you must tell me, you dear, beautiful Sophia, who are the people I must contrive to get acquainted with, in order that I may be sure of meeting you, for it's as plain as daylight to me, that I shall not like any of the London parties unless I meet you."

"Young flatterer," she exclaimed, fixing on him a look half tender, half reproachful, "why should you try to make me believe that? I have told you that I scarcely know anyone in London; so if you really wish to see me, you must come and look for me in my little quiet lodging here. And I will not be so—so untrue, Edward, as to pretend that I shall not be glad to see you."

"And don't you think I shall like to come, Sophia?" he replied. And it is astonishing how rapidly the young man improved under the influence of the beautiful Sophia's affectionate encouragement. He not only enjoyed the full power of speech, but used it, too, without any great symptoms of shyness, and became as conversable as it was in his nature to be. And then there followed a well-managed scene of flirtation, such as may, perhaps, have occurred before, and may possibly occur again, between a married woman (one who has been married is meant, of course) and a lad. It was love-making made easy, and Lord Goldstable had never been in such high spirits before. And then she warbled a few notes, and reminded him that she had promised to sing " Old Robin Grey" for his amusement, to which he replied, very eagerly : " Oh, yes, do ! sing it to me this very moment, my dear, dear Sophia !"

And then she led him into the other drawing-room, and having placed him very comfortably and very advantageously as to both seeing and hearing, she kept her promise, and sang to him the touching ballad of " Auld Robin Grey," from the first word to the last. Her voice was rich and sweet, and though she had little science to help her, she gave the song in a style which might have enchanted more learned ears than those which now listened to her. Moreover, the performance altogether was of that peculiarly captivating kind, which can be only achieved by ladies of her peculiar style of attraction.

After " Robin Grey" had been thus performed, there was a pause of perfect silence, which lasted for a minute or two; it seemed, indeed, as if Mrs. Fitzjames shed tears, for a fragrant handkerchief was pressed for a short interval to her eyes, and her bosom heaved with a plaintive sigh. Then, suffering her handkerchief to fall (not unheeded) on the floor, she again ran her slender fingers over the keys of the instrument, and warbled mournfully, but very sweetly :—

" Oh ! think not my spirits are always as light."

And with every word she said, and every look she looked, and every note she sung, and movement she made, the doomed Lord Goldstable fell more and more desperately in love with her; a process of which she was as perfectly cognizant, as the angler is of the nibbling which his destined prey is making at the bait.

While this fascination lasted, Lord Goldstable forgot all about the social and legal penalties with which Lady de Paddington had threatened him, in case he should break his troth to Miss Harrington. But when, at length, at about five o'clock in the afternoon, he left Jermyn Street (not, how-ever, till he had given a gently asked-for promise to return ere long', his mind reverted with very considerable uneasiness to the dreadfully precipitate proposal which he had been rash enough to make to Miss Harrington, and then followed a terribly distinct recollection of all his aunt had said upon the necessity of abiding by it.

What shape his profoundly ignorant fears assigned to the vague denunciation of Lady de Paddington he would himself have been puzzled to say; but the general notion of being exposed and exhibited to all the great unknown world, as having done something shocking and disgraceful, nay, contrary to its usages and fashions, was really dreadful to him; and, despite his violent love-fit, he felt that, come what would, he could not bear it. It might be supposed, certainly, that this all-pervading fear of the world's ban would scarcely have penetrated to the remote seclusion in which this poor blundering boy had been educated; but this is decidedly one of the cases in which, as the learned express it, the *omne ignotum pro magnifico* principle is particularly active.

The power of this often heard of monster, "The World," seems greater, from its indefinite vagueness, to those whose lot has been cast at a distance from its great tribunals; just as the judges of the land are objects of far greater awe to the village rustic, than to the familiar *habitué* of the Old Bailey. And thus during poor Lord Goldstable's thoughtful walk homewards, the consequences of being held up to the world's scorn, presented themselves to his imagination in shapes and forms equally undefined and tremendous.

Meanwhile, the long morning which his Lordship had passed with the too-enchanting Mrs. Fitzjames, had not been permitted to wear away in idleness by Lady Augusta Harrington. She was determined that her ill-judging daughter's destiny should not be marred for want of hearing good, and what must be considered as highly authoritative advice, and, therefore, about two o'clock, having previously dispatched a note to her friend, informing her how matters stood, she sent to inform her daughter that the carriage would be at the door in half an hour, and that she must get ready to accompany her in her drive.

To refuse her attendance was quite out of the question, and the suffering Kate meekly prepared herself for the penance she was thus commanded to undergo. But although she had certainly anticipated anything than a pleasant drive, she was, nevertheless, rather startled and rather shocked at hearing her mother give the order:—"To Lady de Paddington's."

As the carriage drove off, Lady Augusta turned to her daughter, and said:—

"Lady de Paddington has shown herself so true and valuable a friend in this business, that I think it due to her to let her know exactly how matters stand."

And these exceedingly disagreeable words, were the only ones spoken till the mother and daughter had arrived at the dowager's door.

Lady Augusta sent up her card, which instantly reversed the standing order against morning visitors in her favour, and they were forthwith shown into the brown-holland clothed drawing-room.

"My dear Lady Augusta!" exclaimed the old lady, meeting her at the door with an extended hand, "you have arrived just in time to prevent my setting off to call on you. My dear Miss Harrington," she continued, turning with a most affectionate smile towards Kate, who was looking as pale as death, "I congratulate you most sincerely on having secured the prize, for which all the beauty and fashion of London are on the look-out. And I assure you, that I have no little pleasure in thinking that this happy event is, in some degree, owing to me."

"Kate will feel all the gratitude she owes you, my dear Lady, when she has sufficiently recovered her startled senses to become aware of what she has to thank you for," replied Lady Augusta, taking upon herself to answer for her mute daughter. "But at present," she added, "I am sorry to say, that she appears utterly incapable of forming a rational judgment on this or any other subject! It is not without a profound feeling of shame and humiliation, Lady de Paddington, that I confess to you how little all the care and affection I have bestowed on this ungrateful child, has availed to teach her the duty she owes to her parents. You will hardly believe it possible, my good friend, that a girl so carefully brought up as she has been, should declare that it is her wish to reject Lord Goldstable, and that she positively refuses to obey her father's will and mine, on this most important affair of her life!"

"It is, indeed, almost impossible for me to believe that any young lady, not absolutely depraved in heart and mind, should so conduct herself," returned Lady de Paddington, solemnly. "Nay, I will not believe it!" she added, fixing her, large, dull eyes with a sort of indignant glare on Kate. "I will not believe that she will persevere in such desperate wickedness, and such desperate folly. Let her be very careful that her sudden change of sentiments respecting my nephew, does not get abroad before she has well weighed the consequences! I can tell you, Miss Harrington, that the news of your engagement to Lord Goldstable, is at this very moment the talk of the whole town. Enchanted and happy beyond concealment, poor fellow, from the very moment that you listened to his proposal without rejecting it, he not only considered himself as engaged to you, but he poured forth his joy to me, and I considered myself as fully at liberty to spread the news. If you have any regard for the honour of your family, and, let me honestly add, for your own reputation, Miss Harrington, you will reflect deeply before you give the world cause to believe that this greatly envied engagement is broken off. You can scarcely be ignorant, I think, of what must be the inevitable consequences of your breaking off this marriage? Trust me, young lady, that if you persist in your present line of conduct, it will be sedulously spread throughout the whole of what deserves the name of society, that Lord Goldstable has renounced the alliance '*for reasons;*' and we all know, I presume, the sort of construction, or, I might say, the natural interpretation that will be put upon this ——"

Lady de Paddington suddenly paused, clasped her hands together with an appearance of very strong emotion, and fixed her eyes upon the carpet as if she dared not look up to witness the misery of her unhappy friend, Lady Augusta.

Poor Kate, however, turned an appealing glance upon her mother; but she found no comfort in the stern look she encountered in return.

"You begin, perhaps, to perceive, Kate, some of the ill-consequences likely to arise from disregarding the wishes and the counsels of your parents," said Lady Augusta, in answer to her mute appeal. "Believe me," she added, with great solemnity, "if you were now permitted to follow your own childish whims and wishes in this most momentous affair, new mischief and new danger would arise around you with every passing hour, and would dog your steps through life. It will be a cruel return to your father and myself for all our affection, if an only daughter should make her first step in life, by blasting her own reputation! Yet this must be the inevitable result, if we were to be weak enough to permit your acting according to your own caprice in this business."

Kate did not attempt to reply to this; it was not that, after

what she had listened to from her Uncle Walter, she entertained for a moment any doubt as to what it was her first
duty to do, but the difficulty which now beset her was a new
one. The idea of so conducting herself, as to blast her own
fair fame upon her first entrance into the world, was certainly
very terrible to her; and the only touch of comfort that
cheered her heart at that very miserable moment, arose from
the thought that she would consult Uncle Walter, and be
guided entirely by his advice. But though she knew it not,
this blessing was not at present within such reach as it had
been; and she had a good deal of suffering still to endure
before it would be so again.

Lady Augusta's next move was to utter a very dismal
groan, and then to turn towards her friend and say: " But
you know not yet, dearest Lady de Paddington, the whole
extent of this misguided child's perversity. I blush, I blush
with shame, as I resolve to tell it you; but I owe it to
your well-tried friendship to have no concealments from you.
You will pity me when I tell you, that at the same interview
in which my daughter thought proper to inform me that she
had changed her mind with respect to the proposal of Lord
Goldstable, and that she now wished to refuse it, she also
thought proper to announce to me that she had formed another
attachment, and was engaged to Mr. Caldwell, the briefless
young barrister! "

" My dear Lady Augusta! I do indeed most sincerely pity
you," replied her sympathizing friend, throwing up her eyes
and hands in a style expressive of the deepest sorrow and
dismay. " I certainly should have hoped that your daughter
would have been incapable of forming a low attachment
under any circumstances."

Kate had determined within herself to bear the martyrdom
her two executioners were inflicting on her, in silence. But
this attack upon her lover was more than she could bear, and
she replied, haughtily enough: " Mr. Caldwell, Lady de
Paddington, is not only a gentleman by birth, but also by
education, conduct and manners."

" And fortune, of course?" sneered the exceedingly vulgar
peeress in reply; but to this Kate did not vouchsafe any
answer.

" Under these most unforeseen and unfortunate circumstances, there is but one course for me to pursue," resumed
the indignant Lady Augusta. " Of course, she will not be

permitted to see the insolent and presumptuous person, who has thus basely abused the hospitality that has been shown him. Neither shall I permit her, for the present, to hold any communication with that very wrong-headed and eccentric individual, Dr. Harrington's brother; for I am by no means quite sure of his principles on such a subject as this."

Kate started, and changed colour very visibly on hearing this, of which her observant mamma was quite aware; but taking no notice of it, she continued the confidential statement of her intentions to her friend, by saying, with a good deal of decision and firmness of manner: "My purpose is to remove her at once from all possibility of mischief from this source. I shall keep this rebellious young lady strictly under my own eye, till I have arranged something with her father about sending her immediately into the country, and I flatter myself that I shall be able to achieve this, so that she shall leave town to-morrow. Meanwhile, dear Lady de Paddington, I trust implicitly to your good sense and discretion. Lord Goldstable need not, I think, know anything of her capricious change of mind for the present."

"Never fear me, my good friend," responded her worthy ally. "I think you have acted with admirable judgment, in deciding as you have done for the present. And for the future, let us hope that we shall not always find this young lady so obstinate. I trust that the time will come, when she will be aware of her own great good fortune in having had such a mother!"

And thus they parted; Lady Augusta ordering Kate to go down before her, as if she feared to lose sight of her for a moment.

CHAPTER XXI.

Not a word was uttered between the mother and daughter, during what probably appeared to both of them their long drive home. On reaching the mansion, Lady Augusta descended first; but waited in the hall till the young lady stood beside her. "Come with me into my own room, if you please," said Lady Augusta as she mounted the stairs; and Kate, without saying anything in reply, meekly followed her. Lady Augusta rang the bell as soon she entered the room, and inquired if Dr. Harrington was in his study.

"Yes, my Lady," was the prompt reply; "my master is just come home, and I saw him go in there."

Lady Augusta then submitted herself to the hands of her maid, for the removal of bonnet and cloak and so forth, and then dismissed her.

"You can take off your bonnet, I presume?" said the sarcastic lady. "It is probable, that you do not wish to accustom yourself to such personal attendance for the future. And now I shall leave you, in order to settle with your father in what manner it will be best for your unfortunate family to act, so as most effectually to protect themselves and you from the obloquy and disgrace which your present line of conduct must infallibly bring upon them, if not guarded against by all that watchful affection and enlightened good sense can achieve to prevent it."

"Do not fear me, mamma," said poor Kate; "I will do nothing, I will never do anything clandestinely. All I ask for, is the permission to refuse to make a man I can never love, my husband. Grant me this privilege, my dearest mother, and I will trust to time for bringing you to treat me in all respects, not as a naughty child, but as a reasonable woman."

"A reasonable woman!" repeated the angry mother, in an accent of bitter contempt. "With your Uncle Walter, like a wild man of the woods, to counsel you, on one side, and an audacious lover running away from his dirty desk and his musty books to invite you to elopement, on the other, you are vastly likely to become a reasonable woman! But, thank

God, you are *not* a woman yet; and thanks to the wisdom of our glorious country, you have very nearly three long years to wait before you will have any more right or power to act for yourself, than if you were an infant in the eyes of your lover as well as in the eye of the law. There lies our safety, Kate, and not in your wisdom, you poor, silly, vain, deluded, creature! Your Mr. Caldwell is, of course, quite ignorant of the unimportant fact of your having a handsome independent fortune! He never heard of such a thing, I daresay. Nothing but the most generous and disinterested attachment could have induced him to neglect all the amusing duties of his profession, in order to make love to you! But you do no good by weeping, Kate. I am now going to leave you to your own thoughts, and it will be more profitable for you to sit down quietly, and paint to yourself the difference between taking your place in society as a peeress, with eighty thousand a-year, or living gloomily under the displeasure of your parents, waiting year after year, till the time shall come when you will be old enough to throw youself into the arms of a needy lover, without their having any longer the power to prevent it!"

Having thus finished her harangue, Lady Augusta left the room, and poor Kate had the mortification of hearing her lock the door after she had closed it upon her. This was a species of degradation for which she was by no means prepared, and its effect upon her was extremely painful in every way. The most substantial evil it brought with it at the present moment, was the depriving her of her Uncle Walter's advice. It was her wish to put him more fully in her confidence than she had yet done, on the subject of her positive engagement to Mr. Caldwell. She knew, indeed, that Uncle Walter was already aware that she was attached to him; but she had not, as yet, fully communicated the particulars of the decisive little interview which had taken place in the conservatory, and one result of her meditations during her silent drive home, had been the determination of mounting to the philosopher's garret immediately after her arrival there, and telling him everything. But now she became very painfully aware, poor girl, that all comfort and all benefit of any kind from that source was effectually withdrawn from her.

Meanwhile Lady Augusta descended the stairs, with the key of her room in her pocket; and feeling as great certainty, as that of Kate herself, that save for this precaution, her

daughter would have passed the interval with the elder
brother, which she was about to pass with the younger, she
went to the door of her learned husband's study, and entered
it "with the boldness of a wife," without even the ceremony
of knocking, which was exacted from all others.

A restorative luncheon, accompanied by two bumper glasses
of his favourite sherry, had done much towards restoring the
Doctor to his usual comfortable condition of mind and body,
and it was with his usual polite placidity of manner that he
welcomed her Ladyship, exclaiming as she closed the door
behind her :

"Well, my dear! I trust you have come to tell me that
your admirable management has overcome all difficulties,
and that our dear Kate has been brought to a sense of her
duty ? "

"Not exactly that yet, Dr. Harrington. I am sorry
enough to tell you, that there are difficulties in our way of
which we never dreamed," replied the lady ; "but we must
be firm, my dear Doctor, and then I trust everything will go
well at last. You may guess the state of my feelings at the
present moment, when I tell you that the principal result of
my interviews with Kate, was the receiving a confession from
her that she was engaged, as she chose to call it, to be married
to—who do you think, Dr. Harrington ? " The Doctor shook
his head impatiently. "Nay, you need not be in a hurry !
You will hear it quite soon enough, Mr. Warden ; and it may
be that you will then become aware of a fact I have more
than once remarked upon—namely, that you are not quite as
cautious as you ought to be in giving invitations to young
men. Your daughter tells me, Dr. Harrington, that she cannot possibly marry my Lord Goldstable, because she has
engaged herself to marry Mr. Caldwell."

"Infamous blackguard !" thundered the enraged dignitary,
utterly losing all power of self-control, and becoming almost
purple with passion. "Infamous scoundrel! who would
abuse a father's confiding hospitality by robbing him clandestinely of his child ! And as for her !—if she marries him—"
and his uplifted arm seemed to give warning that some
terrible denunciation was coming; but his less vehement,
though fully as resolute, companion, stopped him.

"Do not expend your just and most perfectly righteous
anger in words that may shock my ears, and your own too,
perhaps, and which can do no good you know, when they are

spoken. Moreover, I flatter myself that I have already arranged matters in such a way, as to render any such odious sin and folly as you fear, absolutely impossible. I have already told Kate that no such marriage ever shall, or ever can take place under any circumstances whatever! And now, if you will give me leave, I will just tell you the measures I have already taken, and those which I mean to take, if your ideas on the subject accord with mine. Fortunately, a word which dropped from Kate opened my eyes in time to another difficulty with which we have to contend. She hinted pretty plainly, that your brother would not be likely to agree with us in his opinion of Mr. Caldwell as a husband for our daughter! and I immediately decided upon removing her from the danger of such very mischievous influence. In fact, I felt it to be extremely important that Kate should not be allowed to communicate at all with her Uncle Walter for the present."

"I agree with you perfectly, my dear, as to your theory on the subject; but I hardly know how you can put it in practice. How are you to prevent her communicating with him?" said the Doctor.

"A moment's patience, Doctor, and I will show you," she replied. "A good manager," she added, "will always find ways and means. But it was, as I am sure you must perceive, quite impossible for me just now to stand on any ceremony with our rebellious young lady, and accordingly, I hold her at this moment safely locked up in my own room."

"Admirable! my dear, you have done exactly the right thing!" replied the admiring husband. "It is precisely the right mode of teaching her what she is to expect if she attempts to persevere in her abominable folly. And as to poor Walter, I must confess that I perfectly agree with you, in thinking that he is not to be trusted on such a subject. His notions upon nearly every subject seem to be adapted to savage rather than to civilized life, and and we must guard against his influence accordingly."

"Decidedly so," replied Lady Augusta, firmly. "But it will not do to keep her locked up, you know, and I therefore purpose, with your good leave, to send her into the country to-morrow morning, accompanied by my sister, Lady Juliana; and there she must remain till we have effectually made this audacious young lawyer understand that he will no longer be received here as a guest."

"Quite right! Perfectly well arranged, my love," returned the Doctor; "but Lady Juliana must, you know, be cautioned."

"She shall be made acquainted with the facts, Dr. Harrington, and then there will be no cause whatever to fear her being indiscreet. I know she has many odd religious notions; but upon a subject of this kind, I will do her the justice to say that all her feelings will be quite in accordance with your own."

"Very well, then," returned the reasonable divine, perfectly satisfied. "So let it be, my dear; and you may follow them into the country very shortly yourself. We shall all be going down to Glastonbury, you know, very soon, and I see no objection whatever, to her preceding us."

"I think I can suggest a better plan than that, Dr. Harrington," returned his wife, "and one which, if I mistake not, will remove her much more effectually from *all* pernicious influences. For you know it would immediately be conjectured that as we are going to Glastonbury, Kate would be going there too; and she might very easily be pursued thither. What I would propose is, that she and my sister, should set off to-morrow morning by the early train, which starts even before your brother can have left his room, and pay James a visit at Stanton. He too, as we both know, has some odd and objectional doctrines in his head, but he also may be trusted to feel exactly as he ought to do upon the matter in question. Both in his case and in that of my sister, I am quite sure that their abstract religious notions would have no effect whatever in influencing their opinions on any point, where the advantage of the family was concerned. I know too, that their religious opinions differ, nay, that they are in precise opposition to each other; but on this subject they are sure, nevertheless, to think alike, and both together, they are likely to urge the thing upon her mind with a degree of perseverance which, in the complete absence of all adverse influence, must, in the long run, tell upon her mind."

"Most true, my dear wife,," said her approving spouse, with a look of the most benignant admiration. "I consider the idea as perfectly providential, and much may be expected from it. I will write to James instantly to announce his visitors. He will get the letter at his breakfast-table to-morrow, and his aunt and sister will be with him in good time for dinner. And now you had better go and prepare Lady Juliana for her journey."

* * * * *

And thus it was authoritatively decided that Kate should be delivered over to the keeping of her Puseyite brother, and her Evangelical aunt, in order to be ground down to the necessary point of obedient submission by their joint efforts.

CHAPTER XXII.

It was not many minutes after Lady Augusta had left the Doctor's study, when another knock was heard at its door; but on this occasion it was only the footman, who announced that Mr. Caldwell was in the hall, and begged to know if he might be admitted then.

But scarcely was the man allowed to make this announcement, before the sonorous voice of the dignified divine was heard in reply, and in a tone that might have been perfectly audible to anyone at double the distance from which it was heard by the visitor in question.

"No, Sir!" it thundered, "I am not at home to Mr. Caldwell, and I beg you to observe that I never shall be at home to that individual upon any future occasion whatever!"

The first movement of surprise and indignation which this unexpected reception occasioned to the object of it, prompted him to turn on his heel, and quit the house. But before the servant had fully delivered this message, modified in its transmission into a civil "Not at home, Sir!" the anxious lover had changed his mind, and now demanded if he could see Mr. Walter Harrington.

"I will see, Sir," said the man, and as soon as it was well possible, he returned from the lofty quarters occupied by the old gentleman, with the assurance that Mr. Harrington would be very glad to see him.

In climbing to the abode of the attic philosopher, Mr. Caldwell had to pass before the door of Kate's cell, which

11

had been rendered henceforth and for ever a sacred spot
to him.   But he little guessed that the jewel had been already
removed from its casket; and that his own destiny, and
that of her who was at least equally dear to him, would have
undergone most important changes before this same precious
jewel was restored.

On reaching Mr. Harrington's room, he found him, as
usual, exceedingly busy; but nevertheless he was received
with hearty cordiality.

"I think I know all about it already, my dear fellow,"
exclaimed Walter, affectionately shaking the hand that was
extended to him; "and though we may meet with some little
difficulties and impediments in the way, I think we shall
manage to make things all right at last."

"You know then, my dear Sir, that I was bold enough
last night to confess to Miss Harrington that I love her?
That I dared to offer her my hand? And that she did not
refuse it?"

"Yes, Caldwell, I think I may say that I know all that
already; though I cannot exactly say that these important
facts were very distinctly communicated to me either. But
knowing that my niece had just reached her room when I
was approaching my own—for, in fact, I had followed her up
the stairs—I went in to wish her good-night; and then I
perceived such symptoms of agitation, as she threw her arms
around my neck and kissed me, that I did not leave her till
she had given me some little insight into what had been going
on.   Her account was not, I confess, a very clear one; but I
think I made out that she had promised to marry you, and
that there were difficulties in the way of her keeping her
promise.   This morning I have heard still more about these
said difficulties; but I flatter myself, Caldwell, that we shall
be able to master them."

"You know then, my kind friend, that my suit is not
acceptable to Miss Harrington's family?" said the young
man, looking considerably paler than usual.

"I know," replied the old gentleman, "that some part of
her family, at least, are very likely to oppose it; for I know
also that within a very few minutes after my charming niece
had accepted you, she assumed to herself the privilege of
refusing a peer of the realm, with a yearly revenue of eighty
thousand pounds. And I will not disguise from you, my dear
Caldwell, that I suspect there may be some among us who

will be of opinion that the second proposal ought to super-
sede the first."

"And Miss Harrington herself?" faltered the lover.

"I do not suspect that she will bo one of them," replied
Walter. "Do you?"

"No, Mr. Harrington, I do not," said Caldwell, firmly.
"I know her too well to believe it possible, after what passed
between us last night. Yet how can I dare to hope, that so
young and so gentle a creature will be able eventually to
resist the authority, which will be exerted to prevent her fulfilling the hope she has given me?"

"It would be difficult for me, Caldwell, to give you any
very satisfactory answer; but I see no reason why I should
conceal from you that I have great confidence in Kate. It is
quite true, as you say, that she is both young and gentle,
nevertheless, I am greatly inclined to think that she is not
weak. We shall see, Caldwell! we shall see! I will venture
explicitly, however, to assure you of two important facts,"
continued Walter, seizing the agitated young man's hand,
with a friendly grasp. "The first is, that my niece Kate will
never marry any man whom she does not thoroughly love and
esteem; and the second is, that she neither loves nor esteems
poor silly Lord Goldstable in any degree whatever."

"I need not tell you that your words fall like balm upon a
very troubled spirit. But though I have implicit faith in
what you say—for I should wrong her vilely could I doubt it
—yet I think that you will be equally ready to agree with
me, when I state my conviction that Miss Harrington will
never marry against the consent of her parents. And how
can I ever hope to obtain this, when such a proposal as that
of Lord Goldstable is put in competition with mine?"

"Patience and courage, my young friend, may accomplish
much," returned Walter, calmly. "Do not let us despair."

"Dr. Harrington refuses to see me now, in the very
harshest manner possible," said Mr. Caldwell, colouring as he
remembered the offensive words to which he had been an
involuntary listener; "and knowing this, I feel that it would
not be right to attempt seeing his daughter in his house. For
the present, therefore, dear Mr. Harrington, I must leave my
cause in your hands. Make her understand—make Miss
Harrington understand—how deeply it pains me to know
myself the cause of discord between her and her parents.
But I should like her to know, too, that I feel perfectly sure

11—2

that her manner of treating Lord Goldstable's proposal would have been the same under any circumstances."

"And she shall know it, my dear Caldwell," replied the old man, kindly. "But poor Kate is over-tired by the ball, they tell me, and is gone to bed. Do you go to Miss Wigginsville's to-morrow? If so, I will see you there, and shall then be able to report progress, and tell you a little how matters stand."

"Assuredly I will go there," replied Caldwell; "and now I will leave you, carrying with me a heavy load of anxiety, yet not altogether unmixed with hope, for which I ought most devoutly to bless you. Let Miss Harrington understand the motives which prevent me from attempting to see her. I think she will appreciate them."

"Be very sure of it," replied Walter, cordially. "If everyone concerned in this business behaved as well as you do, Caldwell, our difficulties would be very soon over. Farewell for the present. We shall not, as I flatter myself, be always obliged to part by necessity as we do now."

CHAPTER XXIII.

GREAT was the surprise of Walter Harrington, on being told at the breakfast-table, on the following morning, that Kate had left town at a very early hour of the morning, accompanied by her aunt, the Lady Juliana. He had spent the whole of the preceding evening at the meeting of one of the numerous scientific societies to which he belonged, and had this day left the house at his usual early hour, in order to take his accustomed morning walk.

Under all the circumstances of the case, it might have occurred to anyone, save Walter Harrington, that matters had been exactly so contrived, on purpose to prevent any interview from taking place between him and his niece, previous to her departure. But he was much too inartificial himself to suspect any manœuvring in others, and no suspicion of the kind ever entered his head.

"Gone!" he exclaimed, in reply to Lady Augusta's announcement of the fact, "surely she might have waited until I returned from my walk. She knows the time of my coming back so well, because we have always had a little talk together before going down to breakfast. Surely she might have waited to shake hands, and say good-bye."

"My sister, Lady Juliana, is very particular about always setting off early, and, of course, her niece would on no account propose to change the hour of her departure for her own especial gratification. You must, therefore, acquit Kate of any intentional neglect, Mr. Harrington."

"There is no danger that I should accuse her of it," replied the old man, with something more nearly approaching a frown on his brow than was often seen there. "If Kate ever does wrong in any way, it will be at the suggestion of others, and not at her own. I have studied the character of your daughter carefully, brother Henry," he continued, turning to the Doctor. "Her heart is pure, and her head is clear. If she goes wrong in any way, it will be because the way was not chosen by herself. Above all, brother Henry, be careful to let her marry the husband of her choice."

Between rage and muffin, Dr. Harrington really appeared at that moment to be in considerable danger of apoplexy, and as from sheer necessity he was obliged to remain speechless, the task of replying to Walter's very startling speech devolved on Lady Augusta.

"I must confess, Mr. Harrington," she said, with a degree of dignity that perhaps had some little mixture of austerity with it, "I must confess that your words surprise me. Perhaps if I said shock me, I should be guilty of no great exaggeration. It is very possible, Sir, that your long absence from Europe may have disqualified you from justly estimating and appreciating your brother's position in the world. Were this otherwise, were you more capable of comprehending his high responsibilities, and, through him, of the responsibilities of his family also, you would never have permitted yourself to utter such a phrase as that which we have just heard from you. To my ears it sounds, I must confess, very like the sort of language and the species of advice which might be heard and listened to with impunity by the lower orders of the people. But when referring to the daughter of Dr.

Harrington, and the grand-daughter of the Earl, my noble father, it has the effect of very painful coarseness. Surely, Sir," she continued, "you cannot think it right that parents should abdicate all control over a child, in a point the most important to her happiness, and that, too, in which she is least able to judge for herself?"

"Assuredly not, my dear sister-in-law," replied the old man, "but I will tell you in a few words what I do think. It is undoubtedly true that marriage is to a woman the most important step in life, the most awfully fraught with lasting weal or woe. True it is likewise, that at the age when most women marry, they are not likely to be very competent judges of the real, genuine characters of those who propose to them, and most assuredly I do think that parents are right in using their influence, and even their authority, over a child of tender years to prevent her marriage with a man whom they consider as unworthy, and that any girl who should act in defiance of such authority, exercised on such grounds, would be most culpably imprudent."

"I was sure," interrupted the Doctor, "that my brother would, upon reflection, be found the advocate of that due submission and obedience to constituted authority which is the only bond and bulwark of society, which religion and polity alike require, and which divine and human laws equally enforce."

The Doctor was always apt to become wordy and pompous, when he got upon the favourite topic of the submission due from all classes and individuals in Church and State, who occupied positions beneath his own; but Walter listened very meekly, till his brother had reached a full stop, and then he said :—

"I never was so unfortunate as to meet with anyone who was not an advocate for *due* submission ;"—there was something rather sly in the look and emphasis with which he said it, but the significance of this was not caught by either of his auditors—"however," he continued, "I must confess, brother, that a parent who undertakes the duty of thus constraining the wishes of a daughter, assumes a very grave responsibility, and one that should be exercised with very strict self-scrutiny, as to his own motives in the matter, in order that he may be quite sure that no consideration of what would be most personally agreeable to himself has any influence on his judgment. Under no conceivable circumstances, can it be otherwise than a most wicked and horrible tyranny to urge a daughter to a marriage that was repugnant to her, nor do I hesitate to say that a young girl would act well and wisely if, in defiance of the wishes of her parents, she married according to her inclinations, if the doing so were a means of escaping from a marriage in which her affections had no share."

"I am truly pained, brother Walter, truly pained, to hear you give utterance to theories so utterly subversive of—of—of everything. Very dangerous doctrines, brother Walter! Highly dangerous doctrines indeed!" groaned forth the scandalized and alarmed Doctor.

"I own that I am not sorry," said Lady Augusta, with a frown of considerable severity, "that the absence of Kate should have saved her from hearing such dreadful sentiments advocated. Utopian fancies will not do in civilized life, Mr. Harrington, and I must beg you to understand, that I do not wish to have my daughter's mind disturbed by them."

"I am afraid, my good lady," replied Walter, "that you will find everything in the way of mischief, which my notions on this subject can do my niece, has been done already. She knows what I think about marriages made from other motives than those of affection. But will you tell me the grounds on which you consider a marriage between Kate Harrington and my young friend, Frank Caldwell, to be a *mésalliance*, as you call it?"

"In the first place, my dear Walter," replied the Doctor, with infinite dignity of manner and of accent, "in the first place, I might tell you that the name we bear would disgrace no family in the realm by intermarrying with it. A Harrington came over with William from Normandy; a Harrington is recorded as having fought bravely at Cressy, and at Agincourt. I own I am surprised that even you should have so thoroughly adopted the feelings of savage life, as to be insensible to the pride of bearing such a name."

"Nay, Harry!" replied the elder brother, laughing, "I am not even yet philosopher enough to merit all your reprobation. I will be honest enough to confess, that I have still enough of old world notions hanging about me, to make me value an old and honourable name. But surely you have struck a very random stroke, brother, as regards the matter in hand. Caldwell's father was an estated gentleman, and his grandfather to boot; ay, and rotulorum too, and a gentleman born, brother parson, who wrote himself armigero in any

bill, warrant, quittance, or obligation. Now Lord Goldstable's grandsire, brother Harry, was a Bristol merchant,
who made the principal part of his huge fortune by trading
in slaves."

"Lord Goldstable, Walter, is a peer of the realm," returned the Doctor, reddening, or rather purpling. "The
Sovereign," he added, solemnly, "is the fountain of honour,
and the inherent power and faculty of ennobling resides in
the monarch, as a portion of the divine right which not even
the levelling heresies and aberrations of our sadly degenerate
days have yet dreamed of disputing."

"It is at all events a power which monarchs of late years,
or their heaven-born ministers for them, have laboured hard
to discredit," replied the old man. "It would be a curious
examination," he continued, "to go carefully through the
true Englishman's *vade mecum*, the peerage, and to observe
how large a portion of the names inscribed there have obtained
this glory under circumstances involving anything but honour
to the individuals so distinguished."

"What *can* you mean, brother Walter?" returned the
Doctor, with every appearance of the most genuine astonish-
men. "I protest to you that I have not the remotest idea of
what you mean to insinuate by so startling and monstrous a
suggestion."

"My meaning, Harry, is simply that no honour can be
reflected on any man by the circumstance of his having been
the unscrupulous agent of a bad king's worst designs—or a
judge corrupt enough to make justice bend to the wishes of
the court—or lastly, though not leastly, from his having
backed a ministry through thick and thin by unconstitutional
influence in the House of Commons."

"My dear brother! my dear brother!" exclaimed the
scandalized dignitary, looking positively terrified. "It is
painful—it is very painful to me to hear you use such
language. Trust me," he added, with a warning gesture of
his upraised hand, "trust me, you are treading upon very
dangerous ground, very fearfully dangerous ground, indeed!
For myself, inividually, I am happy to say that the convictions of my reason, and the duties of the important position
which I hold, alike forbid my attempting to follow you in so
frightful a course of speculation. But it must be evident to
the most obtuse comprehension, that such ideas lead to conclusions subversive of all that mankind holds dearest and

holiest. The most sacred bonds of society, and the most holy
sanctions of religion are alike—"

"Hold! enough, my dear Harry!" cried Walter, laughing.
"To save you the trouble of a provocation, I will plead guilty
at once—guilty of holding many opinions which, if followed
out to their consequences, might lead to the overthrow of
many things that some men deem dear, and well-nigh holy.
But, as you well observe, the duties of your position forbid
you to speculate on such themes, for which reason we will
pursue them no farther. To return, however, to the point
from which we started, let me ask you seriously, my dear
brother, whether you are really bent on marrying your
daughter, who loves another man, to this silly young nobleman, because he has an income of eighty thousand a-year?
If this be so, I can only say that I am truly sorry you should
have set your heart upon such a scheme, for I am quite sure
you will never succeed in it."

"And may I ask, Mr. Walter Harrington, on what grounds
you predict what, under the circumstances of the case, we
must consider as a heavy misfortune to your brother's family?
Kate has hitherto on all occasions shown herself well disposed
to be a good and obedient daughter, and I see no reason to
doubt her being so still."

"She is a dear, good child!" returned the old man, not
without emotion, "and I feel strongly persuaded that in this
important matter she will act in strict accordance with what
she believes to be her duty. But are you quite sure that you
know how his youthful Lordship will act after Kate's abrupt
departure, upon receiving his proposal?"

"On that point," replied Lady Augusta, with a slight toss
of her head, "no one can reasonably entertain the slightest
doubt. It is impossible that any young man could manifest a
more decided determination to win a lady's hand than Lord
Goldstable has done, and there was nothing in her manner of
receiving his proposal that ought to discourage him. The
timidity of a very young girl on such an occasion, is not very
likely to discourage any man."

"Well! we shall see," replied Walter. "Let the affair
end as it may, we shall none of us have anything to regret, if
the result be the lasting happiness of our dear Kate. But
tell me," he added, "where is she gone,? and when do you
expect her back?"

Lady Augusta directed a meaning look towards the Doctor,

who had been discussing his breakfast in silence during the above conversation between his wife and brother, well pleased to be relieved from the necessity of taking any part in it; and having by this expressive glance put him upon his guard, she replied to the old gentleman's queries by saying vaguely:—

"Both will depend very much upon circumstances, Mr. Harrington. My sister has *carte blanche*. We wish Kate to change the air, and to be amused, for she certainly, like most other young ladies, has been made rather nervous by this sudden proposal. They may go to Glastonbury, or they may go to Stanton, and probably they will visit both."

"So then the Lady Juliana has what we may call a roving commission," replied the old man. "Well! I suppose you will hear from them shortly, and I trust it will not be very long before we have our pretty Kate amongst us again. Meanwhile I, for one, shall miss her sadly at the party to-night. I fully intended to make her my cicerone."

"What party is there to-night?" inquired her Ladyship; "I am aware of none."

"What, sister! have you forgotten the conversazione at Casa Wigginsville, as Caldwell calls it? Of course you mean to go?"

But in reply to this, Lady Augusta protested that the Wigginsville parties were the greatest bores known in the civilized world, and that positively her health and spirits were not equal to the exertion of appearing at them. So it was settled that the Doctor and his brother should go as representatives of the whole Harrington family; and the trio at the breakfast-table broke up, the Doctor to doze over the newspaper in his study, his brother to be present at the reception of some new inmates at the Zoological Garden, and the Lady Augusta to pay an early visit to her friend Lady de Paddington in quest of the latest news of Lord Goldstable's movements.

CHAPTER XXIV.

But neither the splendid specimens at the Zoological Gardens, nor yet the brilliant mixture of science, art, wit, and wisdom assembled at Casa Wigginsville in the evening, could do much towards making the warm-hearted philosopher happy in spirit or easy in mind. Kate and her difficulties haunted him, not only through the day, but through many hours of the night also. The more he meditated on the subject, the more fully he became convinced that all his own feelings and opinions were too completely in opposition to those of his brother and his brother's wife, to leave any rational hope of his being able to influence them in the manner he wished; and the final result of all his meditations on the subject, was resolving to seek an interview with Lord Goldstable himself.

The old man felt that the interview would be a strange one, and that the awkwardness of it would certainly be considerably increased by his not being the nearest of kin to the fair lady, to whom the noble and wealthy suitor had so impetuously declared himself; but, nevertheless, he resolved upon the measure, as offering a better chance of a successful issue than any attempt he could make to convince his reverend brother and noble sister-in-law, that they would be committing a grievous sin by compelling their gentle daughter, either to marry the man she did not love, or give up the man she did.

Having made up his mind to this spirited, but somewhat eccentric, course of proceeding, he felt more tranquil, and slept as soundly through the night as he was wont to do of old, after a long day of forest wandering. The next morning, the old gentleman rose at his usual early hour as ardent and eager to act upon the resolution he had taken on the preceding night, as if he had been a score or two years younger; so he directed his early walk to the lodgings of the young peer, never doubting that he would find him up, but rather fearful that he might not be early enough to catch him before he went out.

It was a pretty considerably long time, however, before his

stoutly reiterated summons at the young man's door succeeded in obtaining any notice whatever; but at length a yawning, half-dressed servant presented himself, who after staring at him for a minute or two, such as he might have done if holding enforced communication with a madman, condescended at length to inform him that Lord Goldstable breakfasted at twelve, and never left his bed-room earlier.

"Poor lad! poor lad!" ejaculated Walter. "Well, my man, give him this card, with my compliments, when he does get up, and tell him I will call upon him again between twelve and one."

And so saying, the old forester turned to pursue his morning walk, meditating as he went, on the strange perversion of all natural feeling which must take place, before a young fellow of Lord Goldstable's age could be induced to lie in bed till mid-day. And having heaved a kindly sigh for all such unfortunates, he turned his thoughts towards the delicate interview which he was seeking, and upon the probable results of it.

But if the old gentleman looked forward with some degree of anxiety to this interview with the sluggish stripling, that of Lord Goldstable upon the same subject was infinitely greater. When, on ringing his bell at about eleven o'clock, his valet handed to him Walter's card, and very distinctly delivered to him the message by which it had been accompanied, his young Lordship betrayed a degree of surprise, or, more correctly speaking, of alarm, which very considerably astonished and puzzled that usually very intelligent functionary. It could scarcely enter into this reasoning individual's philosophy, to believe it possible that a nobleman of his master's rank and revenue could greatly care for the coming or going of any mortal man: but that he should be thus strongly moved by a card and a message from such a decidedly unfashionable old codger as the early afoot old forester, had something in it absolutely revolting to all his principles and all his feelings; and when his master asked him with nervous eagerness why he had not waked him immediately, the indignant valet replied, with evident disgust: "Indeed, my Lord, I should never have thought of such a thing. It would be a deal more fitting, that such a queer-looking old fellow as that should wait your Lordship's time, let him be whom he may, than that your Lordship should put yourself out of the way, and be waked up from your sleep to see him."

" Well, Simpson, perhaps that's right too, seeing that I am come of age, and altogether my own master. But I say, Simpson, he didn't seem angry, did he ? "

" Angry, my Lord ? " replied the man, who almost began to suspect that the golden calf he so devoutly worshipped must have some portion of lead in it. " I am sure, my Lord, I don't know whether he was angry or not. It never came into my head to think that your Lordship could care whether such a sort of person as that was angry with your Lordship or not."

" I did not mean angry with me, Simpson, of course," returned the corrected nobleman, turning very red. " But he might be angry with you, you know, for not waking me ; that is what I meant."

" I know my duty, my Lord, too well to care whether such a person was angry or not ; and, asking your Lordship's pardon, I should say that them has most cause to be angry who is waked out of their natural sleep, and called from their beds at such undecent hours. Why this old person, my Lord, was here, knocking at the door, between six and seven o'clock this morning," added the civilized London domestic, shivering from head to foot, as he rehearsed this thoroughly savage trait of the wild man of the woods. " I can't say that it ever came into my head, that he ought to be angry with anybody."

Lord Goldstable did not dispute the point, but proceeded with the business of dressing himself, in silent, but by no means pleasant, meditation, on the coming interview ; while his valet performed his share of the business in equal silence, his temper being rather disagreeably affected by the suggestion that such an individual as the grey-haired old forester should have presumed to feel angry with him.

While stating the mutual anxiety of Lord Goldstable and Walter Harrington, as they were each occupied in meditating on the difficulties of their approaching interview, it is impossible not to recal the pithy lines :—

> " ' A different cause,' said Parson Sly,
> ' A like effect may give ;
> Poor Lubin weeps lest he should die,
> His wife, lest he should live.' "

For their anxieties arose from views as diametrically opposed as those described by the poet. The reader can be at no loss

to understand the honest and kindly hopes and fears which
harassed the mind of Walter; but it may be necessary to
recall the conversation which passed between the young peer
and his intriguing old aunt, when his Lordship first showed
symptoms of uncertainty respecting the durability of the
tender passion he had professed for Miss Harrington. The
present emotion of the noble, but inconstant youth, arose from
the remembrance of Lady de Paddington's very solemn
assurance, that if he now declined to marry the beautiful
young lady whose hand he had so abruptly solicited, he would
lay himself open to all the pains and penalties consequent
upon an action of breach of promise of marriage.

The idea of being immediately obliged to marry the shy
young lady, who had been so over-modest as to run away from
him, instead of going on making lots of love to the beautiful
widow of Jermyn Street, was exceedingly disagreeable to
him : nothing, perhaps, could appear more so, except the
being held up as an object of universal scorn and ridicule, by
means of being brought into a public court for breach of promise of marriage.

This last was indeed a misery which he felt himself totally
unable to face.

He longed for the world's admiration, and dreaded its
censure with a vehemence in exact proportion to his ignorance
of the real value of either ; and he was now working himself
into a perfect agony of nervous agitation, from believing that
the Mr. Harrington, whose card lay before him, and whom
he well remembered to have seen pointed out with his stately
stature and flowing grey hair, as the uncle of the young lady
to whom he had offered his hand, was now come to demand
explicitly whether he were ready to proceed with the matri-
monial contract he had so impetuously begun.

At length, within a very few minutes after twelve o'clock,
came the expected knock at the house door, and the heart of
Lord Goldstable immediately leaped into his throat.

" There he is ! " exclaimed the terrified youth, jumping up;
" and I have not even thought yet of one word that I am to
say to him ! What a confounded fool I was to want to be
made into a man of fashion, by marrying the very first handsome girl I looked at ! How I wish that my confounded
Aunt de Paddington had been at the bottom of the sea, before
I ever set eyes on her ! "

And as this vain wish exhaled itself, accompanied by a

suppressed groan, the door of the room opened, and Walter Harrington entered. There was no door at which the very unfortunately silly young peer could creep out, and therefore he faced him, with his light hair, through which he had just passed his agitated hand, standing very much on end, and his fair young face as red as scarlet.

But Lord Goldstable's first terrified glance at him was the last that expressed any mixture of pain. Walter entered, holding out his hand to Lord Goldstable, with such a frank and cheering smile upon his kind face, and with such a cordial friendliness of manner, that one moment was quite sufficient to tranquillize all the terrors of the poor peer, and almost to set him at his ease.

"I have taken the liberty of calling on you, Lord Goldstable," said he, coming to the point at once, "in order to have a little conversation with you respecting my niece. I rather suspect that you have fallen into a mistake about her."

"It is very true, Mr. Harrington; I will not deny it for a minute," said his Lordship, eagerly interrupting him. "But when my aunt, Lady de Paddington, told me it was a mistake, I never stuck to it—I didn't, indeed; upon my word and honour I didn't. I gave in directly, and took her running away in that shy manner, just in the sense that my aunt told me I ought to take it. And I am not so ignorant, Mr. Harrington as not to know that your niece has all the right on her side; and of course, Sir, I am sure—that is, I mean to say, as a man of honour and a gentleman, I am ready to do all that is expected of me."

"Expected of you, my Lord! What can you be talking of? What do you suppose is expected of you? And by whom, my Lord?" repeated Walter Harrington, thoroughly puzzled.

"Why by all London, to be sure!" replied his young Lordship, rather querulously. "By all the fellows at the clubs, and the opera, and the House of Lords, and all the rest of 'em. I know all about it, Sir, though I am so newly come to London. I have not forgotten one single word of it. But you may depend upon it, Mr. Harrington, there shan't be wanting any action of *crim. con.*, or anything of that sort to bring me up to the scratch. There shan't, indeed, my dear Sir. You seem inclined to behave very politely to me, and you shall see I deserve it."

Walter Harington opened his eyes to their utmost extent, and for a moment stood silently staring at him in utter amazement. "Action of *crim. con.*, Lord Goldstable!" he exclaimed at last. "What on earth have you got into your head? Are you dreaming?"

"No, no, that's not the name of it either," rejoined the puzzled boy, looking vexed, irritated, and bashful, all in one. "But whatever the name of the law is, don't think of it, pray, Sir; for I do assure you, upon my word and honour, that I fully intend to do everything that is right, and everything that the world expects of me."

Walter now looked at him with vastly more of kindness than of anger, for he really began to doubt whether his simple-looking companion had not, somehow or other, been frightened out of the little wit that niggard nature had bestowed upon him. "My dear young friend," said Mr. Harrington, kindly, "depend upon it, we shall be more likely to understand each other, and more able to put everything in its true light so as to conduce to the happiness of all the parties concerned, if you will consider the subject of this projected marriage between you and my niece, solely with reference to the two parties principally concerned, leaving altogether out of the question, the expectations of the world in general respecting it."

"I am sure it is very kind of you to say so, Mr. Harrington," returned the young man, struck by the unmistakably friendly and sincere manner of the old gentleman. "You really are very kind, indeed, and I am sure I would wish nothing better than just to listen to you and follow your advice. But you know, Sir, that even putting the case that I no longer wanted to marry Miss Harrington, I could not draw back. I am not going to deny that I certainly did make her an offer; and we all know that as a gentleman and a man of honour, I ought to stick to it."

"Allow me to assure you, my dear Sir," returned the kind, but now proud-looking, old man, "allow me to assure you that you have, somehow or other, been led to conceive extremely mistaken notions on this subject. Why do you suppose that, if you were no longer desirous of marrying Miss Harrington, you would still be under the necessity of doing so?"

"Why, because all the fellows would point at me if I did not; and, besides that, of course her father would take the law of me."

"You have been misinformed on this subject, Lord Gold-stable," replied Walter, gently but very gravely. "I will assume the responsibility of assuring you myself, my Lord, that you may wholly dismiss from your mind this very mis-taken and preposterous apprehension. I will undertake to say, that my brother, Dr Harrington, will not seek to com-pel you in any way to marry his daughter," said Walter, with a voice and manner which made it clear, even to the dull comprehension of his startled young companion, that he had, in some way or other, said something that he ought not to have said. So he hastened, poor youth, to reply, in a greatly humbled tone :—

"Well, then, I am sure it is very handsome of him, very; and it's very handsome and very friendly of you to come and tell me so. And I won't deny that it's more than I had any right to expect. And what's more, Mr. Harrington, it is a great deal more than some of his friends expect of him."

"And may I ask you, Lord Goldstable," returned Walter, whose momentary feeling of indignation was now giving way to a strong desire to laugh, "may I ask which of Dr. Harrington's friends expected that he would have recourse to legal coercion, in order to compel you to become his son-in-law ?"

"Why my aunt, Lady de Paddington, did," replied the young man, eagerly. "She said that for a certainty, and without any shadow of doubt about the matter, Dr. Harring-ton, the father of the beautiful Miss Harrington, would bring an action of *crim. con.* against me, or whatever the newspapers call it. I am not quite certain about the name of the law, but she said most positively that nothing in the whole world could, or would prevent it, if I gave the very least sign of going back from the offer of marriage."

"Well then, my dear young man, I must take the liberty of telling you, that your aunt has endeavoured to influence your conduct by uttering a most unjustifiable fiction. What her motive may have been, I will not pretend to guess; but believe me, when I assure you, that she has thought proper, for some reason or other, most deliberately to hoax you. I flatter myself that you will at once, and for ever, dismiss this most absurd statement from your mind."

"Well, Mr. Harrington, I shall always be ready to say as long as I live, that you have behaved in the very kindest way to me that any gentleman ever did, and I don't think

12

I ever felt so grateful to anybody in the whole course of my life."

"Then, if I understand you rightly," returned Walter, with a merry smile, "you are not now quite so desperately in love with my little niece as you thought you were, eh?"

"Oh! I never said that, Sir!" exclaimed the young man hastily, and colouring to the very tips of his ears. "I am sure I ——"

"Nay, nay," returned Walter, now laughing outright, "there is no harm done. You are not the first man who said over-night, what he was sorry to remember the next morning. But in this case, at least, there will be no broken hearts to lament over."

"Indeed, Sir, you are very kind. I really do take it very kind of you," said the greatly relieved, but still embarrassed peer; "and if—that is, suppose I was to—I mean, if Miss Harrington did not—in real truth, then, if I was to cry off, should not I behave very bad? What would Dr. Harrington say? and what would Miss Harrington say? and what would the world say?"

"My good young friend," returned Walter, more gravely, "once more let me advise you to leave the world altogether out of the question. Depend upon it, the world would not be greatly troubled about the matter. If half-a-dozen gossips talk about your falling in love with my niece to-morrow, they will be talking about something else the day after. And as to what my niece will say, I think you must forgive me if I remind you, that you have pretty good grounds upon which to form your opinion of what she will say, if you will only remember what she *did* at the time you honoured her with your proposal."

"What did she do?" demanded his Lordship, eagerly.

"I think your Lordship must remember," replied Walter, with a quiet smile, "that her only reply was running away from you."

"She *did* mean to refuse me, then," replied the delighted lover, with sudden exultation, "and I was right then, though nobody would believe me. Aunt de Paddington positively declared that her running away without saying anything, wasthe most perfect acceptance possible, and that all well-behaved young ladies always did so when they were too modest to say *yes* outright. And you really do think that she meant to refuse me out and out, in real earnest?"

"However incredible it may appear to your Lordship's friends," returned the old man, smiling, "I am afraid that such was unquestionably the fact."

"It was my old aunt, Lady de Paddington, who contradicted me flat when I said so," returned the young man, "she did, upon my word and honour; and she said that girls always did so. Well, then, Mr. Harrington, I *was* refused and we're all right, and there is no more to be said about the matter."

And as his young Lordship uttered these satisfactory words, he rubbed his hands with an air of the most joyous exultation.

"I am afraid," returned the old man, with a degree of severity that was very unusual to him, "I am afraid that I now see through the whole affair. There has been a regular conspiracy to bring about a marriage between you and my niece. But thanks to a little plain-dealing and honest sincerity, both on her side, and on yours, the plot has failed. But, my dear Lord, the matter is not, as you fancy, wholly at an end. Some little care must be taken to prevent the young lady from suffering any further inconvenience, and I trust to your good-nature for acting in such a manner as to spare her, as much as possible, from suffering from the consequences of your thoughtless offer."

"Well, now, Mr. Harrington, I thought it all seemed quite clear," returned the young man, in a tone that indicated great disappointment. "However, I am sure I am ready, as I ought to be, to do anything and everything that you tell me it is proper I should do."

"I am confident, Lord Goldstable," replied Walter, "that when I have explained to you a little how the matter stands, you will readily do what is necessary to spare Miss Harrington from any further annoyance. You asked me just now what my brother, Dr. Harrington, would say if all question of this marriage were given up; and I will frankly tell you that he will be very much disappointed. Your rank and fortune, my young friend, are such as would make most parents, who are ambitious of a great match for a daughter, exceedingly unwilling to give up the chance of catching you. Now the fact is, that though my good little niece did most unequivocally and decidedly wish to make you understand that she declined the

12—2

flattering offer of your hand, her parents still persist in
declaring that, on account of her youth, this refusal is not to
be considered by you as final. She has already suffered very
severely from this very foolish and very unfortunate affair,
having fallen under the heavy displeasure of both her parents
for wishing to decline your proposal. It has, believe me, my
Lord, been a source of great distress to her; and if she is
compelled, by your Lordship's persisting in your suit, to continue to refuse your hand, in defiance of the wishes of her
father and her mother, it will infallibly be the cause of much
increased suffering to her. I do not and cannot doubt, that
you must be sorry for having brought this unhappiness
upon her by the idle offer which you so thoughtlessly made;
and the only mode by which you can protect her from the
effect of her father's anger, and indeed from all further
molestation of any kind, is by frankly stating to Dr. Harrington, that upon further consideration you desired to withdraw the offer you had made, having reason to believe that its
acceptance would not be likely to contribute to the happiness
of either party."

"Oh, goodness gracious, Mr. Harrington!" ejaculated the
terrified young nobleman; "how in the world shall I ever be
able to say that? Only just think of the rage of my old
aunt! Oh dear! oh dear! what will Lady de Paddington
say? And what will Dr. Harrington say? And how do
you think I shall ever be able to answer them? Is there
no other way? Couldn't you say it for me, dear, kind Mr.
Harrington?"

"I am afraid that would not answer the purpose, my
Lord," replied the old man, with as much solemnity of
manner as he could assume. "My brother is already aware
that my opinion on the subject does not agree with his, and
that I am, on the contrary, strongly opposed to the scheme of
forcing my niece to consent to a marriage which she confesses
to be contrary to her inclinations, so that I know beforehand
that he would not listen to me on the subject. Besides,
Lord Goldstable, it is, in my opinion, more proper in every
way that you should yourself undo the mischief you have
done."

"Well, then, I will do it, Mr. Harrington; I will, indeed,
because it would be my wish to do exactly what would please
you, on account of the great kindness you have shown me,
and your taking it for granted that I would not go on acting

wrong, if I did but know what was right. I am quite
willing to do whatever you would have me. But you will
stand by me, eh, Mr. Harrington? You will tell me what I
ought to say, and take my part afterwards, won't you?
Come now, Mr. Harrington, promise me one thing, and then
I shan't mind my Aunt de Paddington a single straw. It
would be so monstrous kind of you! I am going the day
after to-morrow to my place in Derbyshire, called Brandon
Abbey, you know. I have never been there yet, and everybody tells me that it really is a monstrously fine place, and it
is only a mile or two from the railroad station at Barnley.
Now if you would be so very kind as to go down with me,
and stay for a little time, I would write to Dr. Harrington
from the Abbey, and say everything that you tell me I ought
to say. It will make everything easy and right, if you will
only stay with me for a little while, just to show, you know,
that I am not a good-for-nothing, false-hearted fellow in
your opinion. Now do come, Mr. Harrington! Do, pray
come!"

Walter paused for a moment to consider this unexpected
proposition, which notwithstanding its startling abruptness,
was not altogether an absurd one. His presence as a guest in
the house of Lord Goldstable, would certainly have the effect
of countenancing the steps he was urging the young man to
take, and must testify very decidedly, that if in truth there
had been any notion of a marriage between the young peer
and Miss Harrington, it had passed off without offence on
either side.

Moreover, it so happened that Brandon Abbey was in the
immediate neighbourhood of Stanton Parva, and he should,
therefore, by going there, be close to his unknown nephew
James, whom he was anxious to see; this expedition, too,
would enable him to visit his own long-forsaken ancestral
mansion, which he was well enough inclined to visit, if
he could do so without making any fuss or parade about
it. So after the meditation of a minute or two, he very
frankly and cordially accepted the invitation; and in about
five minutes more, it was settled that on the next day but
one, they should leave town together at eight o'clock in the
morning.

The young man was evidently delighted by the project, and
the old one considerably amused both by the suddenness of the
arrangement, and the seeming incongruity of the circum-

stances which led to it. But, notwithstanding both the strangeness and the incongruity, Walter Harrington was inclined to think, as he deliberately meditated on the scheme, that it would be difficult to find another equally well calculated to smooth the somewhat thorny path which lay before them.

～～～～～～～～～～～

CHAPTER XXV.

THE interview recorded in the last chapter, left Lord Goldstable a very much happier man than he had been before it took place. He now, as he very triumphantly told himself, saw his way clearly before him, and perceived no reason to doubt that if he did not immediately become the most fashionable man in London, he was in a very fair way of being the happiest. He snapped his fingers in the most light-hearted style as the recollection of his old aunt, and all her legal threatenings recurred to him, and actually whistled " Polly put the kettle on," from excess of glee, as he thought of the contrast between his actual situation, and the glory of taking that famous old fellow, Mr. Harrington, down to Brandon Abbey with him, and the having to be taken before all the judges and justices of peace in London, to answer to an accusation of *crim. con.* or *felo de se*, or something of that sort.

In short, he was a vast deal happier than he had ever been in the whole course of his life before, and the delightful consciousness that there was no longer any impediment to his throwing himself, his coronet, and his fortune at the feet of the enchanting widow, gave the last bright finish to the delightful future which appeared opening before him.

With the instinctive reverence which feebleness ever feels for strength, he both clung to, and bowed before, the straightforward manly influence of Walter Harrington; he felt at once he was his shield and buckler; and he would willingly have sacrificed many of his annual thousands, rather than have lost the friendship which Walter's kindly eye had seemed to promise him.

For, in truth, the young man (as the phrase goes) had no harm in him, and his natural impulses were almost always rather good than bad; so that if he really had the immense good fortune of inspiring the warm heart of the old forester with a friendly feeling towards his youth, and his guileless folly, it was quite on the cards that as an eating, drinking, digesting, and legislating individual, he might do his duty in that state of life wherein fate and our social system had placed him, quite as satisfactorily as many other peers of the realm.

But while Lord Goldstable's good genius was thus making a benign effort in his favour, the young man himself, as often happens to poor blundering mortals, was bent on making a move in a diametrically opposite direction.

No sooner had Walter left him, than Simpson, the valet, was again summoned, and a second toilette was commenced, with infinitely greater alacrity than the first had been, on that eventful morning. And when it is confessed that the end and object of this was an immediate visit to the fascinating widow in Jermyn Street, it will be readily understood that the process, though gayer, was nevertheless, infinitely more elaborate than the former one.

And off he set, poor boy, as soon as it was completed, with all the wilful eagerness with which a moth sweeps onward, with all its strength, towards the bright but baleful light, which is sure to scorch if not absolutely to consume it.

His present visit was very deliberately intended to be of a different and much more decisive character than that which has been already described. The heavy consciousness of his entanglement had then stood in his way, and prevented his opening his heart to the bewitching object of his affections, in the manner he now fully intended to do.

It will easily be believed, that Mrs. Fitzjames had not been slow in perceiving that, for some reason or other, the boy was under restraint with her. But as he had made no effort to conceal his passionate admiration of her charms, she was quite contented to "bide her time," which she felt very comfortably certain would not be far distant, let this troublesome restraint proceed from what cause it might. She was very

comfortably assured that he was not married already, and short
of this obstacle to her noble projects, she feared none.

The clever creature failed not to discover, almost as soon
as he appeared before her, that some change had come over
him. The tempered light of her rose tinted and delicately
scented little drawing-room, was quite sufficient to enable her
to see that his smile was more gay, and his step more buoyant,
than they had been before. She wasted not a moment in
meditation as to what the cause might be; that so it was,
was fully enough for her. It was exactly all she wanted, and
she already felt that the struggle was over, and the victory
well nigh achieved.

As usual, she was reclining on her *chaise longue*, precisely
in the position most favourable to the display of all the beauty
and of all the grace of which she was so triumphantly conscious. A soft, low chair, stood ready for the visitor to sink
into, at no great distance; and even that distance might
be easily lessened, for the chair rolled smoothly on its castors.

Of course she was reading. Such ladies always are reading, if they do not happen accidentally to be half asleep.
She started violently as he approached her, as if the seeing
him was exactly the last thing in the world that she expected.

"You are come to me again, dear old friend;" she exclaimed, with a sort of plaintive pleasure; as if the happiness
caused by seeing him could neither be denied nor concealed,
but as if it was accompanied by a bashful, timid, trembling
sense of danger.

"Ain't you an angel then, to look so beautifully glad to
see me? and that, too, before you have got the least bit of a
notion whether I am a false-hearted fellow or not!" he exclaimed, seizing her hand, and hugging it very lovingly.

"False-hearted, Edward!" she replied, indignantly. "No!
Your father's son could never be false-hearted to my father's
daughter! And yet," she added, mournfully, laying the hand
which he had left at liberty upon his shoulder, "a woman
may be made very miserable, even though no false heart
responded to her true one!"

"You ain't the woman that is to be made miserable: that
is to say, if you really feel about me as you seem to do," said
he. "You certainly do seem to like me a little, Sophia—
only a little, you know. Don't suppose that I am such a fool
of a puppy, as to fancy you like me a great deal."

"Oh! Edward, Edward! How wildly you talk! And how gaily, how jestingly! Alas, alas! the heart of a woman and the heart of a man are things so widely different."

"Well, I don't know about that," he replied. "And it is very possible you may be right, Sophia; because I am sure that a man's face and a woman's face are no more alike than a coal shovel and a lady's fan. Now if you could but just see our two faces put close together," pursued the bold boy, suiting the action to the word, "you might say there was a difference."

"Ah! dearest Edward!" returned the beautiful widow, gently interposing her delicate hand between his cheek and her own. "How well you know the power that years of friendship between our families has given you. But be generous, Edward! You know I cannot be angry with you. It would be perfectly unnatural in me if I were to attempt it."

"Then don't attempt it, my beautiful Sophia!" replied the not much discouraged youth, audaciously saluting her lips in a style very nearly approaching that of a cow-boy when catching a juvenile dairy-maid at a disadvantage.

"Edward! too dear, too daring Edward! Be generous! oh, be generous! and protect me from myself!" she murmured, burying her face, whether blushing or not, on his shoulder.

"Generous!" replied the young noble, repeating the offence. "I don't know whether it is generous or ungenerous to tell the truth without fear or favour. But I say you are an angel, and I'll knock down any man in England, or Scotland either, who would dare to contradict me."

"Edward! dear Edward! oh, do not jest! oh, do not trifle with me!"

"Trifle—jest?" exclaimed the impassioned peer. "Upon my life and soul, Sophia, I never was more in earnest in my life. And now, then, if you will but listen to me patiently, and not put yourself into such a tantivy, I'll tell you what I am come here for. I am come here, Sophia, for nothing else in the whole world, and for no other reason upon God's earth, but just to tell you downright and straightforward that I am over head and ears in love with you; and that I want you to be mine, Sophia, for good and all. Do you understand me, my darling? I want you to be Lady Goldstable, you know. You understand that, don't you, Sophia?" he added, in rather a business-like tone, very evidently for fear of her making any mistake as to the extent of his generosity.

But his young Lordship was by no means prepared for the reception that awaited his generous proposal. Scarcely were the important words pronounced, before the lady's head fell back upon the sofa, and her eyes closed, while a convulsive working of every feature, and a most tumultuous heaving of the thinly-veiled bosom, proclaimed to the greatly terrified young nobleman that his adored Sophia was either in a fit, or else in the crisis immediately preceding one.

It is true, indeed, that the lovely lady did not change colour; but this did not prevent the inexperienced gentleman from being horribly frightened, and he would have infallibly spoiled a very pretty "situation," by violently ringing the bell, if his Sophia had not clutched him very vigorously by the hand which still held hers.

And in this attitude he was, perforce, obliged to stand quietly by her side for a minute or two—for no shorter interval would have sufficed to enable her to take such a view of present circumstances as could enable her to decide, definitively, upon the best course for her to pursue under the existing exigencies of the case. Though the first great object was gained, *videlicet*, the positive offer of marriage, everything was not yet quite plain sailing before her. Her position, for the attainment of her object, was not at all points a very strong one. She would have said herself, if asked to explain it, that she was suffering, like every other woman gifted by nature with more attraction than their neighbours, from cruel, unmitigated, and totally unfounded slander.

Not few indeed, were the equivocal adventures of which she was said to have been the heroine; and though London had never, as yet, been the scene of these, and though, moreover, she had, by excellent good management, obtained an *entrée* into other *salons* as much *comme il faut* as that of Lady Augusta Harrington, she knew perfectly well that great danger would be likely to attend the notoriety, which would be sure to attach to the name of the lucky lady who would be proclaimed as the fortunate winner of the great Goldstable stakes.

The question which suggested itself to her at this important moment therefore, was whether she should at once confess her love and joy, and then fall into such a paroxysm of timid tenderness as would prevent her knowing a single moment's peace till she felt his *written* promise resting in her bosom, and for ever pressing, with delicious certainty, against her throbbing heart; or, should she venture to postpone this precautionary measure for a little while, so as to afford time and opportunity for wrapping her fascinations closer and closer still about him, till such a promise could be asked for with still greater safety than at present.

In considerably less time than would have been necessary to convert the trembling alarm of the novice lover into any feeling bordering upon common sense, the enchanting Mrs. Fitzjames, deciding upon the bolder course, determined upon postponing, at least for the moment, the important business of the written promise, whilst she gave herself up wholly to love and rapture.

And the moment this bold decision was arrived at, a sweet, but very languid, smile, stole over the working features of the beautiful widow. Her closed eyes opened, and were raised to her enraptured lover's face with an ineffable expression of tenderness and gratitude; the convulsive heaving of the fair bosom became less vehement, and Mrs. Fitzjames "came to."

"Bless your dear, beautiful face!" exclaimed Lord Goldstable, with a joyous laugh. "Now you look like your own angelical self again! You mean to have me then, Sophia? You are not going to send me off with a flea in my ear? You will be mine, darling, won't you?"

"Will I be thine, my Edward?" she exclaimed, in an accent of the most thrilling tenderness, her large, liquid, dark eyes fondly fixed upon his. "Oh, what is there that the earth can offer, that I would take in exchange for the dear hope of being thine—thine only, wholly, and for ever?"

"Well said, my beauty!" returned her adorer, giving her a very unceremonious hug. "That is what I call speaking frank and free, and straightforward. And I should like to see the old woman, or the young one either, that would make me give you up!"

"Alas, my Edward! Those words—dear and delightful as they sound to me—prove but too clearly that you are not unconscious of the efforts which will be made to part us. And have you really strength of mind enough—tell me, my too dear Edward—have you really sufficient strength of mind to resist, and resist effectually, all the intrigues which will be put in action to part us? Remember, the whole set of Harringtons are leagued against us!"

"Not a bit of it, Sophia! There you are out altogether," cried Lord Goldstable. "That old man, Walter, is a trump, I can tell you; and if I wanted anybody's help to enable me to have my own way about marrying you, or anything else, it is to him I should go, sooner than to anybody else, I promise you. So don't you take it into your dear, beautiful head, that my marrying you will be hindered by the Harringtons. By what that fine old fellow says, I don't think that there would be much danger from any of them. But even if there were danger, the dear old man would take care that it should not hurt me. So now, Sophy dear, it is all settled between us, isn't it? I never did see any woman that I thought so beautiful as I do you, in the whole course of my life before; and it would be very hard, indeed, now I am come of age, if I might not marry you if I like, and you seeming so fond of me, too, into the bargain."

"Alas! my Edward!" replied the widow, her trembling arms clasping themselves for one moment of irrepressible emotion around his neck. "Alas! my Edward!" she re-iterated, "your generous nature is incapable of suspecting all the mischief that lies hid behind the saintly seeming of those odious Harringtons. I fear, I fear, that you do not know your own danger. Such a set of sly, artful, practised intriguers might undermine the noblest feelings that ever existed in the heart of man!"

"Well, my darling, perhaps you are right about some of them, for I won't deny that they seem to have got scent of my money and title, you know, and all that; but that's no reason why they should have their way instead of my having mine; so don't you put yourself in a fright about it. Besides, as I told you before, the girl's old uncle is a right down good old fellow; and he would not let the others grapple me if they wished it ever so much."

"Grapple you, my Edward! Yes; that's the proper word for it," replied his Sophia, with a groan. "And how, then, can my heart be at rest, when I know that the man my soul adores is the object of their mercenary machinations?"

"Oh, then, my dear, you are altogether mistaken about machinations, as you call it. Whatever they might have got into their heads at one time, about—about all the stuff my aunt, Lady de Paddington, talked about," said the young man, colouring, as he remembered his blundering statement to Walter, "I am sure and certain that it is all over, and that there is nobody now that will want to stop our marriage in any way—and married we will be, my beauty, as soon as ever we can get everything ready; and the sooner the better, say I."

This satisfactory assurance was accompanied by so tender a caress, that it was some minutes before the agitated Sophia could recover her composure sufficiently to renew the conversation; but at length she said:—

"How would it be possible for any woman to doubt such love as yours, my Edward? My heart, at least, is utterly incapable of it! Its own truth teaches it to believe in yours. And yet, dear love, the tenderness of a woman for ever is, and for ever must be, accompanied by a thousand trembling fears, to which the firmer spirit of a man would never listen. But bear with me, dearest Edward! Bear with me, even if you think that I love you too well!"

"Don't you be afraid of that, Sophia," replied the young man, very affectionately. "The more you love me, the better I shall be pleased, take my word for that, my dear."

"Oh! how delightful is it to hear you say so, my own— own affianced husband!" she replied, with a gentle caress. "But tell me, dearest," she added, earnestly, "tell me everything that has passed between you and these hateful Harringtons. Think what I must have suffered when I overheard your aunt say at that eventful ball: 'That it was quite plain her nephew was caught already: and that it was her young friend, Kate Harrington, who had carried off the prize.' Think what I must have suffered, Edward, at hearing this! and soothe my anxious heart, by telling me exactly everything that passed between you and these dreadful Harringtons, from first to last."

"Well, then, Sophia, you shall hear all about it, at least as far as I can remember," he replied. "And all that really signifies was what passed this very morning, and I am quite sure I shall remember that. Quite early this morning, before sunrise, I believe, who should come to my door but the old boy, Walter Harrington himself!"

"Oh, Edward! did that look as if he were not interested?" exclaimed Mrs. Fitzjames, hiding her face upon his shoulder.

"Don't be in a hurry, my dear," replied her lover, "but hear all I have got to say; and don't cry out before you are hurt. Well, Sophy dear, the old fellow knocked up Simpson, my valet, you know, and frightened him as much as he seems to have frightened you; and he, Simpson I mean, got as sulky as the devil. The old gentleman asked to see me, and got for answer that he must come again at twelve. Cool of Mr. Simpson, wasn't it? Well, there was I thinking, of course, that he was coming to insist on my fulfilling my offer. For I don't deny, you know, that I did make an offer; but it was before I got a sight of you, my darling."

"Offer! Nonsense!" exclaimed the indignant beauty. "No people of honour would dream of taking advantage of such idle words."

"Well—but listen now," he resumed, eagerly. "There I sat waiting and waiting, till twelve o'clock, trying to think what it would be best to say to him, and wishing heartily that the whole Harrington race were at the devil, so that I might be free to throw myself into the arms of a certain beautiful person, that shall be nameless. At last the clock struck, and bang, bang, went the knocker, and in walked the old fellow, as punctual as time itself. I can tell you, my dear, that I wished myself anywhere else upon God's earth; but face him I must, and so I did. And would you believe it, my darling, in about five minutes I felt exactly as if I was talking to an old friend, ay, and the best friend too, that I ever had in my life."

"Alas, my own dear love!" exclaimed his Sophia. "Your own noble nature is too far removed from every species of guile and hypocrisy, for you to be capable of suspecting it in others. But oh! my Edward! beware—beware this seeming friendliness! Trust me, sweet friend, that old and artful man hopes to bend you to his purpose, by leading you to forget what that purpose is."

"You are a monstrous clever creature, I am quite sure of that," replied her lover; "but yet, somehow or other, I don't quite think you are right this time, either; and if you will hear me to the end, you will agree with me in thinking that the fine old fellow does not want me to marry his niece a bit more than you want me to marry her. Just fancy my surprise, my dear, when it came out that his only reason for taking the trouble of paying me a visit at all, was just to make me understand that he particularly wished I would be so obliging as to put all idea of marrying his niece out of my head altogether. What do you think of that, Sophia? I don't feel inclined to quarrel with him for that. Do you?

And so I answered him frank and free, that I was quite willing to say no more about it, if he would stand by me to prevent the old big-wig of a father from making a fuss. And he promised that it should all go off as smooth as silk. And in order to make this quite sure, he has also promised to go down to my place, Brandon Abbey, with me, the day after to-morrow; and if he will do that you know, it is not very likely that they will any of them want to go to law with me afterwards, is it?"

"It certainly does not seem likely," replied the widow, musingly; "but there are many characters so deeply artful as to make it almost impossible to discover their real meaning. I do not say that this old man is one of them, my dearest Edward, but we ought not to forget that it is possible he may be. But are you really going to leave town, dearest?" she added, her voice trembling with emotion, and her beautiful eyes speaking volumes of tender sorrow. "And going too," she added, almost with a groan, "going too in company with the artful uncle of my dreaded rival."

"I tell you once for all, Sophia, that the old man is a very good old man, and no more artful than a baby. And as to your having a rival, my beauty, that is downright impossible; for in point of beauty, and kindness too, the Harrington girl is no more to be compared to you than the moon is to the sun. And I don't think I should have thought so overmuch of her beauty, even before I saw you, if my cunning old aunt had not told me such a lot about her being the fashion. But I'll be hanged, Sophia, if it won't be easy for you to be more the fashion than ever she was, if you do but set the right way to work."

"Oh! what is there that I would not do to please you, my beloved Edward?" replied the fair creature, suddenly pressing her lips to the young man's forehead. "Tell me, only tell me, what you would have me do, and if I fail to do it, then say, dearest Edward, that I love you not."

"And that's what I would not believe, nor say either, for more then you'd believe, perhaps, my beautiful Sophia. But what I want you to do in the way of making yourself as much the fashion as Miss Harrington, would have nothing very disagreeable in it, my darling. You would only have to dress yourself as fine as possible, you know, and have the very finest carriage, and the very finest house, and then get all the very finest people in London to come and dine, and dance, and all

the rest of it. There will be no great difficulty in that will
there, my treasure? And when we have got to that point,
Sophia, we'll soon see whether my fusty musty old aunt, Lady
de Paddington, will be able to prove that I am not as much
the fashion as if I had married all the Miss Harringtons that
ever were born."

CHAPTER XXVI.

THE conversation had, up to this point, gone on very
delightfully, as it seemed, to both parties; for the little
picturesque weakness displayed by the lady had passed away
too rapidly to produce any serious uneasiness in the gentleman. But now it appeared as if a very painful change was
likely to take place, for Mrs. Fitzjames burst into a most
vehement paroxysm of weeping.

"My eye! What's the matter now, Sophia?" ejaculated
the terrified young man. "If I didn't think we were two of
the very happiest lovers that ever sat down side by side
together, I'll be hanged, drawn, and quartered! And now,
for no reason in the wide world that I can think of, hocus-
pocus, presto, behold! If you ain't sitting there crying like
a church spout. What is the matter with you, Sophia?"

"Forgive me, oh, forgive me!" cried the beautiful Niobe,
sinking with unspeakable grace on her knees before him.
"Edward, beloved Edward, forgive and pity me! Nay,
more, my Edward, you must listen to me with patience or
you will never understand the heart you have so completely
won."

"Don't cry then, Sophia; only don't cry," said the really
agitated young man. "I don't mind your kneeling and looking
up at me in that way, if you like it, because it makes you
look so excessively beautiful; but I won't have you cry, my
beauty, and I don't see why the devil you *should* cry, if it is
really true, Sophia, that I have won your dear little affectionate heart—for havn't I just said, out and out, that I wish for

nothing in the world so much as to marry you, and make you
Lady Goldstable at once, my beautiful darling? Why should
you fear anybody then, Sophia? Is not everything settled
between us just as safely as if we were married already?"

"Ah! my Edward," replied the fair, trembling creature,
as she lent with bewitching weakness on his bosom, "to
your strong and manly mind, it may seem so; but to me, alas!
the difference between us on this point is most awfully great,
my Edward! The idea of this journey is terrible to me,
dearest! At your age, dear love, absence is, indeed, a
dangerous test of affection—so dangerous, Edward, that my
woman's heart sinks and droops before it! Think for one
moment—think what would be my feelings if any cause of
any kind were to make you forget your poor Sophia! If
some fairer face should attract your truant fancy, my beloved
Edward, what think you would be my fate were this to
happen? Do you, can you, doubt for a single instant that I
should die? Oh! do not doubt it, Edward! Commit not
such injustice to the heart that loves you so fondly! As
surely as my hand now presses yours, my Edward, so surely
should that hand lie cold beside me in my early coffin did you
cease to love me!"

"My darling angel!" he replied, "I never can, and I
never shall, cease to love and doat upon you; upon my life
and soul I never shall. So don't shake and tremble so; and
for goodness sake don't cry any more about any such ridiculous idea, for the thing is impossible, and there's an end of it.
I never can see anybody's face that's fairer than yours. Your
skin's just like alabaster, my darling, and it's as smooth as
silk into the bargain. So don't take any more such silly
fancies into your head, my dear. Isn't everything settled
between us, Sophia?"

"Alas, *no!* my Edward!" replied the widow, with sad
and solemn emphasis. "Nothing, nothing is settled. And it
is this which terrifies my too fond, too timid heart! If only
this were done, if the settling you speak of—settlement, I
believe they call it—if this only could be fixed, and made;
my poor heart would be comparatively at rest, for then I
should know that neither the Harringtons nor anyone else
could come between us."

"Oh! settlements? Yes, to be sure, my dear. I know
people always do make settlements when they are going to be
married," said he; "and we can set about making ours just

13

as soon as you please. The sooner the better, darling, I say, for the sooner I am your husband my beauty, the better I shall be pleased. But how does one set about it, Sophia? Hang me, if I know anything at all about the matter."

"Why, first, you know, dearest, you send for a lawyer—at least, that is what Colonel Fitzjames did, when he settled. I mean, you know, when he settled everything about his marriage with me," replied the lovely widow, with a childish innocence of tone that was indescribably bewitching.

"And then I presume," returned the gentleman, laughing, "that he binds us over to keep each other. Is that it?"

"Just so," she rejoined, nodding her pretty head and echoing his laugh; "and then you know you will have to say how much you would choose to allow your poor little wife if she was to live longer than you; but that I should never, never do, Edward! No, never, never! If you were to die to-morrow, I do believe in my heart, that I should follow after, quite soon enough to be buried on the same day. I do, indeed, Edward," and here her pretty, nicely-embroidered handkerchief was pressed for a moment to her beautiful eyes.

"I will not have you say so, my darling?" cried the greatly-touched Lord Goldstable, with an affectionate hug. "I can't bear it, Sophy, I can't indeed: and I won't go on a bit farther about these stupid settlements, if you are to cover up your beautiful eyes so that I can't see them, and I knowing all the time that you are spoiling their brightness by crying like the rain. If you don't kiss me this minute, and promise not to do so any more, I will go away without talking any more about our settlement, or about sending for the lawyer that is to bind us over to one another. And what shall you say to that, dear?"

"I shall say that you are a cruel tyrant," she replied, obeying his command as if too much frightened to disobey him; and then after giving him the kiss, and an enchanting smile besides, just to prove that she had ceased to weep, she suddenly clapped her little hands with the prettiest air of childish glee imaginable, and said: "Now, then, I have obeyed you, and I am quite determined that you shall obey me. What I should best like would be, to command you not to go out of town at all; but I suppose I must not dare to do that, because you have promised that tiresome old man to go with him. But if you must, and will leave me, Edward, you positively shall not go without leaving something behind to comfort me." This was a sudden thought, and a very clever one.

"What can I leave my darling?" said the fond youth, rapturously gazing in her beseeching face. "I would leave you my picture, Sophy, if I had got it. I will have it done for you, though, as soon as ever I come back to town; but it can't be done all in a minute, you know. What can I leave to comfort you when I am gone?"

"I will tell you, dearest," she replied, half-tenderly, half-playfully; "and it will be a comfort, I can promise you; and I shall kiss it, too, but I hope you won't be jealous."

"What do you mean, Sophy?" said his puzzled Lordship. "I never will let you kiss anybody but me—that's flat; so mind your hits, my darling."

"Oh yes, Edward; you will let me kiss what I am talking about, and without being jealous at all; and it will be such a comfort to me. Oh! how very lucky it was that I happened to read that beautiful new novel the other day. I should never have thought of such a thing, if I had not seen it there."

"But what is it, Sophy? Why won't you tell me at once what it is that you want to kiss?"

"You shall know all about it this very minute," she replied, springing from the sofa with the agility of a young gazelle, and running to a table at the farthest corner of the room, on which stood a miniature writing-desk. "This is what you shall leave me; and this is what I will kiss; and this is what shall comfort me, and keep me alive during your absence, Edward."

And as she spoke, she opened the desk, drew from it a sheet of delicate miniature writing-paper, together with a pen and a tiny ink-bottle.

"Don't move; sit just where you are," she continued; "just where you so tyrannically made me give you a kiss; and write on this bit of paper: 'I hereby solemnly promise to marry you, my dearly beloved Sophia Fitzjames. Witness my hand, GOLDSTABLE.'"

The thing was no sooner asked than done. And how could it be otherwise? For did not the beautiful Sophia kneel down before him as he sat on the sofa? and did she not put the pen into his hand? and did she not spread the paper smoothly on a little book, and hold it most commodiously before him?

She did all this; and he also did the little that was required of him; and having placed the bit of paper in her hands, inscribed with the few words she had dictated, he had the unspeakable satisfaction (as soon as she had sprinkled a little golden sand upon the words, to prevent their being blotted) of seeing her press the paper to her ruby lips, and then tenderly deposit it in her bosom.

"What a fool you are, Sophia, to be sure," said the youth, laughing heartily. "I have heard over and over, that people in love always are fools; but, upon my soul, I think you beat me hollow. Catch me kissing a bit of paper, when I might be kissing you instead. And you seem to have forgotten, you silly thing, what we were talking of before—it was about the settlement, you know; and there was something like sense in that; for I don't believe that we can be married lawfully and properly without that being looked after, and attended to, really, by lawyers and men of business; and to my thinking, my dear, it would be much more to the purpose, for me to send to my lawyer about that, before I go out of town, instead of giving you a bit of paper to kiss."

"Of course, Edward, I know you are right there," she replied; "but women, poor souls, will be thoughtless and silly sometimes; it is part of their nature, I believe. But certainly, now you remind me of it, I should be very glad that you should send to a lawyer before you go out of town, because they always take a monstrous long time for their work; and I can't say that I want to be parted from you at all longer than is absolutely necessary."

"And how much do you think I should like to be parted from you, darling?" responded the young man, very fondly. "But you must lend me a helping hand, you know; for of all things in the wide world, I believe law is what I know the least about. Upon my life and soul, Sophy, I don't think I ever saw a lawyer above twice in my life. However, I know the name of my own lawyer. It is Barlow, Lincoln's Inn Fields. I'll send to him directly, and he will know how to do everything all right."

"Oh, you dear, darling boy!" cried the lady, laughing heartily, "why, it is the *lady's* lawyer, and not the *gentleman's*, who is always sent to about making marriage settlements. My poor dear father's old friend—mercy on me! I forget his name; but I shall be sure to remember it presently—it is he who has always done all my business for me; and he has always been so friendly and attentive, that I think he would feel quite hurt if I were to be married without sending to him to make the settlements. You had better write at once to your lawyer, my dear Edward, and tell him to confer with mine on the subject. Stay! I will give you another sheet of paper, a little bigger than the last, and you shall sit down at once, to write your instructions, and I will write as soon as I can recollect his name, to my lawyer, and make him understand that he is to meet your Mr. Barlow."

"Well, then, that is all that need be done at present, isn't it?" said the young peer, looking as if they had been talking of business quite long enough, and that he should greatly prefer a little more love-making to any further discussion upon law and lawyers.

"And who's the silly goose now?" returned the widow, again clapping her hands and laughing heartily. "What do you think they can do together when they do meet, if you don't tell them?"

"Why, what in the world can I tell them, Sophy dear, that they won't know a great deal better without my telling them anything about it?"

"But they can't know, my darling Edward, exactly how much you may choose to settle upon your wife; that depends entirely upon your own dear self, and your own generous nature. You must tell the lawyers, darling, how much you choose to settle upon me, and then they will take care that it is properly done. I know quite well that the doing that is all they have got to do with it. It is you, Edward, who must say how much you choose it should be."

"And how on earth should I know, Sophy? I don't think I ever heard any human being say a single word about it in the whole course of my life. Do tell me, dear! you must know more about it than I do."

"As to knowing anything about it, Edward, I do assure you, upon my word and honour, that I am as ignorant as the babe unborn; so, for goodness sake, don't ask me to tell you. All I ever heard about it, was hearing somebody say that the marriage settlement was always made in proportion to the person's income who made it, and that the usual custom was to settle a tenth of the whole income."

"Well, at least, that's knowing something, my darling, and a great deal more than I ever knew before. If I was to follow that rule, Sophia, I should settle eight thousand a-year

upon you, for my income, they tell me, is exactly eighty
thousand—and a very beautiful fine income it is, everybody
tells me. But that's the very reason, isn't it, why I should
settle more than a tenth upon my beautiful darling of a wife?
and so I will too; I shall settle just double—I shall settle
two-tenths upon you, my beauty, instead of one. Nobody
shall say that I was a stingy fellow, at the very moment that
I was going to marry the most beautiful woman in the whole
world. You will love me all the better if I settle two-tenths;
won't you, my angel?"

"I am sure I don't know. People, I know, say that
women always do love the most generous men the best; but
it seems to me, Edward," she replied, with a very fond caress,
"that I love you already as much as it is possible for any
woman to love any man."

"God bless you, my angel! you are quite mistaken then, I
promise you," he rejoined, with an answering caress, "for I
mean to be so generous to you in everything, that you will be
obliged to love me ten times more than you do now—you will,
indeed, Sophy. And now, let us just put our two heads
together, my darling, and see if we cannot think of something else that I can do, or settle, as you call it, that may just
show the truth of what I say, and prove to the lawyer, and
to you, and to everybody else, that I am a great deal more in
love with you than ever anybody was in love before; but you
must help me about it, Sophia, because I am so stupid that
I cannot think of the things. What else shall I write down
besides the two-tenths that I have promised you? Do tell
me something to write."

Mrs. Fitzjames laughed heartily, showing the beautiful
range of her ivory teeth to a greater extent than he had ever
beheld them before, and for a moment or two she seemed too
much overpowered by the merry convulsion to be able to
answer him, but at length she recovered herself sufficiently to
say:—

"Oh yes, Edward! I know perfectly well how lovers that
are very much in love indeed order their settlements to be
made, and you may do so too if you like it, dearest. Though,
to tell you the truth, I think the whole business of settlements is nothing but nonsense. However, you are quite
right, dear love, to do like other people about it; for if you
did not, everybody would be sure to say that it was because I
had no large fortune myself."

"And *that* they shall never say," exclaimed Lord Gold-stable, with a degree of eagerness which showed that there was a strong touch of generosity in his character, however deficient it might be in other respects. "But tell me," he added, "what you were going to say just now? What is it, my beauty, that the lovers who are very much in love order their lawyers to put in their settlement?"

"Oh, it is something so ridiculous that you will scarcely believe it, and yet, upon my word and honour, Edward, it is quite true. They order it to be put in the settlements that the lady is to have—oh, I don't know how much—but about two thousand a-year, I think, for pin-money. Just fancy, a woman having two thousand a-year to spend in pins."

"Oh, that is too silly, Sophia," replied his Lordship, laughing. "I am sure that you are only making fun now, and that is very wrong of you, my dear, because I really do want to have the settlement all ordered before I go out of town."

"And do you think I want to delay it, Edward?" she replied, with touching tenderness. "Do you think that I wish that we should live asunder longer than is absolutely necessary? Ah, Edward, you little know how fondly you are loved."

"Well then, be serious, Sophia," he replied, taking up the pen and placing a sheet of paper before him: "tell me at once, and without any more joking, exactly what I am to write down upon this paper for the lawyer."

"Indeed, and indeed, Edward, there is no joke in what I said," she replied, in a plaintive voice, and very much as if she were going to weep because he scolded her so harshly. "I do assure you, upon my word and honour, Edward, that I said exactly the real truth. Every woman, when she is going to be married, unless the man is very, very poor indeed, has a sum of money settled on her for clothing herself; and there is nothing ridiculous in that, you know. It is only because the lawyers will call it pin-money, that it was so very absurd. There is nothing foolish in a woman having money to pay for her dresses, is there, dear? You would not like that your wife should go without dresses, I am quite sure of that."

"I think not, indeed," replied his Lordship, evidently disgusted at the bare idea of such barbarity. "Pin-money, two

thousand a-year?" he added, interrogatively. "That was
what you said, wasn't it, dearest?"

"Yes," she replied, opening the volume which lay on the
sofa with an air of the most lazy indifference. "That is
what one or two of my friends have had named for that
purpose in the settlements. But I suspect that it is only a
mere form after all."

"At any rate I won't leave it out, dearest, if it was only
because of what you said just now about lovers that were
very much in love. And where was there ever a lover more
in love than I am, I should like to know? No, no, my dear,
neither the lawyers nor anyone else shall ever misdoubt me
on that point."

The only reply which suggested itself to Mrs. Fitzjames,
in return for this loving assurance was another kiss, rather
more tender than any of those which had preceded it; and
when this had been performed, the instructions were given
with a pretty air of much gravity by the lady, and written
down with a very painstaking degree of real gravity by the
gentleman.

And this being achieved, a few more playful caresses followed, in the midst of which the discreet Sophia declared that
it was high time he should go, for that if he stayed any longer,
the servants would be sure to begin talking about the extraordinary length of his visit.

"And that won't do, my dear Lord," she said, with an air
of almost solemn gravity. "I never have been talked of yet,
Edward, and I never will."

"I should like to hear anybody dare to say a word against
you. You should see if I would not knock 'em down as flat
as flounders in no time," rejoined the young man. "However, my darling, if you tell me I must go, go I will, just to
prove that I don't mean to contradict you in anything. So
good-bye, dearest. Of course, I shall pay you another visit
to-morrow, so take care that you are not gadding, my beauty.
One kiss more, Sophy, and then good-bye, my own dear,
beautiful wife."

"Good-bye, Edward," returned the fair creature, very
plaintively. "Good-bye."

But while she said this, she still held his hand very firmly
clasped in hers.

"Dear little soul! you don't like to part with me, do you,
my darling? Tell me before I go, Sophia, if there is any-

thing I can do for you? Can I be useful to you in any way?" said the enamoured youth, looking very much as if he had not the courage to depart.

The widow raised her delicate hands, and for a minute or two stood still, her face concealed behind them.

"What is the matter, darling?" said her lover, endeavouring to remove the barrier which hid the features he so greatly loved to look upon. "You are not got to crying again, are you? I positively will not let you cry, Sophy, for I can't bear it."

"No, Edward, no; I am not crying, I should be very foolish to cry when I know that the man I love, loves me; but I was hiding my face that I might have time to think, and make up my mind whether it would be right or wrong to tell you a secret that I have got heavy upon my heart, and which gives me a good deal of uneasiness."

"Tell me what it is this very moment, my darling angel!" he exclaimed, in an accent of very true affection. "Think what a delight it would be to me, if I could help you out of your trouble."

"But I am afraid that it will appear as if I was so very careless, and such a very bad manager. But indeed, dearest Edward, it was a series of unlucky accidents, and no fault of mine, that occasioned it," she replied, with a pretty air of timid embarrassment, that touched him to the very heart.

"You don't mean that you are afraid of me, my beautiful darling!" he exclaimed, throwing his arms fondly round her, and pressing her trembling but unresisting form to his heart. "What can I say to you, Sophy, to make you know how dearly I love you?"

"I do know it, Edward," she replied, gently returning his caresses; "indeed I do, and I should not be worthy of your love if I doubted it. But I don't feel quite certain that it is right to trouble you with all my troubles. I have been very cruelly robbed, dearest Edward, by a servant whom I trusted, and the consequence is, that at this moment I am greatly in distress for money."

"Oh, Sophy! Sophy!" he vehemently replied, "what a silly creature you must be to fancy it would be more right to hide such a thing from me, than to tell me of it! Do you really think, you naughty little goose, that it would be better for either of us that you should go on positively suffering for want of a little money, instead of letting me have the delight of giving you some? Tell me how much I shall give you, my beauty. I have got my cheque-book in my pocket, because I wanted to pay my tailor's bill to-day, before going out of town, you know, that he might not think I was running away; and here is the pen and ink, darling, all ready. Tell me how much you want, you beautiful creature, and let it be as much as it will, I promise to give it, provided you will promise to give me a kiss of your own accord the moment after."

"Dearest Edward, if a kiss be indeed a token of love, I should not find it very easy to refuse it."

"Dove! Then that's a bargain!" cried the youth, gaily seizing the pen with his right hand, and extracting his cheque-book from his pocket with his left. "Now then, pretty one, how much?"

"I am half afraid to tell you," she replied, "I am, indeed! I could not bear that you should fancy me thoughtless or extravagant; but the truth is, Edward, that less than five hundred pounds would not suffice to relieve me from my present embarrassment."

Lord Goldstable said nothing, but wrote the cheque with as much rapidity as any man could be expected to write who used a pen as rarely as his Lordship; and when he had fairly filled up the cheque, and duly signed his name thereto, he approached the lady, and gazing at her bright and curious eyes, into which she instantly threw a look of tender softness, that in some degree tempered the eagerness of their glance, he said:—

"Fair play is no robbery, my darling. You are to give me, of your own free will, without my taking it, one dear, beautiful kiss for five hundred pounds; and if you act fair, and no cheating, you will let me take five more on my side for the other five hundred pounds, for I have drawn for a thousand, my sweet one! What do you say, is it a bargain?"

"Oh, Edward! what can I say to you?" she exclaimed, throwing her arms very frankly round his neck, while she performed her part of the compact.

"Now then, my dear, it's my turn!" he gaily replied; and not having met with any absolutely unconquerable resistance, his part of it was accomplished likewise. The precious manuscript was playfully thrust into her hand, and the lovers parted, equally, perhaps, enchanted with each other.

CHAPTER XXVII.

MRS. FITZJAMES, notwithstanding her rapidly-increasing attachment to, and admiration of, her young lover, was decidedly very glad when she heard the house-door close behind him. She was, in fact, exceedingly fatigued: and no wonder. She had achieved much, and very important business, and this is rarely or never done without some feeling approaching to fatigue succeeding. As soon as this welcome sound had greeted her ears, she rang the bell, and then she threw herself at full length upon the sofa, two very well-stuffed cushions under her head, and Lord Goldstable's draft for a thousand pounds in her hand; so that, although decidedly fatigued, she felt on the whole very comfortable. The maid who answered the bell was her own personal attendant, and, in fact, the only servant of any kind who belonged to her. She was a French girl, and clever in many ways; and had Mrs. Fitzjames been describing her character, she would have ascribed to her, among many other good gifts, all the rare qualities that constitute a perfectly confidential servant. Nevertheless, the beautiful Sophia placed the hand which still held the precious draft, very snugly out of sight behind her back, and there let it remain as long as the interview lasted.

"I know not what is the matter with me, dear Lisette," she said; "but I am dreadfully tired and languid. Do let me have a cup of coffee. I left more than a cup at breakfast: and bring me a bit of toast with it. And don't let anyone in, for your life."

To all which the intelligent handmaiden promised obedience; and after curiously gazing at her beautiful mistress, for about half a minute after she had ceased speaking, she made her exit, gently closing the door after her, and very certain that she should hear something or other about the young visitor and his long visit, as soon as her lady had refreshed her spirits by the coffee and toast.

Far, however, was the acute waiting-maid from guessing the immense importance of the news that the lady was now very truly and literally too tired to tell. Had she been a little better informed, she would not have blundered so egregiously in the performance of her duty, as she did; and in that case, the events which followed might have been very dissimilar to what they were.

The widow had again thrown her languid limbs upon the sofa, and was enjoying with eyes half closed, the almost dreamy but most delicious consciousness, that she still clasped within her little hand a cheque for one thousand pounds, when just about the moment that the coffee and toast were expected, the door of the room was again opened by Lisette, who, instead of presenting a tray, pronounced with great distinctness the words, "Captain Fowler."

The effect produced by this announcement on Mrs. Fitzjames was very vehement, and certainly at the moment extremely startling and unaccountable to the gentleman who produced it. No sooner had his name reached her ears, than suddenly starting, with a vigorous spring, from her recumbent position, and darting with the rapidity of lightning across the room, she cleared, as it seemed with one bound, the space between the sofa and the table on which Lord Goldstable had deposited the instructions she had dictated for his lawyer, and while with one hand she thrust this into her pocket, she hastily placed the cheque she still held in the other, into her bosom.

This marvellous display of agility sufficed to enable her to secure possession of the papers; but not without being perceived by the tall personage who still stood, startled into silence, as it seemed, by the vivacity of her movements, immediately behind the servant who had announced him. As soon, however, as the flying figure of the lady had ceased to flit before his eyes, and had resumed its position on the sofa, the tall gentleman made a step in advance, whereupon Lisette disappeared; and then the stranger, before he uttered any salutation whatever, turned again towards the door, and with his own hand effectually closed it—an operation Lisette was rather apt to leave imperfectly performed. This being done, he turned again, and drew near the lady.

He was, though very tall, a very well-built man, of some five and forty years of age, or so. His upright figure was clothed in a military-looking blue frock-coat, single-breasted, and buttoned to the chin. Though a good deal approaching towards being bald, he would probably still have been deemed a very remarkably handsome man by all those persons, whether male or female, who look at the form of a human being, precisely as they would at that of a horse, and who are wholly unable to see or feel the beauty, or absence of beauty, which the inner man so mysteriously and so infallibly impresses on the outward casing. Despite his handsome features, anyone who was endowed with the power of seeing more in the human face divine than its mere form, would have pronounced Captain Fowler to be a singularly ill-looking person.

And yet the most skilful and practised physiognomist might have failed to read Captain Fowler aright, had the said Captain's eyes been hidden from their scrutiny. His smiling, well-formed mouth, might have been thought to express only good humour and a kind temper. But the eye rarely succeeds in lying; and there was a cold, doubtful, sinister expression in his, joined to a sort of calm audacity, which had no mixture of frankness in its boldness, which produced an effect inexpressibly repulsive.

For the rest, Captain Fowler might perhaps have been mistaken for a gentleman as long as he remained silent, had it not been for a peculiar look of smart "seediness" about his habiliments, totally different from the impoverished shabbiness of a gentleman under any circumstances.

Mrs. Fitzjames having performed the feat of activity which has been above described, had resumed her place on the sofa; but her whole attitude and bearing were changed to a degree which seemed to have converted her into a totally different person from what she had appeared ten minutes before. She positively, and without the slightest exaggeration, looked ten years older. Her features no longer expressed softness, delicacy, or refinement of any kind. Her aspect was now that of determined endurance, and settled, obstinate firmness of purpose. She had evidently made up her mind as to the manner in which she intended to act under existing circumstances, and it was evident also, that she expected, and was resolved to endure a sharp struggle. She sat with one knee crossed over the other, and her hands firmly clasped round the upper one. Her head was somewhat bent down, but not so her eyes, which seemed to watch furtively every movement of the new-comer.

" I am quite delighted to observe, my dear, that you possess anything which you think of sufficient value to justify so much anxiety, and so much activity to remove it out of—out of harm's way," said Captain Fowler, demurely, as he

majestically marched up to the fireplace, and took his stand
on the rug before it, by which means he found himself exactly
opposite the lady.

"There may be secrets, Fowler, which I have no wish to
entrust to your discretion, without there being anything of
value in question," she very quietly replied.

"Scarcely so, my fair Sophy, at this time of day," was his
answer. "Time has been, certainly," he continued, "when
something of this sort might have been the case. But after all
that has come and gone between you and me, my fair friend,
I am inclined to think that there is nothing you would be so
very anxious to keep from my cognizance save and except *cash*,
my charming Sophia, or something thereunto conducive.
Pray observe, and be grateful for it, how highly, with that
one trifling exception, I rate your connubial confidence in the
man of your choice, my dear Mrs. Fowler."

"Idiot!" she exclaimed, with a grimace indicative of the
most profound contempt. "I know of no folly so disgusting
as a worn-out jest."

"Did you know how, beyond all else on earth, the dear
and solemn subject to which you allude as a jest, is precious
to me, my divine Sophia, you never would venture to use so
peculiarly inappropriate a phrase. A jest, my love? How is
it possible that you can think I consider as a jest, that dear,
that darling, that inestimable privilege which I have enjoyed
so long? Oh no, you cannot think it! You call me idiot,
now; but what would you call me if your cruel suspicion—
that I could cease to consider you as my wife—were just?
It is you who jest, Sophia."

"Let me advise you, Captain Fowler, not to amuse yourself by these most ridiculous airs at a moment when my most
important interests are at stake. Not content with endangering every hope I have, by showing yourself here at all, you
must needs shout out words which, if heard, must inevitably
destroy me, in a tone loud enough to be audible by everyone
in the house." And then suddenly sinking her own voice
to a low whisper, she added: "You know not what you do,
madman! you know not what you risk!"

"Risk, child? Bless your little tender heart, I risk
nothing. You know as well as I do, that my calling you
Mrs. Fowler has, many a time, been the best protection I
could give you against being called something worse. No
nonsense, if you please, Sophia—no nonsense, and no airs.

If you have any good news to tell me, let me hear it; and you know, perfectly well, that I am not the sort of man likely to be in your way—that is to say, upon proper conditions, you know; but we must share and share alike remember. I am devilish hard up, I can tell you, and if I were not, I should not be prowling about to find you out. But circumstances have made it inconvenient for me not to stay in Paris any longer, just at present; so here I am again at your feet, my beauty, and if you have really anything hopeful to communicate, pray let me hear it."

"Captain Fowler!" returned Mrs. Fitzjames, knitting her brows into a very threatening frown, "you know not what would be lost to me, nor what would be lost to you either, Sir, were the inmates of this house to overhear you when you thus absurdly and madly address me by your own name!"

"Go on, my dear love; I am really listening to you with intense interest. Go on, Sophia! What you might lose I can, perhaps, conceive, by a vigorous exertion of my invention, though I do not as yet see how, or where; but as to what I should lose, I profess that I have not the very slightest idea. You are permitting yourself, very foolishly, I fear, to lose sight of that part of the subject. Now, once for all, my very dear wife, for such you were once most happy to be called, and shall be so called still, if it suits my convenience, let us understand one another, as all such good and well-matched couples should. You evidently think it desirable, and no doubt for admirably good reasons, to sink, blink, forget and deny all remembrance of the blissful period during which we enjoyed an interval of such supreme felicity at Passy. I, on the contrary, shall never sink, blink, forget or deny the remembrance of so extremely agreeable a portion of my existence. It is, no doubt, possible, that there may now be reasons for your denying that you ever were called Mrs. Fowler, as powerful as there were then for declaring that it would have been a cruel outrage to call you anything else. Well, my dear, if that be the case, you have only to explain the matter to me, in order to make me conform to your wishes in every particular, provided, you know, that I could see my own benefit in it, as well as yours. You know me far too well to suspect that I should be so unreasonable as to make any objection to what I should, of course, in that case consider as a perfectly rational line of conduct."

"Have you not sufficient common sense to perceive the benefit of breaking a tie which no longer holds either, but which still may gall both?" returned Mrs. Fitzjames, with very solemn earnestness. "Would it be no benefit to you to be rid for ever of a galling entanglement which, like the clutch of some desperate drowning wretch, may effectually frustrate your own struggling efforts to swim?"

"But you seem to forget, my sweet, that it is I who am the desperate drowning wretch," said the Captain, with a bitter laugh; "and the species of discretion to which you allude never, I believe, arises with the individual so circumstanced, whatever it may do in the case of his more desperate associate. Keep this in mind, will you, dearest? for the forgetting it will infallibly lead you to draw false conclusions."

"You are very idly playing with words, Captain Fowler," she replied. "The *fact*, the important *truth* which I wish, for both our sakes, to point out to you is, that there can be no advantage to either of us in remembering or alluding to the imprudent connection which we were weak enough to form when we were some years younger, and many degrees less experienced, than, I presume, we both are at present."

"Well, Sophia, you need be under no alarm from fearing any desperately imprudent fondness on my part. I will not attempt to deny, my dear, that despite these still unfaded charms, which some five long years ago so completely subjugated my too tender heart, I will not, I say, pretend to deny that it is, *par le temps qui court*, considerably more convenient to me to be without you. I own it candidly; and this of itself ought to convince you of my unvarnished sincerity. Nevertheless, I am still disposed to consider the terms on which we have lived together as forming a tie that may, by possibility, be very advantageous to me. It constitutes a sort of partnership, you see, which gives me a fair claim to share in whatever advantages you may derive from dropping all allusion to it. Observe, my dear, that you cannot realize these advantages of oblivion, without my being a consenting party, and I am by no means disposed to abandon the vantage-ground which this gives me, without a fair share of the benefit to be derived from my silence and discretion. Do you comprehend me, my dear Mrs. Fowler?"

"Oh, very clearly, Captain Fowler," replied the lady, quietly. "For a long time past you have made yourself quite well understood, and well known to me. I only wish, Sir, I had always known you as well."

" I, too, think that our connection, formed, too, so broadly in the face of day, was a very imprudent one, and that we should both of us, probably, have been better off, if we had never happened to fall in love with each other. To say the least of it, we must confess that it was a very great imprudence ; I, too, having an old wife alive at the time in Brussels. But all these moralizings, my dear, though they may sometimes form a very agreeable little domestic pastime, will not help us at all forward in the solution of the present question. Make an effort, Sophia dear : do now, for once and a way, make an effort to be frank and honest. It will save you time and trouble, depend upon it, though I am aware that it may be inconsistent with your principles."

The lady looked at him earnestly, as if reading the strong large characters in which his soul was written in his face, and she gave a minute or two to meditation, after which she replied very quietly :—

" I am sure I have no desire to be otherwise, Captain Fowler, especially as such frankness will, I doubt not, convince you of the prudence of keeping yourself at a convenient distance henceforward and for ever from my whereabouts. Do you see that letter yonder ? That paper I mean, that is lying unfolded there, on my writing-desk. Have the goodness to give yourself the trouble of reading it."

The obedient Captain lost no time in complying with this request. On the contrary, it was with a very rapid stride that he transformed his person to the other side of the room, and seizing upon Lord Goldstable's letter of instructions to Mr. Barlow, read it with every possible appearance of interest, from beginning to end. He then replaced it on the desk, and stood profoundly silent, but evidently in wide-awake meditation for a minute or two. At length he said :—

" I do believe, Sophy, that you will force me to confess, after all, that I might have done worse than devote myself to you as faithfully as I have done—devil's imp, as I have often thought you. But it is beyond all question, a very fine thing to be closely connected, either as father-in-law, or anything else, to the three-tailed portion of the human race. Eighty thousand a-year. Upon my life, Sophy, you seem to have driven your pigs—I beg pardon, my dear, your smiles I mean —to a famously good market at last. Well, Sophy, for my

14

part, I say *done* to my share of the bargain. I would not
permit my attachment, overpowering as it is, to interfere with
your present admirable scheme for the world. I am content
to sink our connection in eternal oblivion; I am quite ready
to march off, and evacuate the place to this Lord Goldcalf, or
whatever his name may be. Bag and baggage I'll be off, my
dear, for a proper and sufficient consideration. You understand me, my fair friend? I am sure you do. I have always
observed in you an extraordinary degree of intelligence, on all
points connected with what is vulgarly called the main chance.
All we have to do, therefore, is to take care before we part,
that no mistake is likely to arise between us, respecting the
amount of the consideration which I am to receive for consenting to absent myself for ever from the light of my eyes,
and the joy of my heart. If you will do the thing handsomely, Sophy, I will never come near you, and especially
never near enough, my dear, to eat or drink cup or platter of
your catering. Eh! upon my soul, my beauty, it makes me
shiver to think how delighted you would be to see me fairly
on the road to kingdom come. But never mind, my dear,
don't look cross. Looking daggers will do no good, you
know."

"If I were to pay you for your absence, Fowler, in proportion to the disgust your presence causes me, you would be
rich enough," replied the lady "But go, only go, and go
far enough, and never doubt that I will make it worth your
while to stay away. Cannot you guess, Sir, how I loathe the
sight of you?"

"Oh, dear, yes; perfectly, my dear, perfectly. I can quite
enter into your feelings, and fully sympathize in them. But
before this blissful going is performed, I have one or two
rather important observations to make, which are indeed
absolutely essential to a right understanding between us of
the matter in hand.

The first is, that in determining the amount of the provision you intend to make for the fond lover, who thus
generously consents to resign you to another, it will be necessary for you to lose your calculations, not so much on what
it might seem to be worth my while to take in order to keep
me silent, as what it would be worth your while to give, to
reward that precious silence. For you will do wisely to
remember, Madam," and here, for the first time since the
colloquy began, his manner changed from sneering raillery, to

savage intensity of earnestness; "you will do wisely to remember, that as you have bestowed yourself upon me, my power over you in such a case as this is absolute, and pretty nearly unlimited. Therefore we must share this fool's wealth together, fairly and evenly; or, by Heaven, we will sink together into the abyss which the slightest disclosure of bygone facts on my part, would cause to open before us!"

In reply to this, the only answer he received was a slight inclination of the head from Mrs. Fitzjames.

"That is enough," said he, resuming his former free and easy manner. "I am, indeed, aware that you know me well enough to make any further observations on the subject quite needless; now, then, fair Sophy, I have only to remark, that though these golden prospects are very charming, and highly satisfactory in every way, yet, nevertheless, they are not available assets for the payment of my dinner, and so forth, to-day; and this brings me back to the subject from which we started, and which I have by no means lost sight of, namely, the bit of paper, my dear (it was a cheque, if my eyes did not greatly deceive me), which you made such very vehement efforts to conceal when I came in."

"And from whom do you think it was likely that I should receive a cheque?" she replied, with a weak attempt at evasion, which she herself knew was hopeless.

"From whom, my dear? why from your noble lover, to be sure; from your glorious golden calf, Sophy! The story tells itself, and a very amusing one it is. His soft Lordship having written the very interesting letter which I have just read, my Sophia—I beg pardon, my *ci-devant* Sophia, I mean —would have acted in a manner totally unworthy of herself, had she suffered him to depart without a little gentle bleeding; I would have bet two to one upon the chance of this, even if I had not seen the cheque. Come, my dear, hand it over!"

"It is true, Captain Fowler," she replied, "that I did get a draft from him for twenty pounds to pay my lodgings here; and you shall have half of it, Sir—I will send it to be cashed immediately," and as she spoke she rose from the sofa, and with a very quiet movement approached the door.

Her smiling companion suffered her to proceed without interruption for a step or two, and then, with one long stride, overtaking her, he very politely took her hand, and having performed a courtly bow, led her back to her seat.

14—2

"It was well tried, Sophia. Very well tried. But I suspect, my pretty one, that your former lover is not so easy to deal with as your present one. Just lay your fair hand upon your tender heart, sweet Sophy, and draw forth the cheque that is nestling there! But do it at once if you please, and do it quietly, there's a good girl! In which case I swear I will take only half; but if you make any bother about it, Sophy, upon my soul I will take the whole."

The unfortunate lady knew him too well to doubt his keeping his word, and the cheque for one thousand pounds was drawn forth, and placed in his hands.

"A thousand pounds, by all that's holy!" exclaimed the ruffian, greedily clutching it. "But, upon my life, I envy you the pleasure of plucking such a pigeon as this. It positively ought to count as at least ten per cent. upon every hundred we divide. But come, don't look frightened! Fair play's a jewel! Honour bright, my dear, you shall have half of it; if it was only to teach you the principle of fair *half-and-half* division for the future. And really, Sophia, you need not look blue about it. If ever any woman could afford to let her lord and master go shares, it is you, Sophia; for it needs no conjuror to tell one that you will find it easy enough to make another pull on the same bank, and without danger of breaking it either."

"But it may stop payment, Sir; an event extremely likely to happen, if it has to guard against a claimant as ravenous as yourself," replied the lady, bitterly.

"Not a bit of it, Sophy," was the rejoinder, "as long as you look as beautful as your virtuous indignation makes you look at this moment, the bank of Gold-calf will not stop payment. And now, good-bye, my dear. I will call on you some time to-morrow, in order honourably to pay over to you your share of the dividend; and I hope I shall find you disengaged. But do not stand upon ceremony. If you are occupied, I can call again. Good-bye."

The overpowered Sophia spake not a word in reply; and thus they parted.

CHAPTER XXVIII.

If the first of Mrs. Fitzjames' visitors had left her food for meditation of a nature that appeared of the greatest possible importance, the apparition of the second awakened and left with her thoughts so heavy, in their terrible consequences, as to make all else appear too light and too uncertain to be any longer dwelt upon as a grave reality. The train of thought which Lord Goldstable had left behind him, had been all *couleur de rose*; whereas, that which succeeded the departure of Captain Fowler, might be said to have palled itself in the very dimmest smoke of hell, so dismally dark did it appear to her.

For the man had uttered no vain boast, when he said that she knew him well enough to be certain that he would act up to all he threatened. She had become fully awake to the tremendous peril which had now beset all her brightest hopes; yet still she thought that if she could but bribe him to keep off and remain quiet till the marriage was achieved, she might afterwards, in a great degree, defy him.

It was certain that he must for ever, as long as life was left him, command the power of blasting her reputation; he might, too, there could be no doubt of it, have power to cause a separation between herself and her future husband; but, even so, she would still be mistress of wealth far, far beyond all she had ever dreamed of possessing. Nor did she yet quite lose sight of the rainbow brightness of the tints in which her destiny might still be traced, could she but succeed in bribing her tyrant to lasting silence.

More than once during the dreadfully painful hour of meditation which succeeded his departure, did she feel inclined to think she had been wrong in trusting to him the secret of her splendid hopes; yet, on the other hand, she felt that it would have been almost impossible for the marriage to have actually taken place without his hearing of it; and she felt also that, even if he had not arrived at so critical a moment, her misery from his approach would only have been delayed till rumour, or a newspaper, had announced to him

that she was in a position which might make it worth his
while to persecute her.

But Mrs. Fitzjames was much too clever a woman to waste
in profitless meditation, moments which might be more advantageously employed in action. She sat quietly on the seat
where the detested Captain Fowler had left her, just long
enough to contemplate the actual position in which she was
placed, from every point of view at which her active sagacity
could place her ; and the result of this was, that, instead of
wasting another moment in lamenting the ill-timed re-appear-
ance of her ruffian lover, or in mourning over the robbery he
had perpetrated, she suddenly, but firmly, resolved to hurry
forward, by every possible device, the irrevocable ceremony
which should make her Lady Goldstable, let the subsequent
dangers which might threaten the tranquillity of her wedded
life be what they might.

"Once his wife," she murmured, "and he cannot divorce
me for anything that happened before I became so. I am
lawyer enough to know that. And my heart being very considerably less tender than it has been in days of yore, I shall
continue to be his wife as long as we both shall live ; unless,
indeed, accident and my fair face should lead me within reach
of some position that I might like better. But, at any rate,
I may soothe myself with the comfortable assurance, that no
tender weakness on my part towards Captain Fowler will
endanger the tranquillity of my noble nuptials."

Having reached this point, she rose, in order immediately
and literally, without a moment's delay, to put into execution
a scheme which had suggested itself to her bold and fertile
imagination, even before Lord Goldstable had left. The project was a daring one, being no less than making a visit to
Lady de Paddington, and trying the power of her winning
ways in converting that highly respectable old noblewoman
from a furious enemy into a useful ally.

The move was certainly a very bold one, and required no
small portion of courage and self-confidence. But in neither
was Mrs. Fitzjames deficient. Moreover, she enjoyed the
advantage of having heard some of the peculiarities of her
ladyship's character, discussed by a woman who now carried
on the business of buying and selling second-hand dresses,
but who had formerly lived with Lady de Paddington as her
maid. From this source, she had learned that the old lady
was both poor and avaricious, and well disposed either to save

or to make money by every opportunity that came in her way. On this hint she determined to act; and the result proved that she had neither blundered concerning the information she had obtained, nor in the confidence with which she trusted to her own talents for making the most of it.

If the reader will take the trouble of following the lovely widow across Piccadilly, he will soon find himself at the door of Lady de Paddington's aristocratic, but gloomy old mansion; and when he has learned how she sped when she got there, he may be tempted to give her credit for some cleverness.

To the gruff answer of "not at home," which was flung to the walking visitor by Lady de Paddington's servant, with about as much civility as he would have thrown a bone to a dog, the lady replied by drawing from her pocket a little note, which she extended to him with one hand, while between the finger and thumb of the other she held a golden sovereign very visibly displayed.

"If you will deliver this note to your mistress, Sir, this sovereign is yours," she said. "It is very important to me that I should see her, and if you will give her this note, I think it very likely that she may wish to see me as much as I wish to see her."

"Well! I don't know, ma'am, how that may be; but I'll do my best," returned the man, extending his hand, into which both note and sovereign were given. "If you will please to walk in for a minute, I will see what I can do."

And on receiving this answer, the beautiful Mrs. Fitzjames walked in, perfectly well contented to take her station at the bottom of the stairs, to await the result of her experiment.

Lady de Paddington, meanwhile, received the note, and read as follows, with mingled indignation and astonishment:

"Mrs. Fitzjames presents her compliments to Lady de Paddington," it began.

"To me! the creature dares to present her impertinent compliments to me!" muttered the old lady, between her teeth; and for a moment she felt exceedingly disposed to tear the document to atoms before the eyes of the messenger, by way of enabling him to deliver a fitting reply to it.

But a strong feeling of curiosity changed her head and checked her pride. And so she read on:—"And has taken the liberty of calling on her, for the purpose of communicating some important intelligence which it may be advantageous to Lady de Paddington to hear. Should this statement be proved erroneous, Lady de Paddington may resent the step now taken, by causing Mrs. Fitzjames to leave her house immediately. All that her Ladyship can lose, therefore, by admitting her, is a minute or two of time. What she may gain by it, may be less easily stated, and may be more worth inquiring about."

"That's true; let who will say it," was the next phrase muttered; and after the silent meditation of about a minute, the old lady dismissed the man by saying: "Show the person up."

She then seated herself with an air of very imposing dignity in the middle of a large sofa; and in this attitude awaited the entrance of her mysterious visitor.

Mrs. Fitzjames, however, entered her magnificent presence with every appearance of the most perfect ease; and on receiving, in return for her graceful courtesy, a slight movement of the head, which seemed to indicate that she was to place herself on a chair which stood on the opposite side of the table, she obeyed it, and sat down.

"It was in reference to your nephew, Lord Goldstable, that I wished to speak to you, Lady de Paddington," said she, gently and quietly.

"And may I ask to be informed, madam, what it is possible you can have to say to *me* on such a subject?" said the noble and indignant dowager. "And how can all and everything you can say concerning it, justify the language of your note? unless, indeed, it may be that, conscious of the wickedness of which you have been guilty, by enticing this poor weak young man away from his proper friends and connections, you have come here to promise that you will see him no more."

Mrs. Fitzjames smiled, and really looked excessively pretty as she did so.

"No, Lady de Paddington," she replied, "that is not exactly the object of my visit. On the contrary, I am come expressly to inform you—and you are the first person to whom I have considered it as my duty to communicate the fact—that I am about to be married to Lord Goldstable immediately."

"Audacious woman!" screamed Lady de Paddington. "And do you really dream that such a marriage is possible? And not only that, but you have the inconceivable effrontery of coming here to tell me of it, as something greatly to my advantage!"

"I did not mean, Lady de Paddington, that it would be for your advantage that I should marry Lord Goldstable," replied the quiet, self-possessed Mrs. Fitzjames, "though I have great pleasure in thinking that eventually it may turn out to be so. But what I meant in the present instance was, that it might be for your advantage that you should be made aware of the fact that he is about to contract such an alliance."

"Heaven grant me patience!" exclaimed the old lady, passionately. "What do you mean, young woman, by making such an outrageous statement? Are you not aware that Lord Goldstable is on the very eve of marriage with Miss Harrington?"

"I do assure you, madam," replied Mrs. Fitzjames, gently, "I do assure you, that he has already broken off that engagement, at once, and for ever. It will save you much trouble and inconvenience, dear lady, if you will receive this statement as being true—for true it is, you may depend upon it."

"It is very possible he may have told you so, and it is very possible that you may have been fool enough to believe him. But an engagement of this kind, as the infatuated boy will find to his cost, is not so easily got rid of. What does he suppose her family will say to such conduct?"

"He has already the satisfaction of knowing, Lady de Paddington, that the most influential individual of the Harrington family perfectly approves his withdrawing his proposals," returned Mrs. Fitzjames, with the air of a person perfectly well acquainted with all the particulars of the affair of which she was speaking.

"What! the vulgar savage, I suppose, who has possession of the family acres? He is a party in your plot, is he?" returned the old lady, scornfully.

"I have not the slightest acquaintance, Lady de Paddington, with the person to whom you allude; nor have I any reason to believe that he has been made acquainted with Lord Goldstable's engagement to me," replied the widow, with the most philosophical composure of manner, "nor does it appear to me that it can be a matter of any interest to him. That the union which had been proposed between your nephew and his niece was so, can surprise no one; for I know that it is said she will be his heiress. The young lady's family—that

is, her father, I believe,—threatened to bring an action against
poor dear Edward for breach of promise. But old Mr. Harrington appears to be a more reasonable person, and has set
Edward's mind quite at ease on that subject."

Lady de Paddington stared at her, and listened to her with
equal astonishment and indignation. The cool effrontery of
the beautiful widow seemed so completely to pass her comprehension, as to leave her in doubt as to what her actual position was, and how she ought to be treated. After a pause,
which Mrs. Fitzjames interpreted greatly to her own satisfaction, the old lady said, but with considerably less vehemence
of manner :—

"Go on, ma'am, if you please : I beg that I may hear the
whole of your statement."

"You have heard it already, Lady de Paddington," replied
the unblushing widow, in the gentlest and most lady-like
accents imaginable, "and it really will be better for you to
understand at once, that Lord Goldstable and myself are about
to be married, and that you will find it wholly out of your
power to prevent it. You call your nephew a weak young
man ; it is possible he may be so. You have called me an
audacious woman ; this, too, may possibly approach the truth
—that is to say, that it is possible I may be a person, not
easily daunted or turned away from any resolution I may
have formed. If you will add to the information afforded
by these acknowledged facts, a careful consideration of this
document—which is a copy that I have just made of Lord
Goldstable's instructions to his lawyer respecting the settlement he is about to make on me—I think you will no longer
doubt the truth of the statement which I have had the honour
to make to you."

"And if I were to believe it, ma'am?" returned the old
lady, receiving the paper, and frowning very majestically as
she read it by the aid of her spectacles from beginning to
end. "What do you expect me to say to you, even if I do
believe it ?"

"That must depend entirely, madam, upon the degree of
influence which your good sense may have upon your temper,"
replied the impassable widow. "If you permit your sober
judgment to dictate to you, I think that you will very soon
be brought to acknowledge that, even if you had the power of
making Lord Goldstable marry Miss Harrington instead of
marrying me, it would be greatly more for your own interest

that he should become my husband than hers. Examine the question dispassionately, Lady de Paddington," continued the beautiful widow, in the clear, distinct accents of deliberative wisdom, "examine the question dispassionately, and I am greatly mistaken if you do not arrive at the conclusion that it would be much more for your advantage that your nephew should marry me than Miss Harrington. Depend upon it, that the family of Miss Harrington would all claim, and no doubt enjoy, a large share in the profitable and agreeable duty of guiding and influencing a weak, easy-tempered young man, possessed of eighty thousand a-year. I have no family connections of any sort to interfere with that influence, which you might so easily and beneficially exercise. Standing alone in the world as I do, and have done since the death of my ever-lamented husband, Colonel Fitzjames, and almost perfectly a stranger as I am in London, it will be of most material advantage to me, as Lady Goldstable, to have the immense benefit of your Ladyship's countenance, advice, and protection. And I scarcely need point out to you," she added, in a sort of earnest whisper, "that I shall be in a situation to repay, with very solid value, all such support and assistance. Remember, too, while it is yet time, that by attempting to force him into marrying Miss Harrington, you will make your greatly irritated nephew your enemy for life; while by countenancing me, who, in the eye of the world, may seem really benefited by your doing so, you will secure his gratitude and affection to the end of your days. And if, in addition to those considerations, you keep in memory the fact, that you have no power whatever of preventing our marriage, I cannot but think that a little quiet meditation on what I have said, may lead you to change your opinion concerning it."

There was a long pause after the widow reached this point, for she herself very judiciously thought that it would be difficult for her to place the question in a better light; and the dowager also evidently felt, that the arguments to which she had listened, deserved more attention than would be consistent with a very prompt reply.

At length she said, but in a tone considerably different from what she had used before: "Has the original of that letter been sent to Mr. Barlow, Mrs. Fitzjames?"

"Yes, Lady de Paddington. I put it into the post myself as I came hither," she quietly replied. "It was left in my hands for the purpose of inserting the name of the legal gentleman whom I might wish to apppoint to meet Lord Goldstable's man of business, and I have done this. But if your Ladyship has any doubt of the fact, it would be very easy to ascertain it by an application to Mr. Barlow himself."

And then followed another long pause, during which Lady de Paddington sedulously employed herself in wiping the glasses of her spectacles with her pocket-handkerchief, while Mrs. Fitzjames amused herself by arranging the relative positions of her coral bracelets, and her embroidered cuffs."

"It may be admitted, certainly, and I have no intention of denying it, Mrs. Fitzjames," resumed the old lady, at length, "that there is at least the appearance of good sense in much that you have just said; and I will not deny, moreover, that you have on the whole, appeared to behave towards me with very praiseworthy and judicious candour. Neither do I see any objection to my confessing to you, that I think it very possible that you would make a better wife for my poor dear Edward, than that very young, and decidedly very silly girl, Miss Harrington. And, being aware of this, it certainly becomes my duty to weigh the question deliberately, whether it may not, on the whole, be advisable for me to remove the principal objection to your becoming Lady Goldstable, by at once openly showing the world that I, his only near relation, approve and encourage the match."

"Your doing so frankly, openly, and courageously, Lady de Paddington, would deserve, on my part, a very liberal demonstration of gratitude in return; and at once, let me tell you, that I am fully prepared to offer this. Name your own terms, and if they appear to me to be at all reasonable, they shall be complied with. You will perceive by my thus expressing myself, that I am disposed to waive all affectation, and all false delicacy, in this negotiation. It is quite certain that we are about to be very nearly connected; and, in my opinion, we shall both of us be giving the best proof of sound judgment and good sense, by dismissing everything like ceremony and reserve from our intercourse.

"Upon my word, Mrs. Fitzjames, I believe you are right," replied the conquered dowager. "It is impossible not to perceive that you are a person of no ordinary ability, and this is a consideration that is likely to have great weight with me, for I hate fools, and detest nothing so much as being involved in any affair of business with them. Of course you know

that my first object is the poor dear boy's happiness ; but as I
have suffered an immense deal of anxiety about him, and have
always held myself ready to make any sacrifices in the world
in order to secure to him the advantages of good society, to
which, as you must be aware, his rustic bringing-up has
hitherto been a great impediment—I confess I feel that I have
a right to look for some advantages in return. My jointure
is a shamefully small one, Mrs. Fitzjames, and I really think
that, as his nearest relation, I have some claim to assistance
from his noble revenue."

" I was fully aware, my dear madam, that your jointure
was much less than it ought to have been," replied the widow,
with a business-like air, which showed her to be perfectly
au fait of the subject before them. "And it was in consequence of this, that the obvious advantages of a clear understanding between us become so apparent to me. The fact is,
Lady de Paddington, that we can be mutually useful to each
other, and I believe it is equally a fact, that we are neither of
us so deficient in common sense, as not to make use of this
common stock of utility."

" You are quite right, Mrs. Fitzjames, in your estimate of
my understanding, and I therefore flatter myself, that you
will be equally so in your estimate of my heart. It is a truly
affectionate one, I do assure you, and nothing but my belief
in the strength of dear Edward's love for you, could induce
me to act as I now intend to do."

" Mrs. Fitzjames really was a very clever, sharp-witted
woman ; she perfectly understood the character of the highly
respectable old lady she had to deal with, and was a good deal
amused at her highly respectable mode of doing business.
She had been all her life accustomed to see iniquities of all
sorts openly proposed, and openly assented to ; but she found
that in the superior circle within which she now hoped to
enter, there was so strong a sense of propriety existing, as to
render it necessary that the *tête-à-tête* plotting of two confidential compeers should be decorated with a little hypocrisy.
It was clearly evident that Lady de Paddington was so much
used to humbug, that she could not do without it ; and
the less respectable sinner laughed in her sleeve at the
weakness, but immediately complied with this decorous demand for drapery by replying with admirable aptitude of
manner :—

" Indeed, indeed, Lady de Paddington, I would not under-

take this grave responsibility did I not think that I should
be able to make our dear Edward happy. I shall, believe
me, enter on this solemn engagement with the most earnest
desire to fulfil all the duties of a good and affectionate
wife."

"This ought to satisfy me, my dear Mrs. Fitzjames; and
under the full persuasion that this solemn promise will be
kept, I frankly promise you my countenance and assistance.
I certainly had been much prejudiced against you, and it was
under the persuasion that you were a very different person
from what I now find you, that I so strongly opposed your
union with my nephew. But your admirably frank and loyal
manner, and conduct, have completely disarmed me. And
now tell me, my dear, do you know anything of Lord Goldstable's present movements?"

"Oh yes, my dear lady," replied the beautiful widow, with
a look of pretty innocent confidence. "Edward sets off the
day after to-morrow to Brandon Abbey. He has invited that
very eccentric old gentleman, Mr. Walter Harrington, to go
down there with him, and the odd old man has agreed to do so,
though dear Edward told him explicitly that he had no intention whatever of marrying his niece. And this strange arrangement has suggested to me a plan which I should like to submit to your judgment. The fact is, dear Lady de Paddington,
that though this whimsical old man has decidedly done me
an acceptable service by persuading Edward to break through
his entanglement with Miss Harrington, I by no means wish
that my dear innocent-hearted Edward should be left altogether in his hands. I will confess to you, that I have an
instinctive dislike to that old man, amounting almost to
antipathy. And, in short, I shall not be easy in my mind,
unless I can contrive to be near enough to counteract his
influence."

"You are quite right, my dear—quite right," replied the
dowager, knitting her brows with an expression which showed
her to be very much in earnest. "There is something about
that Mr. Walter Harrington which inspires me with fear
whenever I approach him, as if I were coming within reach
of some noxious animal. I am extremely sorry to hear of
Edward's becoming intimate with him."

"Well then, dear lady, listen to my little scheme, which,
as I flatter myself, will effectually prevent his doing your dear
nephew any permanent injury. Your Ladyship has doubtless

heard of the new water-cure establishment that has been so much talked of lately at Doucham? Well, Doucham is only three miles distant from Brandon. Now it strikes me, that if you and I, my dear lady, were to make a little excursion to Doucham for the sake of your health, we should be quite near enough to watch over the interest and happiness of our dear Edward. It is a very healthy and very beautiful place, and the excursion might really do you good, my dear Lady de Paddington, even if you did not put yourself into the hands of the professor."

"Oh! as to that, I should as soon think of being tied, neck and heels, like a blind puppy, humanely prepared for drowning. But that would not signify a farthing. Wherever a great many people go, a great many more people will be sure to follow them. It is the fashion, you know, among all people of distinction to do so. But there is one great objection, Mrs. Fitzjames, and one which must prevent me from agreeing to the plan, though I will not deny that it has a good deal to recommend it. I have heard that Doucham is a very dear place, and the fact is, that I cannot afford such an excursion."

"On this occasion," replied Mrs. Fitzjames, eagerly, "your Ladyship must forgive me if I take the liberty of saying that if my proposal is acted upon, it can only be upon one condition—namely, that you should consider yourself as my guest from the moment you quit the door of your own mansion till you return to it. It is impossible that I can consent to go on any other terms. Is it not to secure the happiness of my life, that this journey will be undertaken? And will not the obligation you will confer on me be of the most important kind? Besides," added the clever creature, with a sweet smile, "the relative positions we are about to stand in to each other, my dearest lady, will often make our purse a common one, so it will be surely best for us to put aside all idle scruples at once."

It would have been evident to a much less acute observer than the wily widow, Fitzjames, that this last hit had decided the victory in her favour. In fact, the temptation she now held out would have proved irresistible to the needy and penurious old dowager, even if the scheme itself had been disagreeable to her; but this was very far from being the case. She paused only long enough to perform a most benignant smile, which acted upon her visage like the drawing up of a curtain upon the stage, displaying a complete change of scenery and decorations.

"Indeed, my dear Mrs. Fitzjames," she replied, in the most friendly tone imaginable," your plan is much too agreeable a one for me to object to adopting it. And, moreover, it is perfectly true that, under the circumstances, our presence near Brandon Abbey, may be of the most important service to our poor dear Edward. I will, therefore, go with you to Doucham with great pleasure. When do you think, my dear lady, that we ought to start?"

"As soon after he leaves London as possible," answered the active widow with great promptitude. "Suppose we say Monday next, my dear Lady de Paddington? I know that he goes on Saturday."

"With all my heart, my dear. So be it then. On Monday morning I shall be quite ready for you. I suppose you will be able to call for me, that we may drive to the railroad station together?"

"Oh, yes, dearest Lady de Paddington. It is now, as it ever will be, equally my duty and my pleasure to wait upon you."

"You are a very charming young woman, Mrs. Fitzjames; I promise you that I can see that as plainly as my nephew," returned the old lady, shaking hands with her very cordially. "On Monday morning then, at about ten o'clock I shall expect you. The half-past ten will be the train for us, I think."

"Exactly," replied the fair Sophia. "And now, dear lady, I will leave you, infinitely happier, as you will readily believe, than before I had the happiness of knowing you as I do now. Such a noble heart as yours, Lady de Paddington, must be thoroughly studied, in order to be properly appreciated."

"God bless you, my dear child! Good-bye," returned her Ladyship. "Take care of yourself. I really doubt if all England could furnish a wife that I should more cordially approve for my dear Edward."

The state of mind in which the beautiful widow walked back to her lodgings in Jermyn Street, after her perilous interview had reached this happy conclusion, might be easily described, but it may also be easily imagined, and therefore we will leave her for the present—not without mentioning, however, that the half of poor Lord Goldstable's tender effusion was faithfully delivered to her on the morrow by her "honour-bright" friend, Captain Fowler; and the flattering persuasion that her sudden withdrawal from London would effectually puzzle him as to her whereabouts, made his visit upon this occasion as every way agreeable as his last appearance before her had been the reverse.

CHAPTER XXIX.

WHEN Walter Harrington returned to Vale Street after his visit to Lord Goldstable, he found his nephew Henry waiting to see him. The venerable traveller had been too early for him in the morning, but the servant who admitted the active old gentleman on his return, told him that his nephew had inquired for him at least a dozen times since ten o'clock.

"What is it, Harry, my boy?" said the cheerful old man, as his nephew entered his attic *sanctum*. "There is nothing the matter, I hope. You have been waiting to see me all the morning, Robert says."

"If you are at leisure, my dear uncle," replied the young man, "I must have a long talk with you upon an important subject, but far from a pleasant one."

"My time is yours, Henry," replied Walter, kindly, "and my services, also, if the disagreeables you mention admit of mending by anything I can do. I hope you have nothing very bad to tell me."

"Why, I am afraid that it is rather a bad business," said the young man, gravely, as he seated himself opposite to his uncle. "It is about Caldwell, Sir, that I wanted to speak to you. I greatly fear that he is not what we have supposed him to be; and I more than fear that if my suspicions are well-founded, and if, indeed, he proves to be unworthy, it will be a tremendously heavy blow to our poor dear Kate."

"Proved unworthy?" said the old man, with a greatly altered countenance. "Be careful what you listen to,

15

nephew Harry! Be careful not to do an honourable man
injustice by believing slanders. I tell you fairly, that it will
be no easy matter to make me believe that Frank Caldwell is
unworthy. I have seen more of him, Harry, than you have,
and I think I know him. Yes, my young Sir, I think I
know him. Nay, at this very moment, before listening to any
of your reasons for judging otherwise, I shall be ready to hold
a heavy wager that you have been somehow or other led
into an error, and that Frank Caldwell will eventually prove
to be all that I think him."

"Heaven grant you may be right, my dear uncle," replied
young Harrington. "I should confess my blunder with a
feeling more like triumph than defeat, for I most sincerely
liked and esteemed the man, and thought him in every way
suited to Kate, and likely to make her happy; but if all I
have to tell you be not a dream, I shall no longer be able to
deny that even that gilded oaf, Lord Goldstable, would be a
more desirable match for her than Caldwell."

"Tell me at once, then! Tell me everything," said the
old man, impatiently. "What are your reasons, Harry, for
thinking thus? At any rate, we will put our heads together,
and sift the matter to the bottom, before we finally decide
upon preferring Lord Goldstable to Frank Caldwell."

"I grieve to say," replied the young man, "that my
suspicions rest not upon hearsay evidence, but upon what I
have myself seen. Now listen to me, Uncle Walter, and
judge for yourself. I was induced last night to accompany a
college friend of mine—who, by the way, I sadly fear, is
going the shortest and fastest road to ruin—to a low hell in
Aylesbury Street. I will not say that I never flung away a
guinea in such a hole myself; but I assure you that last night
I went solely with a view of endeavouring to check poor
Saunderson, who was rather more than half intoxicated when
I got hold of him, and whom I would fain have dissuaded
from going if I could. Well, we were in an outer room,
where they were playing chicken-hazard, and from which we
could see the crowd of *rouge et noir* players around the table
in the inner *sanctum* or rather *profanum*, I suppose I should
say. Well, my dear Sir, we had been in this abominable den
some time, and I was doing my utmost to persuade Saunderson
to cheat the devil and come away with me, when a sudden
dispute in the inner room caused a movement among the
players. This attracted my attention, and I made a step

forward to look in amougst them, when whom should I see
amongst the loudest and most excited of the disputants but
Frank Caldwell! I cau assure you, that I could not and would
not very easily believe my own eyes, and would fain have
made up my mind to disbelieve them ; but then came the
additional evidence of my ears, for as the altercation grew
louder and more vehement, the name of Caldwell was more
than once pronounced with most unmistakable distinctness.
No! Uncle Walter—there was no mistake about it. There
was the man whom we had believed to be so extra-fastidious
in all the niceties of honour, so elevated iu all his notions, so
superior, so refiued in all his tastes and pursuits, there he
was, brawling away among the lowest *habitués* of a low
gaming-house! Hang the fellow! if he had been a frauk
rake, there might be hope for him. Wild oats may be sown,
and done with. Charles Surface might contain the material
of an honest man in him ; but Joseph never! Thiuk of the
deceitfulness and hypocrisy of the scamp ! "

Aud Henry Harrington sprung from his chair and paced
the room with houest, but very painful indiguatiou.

" Did he see you, Henry ? " inquired his uncle.

' No, Sir, he did not," replied the young man; " nor did I
give any iudication of having seen him. What use would
there have been iu doing so ? "

" Perhaps not," rejoined the old gentleman, musingly.
" But that was not what I was thinking of, Harry. I was
thinking that if he had seen you, he might have drawn the
same conclusions respecting you, that you have so naturally
done respecting him ; and if he had, he would, thank God,
have been mistaken, Harry. How do we know that he
might not have been able to give as good a reason for being
there as you have done ? "

" Impossible ! " returned Henry. " You forget, my dear
Sir, that Caldwell was not a looker-on, but hotly engaged
in the game, and hotly engaged, too, iu a brawling altercation
arising out of it! No, my dear uncle, there can be no second
opinion on this point. The man I saw was a vulgar, desperate
gambler, and I believe from the tone of his voice, that he
was half-drunk into the bargain."

" I still do not think the evidence sufficient to convict,"
replied Walter, " though abundantly sufficient to justify,
nay, to necessitate further and very strict inquiry. It is still
possible, in my opinion, that a man may be betrayed into

15—2

going to such a place, and even playing and getting into a passion there, without being, or deserving to be, classed either as an habitual gambler, or an habitual brawler. And if you are right in believing him to have been tipsy, the chances in favour of the whole thing being accidental are greatly increased. No, Henry; I won't give him up yet."

"Yes, Sir, it is possible," replied his nephew, thoughtfully, " though, alas! I assuredly feel that it is not probable. My own conviction is, that the man I saw there, and heard addressed as Caldwell, was a familiar visitor at the place, and was talking to, and disputing with, persons whom he knew and who knew him. It is impossible for me to communicate to you this conviction of mine. Nothing save being a witness to the scene could give this conviction. Yet this is exactly the point which it is most important to ascertain. Was Frank Caldwell in the Aylesbury Street hell last night for the first time ? If this can be proved, I can very readily believe that it will have been for the last also. And this is the question, Uncle Walter, upon which I must satisfy myself to-night, if possible. I will go again to the same house. If it be as I suppose, I shall, in all probability, again find my gentleman there ; and if not, I shall have little difficulty in getting some of the frequenters of the place to speak on the subject of the row that I witnessed last night, and shall then easily learn whether the person who appeared to be chiefly concerned in it, is well-known there or only an accidental visitor."

" I warned you at first, Henry, that you would find it difficult to shake my good opinion of a man whom I have known as I have Caldwell," returned Walter. " And you must excuse me, if I still say that I am not convinced—nay, to tell you the truth, I am not quite sure that I should be, even if your second report appeared to corroborate the first. There are so many sources of error ! "

" I'll tell you what, uncle," cried Henry, eagerly, " by far the best and wisest plan would be for you to go with me yourself. It would decidedly be the most satisfactory course in every point of view. You will then estimate whatever evidence we may be able to obtain for yourself far more justly than you could from any report of mine. What say you, Sir ? Have you any engagement for to-night ?"

" None, I believe, Henry," replied the old man. " But don't you think that I shall look somewhat out of place there, eh ? Will not the entrance of such a grave and reverend senior as your old uncle be apt to cause rather a sensation, and occasion a degree of observation more flattering than acceptable? I take it, that silvery locks like mine do not much congregate around that board of green cloth, eh, Harry? Old age, I am afraid you may have there, worse luck! but such a head of hair as this does not grow by gas-light, I suspect; nor on the top of fevered brains."

"Perhaps not, uncle," replied young Harrington, smiling, "but, nevertheless, you may safely come without fearing any special demonstration of reverence from the votaries of the play demon. Every man there at least, if nowhere else in the world, minds his own business, and takes wondrously little heed of his neighbours. I believe that if the Archbishop of Canterbury were to make his appearance among them in full canonicals, the apparition would not interrupt the monotonous and inevitable 'Make your game, gentlemen,' 'The game is made.' Come, in short, in any form, save that of a policeman, and none will trouble their heads about you."

"If such be the case, Harry," replied the veteran, "I will accept your proposition, and add a London gaming-house to the long list of queer places that I have visited in my time. At what hour ought we to go?"

"At any time after midnight," replied the young man. "These haunts are rarely, I believe, in full operation before. We may leave this house about twelve."

"So be it," said Walter; "and most earnestly do I hope that we may not find what we go to look for. It makes my heart ache to think of the misery which his unworthiness would cause to my dear Kate. She loves him so truly, so devotedly."

"Heaven grant that I may have blundered!" replied Henry, and so saying, he left the warm-hearted old man, with far from agreeable meditations, in the uninterrupted possession of his lofty retreat.

CHAPTER XXX.

It was very punctually a little after twelve o'clock that the uncle and nephew started together, according to their appointment, and took their way to Aylesbury Street, a locality sufficiently notorious as the haunt of a number of those unclean beasts of prey, whose existence is the opprobrium and reproach of our boasted police.

"'Tis said, and I believe the tale," that in the huge world of London there are a vast variety of different districts devoted, as it were, to various specialities. Commerce, law, literature, fashion, all have their well-known haunts. Vice, too, has hers. Vulgar crime has its well-marked lairs, branded and proclaimed to all the world; but, though more aristocratic, sin has also its favourite and peculiar quarters, its geography is less publicly laid down. There is, moreover, as the learned in such matters declare, a very curious district in the vast Babylon where, though it is by no means the region of wealthy ease, the business of life begins at a much later hour of the day, and is continued to a much later hour of the night than elsewhere. It is a district where certain trades, seemingly innocent enough in other localities, are said to be not altogether reputable callings, and where it is avowed more emphatically than in any other civilized region, that no man knows how his neighbour lives. Moreover, whatever may be the cause of the coincidence, beards and moustaches are more commonly seen there than in any other part of the metropolis. It was by a short cut towards this quarter that Henry Harrington now led the steps of his venerable uncle.

Few men, however, who had seen the pair stepping out smartly and firmly, arm-in-arm, would have guessed that there was some fifty years of difference in their ages; and fewer still, could they have rightly read the thoughts and feelings which were passing through the minds of each, would have rightly guessed which was the old man and which the young one. Henry Harrington was most deeply and sincerely interested in the great object of their expedition, but the scene itself which he was about to visit had neither novelty nor interest of any kind left for him. It was all "*connu, connu.*"

But Walter had never, in the whole course of his long life, seen anything of the sort before ; and no young lad, in life's freshest morning, could have felt a keener interest, or more exciting curiosity in the scene he was about to visit.

He asked Henry a thousand questions as they walked towards it : and by the time they reached their destination had worked up his imagination to the utmost, by figuring to himself all the various and strongly-marked manifestations of human passion which he was about to witness.

When they arrived in Aylesbury Street, it was near one. The Cerberus who guarded the approach to this earthly hell made no difficulty about admitting them, being probably propitiated by some open-sesame sort of sop, of which Henry Harrington administered the needful potion ; and having entered unchallenged, Walter followed his nephew to the second floor.

The two first rooms were brilliantly lighted, and thronged with players thickly grouped around the respective tables. The third room contained a variety of refreshments.

Their entrance was as unnoticed as Henry had predicted it would be ; in fact, their approach to the tables did not appear to excite the slightest attention or curiosity in any way. The jingle of cash ; the sharp click of the croupier's rakes, as they gathered in the stakes lost ; and the weary repetition of the ever unchanging formula of the dealers, continued to go on, on, on, without the slightest interruption. Indeed, with the exception of an occasionally short glance from a very un-obtrusive-looking individual, who appeared to be lounging there without any particular object, the new-comers appeared, and in fact really were, totally unnoticed. The short sharp glance was from the eye of the proprietor of the establishment ; but nobody seemed to take any notice of him.

Henry stationed himself and his grey-headed companion close behind the croupier at the table in the outer room ; and while ostensibly occupied in watching the fluctuating chances of the game, they were both anxiously engaged in reconnoitring the features of the players.

The crowded state of the room rendered this a business of some difficulty ; but in about half-an-hour both gentlemen had satisfied themselves that the object of their search was not there. Henry laid his hand upon his uncle's arm and motioned him towards the inner room.

"So far, so good," whispered Walter, as they threaded their way through the crowd.

"Yes," replied his nephew "But remember, that it was in the inner room that I saw him last night."

By the exercise of a little patience, they succeeded in establishing themselves in a similar situation at the second table, where *rouge et noir* was the game played; and again they cautiously commenced an investigation of every face in the room. Gradually they had acquired almost the certainty, that the man they so dreaded to see was not in this room either; and Walter's confidence and hopes were mounting fast, when a sudden burst of loud voices and laughter reached them from the third room—in which were materials for supper, in the proportion of a pennyworth of bread to a terribly abundant supply of sack, in the shape of London-brewed champagne— and caused both the uncle and nephew to continue their examination in that direction.

In the very next moment they saw Caldwell in the doorway, hastily advancing into the playroom with a face flushed with wine, and a step lamentably far from being steady. He paused on the other side of the table, and stood for a minute or two exactly opposite to them, and one would have thought that he must have seen them; but either from intoxication, as it seemed, or else from his eagerness to watch the table, he did not appear to have noticed them.

Walter made an immediate movement to approach him; but his nephew, divining his intention, caught him by the arm, and drew him towards the outer room, whispering as he did so:

"Not now! not here! What use would there be in speaking to him in the state he is now in? Remember, too, where we are! Think of the effect of making a scene here! Look at the people round you!"

"I see, I see! you are right, quite right! Let us get out of this accursed den!" said the old man, dejectedly. "Alas! alas! I have had enough of it. I want to breathe God's atmosphere again, though it be but in the streets of London, instead of this hot, thick breath of hell! Come, Henry! come!"

"One moment's patience, my dear Sir," returned his nephew. "You forget that our painful task is but half done.

Since we have undertaken this most unpleasant business, let us go through with it, and put the matter beyond all possibility of further doubt. Even two nights passed in this abominable place will not, it may be argued, necessarily prove a man to be an utter cast-away. It is still necessary that we should ascertain whether he is known here as an *habitué*."

"True, Henry, true!" said Walter, almost with a groan. "Let us put the finishing stroke to it at once. But where must we seek the information we want?"

"I saw a man in the other room whom I know well enough to speak to. He will, I have no doubt, be able to tell us all we wish to know," replied Henry; and so saying, he steered his way towards a haggard and weary-looking young man, who was leaning against the wall with his arms folded, and seeming to be actually dropping to sleep as he stood.

"What! is that you, Milbury?" said Harrington, touching him on the shoulder. "Why, you really do not look much more amused here, my good fellow, than if you were at home and in bed. You are all but asleep, man."

"Yes," yawned the gambler, "it is such tiring work, always losing, losing, losing, without ever getting a turn of luck!"

"If play can no longer keep you awake, Milbury, I take it you must be used up, old fellow," said Harrington.

"Not a bit of it. That's not it. Try me," replied the hopful youth. "But the fact is, that I am cleared out for to-night, and it is so devilish dull going home so early. You havn't a five-pound note you could lend me, have you? That confounded scamp, Tenbey, does not understand credit, he says. But I suppose you have got nothing left, or you would not be going away so early yourself?"

"I have not been playing at all to-night; I only came to look about me," replied Harrington. "But I say, Milbury, isn't that Caldwell in the next room? He's a Middle Temple man, isn't he? I did not know he was a playing man."

"And I did not know he was a Temple man," replied the other. "What he is after sunrise I neither know nor care. But he's one of the peep-of-day boys here, and would be a very steady player if he did not drink. But poor Caldwell is tipsy half his time."

"Well, good night, I'm off; but here's a couple of yellow boys, Milbury; it is all I have in my pocket, and I wish you good luck with them."

The limed bird, now perfectly awake, returned once again to
the fatal table, and the two Harringtons found their way into
the street as quickly and as quietly as they could.

"And is it possible," cried Walter, with a groan, "is it
possible that this is the man with whom I have so often conversed on all the highest themes that can employ the human
mind? Is it indeed possible that he could be thus engaged,
hour after hour, as the evening stole away, to hasten from such
converse, afterwards, to these accursed orgies? Can it be?
Oh, Harry, Harry! I am more unhappy, more miserable than
I can express to you! Alas! alas! poor Kate!"

"Poor Kate!" echoed her brother, sadly; "I truly pity
her!"

"Poor child! poor loving little heart!" said Walter, almost
with a sob, so vehement was the shock his mind had received.
"But she has escaped a fearful fate!" he added, solemnly: "a
drunken gambler's wife! Thank God, she has escaped it!
But oh, Harry! think of the awful rent made in the whole
structure of one's trust in man! think of the earthquake to
one's whole moral nature! Who can one trust? Who can
one fail to doubt? It is a sad lesson to come upon one at
four-score!"

CHAPTER XXXI.

FOR the first time, during many a year, old Walter Harrington passed a sleepless night, after his excursion to Aylesbury Street. The grief which the painful discovery he had
made occasioned him was indeed profound; and the acuteness
of his distress and disturbance was a striking evidence of the
freshness of the old traveller's mind and feelings.

One deception, and one disappointment the more, can rarely
produce so great an effect on an old man's view of his fellow-
creatures. But it was old Walter's first adventure of the sort.
He now found himself, for the first time in his life, utterly
deceived, and taken in by one whom he had very highly

esteemed, and most implicitly trusted; and his sorrow and disappointment were greatly like those of a quite young man under similar circumstances. He had, in truth, seen wonderfully little of worldly men and their worldly ways in his long and peaceful passage through life; the sort of unnatural hothouse civilization of great cities was, in fact, unknown to him, and he now felt strongly inclined to renounce the race altogether, and fly for solace to the pure companionship of his beloved nature. It was in such thoughts as these that he passed the few, but very heavy hours till it was his usual time to get up for his morning walk.

The fresh morning air of Hyde Park, unpoisoned as yet by its daily potion of smoke, seemed to brace his nerves, and calm his mind, so that by the time he returned to Vale Street to breakfast, he had determined on the course which he thought he ought to pursue. It was clear that under the circumstances, he could no longer for an instant, appear to advocate the pretensions of Caldwell to his niece's hand, and it was certainly due to his brother and sister-in-law that they should at once be made acquainted with the true state of the case.

At this really terrible moment, however, he more than ever rejoiced at having so effectually liberated Kate from the addresses of Lord Goldstable. Had it been otherwise, her difficulties would have been greatly increased, by the weighty arguments which the acknowledged worthlessness of Caldwell would have furnished in favour of his more estimable rival.

It had become quite evident to him, however, from the repeated evasions of both the doctor and Lady Augusta, that it was not intended to let him know where Kate really was. This very disagreeable concealment would he flattered himself cease, of course, as soon as his altered opinion of Caldwell should be avowed; and he hastened to make the painful statement, as he was now more than ever anxious to ascertain the place of Kate's exile, as he particularly wished to be himself the bearer of the news which, he knew would affect her so deeply.

Henry Harrington rarely breakfasted with his family, nor did he make his appearance now, so that the family party consisted only of Lady Augusta, the Doctor, and Walter.

When the breakfast was finished, Walter, who had been unusually silent during the repast, suddenly said:

"Before we separate, brother, I wish to say a few words

on a subject which we all have much at heart, if you and Lady
Augusta can spare me a few moments."

Lady Augusta glanced at her husband and coloured, while
the Doctor fidgetted rather uneasily upon his chair, although
he replied very politely :

" With all my heart, brother ; my time is always yours,
excepting, indeed, when it is forestalled by the laborious
duties and grave responsibilites of my position."

It was very evident that both father and mother expected
that some strong remonstrance, or, perhaps, some gentle threat
respecting the ultimate disposition of the family acres, was
coming, with reference to Kate's present exile, and future
marriage.

" Well then, my dear brother," returned Walter, " to take
up as little of your valuable time as may be, I will tell you
and Lady Augusta in one word, that I no longer wish to see
my niece married to Mr. Caldwell ; but, on the contrary, that
I am as much bent on opposing any such union, as it is possible
that you can be. And, moreover, I wish to assure you, that I
have not the slightest doubt that when Kate hears the reasons
I shall give her for my change of opinion on the subject, she
also will at once and for ever abandon every idea of such a
marriage."

" God be thanked, my dear brother ! " cried the Doctor, fervently. " God be thanked, that your natural good sense has
at last shown you how entirely right Lady Augusta and I
were in this matter. I am, indeed, most truly glad that we
are no longer a house divided against itself on this interesting
subject. Some minds, my dear Walter, are slower in arriving
at truth than others," added the Doctor, in a tone of magisterial philosophy, "although the slower may reach it with
great certainty at last. There are intelligences, brother Walter,
which pierce, as we may say, with one single glance, one single
eagle glance, my dear Walter, to the heart of a subject—
mastering all the bearings of it in a moment, and seizing upon
the truth with an unerring grasp. You may remember that
I was always deemed a quick boy, my dear Walter, and it
may be that the long habit of wielding undisputed authority
in various spheres, may have ripened my faculties, and imparted additional value to my judgment : I merely say that it
may have done so. God only knows what we are ! And his
unerring providence can best select the shoulders capable of
supporting the heavy weight of influence and of power."

" My natural anxiety for my dear child's welfare," said Lady
Augusta, anxious to appropriate her share of the triumph,
" makes me, of course, rejoice to hear that my maternal exertions for her welfare and happiness will no longer be counteracted by the weight of your opinion, my dear Sir.   I trust
that we shall have now no further difficulty in bringing the
poor wrong-headed girl to reason.   At the same time, I cannot
but say, that it is very painful to the feelings of a mother—
and such a mother as I have ever been to her, Mr. Walter
Harrington—to be told that she will yield that obedience to
the authority of an uncle, which she refused to the entreaties
of her mother."

Lady Augusta had not the gift of tears, neither, in truth,
would any such manifestation of tender weakness have been
consistent with the dignified tone of her character ; but there
was, as she was herself fully conscious, a very affecting
expression in her eyes as she raised them to Heaven, slowly
and sadly shaking her head as she did so.

"But you mistake altogether, my dear Madam," cried
Walter, eagerly.   "God forbid that Kate should yield her
own judgment on such a point as this to any authority of
mine !   Believe me I have no intention, no wish to exercise
any—nor even of giving her advice, for I am sure it will not
be needed.   Facts, Lady Augusta, some very painful facts
have, by Henry's assistance, been brought to light respecting
Caldwell ; and these are the stubborn reasoners which will
compel the mind of your daughter to come to the same conclusion that I have done myself—namely, that Caldwell is, in
truth, very far unlike what we believed him to be.   When I
spoke with certainty of her giving him up, I calculated on
my knowledge of her purity of heart, and rectitude of thinking,
and not on any subservience on her part to my wishes, or even
to my judgment."

"That is all very right and proper, perfectly so, my dear
Sir ; but still I cannot help thinking that rectitude, and propriety, and all that sort of thing, are best shown in the conduct of a young lady, by obedience to the will of her parents,"
replied Lady Augusta, with great solemnity.

"But tell me, my dear Walter," cried the Doctor, hastening
to check the eloquence of his lady, which seemed to him, at
this moment, more vehement than judicious ; for he by no
means wished to offend his elder brother, "tell me, what has
led you at last to think of this very presumptuous young man

as he deserves? I always saw through him from the very
first, Walter! You will admit I think, that I showed some
knowledge of character in this, brother? In fact, I saw what
the fellow was at a glance."

"I confess that I did not," replied Walter, humbly. "I
confess that I was most woefully deceived in him. But it is
sufficient that we now agree upon the subject. I never wish
to think of him, nor to hear of him again, if possible."

"Nay, Walter," returned his brother, with a patronizing
air; "I do not think that there is any reason for your feeling
nettled or humiliated at thus finding yourself mistaken. You
really must not suffer any such feeling to make you uncomfortable. Remember that you have not—and indeed few
men have—enjoyed such opportunities of studying all the
varieties of human character, as my distinguished position has
given me. Neither can the same rapidity of intuitive discernment be expected from you. Neither nature, nor education,
my dear Walter, has prepared you for such a task. The good
sense which has at last, though slowly, led your mind to the
conclusion that my opinion was not likely to be erroneous, is
of itself very highly creditable to you."

The elder brother, who was still evidently, in the eyes of
his reverend junior, the naughty boy who would not learn
Greek, received this modicum of approbation very modestly,
and only said in reply: "If I knew where Kate was, I would
myself undertake to communicate to her the change in my
opinion, and give her the reasons which I feel so perfectly
sure will cause her to change hers also."

The Doctor directed a speaking look of inquiry towards his
lady; and seeing plainly that her judgment coincided upon
this important point with his own, ventured, without hesitation, to reply: "Kate is now, I believe, with her brother
James, at Stanton Praya. At least they went there, I believe,
upon their leaving London, and I have no doubt they are there
still. Do you wish to write to her, Walter?"

"I would rather speak to her," replied his brother. "And
if she be really still at Stanton, it will be exceedingly convenient to me, for I have promised Lord Goldstable to go down
with him to Brandon Abbey to-morrow; and Brandon is but
three miles from Stanton, as you must well remember, Henry."

"God bless my soul!" exclaimed the Doctor, not a little
astonished. "I had no idea that you—that is, I mean, that
he—Lord Goldstable is owner of Brandon Abbey, is he? Well,

to be sure, how very strangely things do come to pass! To
think that Brandon Woods, where you and I, Walter, have so
often gone bird-nesting, should come to be—but how did the
property come into the hands of Lord Goldstable?"

"What *can* that signify, Dr. Harrington?" tartly demanded
his practical better half: "and how can a scarcely seemly
allusion to bird-nesting, assist us in examining the important
business before us? I must say, that my brother-in-law has
shown much judgment, and really very great tact, in arranging
this visit exactly at the critical moment when that low young
man's real position became evident to him. It was very
cleverly thought of—quite a master-stroke—and I really
honour him for it."

Again Walter received his laurels very meekly; and having
waited till her ladyship's laudatory harangue was over, he
replied to his brother's question by saying: "The purchase
was made years ago, Henry, when you were the absentee
Rector of Stanton, and I the absentee Squire. And this Lord
Goldstable inherits this property, and a large portion of his
other immense possessions, from the purchaser, who was his
uncle, or cousin, or related to him some way or other. I have
not forgotten, I promise you, our old truant days among those
woods, Henry; and there I was as much your master, as you
were mine in old Ponsonby's school-room. It will be a great
pleasure to me to see those places over again."

"And you start to-morrow?" inquired Lady Augusta,
impatient to bring the conversation back from those unprofitable reminiscences to things of present moment.

"To-morrow morning at eight," answered Walter, "which
was a compromise between the five o'clock start, that I proposed, and the noble young sluggard's eleven."

"Very right, very right!—all very right and proper, my
dear Mr. Harrington. But if you will take my advice, my
dear Sir, you will not try to put the bit in his mouth too much
at first." This was said by Lady Augusta with a greater air
of sisterly confidence, than she had ever used before in addressing her venerable brother-in-law. And she added, in a half
whisper, after a moment's pause: "The great object would be
lost, you know, or at least very much endangered, if he were
to take any dislike to you. You must humour him, my dear
Mr. Harrington—you must humour him, judiciously, and then
we shall have everything in our favour. And I am sure Kate
never ought to forget how much she owes you, my dear Sir."

A great deal of this speech was wholly unintelligible to Walter; but this being the case with much of what fell from Lady Augusta, he had acquired the habit of not listening to her with much attention; and now it was only the last words she had uttered which he perfectly comprehended, and to these he replied by saying: "She has indeed had a narrow escape from the danger of becoming that wretched man's wife!"

"An escape, indeed!" replied the mother, shuddering; "and I trust she will be duly sensible of it! Point out to her my dear Sir, the unremitting anxiety of all her family, your kind self included, for her welfare; and endeavour to make her feel the wickedness and ingratitude of resisting their wishes. And do tell her, my dear Mr. Harrington, to be sure to put a white camilla in her hair when she dresses for dinner. She had one on the night of our ball, and I think it may be important."

"I say, Henry!" suddenly exclaimed Walter, who, during this last harangue, had been indulging his memory by letting it wander back to the scenes of his early youth, "do you remember the old house at Stanton, and those solemn days when we used to pay a grand visit to my uncle? I remember every bit of it, as if it were but yesterday. Tell me, Henry, what sort of fellow is James? Is he like his brother?"

"I am very sorry to say," replied the doctor, solemnly, "that I have of late seen much to reprehend in James's character and conduct. For many years of his life, my son James was really all that I could wish him to be, and never gave me a moment of anxiety or pain. At college he was as regular at morning chapel as the Dean; and I don't think that his name was ever sent up as being out after hours. But latterly, I fear—I very greatly fear—that he has been led widely astray; and many things have been reported to me concerning him, that have pained me greatly."

"It is unusual, too," said Walter, thoughtfully, "for a young man to have passed safely through the temptations of a college life, and then to transgress, in what should seem the much safer position of clergyman in a country parish."

"I can by no means agree with you there, brother Walter," replied the Doctor, knitting his brows into an expression of painful thought. "The isolation of a country parish, where there are no ecclesiastical superiors at hand, is exactly the atmosphere where these grievous divagations are most fre-

quently found. I have been repeatedly told of late that
James has gone to the extent of preaching in his surplice!"

"The lazy dog!" cried Walter, after a short pause, during
which he had been endeavouring to comprehend the nature of
the enormity complained of. "The lazy dog! He will go
to bed in his clothes next, I suppose, to save himself the trouble
of taking them off. I'll give him a *sisserara* for such a trick
as that, you may depend upon it."

The Doctor looked at his brother, much as Mr. Shandy
might have looked at some of Uncle Toby's hopeless manifestations of simplicity; but he very wisely abstained from
what he justly considered would be a hopeless attempt to
initiate him into the mysteries of that curious *ism*, which is
the most recent thorn in Mother Church's vexed side, and
which seems to consist in the power of distilling a heterodox
spirit from the sinews of a too vigorous orthodoxy; for the
Doctor judiciously remembered that Walter's notions of English
parsons, and their affairs, were what they had been sixty
years since, in the old-fashioned days, when every man of
them did his "duty," or it might be the duties, as the case
might be, and eat his tithes in peace.

Perhaps some thoughts of these peaceful days passed over
the Doctor's mind as he remembered this, for he sighed as he
ended the conversation by saying:

"Well, brother, I hope you will enjoy your trip; and
perhaps you will give us a line to say how you find all things
at the dear old place. But now I must leave you, and attend
to my necessary toil in my study."

"And I must go and purchase one or two little feminine
articles, which perhaps you will kindly take down to Kate for
me, my dear Sir?"

"And I," said Walter, "will go and toss the things I shall
want into my portmanteau, where I shall have abundant space,
my dear Madam, for anything you may wish to send to Kate."

CHAPTER XXXII.

AND now it is high time to say something of my gentle
heroine, whom we have too long lost sight of. She herself
knew nothing whatever in her distant banishment, of the circumstances which took place after her departure from London,
and little guessed how much had occurred there, of the deepest
importance to her present happiness and her future destiny.
But though this ignorance certainly spared her much anxiety,
there was little or nothing in the asylum thus chosen for her,
calculated either to amuse or soothe her mind under all the
doubt and anxiety concerning the future which she had carried
away with her.

In truth, her brother James's house was little calculated to
make a pleasant home for anybody, at any time ; nor was its
usual routine rendered at all more agreeable by the presence
there of her aunt, the Lady Juliana. That very devout single
lady had all through her life been conscious of a special aptitude
and vocation to rule and hold authority over some one. But
untoward destiny had hitherto frustrated the gifts of nature,
and repressed very harshly the development of her govern-
mental capabilities. Her residence in the house of her brother-
in-law had, in fact, effectually prevented her from exercising
rule or authority of any kind, over even the most humble of
her species. For not only the Doctor, but his lady too, had
also a pretty talent for governing, so that Lady Juliana's
gift in that line had been hitherto of little or no use to her
fellow-creatures.

It was now, therefore, for the first time in her life, that she
had felt the glory and delight of being intrusted with power
to rule the acts of another ; and she set about performing her
task, not only with hearty good-will, but with a decided
determination of making the most of it.

It is not very extraordinary, perhaps, that she should have
displayed, under these circumstances, a little of the wanton-
ness of power, as well as the consciousness of it. Be this as it
may, it certainly seemed that whatever poor Kate did, had
better have been left undone, and that whatever she omitted
to do, was precisely the only thing that her aunt Lady Juliana

could have entirely approved. The most trivial actions of every hour, appeared of sufficient importance in the eyes of her guardian and monitress to call for special observation and special censure.

This active performance of the important duties confided to her by her sister, began the very moment they entered the carriage which conveyed them to the railroad station, continued with unrelaxed activity during every mile of their transit to the Brandon station, ceased not for an instant during the short interval between that station and the parsonage at Stanton; and was now occupying her every moment, save when she was actually asleep, or when some happy chance removed the poor girl for a short interval beyond the reach of her eyes and her voice.

On entering the usual sitting-room the morning after their arrival, Lady Juliana found Kate seated at the window, gazing listlessly out upon the little flower-garden, while her thoughts were busy enough far away.

This was under any circumstances, a sin in the estimation of the conscientious Lady Juliana, and she began her attack upon it with a groan.

"It is very grievous, Kate," she then proceeded to say, "to find that all the good advice I gave you, when we were coming in the post-chaise from the station, has been so utterly and entirely thrown away. Never, I think, was good seed sown with so small a return. But, thank God, I can truly say I have done my duty; and by His grace, I will continue to do so unto the end. How strongly did I then set before you the guilt of yielding to the desperate sin of idleness! Yet here I see you, on the very first day afterwards, sitting with your eyes wandering about, just as if you did not know that God had given you the blessed gift of sight in order that you might use it in His service. It is this sin of idleness, that is the great and always successful snare of the enemy."

"Had you entered the room a minute or two ago, aunt, you would have found me occupied in reading. But my thoughts wandered irresistibly from my book. I assure you, that I am fully aware of the sin of idleness, and rarely fail to find some useful occupation for my time; but—"

"Oh, Kate! Kate! I tremble as I listen to you. How surely are the elect marked, as with a seal, which will for ever and for ever prevent the worldly-minded from being confounded with them. And how clearly does every word you

16—2

utter proclaim the melancholy fact, that as yet you are wholly
and altogether unreclaimed."

"My dear aunt, you mistake me greatly, if you think—"

"Think? Do I not hear you talk of rarely failing to find
useful occupation? Why should you ever fail? Is there not
the occupation of prayer? Kneel down, Kate! kneel down
this very moment, and pray to be enlightened with the gift of
saving grace. Kneel down, Kate!"

But to this sort of impious mummery, Kate would not submit; and then the indignant aunt appealed to her nephew
James, who at that moment entered the room, upon the obstinate
impiety of his sister, in refusing to comply with a command
which ought at all times to be welcomed with thankfulness.
But the Reverend James knit his brows in very evident displeasure, as he replied, that he was not aware that the Church
had provided any office for such an occasion. He added nevertheless, after a moment of grave consideration, that the
penitential psalms, indeed, are always ready, and always
adapted to every imaginable case of sin.

In his heart, however, James was far more inclined to take
part with Kate than with his aunt, for the unecclesiastical
piety of Lady Juliana was especially distasteful to him;
and, in fact, he would greatly have preferred the flighty
language of the most careless man of the world on serious
subjects, to Lady Juliana's constant reference to "religion,"
without mixing with it the slightest allusion to "the
Church."

In fact, the most peaceful moments that Kate enjoyed during
the first two days of her enforced visit to Stanton Rectory,
were due to the frequent little tilts and tournaments which
were going on between her brother and her aunt.

But while wishing for peace, poor girl, she made a terrible
blunder when, from a good-natured wish to please her brother,
she volunteered the use of her needle to embroider an altar-
cover for his church. This proposal was occasioned by his
lamentations over the great deficiencies in his parish in all
such matters, to which he had contrived to make her listen
before she had been many hours under his roof; the proposal
was hastily made, but still more hastily repented; for the
lady-aunt happening to enter the room just at the moment
that the well-pleased Rector was describing to his sister
the style of decoration he desired, she poured forth such
a copious phial of holy wrath against idolatry, popery, false

shepherds, and blind leaders of the blind, that the really terrified Kate most heartily repented her indiscretion.

But notwithstanding this vehement religious schism between her brother and aunt, it would have been quite impossible for any two people to have been more perfectly in accord upon the subject of Lord Goldstable's proposal of marriage to her than they were. For the Reverend James was by no means a man likely to be insensible to the advantages of being brother-in-law to a nobleman possessed of eighty thousand a-year, and patron of more than one good living.

A strong proof of his feelings on this subject, was given to Lady Juliana the next morning but one after their arrival at the Rectory.

The post-bag was, as usual, put into the hands of the Rector; and, standing apart at a window, while he unlocked it, and examined its contents, he perceived that there was a letter addressed to his sister. It immediately struck him, that this letter might probably be from Caldwell, whom he had already been taught to understand was the *bête noire* of the family clique, established to keep guard over Kate during this perilous period of her existence.

No sooner had this idea occurred to him, than he decided upon retaining the letter till he had held a consultation with the Lady Juliana upon the propriety of delivering it at all. He waited till the poor, unsuspicious Kate had left the room, and then approaching the Lady Juliana, with the letter in his hand, he said: "Just look at this letter, aunt, and tell me if you know the handwriting."

"I am almost sure, James, that it is the handwriting of Mr. Walter Harrington," she replied, after giving the letter as careful an examination as it was possible to do without breaking the seal. "How can he have found out where Kate is?" she added, with surprise in every feature. "You know, James, that one of your mother's principal objects in sending her out of town, was to remove her from the very pernicious influence of your Uncle Walter's principles and advice."

"Exactly so," replied James, eagerly, "and it therefore appears to me very doubtful whether we should not do wrong in letting Kate have this letter at all."

"But how can we prevent it, James? You see he has found out her address, and actually written to her."

"And do letters never miscarry?" returned the Rector. "For my part, I think it may be very important to the object we have in view, that Kate shall not receive that letter from my uncle."

"But don't you think, James, that it might be wrong, perhaps, to suppress the letter altogether?" suggested her Ladyship, hesitatingly.

"No, my dear aunt, for *me* to do it, not at all wrong. This idea of yours results from the pernicious and very dangerous practice of suffering the laity to erect themselves into judges in cases of conscience. In better and more religious days, Lady Juliana, all doubts on such points were referred to the spiritual adviser, who alone is competent and lawfully qualified to solve them with a degree of authority which may be satisfactory to the most scrupulous and timid mind. In the present instance, I have no hesitation whatever in saying, that the object in view, which is the support of parental authority, and with the ultimate hope of securing the happiness of a thoughtless young girl, perfectly incompetent to judge for herself, with such an object in view, I have not the slightest hesitation in saying that we are fully justified in retaining a letter which might do so much mischief from reaching its destination." With these words, the reverend casuist took the letter in his hand, and paused for a moment ere he added: "It will, however, be our duty I think to ascertain the contents of this paper before we destroy it. There is something painful, certainly, in breaking the seal of a letter addressed to another, even though that other is in a state of pupilage. I confess that I am conscious of a disagreeable feeling in doing it; but it must be done, because it is a duty, and it is one that may, and must often devolve upon those who have the charge of young people, and it is one from which we certainly ought not to shrink on the present occasion."

"If you think it right to open it, James, and read the contents, of course you had better do so. It is not necessary for me to meddle in the matter at all," said Lady Juliana, well pleased to have her curiosity gratified at the charge of another person's responsibility.

James, accordingly, with an air of great dignity and discretion, then broke the seal, and read as follows :—

"MY DEAREST KATE,

"I have this instant learned from your father, that you are at Stanton; and I write this hurried line merely to say, that I hope the day after it reaches you, to enjoy the same good fortune myself. I do not propose, however, to make any demand on James's hospitality on this occasion, nor shall I dispute the possession of my own old manor-house with the rats and mice, as I shall be staying at the house of a friend in the neighbourhood. I have scribbled this merely that you may not be too much surprised when I make my appearance. With kind regards to Lady Juliana and my unknown nephew, believe me, my dear child, most affectionately yours,

" WALTER HARRINGTON."

The aunt and the nephew looked rather blankly at each other, after the perusal of this very simple document, and they would both of them, probably, have been very glad had the seal been still unbroken ; for notwithstanding the undoubted fact that letters do sometimes miscarry, there would be something awkward in Mr. Harrington's finding on the morrow that his letter had not been received; nor would the matter be rendered more easy by the necessity of their assuming an appearance of great surprise themselves, at his arrival. Moreover, James felt considerable fear lest his aunt's discretion should not stand the severe trial which thus awaited it, for which fear he had certainly sufficient cause from her present demeanour; for she already began to fidget, and colour violently, under the consciousness of the act she had sanctioned; nor did she fail to remind her uncomfortable-looking nephew that she had said she would have nothing to do with it.

They both felt, however, that the deed was done, and all that was left them in their distress was the recollection, that if they faithfully kept their own secret, there was nobody else who could betray it. So the letter was immediately destroyed, and the noble aunt and reverend nephew, having agreed to forget all about it as soon as possible, began to discuss the very puzzling question, as to where it could be that Mr. Harrington had resolved upon taking up his residence.

The only gentleman's house in the little village itself, with the exception of the unoccupied old manor-house, or indeed in the immediate neighbourhood, was the dwelling inhabited by a Mrs. Cross, the widow of the late incumbent of a neighbouring parish, and her daughter. Now, it is very possible, that as the departed Mr. Cross had held his living for many years, his widow might have been an old acquaintance of Walter's ; and though it certainly seemed rather strange that he should prefer going to her house, instead of coming to that of his nephew, they soon came to the conclusion that it was there he was going.

"If we are right in our guess, James, Mrs. Cross will be sure to tell me that she is expecting him, if I walk over and pay her a visit. And then, you know, there will be no need of—of—of our seeming to be surprised, you know, and all that awkward sort of thing, when he comes over to call here."

"Yes! that is very true. And you can certainly go to call on Mrs. Cross, aunt, if you like it. Only take care that you do not tell *her*, instead of letting her tell *you*. That would be a terrible mistake, you know; so pray, be careful. It must be almost time for me to be off to church. But I daresay now, Aunt Juliana, that you did not even know that it was a red letter day?"

Lady Juliana looked for a moment as if she was in great danger of becoming sick or faint; an effect which every allusion to what she called Popish observances, was very apt to produce upon her. She rallied, however, sufficiently to put on her bonnet and shawl, and to set off resolutely and alone to visit her old acquaintance, Mrs. Cross; while the reverend James proceeded to recite, as pompously and unintelligibly as he could, the service of the day to his clerk, and about half a dozen old pensioners, who depended greatly upon donations from the hand of their priest from the parish oblations, for their snuff or their tea.

CHAPTER XXXIII.

Mrs. Cross's dwelling was a very picturesque sort of cottage. It was not a cottage *ornée*, which means the species of residence that has been described as the fitting abode for the devil's darling vice, "the pride that apes humility;" but it was an ornamented cottage, that is to say, a *real* cottage, which by means of a little expense, and a good deal of taste, had been cleverly converted into a pretty and comfortable dwelling for a ladylike mother and her daughter. There was certainly a little affectation in the name which Mrs. Cross had given to this snug little residence, for she called it "The Widow's Rest;" but, excepting in the name, there was no affectation of any kind about the cottage; it looked like the dwelling of nice, respectable people—and the in-dwellers there were nice, respectable people. The departed Mr. Cross had been a very low-church clergyman, in the days when Calvinism, in its most offensive form, was much more frequently found in our country churches than it is at present. Predestination, election, and reprobation, were the cardinal points of his creed, and these were the features in God's government of the world, on which he best loved to dwell. For the rest, he had been as good a man as it was well possible for any man to be, holding such tenets. But it is difficult to keep the heart widely open to all gentle charities, and awake to all kindly sympathies, when the mind is firmly persuaded that nineteen-twentieths of our fellow-creatures are doomed by unerring justice to eternal torture; and the late Mr. Cross would have felt any denial of this doctrine, to partake of the nature of personal offence to himself, as well as being a deadly sin of the very highest degree, and worst quality.

His good little widow, who had always looked up with exceeding reverence to her husband, as the best, the wisest, and especially the most learned of men, held fast to his doctrine, both as the sole anchor of salvation in the world to come, and as a sort of dignified reminiscence of the proudest days of her life, in the world that was. As the widow of so very learned a divine, she felt that she did herself honour by holding fast to the doctrines which he had taught, although they were no longer very common among those around her; but she seemed to consider these extreme opinions as a work of caste, and at the same time as a very sacred deposit from her departed spouse.

The doctrines of her terrible faith, however, influenced very slightly her individual feelings towards her fellow-creatures. Her woman's heart was too warm, and her woman's head too weak, to permit of her establishing any logical or consistent relation between her principles and her practice. She would have tenderly watched the sick bed, and gently soothed the last moments of those whom her theological self firmly believed were passing from their death bed to eternal fire; nor did she make the least scruple of enjoying a cheerful cup of tea with unregenerate wretches, whom the fore purpose of God had doomed to inevitable perdition from the beginning of the world.

This well-meaning and truly kind-hearted little woman had one only child—a daughter—who had already reached twenty-five years of age. She was tall and well made, and called extremely handsome by those who admire a full development; those who find beauty only in more fragile grace might be inclined to apply to her the disagreeable epithets of "stout," and "coarse;" but for all that, Olivia Cross was a very handsome girl. She had large and very brilliant dark eyes; she had a remarkable abundance of long, thick, but rather coarse black hair, and she had a magnificent set of large, beautifully white teeth, which were fully exhibited between coral lips, of by no means dimutive dimensions.

The *morale* of Miss Cross corresponded very accurately to the style of the *physique*. Her whole nature was vigorous and powerful; her opinions, feelings, passions, were all strong; nor was her intellect weak, though energy, rather than discipline, was the characteristic of her mind; and a very defective education had permitted all her vigorous nature to develop itself as best it might in the tumultuous and confused manner, which in strong and ill-regulated natures, is sure to produce contradictory and unsatisfactory results. It was very natural, therefore, that Miss Cross should be a much less popular person than her more gentle mother. The same religious tenets worked worse on her stronger intellect and sterner nature; moreover, the fact that although she had completed her twenty-fifth year, she was still Miss Cross, operated unfavourably on her mind and character. She was by no means well calculated to endure or adorn a state of single blessedness; on the contrary, a very decided propensity to the tender passion had caused her to plunge into every possible flirtation that came in her way. And this sin of flirtation is especially one of those in the commission of which one person may steal a horse with impunity, while another may not look over the hedge without being exposed to very vehement reprobation.

With one of nature's delicate pet pieces of handiwork, this sin may only be commented upon as "pretty Fanny's way;" but our vehement Miss Cross, with her eager eye and energetic manifestations, did not "do her spiriting gently" in that line. In fact, these doings did not always group prettily with her often strongly-expressed theological sentiments, so that on the whole, poor Miss Cross got a good deal of abuse, and not a little quizzing, in the small quiet world of Stanton Parva. And yet, after all, Olivia Cross was by no means devoid of good qualities. She was warm-hearted and friendly, and most cordially seconded all her mother's little doings, in the way of helping her poor neighbours, and was ever ready with activity of heart, hand and foot, in the service of anybody to whom such an exertion would be a kindness.

And yet the poor dreaded the sight of the managing Miss Olivia crossing their thresholds ; and there were, probably, two to one of those whom she had endeavoured to serve, who would have been more apt to complain of her officiousness, than to be thankful for her assistance.

For the most part, the mother and daughter passed their days and years in greater harmony than might have been expected from their very different characters. Olivia loved her mother, and was always kind, though not always respectful to her ; while on the other hand, the little widow dearly loved her tall daughter, though she was constantly plaguing her with a sort of good-humoured teasing, which meant little or nothing on the part of the cheerful old lady, but which did not always fall so lightly on the hot spirit of the younger one ; and when Olivia lost her temper, her little mother felt a good deal afraid of her.

*   *   *   *   *

When Lady Juliana reached " The Widow's Rest," she was so fortunate as to find both the ladies at home. Olivia was in the parlour, very busily engaged, though with a divided attention—one half of her spirit being occupied by cutting out a polka from rather a becoming pattern, and the other half being given to the perusal of a recently published tract, entitled " Grace before Baptism."

Mrs. Cross was in the garden, but at no great distance from the house, busily engaged in tying up her abounding sweet peas.

" Ah ! Lady Juliana," exclaimed the old lady, on seeing her noble visitor approach, " this is indeed very kind of you. How are you all at the Rectory ? But walk in—pray walk in," and Mrs. Cross threw hospitably open the French windows of her pretty sitting-room.

Lady Juliana entered, and Miss Cross rose to receive her, with a huge pair of scissors in one hand, and her book in the other, saying, with very courteous eagerness :

"How do you do, Lady Juliana? How is Miss Kate?"

"Ah! my dear Miss Cross," replied her Ladyship, "would that the poor benighted child would take a lesson from you! —your life is an example. You are redeeming the time, I see, as usual."

"I am striving to get some edification," replied the young lady, showing her book, "and I have often got to steal time for doing so, from what I am forced to employ on the pomps and vanities of this wicked world."

"Ah! my dear, we have all our trials! If it were not that my path of duty, as you know, had been plainly marked out for me among the great ones of the earth, I often think that I could wish never to move in my own elevated sphere again. But He knows what is best for us."

"And to the holy, we know that all things are holy," rejoined the handsome Olivia, meaning, probably, in the inmost recesses of her secret thoughts, pea-green silk polkas included. "But have you seen this admirable new work, dear Lady Juliana?" she added, displaying the Rev. Mr. Sampson's recent publication on "Prevenient Grace," and having allowed her Ladyship to examine the title-page, she added in a tone of considerable authority, "it is in truth, a most sustaining and comfortable protest against the soul-destroying formalism that is so fearfully growing up amongst us."

"Alas! my good young lady," returned Lady Juliana, with a deep-drawn sigh, "how is it likely that I should be blessed by the sight of any such book as that at Stanton Rectory? You know what James is. Most truly may we call him a blind leader of the blind. God knows, my dear Miss Olivia, that he is a blind leader, if ever there was one. There is not a single book, that can be considered as really profitable to the soul in the whole house; and I really believe if ever he found one, he would burn it. He has loads and loads of those odious big volumes, written in the dreadful days when Popery was rampant, and when God was not known in the world. If ever I do venture to cast my eyes on a new book, it is sure to be the life of some Popish saint or other, with the title printed in red, and a fearful idolatrous sign of the cross in the title-page. Is it not dreadful to see such sights in a Christian-reformed country?"

Old Mrs. Cross had followed her visitor through the open window, with her little gardening basket in her hand, and looked inclined to welcome her as cheerily as if she had not

believed that that the vast majority of her fellow-creatures
were doomed to eternal flames, and had been so for innumerable ages before they were born; and not even the dolorous
tones of her Ladyship had as yet chased the hospitable smile
from her face; her daughter, therefore, who felt conscious
that her demeanour was not in keeping with the tone of their
noble visitor, thought it advisable to·say: "Lady Juliana,
mamma, is complaining of the want she finds at the Rectory
of some reading, comfortable to the soul. Don't you think we
might be able to lend her something that might be a consolation and a redeeming of the time? I am sure you would be
delighted to lend her any of your own good books."

"Certainly, my dear," replied the old lady, "all my small
stock shall be at her Ladyship's service."

"Many thanks, my dear Madam, for your kindness. Alas!
dear Mrs. Cross, you know only too well in what a howling
wilderness of soul-destroying formalism and idolatry we live in
this unhappy parish," returned the visitor. "My poor unhappy nephew seems, I grieve to say it, more and more left to
himself every time I see him, and it is quite plain to me that
he is being led on nearer and nearer towards the worship of
antichrist! It is a sad, sad, spectacle! I wish much he could
have the opportunity of conversing with some of the Lord's
own. Even his father, Dr. Harrington, though very far from
being a shining light, would be greatly shocked, I am sure, if
he were to hear all I could tell him of his son's unfaithfulness.
Indeed, I cannot but think that it would be a very desirable
thing for some member of his family to come here for a little
while, just to see and hear the manner in which he is
going on."

Lady Juliana flattered herself, that in saying this, she very
skilfully gave the conversation a turn which must infallibly
elicit from Mrs. Cross, the avowal that she expected Mr. Harrington, if such, in truth, was the real state of the case; but
Mrs. Cross gave no sign of having any such important observation to communicate, and only replied with a sigh:

"Oh, poor young man! It is indeed most melancholy to
think that he never writes a sermon without having the evil
spirit of antichrist dictating every word."

"And what fearful sermons they are!" groaned Lady
Juliana. "I heard him preach one when I was here last. It
was more like a heathen lecture than anything else."

"And yet," said Miss Cross, in her fine clear voice, and with

her earnest manner, "it is often borne in upon me that Mr.
Harrington is not a brand reserved for the burning, and that
the Lord will in His own good time stretch out His hand and
bring him home."

"I am sure, my dear young lady, it is very charitable in
you to have such kind thoughts of him, but I am sorry to say
that he seems to me to be back-sliding more and more every
time I see him. Think of his keeping all the soul-killing
Romish fasts and festivals, as he calls them. He does, indeed!
Not a single atom of meat is to be seen in the house on a Friday.
And just fancy his making a point of insulting me, by saying
grace before and after dinner in Latin."

"No cast-away ever went farther from real righteous grace
than he does at present. I am quite ready to admit that,"
said Miss Olivia, with decision. "But, nevertheless, there
are so many cases of sudden regeneration on record, that I
think it would be wrong, and unholy, to conclude from any
man's conduct and character, be they what they may, that he
is not one of God's elect. And I confess that, whenever I have
had an opportunity of conversing with Mr. Harrington, it has
always been strangely borne in upon my mind, that so it may be
with him. Upon all those occasions—and they have occurred
repeatedly—I have felt a sort of improving conviction that it
has perhaps been written that I may be the humble means of
leading him to the waters of life. And, oh, Lady Juliana!
To think of the glory, the triumph of bringing such a sheep
into the fold."

This burst was very enthusiastically uttered by this energetic young lady, and there was the least possible shade of
distance and reserve in the tone with which Lady Juliana
replied:

"Indeed, Miss Cross, my nephew ought to be very grateful
for the holy interest you express for him. But I am sorry to
say that I cannot share your hopes of his regeneration. If you
had the same opportunities of knowing his condition that I
have, and saw how all his opinions and practices lean towards
Romish idolatry, I think you would be less sanguine."

"Most certainly," said old Mrs. Cross, "many of his ways
in church are nothing but rank, downright Romanism, and
particularly painful, I may truly say, to a mother in Israel
like myself, who has received the tradition of the faith from a
shining light of better days. For instance, you know, he
turns right round in the reading-desk to bow to the Lord's

table every time His holy name is mentioned in the course of the service, and this obliges us, you know, to turn round short the other way every time he does it, in order to protest solemnly against joining in such shocking idolatry, and as our pew faces the altar, we have got to turn to the great church door. It is very disagreeable, as you will easily believe, my Lady."

"It is dreadful, very dreadful!" rejoined Olivia, "yet still I say again that God's grace may change all that, in the twinkling of an eye."

"But he has got so many shocking ideas," resumed Lady Juliana. "One of them, you know, is that no priest, as he chooses to call a Church of England clergyman, can lawfully take a wife. The Pope himself could not maintain the absolute necessity of the celibacy of the priesthood more strenuously than my nephew James does. He says positively that a priest is not fit to do his duty in a parish, if he is married."

"Lord be merciful unto us!" ejaculated the old lady, very devoutly; "and may He control the rampant power of the Evil One, or we shall see the days of Smithfield fires again!"

Miss Cross coloured violently as she listened to this statement of Lady Juliana; but did not attempt to say a word in defence of her *protégé*, on this point. Whether her emotion arose from her thinking that this last sin put him beyond the reach of grace, or from a fluttering hope at her heart that she might herself be the chosen instrument ordained by Providence to cure him of this most frightful heresy, is uncertain; but it is not uncertain that the sharp eyes of Lady Juliana detected the blush, and that she felt a sort of instinctive appreciation of its significance with an acrimonious feeling of contempt and resentment towards the young lady, greater perhaps than any which the reverend advocate for celibacy himself could have experienced on the occasion.

Moreover, she was vexed at having failed in the object of her visit, so that it was not in a very amiable frame of mind that she rose in order to bring it to a conclusion, saying as she did so: "But now I must wish you good morning, ladies; for I must hasten back to my charge. I can assure you it is no sinecure, Mrs. Cross, to have the entire care of such a young person as my niece. Young ladies, at their first coming of age, must be sharply looked after, as I daresay your own recollections of some years back can tell you. Good morning! Good morning, my dear Miss Cross!" And with these words, and rather a stiff bow, her Ladyship retreated through the still open window.

"What a pleasant, neighbourly sort of person her Ladyship seems to be; and quite one of the Lord's people, which is always a recommendation," said the old lady, innocently.

"Neighbourly!" exclaimed Olivia, with evident marks of disgust. "I wonder, mamma, how you can fancy any such thing. If I am not very particularly mistaken, there is more pride and aristocratic insolence hidden under Lady Juliana's religion, than is to be found in many a professed worldling. I must say that there is something about her very particularly disagreeable to me. She is no more to be compared, in any respect, to her nephew, poor stray sheep that he is, than our cottage is to Brandon Abbey."

"But, my dear Olivia! is it right to speak and think so, when the aunt is a professor, and the nephew a cast-away—surely a brand set apart for burning!"

"Wait the Lord's time, mother," replied Olivia, eagerly. "Wait the Lord's time; and see if there is not more joy over one such sinner that repenteth, than over ninety and nine such folks as Lady Juliana!"

***

CHAPTER XXXIV.

MEANTIME, that noble lady reached the Rectory at a slow pace, and with a discouraged spirit; but news awaited her there, which in some degree restored her good humour, or at any rate restored her to as near an approach to good humour as it was in the nature of her temper to permit. Kate who saw her approach, met her at the door as she entered.

"Whom do you think we shall have here to-morrow, aunt?" she said, eagerly. "See if you can guess!"

"I am sure I shall not waste my time in any such childish and sinful idleness as guessing," replied her Ladyship, with demure crossness, colouring however at the same time with surprise, and also perhaps from the consciousness of her own duplicity. "If you really have anything to tell me," she added, "do it at once, if you please, with the decent sobriety of a Christian young woman."

Thus adjured, and her little outbreak of light-heartedness effectually quenched by her aunt's cold-water reception of it, Kate gravely replied: "My Uncle Walter is coming, aunt! He will be here to-morrow. Old Margery has been here from the Hall. She had a letter from my uncle this morning, telling her that he was coming into this neighbourhood, and telling her, too, that she was to put the old house into something like order, as he wished to go over it, and ascertain what sort of state it is in."

The communication of this piece of news was decidedly a great relief to Lady Juliana, as she had felt many uneasy doubts as to her power of satisfactorily acting the part, which she had thought she should have to perform on the arrival of Mr. Harrington. But she wanted if possible to hear some further particulars respecting this visit.

"Did the old woman show you the letter?" said she.

"No," replied Kate, "she did not bring it with her. But I believe there was nothing in it."

"And he said that he was coming into the neighbourhood?" said Lady Juliana. "Very odd, I think, that he should neither come here nor to the Hall. What house can he be coming to, I should like to know? It is very odd!"

"And still more odd, aunt, is it not," replied Kate, "that he should have written only to Margery, and not a line to any of us?"

"He probably ordered Margery to let us know about it, and thought that would be sufficient," replied Lady Juliana, with an air of great indifference. "Is the old woman gone back again?"

"Oh yes! she would not stay a moment. She was in such a bustle, she said, about opening all the windows, and dusting, and sweeping, and all the rest of it," replied Kate.

James, meantime, had met the old woman hastening back to her duties, as he returned from church, and learnt from her the news, which he too was obliged to receive with an affectation of surprise.

When he met her, he was walking with a Mr. Brandling, who was his great disciple and ally in the parish, and they were in deep and very interesting consultation. Mr. Brandling was a master carpenter, and was one of those men, who

17

are occasionally found now and then, whose natural taste and
artistic preceptions lead them to elevate a mechanical trade into
an art. The study of the fine specimens of woodwork preserved from past ages was his chief delight. Churches and
church architecture, had accordingly become a passion with
him, and this study had made Mr. Brandling, as it had made
many another man, a staunch disciple of high-church principles
as well as high-church architecture. Whether grace comes
before baptism, at the moment of baptism, or immediately after
baptism, the ingenious carpenter did not very anxiously inquire;
but he had extremely strong opinions on the heterodox
tendencies of the practice of dividing a church into penfolds,
called pews, instead of open seats. Moreover, though but
little conversant with the particular points upon which some
have fallen off from the purity of the primitive doctrine, Mr.
Brandling did not hesitate to attach his faith to that section of
the Church—now, alas! more than ever militant—which preferred open timber roofs to whitewashed ceilings.

The subject of conversation between the high-church Rector
and the high-church carpenter, at the moment they met old
Margery and her news, was the alarmingly great expense of
removing the present hideous reading desk and pulpit, and
erecting something less obnoxious in their stead.

"A goodly, well-carved eagle lectern would, I am afraid,
cost more than you dream of, Sir," were the words just uttered
by Mr. Brandling at the moment they were stopped by the old
woman ; and as these words were very important words, the
carpenter repeated them again as soon as she had passed on.

"I hear you, Brandling! I hear you," repeated the Rector,
with a sigh; "and I suppose then it must be given up."

The carpenter sighed too, but answered not a word, for he
had nothing cheering to say; he knew in his conscience that
only a tolerably handsome carved eagle, would decidedly cost
more money than the parish would choose to give, and for a
moment or two the sympathising pair walked on in silence.

But then the Rector made a halt, and suddenly turning round
upon his companion, he said :

"Brandling, why should I not apply to my Uncle Walter to
help me in this? He is the Squire of the parish, you know,
and less than a hundred pounds from him would set us all right,
wouldn't it ? I'll certainly try. And, I say, Brandling, just
look in this evening with a rough estimate, and two or three
of those designs for lecterns we were looking at the other day."

" Yes, Sir, I will," returned the carpenter; "and I was thinking, Sir, that it would be a great thing," he continued, " if we could manage a fald-stool for the litany at the same time. I could contrive something elegant, in the right style, at no great cost; and if old Mr. Harrington has any taste for church matters, Sir, he never would make any difficulty about a few pounds, more or less."

" Well! we will see about it, Brandling. But the want of money is not the only difficulty we have to contend against. We live in times when much care is needed, even in well-doing." And with these words, and a nod, he parted from his companion, and entered the parsonage, perfectly well satisfied with the efforts he had made, and was about to make, in the cause of religion, and deeply convinced he was doing his duty while permitting his exertions to obtain a lectern and a fald-stool to obliterate from his memory all thoughts concerning the having surreptitiously opened and read a private letter addressed to another, together with all the lies, active and passive, necessarily consequent upon it.

But after all, perhaps, there was nothing very much out of the common way in the character of the Reverend James Harrington. He was a man of some taste, but little sense; a narrow mind, though not devoid of imagination; of a cold and selfish heart, though endowed with a feeling approaching to something like veneration; and with a good deal of learning, though marvellously little information. Men of this stamp are by no means very uncommon.

CHAPTER XXXV.

BRANDON ABBEY could scarcely be called a *picturesque* pile of building, yet it was eminently *historique*. The two terms are often confounded, but their meaning is by no means the same. The difference is as great as that so lucidly expressed by Sidney Smith, when he said that the rector's horse was beautiful, and the Rosinante of the curate picturesque. An *historique* edifice suggests ideas of all that we hear called the Romance of History. Not however that historic reminiscences are confined to antiquated buildings. They furnish but a narrow field for the Romance of History. All that recals a particular epoch, or a certain phase of man's past existence, is *historique*. The style of a work of art—the mode of a dress— a gallery of antique portraits. Do they not all carry with them an entire phantasmagorie panorama of the days that are gone?

And such was the case with Brandon Abbey.

The ancient building, which had originally borne that name, had indeed perished in the civil wars of the Rebellion, and the impoverished heir of the ruined Cavalier who had possessed it in the time of Charles I., had, like many others of his compeers, preferred spending what was remaining with him of the family property, in the gay revels of London under Charles II., to making a desperate attempt to restore the old family mansion.

The next in succession thought it better to share the chances of James II.'s sinking fortunes, than those of his own ruined father, who, bankrupt alike in purse, health, and character, was left to die of disease and poverty in London. And so ended the once proud line of the Moultrams of Brandon.

The place, and the neglected property round it, was bought at a marvellously cheap rate by a lucky speculator, who sold it again at a greatly advanced price, a few years afterwards, to Sir Jacob Mansveldt, a newly-created baronet, and a countryman of King William III.; and it was to this gentleman's wealth and ambition that the Brandon estates were indebted for once again having a mansion attached to them. It was because the new Brandon Abbey—for it still retained its venerable name—betrayed in every part of it such unmistakable marks of its Dutch origin, that we have declared it to be less *picturesque* than *historique*. It would be difficult to conceive any imaginable building more unlike all that we are apt to associate with the idea of an abbey, than was this wide-spreading mansion of Lord Goldstable's.

The square compactness of the red brick *façades*, the heavy stateliness of the balustraded roof, and the perfect regularity of its low, answering wings, had altogether a strong savour of orthodox Protestantism about them, amply sufficient to warrant the staunch principles, both in Church and State, of the above-mentioned Sir Jacob Mansveldt.

These peculiar characteristics are certainly not those of architectural beauty; nevertheless, those whose sympathies are not all bespoken for one style of art only, might find somewhat to admire in a structure whose vast extent gave it one indisputable element of grandeur, and which incontestably offered an exceedingly perfect and magnificent specimen of its peculiar class and epoch.

Moreover, Brandon Abbey was fortunate in the nature and features of the surrounding country. The stiff formality of the huge pile, which had been the delight and pride of Sir Jacob Mansveldt, was wonderfully mitigated and softened in its effect by a surrounding landscape of such rich woodland scenery as only England, and England in her most favoured districts, can show. Fortunately, the sudden decampment of King James saved the magnificent oaks of Brandon from the axe. The political crash had precipitated the impending crash of the Moultram fortunes by a year or two, and the place was sold with the old oaks still standing, and there they were standing yet, when Lord Goldstable came into possession of the place.

Of the interior of Brandon Abbey we shall not say much; those who have ever seen a specimen of that style and date—and there are still many such in England—will have no difficulty in forming for themselves a sufficiently accurate notion of it; and it will be enough to say, that most things within the house were very much as they had been left by old Sir Jacob Mansveldt, and were accordingly but little calculated to render the place comfortably habitable at the time it came into the possession of our young Lord Goldstable. If he wished, however, that this portion of his large inheritance should be greatly admired by the guests he brought to visit it, he was singularly fortunate in the chance which made old Walter Harrington one of them.

It was a lovely summer evening that his Lordship's new travelling chariot, which had accompanied him on the railroad, passed through the lofty iron park-gates of Brandon Abbey; and the beautiful woodland scenery of the park was showing itself in its greatest beauty. Both gentlemen were very earnestly engaged in contemplating the scene before them. The younger one was excited by the very natural curiosity of beholding, for the first time, a noble property of which he was the fortunate owner, and really had, as he looked around him, considerably more speculation in his eyes than could be found in their glances on ordinary occasions. "All this is mine," was the prevailing idea which occupied his mind, naturally enough, certainly, and it was so pleasant a one, that he evidently was enjoying himself exceedingly.

To the elder, the scene was productive of far different and greatly more varied emotions. Few romantic youths or land-scape-loving maidens of sweet eighteen, could be found as keenly awake to the beauties of nature as was old Walter Har-rington at near four-score. But it was not only pleasure, it was pious gratitude that he was drinking in, as he enjoyed the gentle holy influence of the calm and lovely landscape. Nor was this all. It was not only present pleasure that he enjoyed, but the sweet memories of many that were past. To him every glade and thicket of Brandon woods was familiar as if this day had been but the morrow of his last truant wandering among them. Nor was the long vista of years through which he looked back upon those joyous hours a blank. To Walter Harrington, this retrospect was not one that could bring pain. The old naturalist had passed neither a sinful nor unprofitable life, and he had no foregone regrets to cast a shadow over the brightness of his present feelings. Yet, nevertheless, there was a sort of sober, though not sombre solemnity which mixed itself with his enjoyment, and kept him silent.

At length they reached the first pair of huge iron gates, which opened upon the splendid avenue which led to the house. They found them widely open, and the post-boys—for his young Lordship had been met by four post-horses at the station —proceeded to display the gallop, which they have not even in these unposting days forgotten, as the necessary preliminary of approaching their employer's mansion. This sudden accelera-tion of speed caused the old gentleman to rouse himself from his delightful reverie; and after looking back for a moment to the gates through which they had passed, he exclaimed:

"How often I have scaled those fine old gates that we have just dashed through!"

"Scaled them? No; you don't say so! Have you, indeed?" cried Lord Goldstable. "What could have made you do it, Mr. Harrington? What could you have wanted inside them?"

"Why, I don't think I much wanted anything inside them," replied the old man, laughing. "You know, my Lord, I told you that this fine old park had been a sort of half-forbidden playground to my brother and myself, some sixty years since, or so. And I suspect, that the incitement to the grand feat

of clambering over the great avenue gates was made up partly
of the especial sweetness of passing precisely where no passing
was allowed, and partly of the pleasure of doing what my companion, I mean my young brother Harry, could not do. But
here we are already at the stately steps of your mansion; and
there, if I do not mistake, is a face I ought to know. I am sure
I remember that old man when I was here last. Let us see if
he knows me?"

The person thus alluded to had been gate-keeper at the park
for many years, unchanged by the change of its masters; and
his father had been gate-keeper before him in the days when the
Rector's two sons had made Brandon woods their holiday resort.

But the remembrance to which Walter now alluded was not
of so ancient a date, referring only to the time when he had
made a short visit to his own property soon after he had come
into possession of it.

Nor was this old man the only domestic who now stood
uncovered on the steps, awaiting the arrival of their new and
unknown master.

Lord Goldstable had given notice of his intended visit by a
letter to his steward, announcing also that he should be
accompanied by a friend for whose accommodation, as well as
for his own, all necessary preparation must be made ; and this
important functionary as well as the old gate-keeper, now
stood in readiness, and with no small portion of curiosity, to
await the carriage, whose approach had been announced by
more than one scout.

The newly appointed steward, who was by no means an old
man himself, while receiving, hat in hand, and with a profound
obeisance, the two gentlemen as they descended from the carriage, was not a little astonished at perceiving that the friend
of his master, instead of being, as he had naturally anticipated,
some gay young man of his own time of life, was a venerable-
looking old gentleman approaching four-score; and it is just
possible, that Mr. Jenkins might have better liked to see
in that position some blooming inexperienced youth, than one
whose appearance seemed to announce something much more
like a Mentor and a guide, than a boon companion.

Old Simmons, the gate-keeper, bowed low to his new master ;
and instantly recognized his venerable companion as he did
so. Whereupon he exclaimed :

"Sure, your honour, I can't be noways mistaken ! Sure,
this is Mr. Harrington of the Hall, at Stanton ?"

"No mistake at all, Simmons," replied the venerable wanderer. "And I made no mistake about you, old friend! I knew you in a moment. And yet it is ten long years, Simmons, since I was last at Stanton."

"But for all that, your honour is just the same as ever you was! And it is a pleasure to look at you."

Meanwhile, two or three servants who had been promptly hired by the active Mr. Jenkins, were seen hurrying forward upon the steps to receive, and stare at their new master; and their salaams, and "my lords," and all other assiduities, were not only abundantly administered, but all in the right direction; for there was no danger of their mistaking the aged commoner for the youthful peer to whom they were proudly conscious of belonging.

Yet somehow or other it soon seemed, notwithstanding all these manifestations, that the principal portion of genuine deference and respect fell to the share of nature's nobleman, rather than to the brilliant creation recorded in the peerage. This might in some degree perhaps have been occasioned by the discovery of the fact that Walter was the representative of one of the oldest families in the county; and this is a claim to respect still too strongly felt in rural districts to fail of producing its effect even beside the newly-arrived splendour of the newly created nobleman. London servants would doubtless have known better how to apportion their reverence, and Mr. Simpson, Lord Goldstable's "own gentleman," was not a little scandalized by perceiving that every servant in the house, excepting himself, evidently considered old Walter Harrington to be a greater man than young Lord Goldstable.

Mr. Simpson, indeed, had previously conceived a special dislike to the old gentleman, whose first appearance in his path had been made by knocking him up at six o'clock in the morning, and who, moreover, since this first offence, had created a still stronger feeling of dislike in the breast of this legitimate prime minister, by the extraordinary influence which he was acute enough to perceive the old man had acquired over his master.

As to Lord Goldstable himself, it is quite certain that his own feelings placed him on the side of the party the most reverential in their demeanour to his strangely chosen new friend. He had gradually, from the first hour of Walter's unceremonious visit to him, conceived for him the deepest feeling of respect, of which he had ever been conscious; but this feeling was so blended with gratitude for the relief he had brought him from the terrible scrape he had got into, and also with a sort of confidential dependance upon his judgment and his goodness (for not even silly Lord Goldstable could doubt the goodness of Walter Harrington), that he felt a degree of comfort in morally leaning for support on his venerable companion, which made him feel himself more comfortably safe and at ease while he was near him, than he had ever done before since the honours and responsibilities attending upon his having attained his majority had fallen upon him.

In truth, the old man might have exercised the most despotic control over every action, and pretty nearly over every thought of his young friend, had he been inclined to do so ; for the poor youth seemed disposed to throw himself upon him in a manner which threatened a far greater degree of responsibility than the old gentleman had bargained for. But there was something so really pitiable in the evident weakness of character of the young man, and in the utterly unfriended condition in which the total absence of any attached friend left him, that it was not in the nature of Walter Harrington to oppose anything like cold reserve to his advances, or to refuse him the council and guidance which he sought, and which it was so very certain that he wanted.

And so this strangely arranged *tête-à-tête* evening passed away in talk between the young host and aged visitor on many subjects connected with Lord Goldstable's future plans : as to whether he should make Brandon, or another large place which he possessed in the north, his future principal residence ; whether he should rebuild, or only alter and ornament either of the two houses ; and many other subjects of the same personally interesting kind ; and before they parted for the night it was decided that they should on the morrow give an hour or two to the thoroughly examining the place they were now in, within and without, in order to decide what degree of temptation there might be for expending a few thousands on its immediate embellishment.

CHAPTER XXXVI.

Long before the hour on the following day which had been fixed by Lord Goldstable for this critical examination of his mansion, Walter Harrington was up and away, upon another errand of far deeper interest.

Rather less than an hour's brisk walking in the delicious air of a fine summer morning, brought the active old man to his native village of Stanton, by the well-known path across the fields so many hundred times trodden by him in the days of his boyhood. But not even the well-loved and freshly remembered aspect of the long ago familiar objects which he passed could now arouse his mind from the painful preoccupation in which it was plunged. He was about to see his darling Kate. But what was the greeting he brought her? How should he bear to look at her? How should he speak to her? How communicate the deplorable tidings which he brought?

It had been agreed between himself and his nephew, before he left London, that Henry should make still further and fuller inquiries as to the whole life, habits and character of Caldwell. The terrible visit they had made together to the den in Aylesbury Street, seemed to leave but little possibility for hoping that anything favourable could result from this farther inquiry concerning facts which already appeared to be proved upon such incontestable evidence; and Henry felt this so strongly when the commission was given him, that no feeling, less imperative than the reverence which he bore his uncle, could have induced him to undertake it; but either from a strongly hopeful temperament, or some other feelings that were at work within him, Walter still clung to the idea that it was *possible* they might have been mistaken as to the identity. And as he meditated upon this last chance, which he saw, or fancied he saw, might yet end favourably, he suddenly asked himself whether it would be wise to inflict a pang which might, by possibility, prove needless? Would it not be better to defer a blow which was certain to destroy the bright hope of a long life's happiness? It might be difficult to say whether there was more strength or weakness shown in the old man's decision, not to mention the subject to Kate till he had received a further report from Henry. But at any rate it was so that he decided.

Walter was fortunate in the hour he had chosen for his visit, for it enabled him to see his beloved Kate alone. James was gone to the church to perform *matins*, in the presence of Mr. Churchwarden Brandling and three old women, to whom the Rector dispensed a daily basin of soup, on condition of their punctually attending all services at the church, and of their never, on any occasion, speaking of the said soup by any other appellation than their *dole*. There was one poor old soul indeed, who was hard of hearing, and she invariably called it her bowl; but fortunately for her, this terrible misnomer had never yet been uttered in the presence of anyone who was not either too ignorant or too charitable to report it, and so she went on receiving her bowl in reward for her prayers with great punctuality.

Lady Juliana was, of course, not absent in consequence of attending "matins;" she would have shuddered from head to foot at the idea of being guilty of such arrant Popery; but fortunately for Walter, she never left her room till a much later hour in the morning. So Kate was in the Rectory garden all alone, enjoying pretty nearly the only moments allowed her of freedom and tranquillity, and she employed this precious interval from annoyance, in letting her anxious thoughts range at will as she strolled up and down the quiet shady path.

She had no idea of receiving a visit from her uncle so early in the day, and it was with a cry of glad surprise that she bounded to meet him, as he entered the garden from the breakfast-room window.

"My dear, dear uncle!" she exclaimed. "Oh! I am so very glad to see you! As usual, you are up with the lark, as cheerful, as cheering, but ten thousand times more welcome!"

"My dear, sweet Kate!" he said, taking her by both hands, and after giving her a kiss upon the forehead, holding her at arms' length, and gazing in her face, he added: "I don't see any of the roses, Kate, that country air and early hours were commissioned to give you. I am afraid you have not been happy here, my dear child?"

"Not very, dear uncle," she replied. "The truth is, Uncle Walter, that somehow or other I do not get on so well with my Aunt Juliana now I am away from home. And then I am spoiled, you know, at home, by having that dear room up stairs all to myself. I don't think Aunt Juliana and I understand one another very well. And then James, too, is so odd in many of his ways; and altogether—in short, it is very, very different from being at home, especially since that home has had you in it."

"Poor little Kate! you shan't be left here long, dearest," said Walter, hopefully. "But where are they, Kate?—James and Lady Juliana, I mean—where are they?"

"My aunt, you know, is never early," she replied. "She will not appear down stairs for at least an hour later than this; and James is gone to church."

"Gone to church, my dear? Gone to church at this hour? What for?" asked the old man, very innocently.

"To perform the early service," she replied. "James has early prayers every morning."

"Really," said Walter, looking a good deal puzzled, "that does not look at all like what his father told me about him."

"I flatter myself that your papa is altogether mistaken about James; and I shall be glad to tell him so when I go back, for he really seemed to be very uneasy about him. Somehow or other, Kate," he continued, "your father has evidently taken up the idea, that James is one of the most slothful, idle, lazy young fellows, that ever lived! Now his getting up, and going to church so very early as this, clearly proves, I think, that my brother is quite mistaken in him. But do all the people here go to church every morning?"

"Oh dear, no!" replied Kate, smiling. "Of course not, Uncle Walter. I went to the early service yesterday to please James; but it made Aunt Juliana so exceedingly angry, that I would not venture to do it again to-day. There were not above four or five persons in the church yesterday; but I do not think James would give it up, if nobody met him there, save dearly beloved Roger, the clerk. But the truth is, you know, dear uncle, that James is a regular Puseyite."

"Oh! brother James is a regular Puseyite, is he?" returned Walter, laughing. "Why, Kate, dear, who taught you to talk about *ites* and *isms*? Who taught you all this, you little seraphic doctor in petticoats? *La polémique où va t'elle se nicher?* In my day, I should as soon have expected hearing the bench of bishops discussing feathers and flounces, as of hearing a girl like you, Kate, discoursing upon divisions in the Church. But I daresay you know all about it, my dear, and are quite competent to instruct me; for you must know, though I suppose the confession will shock you, that till I

arrived in England a few weeks ago, I never had the good or
ill-fortune to hear of a Puseyite."

"In truth, Uncle Walter," replied Kate, very gravely shaking her head, I am greatly tempted to believe that your state
is the more gracious. But we ladies of England, who live at
home, are by no means permitted to live so much at ease. We
should be deaf, indeed, if we could avoid hearing the clash of
polemical arms, even if we are prudent enough to keep ourselves out of the thickest of the fight; and even to do this is
by no means a very easy matter."

"Well, Kate!" returned the old man, "I cannot but think,
that this is one of the few points in which England has not
changed for the better since the days of my youth. But in
that, as in all other things, the change will, doubtless,
ultimately lead to beneficial results. Meantime, however, I
am really and truly very much behind the rest of the world;
I must, therefore, entreat of you, good Doctor Katie, to en-
lighten me a little on the nature of this mysterious *ism*. What
is a Puseyite?"

"Nay, uncle dear! who ever dreamed of asking a lady for
a definition? In sober truth, Uncle Walter, I know wondrously
little about the matter, though I hear a great deal," replied
Kate. "But by what I can make out," she continued, "I
believe that a Puseyite thinks that the world was in its prime
of life somewhere about the year 1500, or thereabouts; and
that it has been going down hill ever since. I know that a
proper Puseyite, thinks it far better to be a Roman Catholic
than a dissenter; and that he wears a particular sort of waist-
coat, generally made of black silk, pinned, without buttons, close
under his chin. This, I know, is a very essential point. He does
not talk much about religion, in the way that Aunt Juliana
does; but discourses very much about 'the Church.' He is
greatly inclined to love and reverence all kinds of ecclesiastical
ornaments; and if anything of, or belonging to the church, has
an old name and a new one, he seems to think it a point of duty
to call it by the old one. He always fasts, as he calls it, on
Fridays; that is to say, he eats no meat; but James, fortunately,
seems to be exceedingly fond of fish, and makes a great point
of having the very finest that can be procured; and it is, I
suppose, a point of conscience with him to have it dressed in
the best possible manner, for he makes quite as much fuss about
that, as about any of his most favourite ceremonies. But there
is some mystery about oil and butter, that I don't quite under-

stand. I once paid him a visit in Lent, and then I heard a good deal about it; but I could never very clearly make out the religious laws, by which the occasional substitution of the one for the other is regulated. And this is really and truly all I know about Puseyism, Uncle Walter, excepting a trifling peculiarity which I remarked in James's pronunciation of the word Catholic. He calls it *Cartholic*, with a strong emphasis on the first syllable. What this means I cannot guess; but I suppose it is intended to mean something."

"Admirably precise and satisfactory, my dear. And so my nephew James is one of these strange gentlemen, is he? It is to me a perfectly new variety of the species, and I shall be curious to talk to him. But I must now run away from you, my dear Kate," continued the old gentleman, drawing from his fob a huge old-fashioned watch, "I must now run back to Brandon without seeing either my reverend nephew or Lady Juliana; if I stay any longer, Lord Goldstable will be puzzled to guess what has become of me."

"Lord Goldstable! uncle?" cried Kate, colouring.

"God bless me, my dear love; I totally forgot that you are as yet in perfect ignorance as to my whereabouts in your neighbourhood. Now don't look so frightened, Kate, and so very much as if you thought I were a deserter to the enemy. Not a bit of it, Kate. I am a true knight as sure as you are a lady fair. Yet, so it is, that I am positively a guest in the castle of the arch foe himself."

"You are staying with Lord Goldstable, at Brandon Abbey Uncle Walter?" said Kate, in an accent of the most genuine astonishment. "Well! I confess this does surprise me."

"And no wonder," returned her uncle. "Perhaps I am a little surprised at it myself. We must presume, I think, that I am under the influence of some potent spell, which has been cast on me by this terrible young English baron. Nevertheless you may depend upon it, that I shall come out from the contest with flying colours, as every bold defender of a distressed damsel always does, and ought to do—though I do not think it is quite *en règle* that the bold defender should be an old uncle. But never mind that, Kate; I shall deliver you from his power at last; nor will I take the red cross and march off to Palestine till I have done so."

I wonder whether this aged uncle will ever be old enough to be serious?" returned Kate, laughing. "But of one thing I am quite sure," she added, more gravely, as she affectionately took his hand, and held it between both hers, "whatever the mystery may be, the *dénouement* will not be an unhappy one, if you are one of the plotters."

"I trust so, my own dear Kate," replied the old man; but as he said so he felt a pang at his heart, as he remembered that the *dénouement* he had in store for her contained, at the very best, but a negative sort of blessing, as regarded his manœuvrings with Lord Goldstable, while he was still, as it were, holding suspended over her head a blow heavy enough to crush all her hopes of happiness. "But in truth, my Kate, I must be off," said he, fondly kissing her hands before he withdrew his own. "Tell me, before I go, when I may see you all? Do you think that, without indiscretion, I may volunteer to come over and drink tea with you this evening? And, Kate dear, if I find, which is extremely likely, that my good friend, Lord Goldstable, does not like to be left alone in his glory, in his old Dutch palace; in that case, Kate, I will bring him with me. But don't be alarmed, he shall be muzzled."

Kate coloured a little, and laughed a little, at the idea of such a visit; but she had almost as much confidence in the tact of her old uncle, as in his affection, and she very courageously declared herself ready to stand the encounter, provided her old champion-knight stood by to protect her. She ventured also to promise, on the part of her brother, the required amount of hospitality; and it was accordingly settled, that if no special message reached her to the contrary, he should make his appearance at the Rectory in the evening, accompanied by his noble host, provided the said noble host preferred making the visit, to remaining in the solitude of his own splendid mansion.

CHAPTER XXXVII.

GREAT, as may easily be imagined, was the astonishment of the Rector and Lady Juliana at learning from Kate, at the breakfast-table, that Walter Harrington was the guest of Lord Goldstable, and, moreover, that he proposed bringing his young Lordship to share the hospitalities of the Rectory tea-table, that evening.

James was really much too thoroughly a gentleman to feel any trepidation at the idea of so unceremoniously receiving an enormously wealthy peer in his modest home. The consciousness of being a Harrington, guarded him from any feeling of the kind; but even had it been otherwise, there was another element in the character of James Harrington which would very effectually have produced the same result.

With the most intimate and profound conviction of his whole heart and soul, he believed himself elevated, by the priestly character with which he was invested, far above the level of all peers, potentates, princes, or any other lay grandees whatever; no other relationships of man to man could be said to make itself practically felt by him; no other was really influential on his conduct in life, save only that between priest and layman. The relative position of youth to age, of simple to gentle, of poor to rich, were all swallowed up in the contemplation of the one great division of the world into *clerical* and *lay*.

Not the most exclusive Levite, not the most spotless Brahmin, not the most untarnished green-turbaned descendant of the Prophet, ever regarded his order with more pride of caste, or looked down from a more sublime height on those of the laity, than did James Harrington the youthful Rector of Stanton.

The one cherished picture which ornamented the small but comfortable dining-room at the rectory, was a representation of that celebrated scene at Canossa, where the offending Emperor, Henry IV., was made to stand for three days, bareheaded and barefooted, in the snow, waiting till it should please Pope Gregory VII. to admit him to his presence. And as the young "priest" of Stanton sate within sight of this edifying exemplification of the power of the Keys, it would have been difficult for any combination of persons, or of circumstances, to have shaken the lofty sense of dignified superiority derived from the conscious possession of the awful power to bind, and to loose.

But the spirit of ecclesiastic domination, like every other spirit, must operate according to the capabilities of the element it has to work in; and, accordingly, the same pretensions which made Hildebrand almost sublime in the audacious flights of his enormous self-assertion, served only to make the Reverend James Harrington *a prig*.

Of course nothing could be more abominable, disgusting, and disgraceful in his eyes, than the innovation which, in these backsliding and degenerate days, has permitted the arrangement which has placed so much valuable church preferment in the hands and in the gift of laymen; yet, nevertheless, it is not impossible that the satisfaction which he very decidedly felt at the idea of entertaining his noble, intended brother-in-law in his parsonage, might have arisen from the recollection that this noble, intended brother-in-law, had more than one capital good living in his gift.

No doubt, for a single instant, suggested itself to his mind as to the motive which had induced his Uncle Walter to become the guest of Lord Goldstable, and to give himself the trouble of so early a morning's walk in order to arrange the introducing the noble suitor to the Rectory with as little delay as possible.

It appeared so clearly evident to James, that the old gentleman had been brought to perceive the great folly of opposing so very desirable a match for his niece, that he would scarcely have thought it worth while to ask him if it were not so, had they found themselves *tête-à-tête* together; and, moreover, it was quite clear, in his estimation, that he had not only withdrawn his opposition, but that he was putting himself very much out of his way to make amends for the mischief he had done by encouraging his over-indulged niece Kate in her absurd opposition.

He was, therefore, for more reasons than one, exceedingly well pleased at the prospect of this offered visit; and he proposed to himself to receive the Squire of his own parish, and the man of the highest rank in his neighbourhood, in such a manner as should clearly set before their eyes the nature of their relationship to the Church as represented in his humble person; and moreover, he was certainly not without hopes that

18

he might possibly, by the exertion of a little skilful management, obtain something in aid of the great object of his and
Mr. Churchwarden Brandling's ambition, in the way of decoration for their beloved parish church.

The speculations of Lady Juliana, at hearing of this most
unexpected arrangement between the head of the Harrington
family, and the noble suitor of her undeserving but most fortunate niece, were more single-minded. She had no dreams
about decorating churches, neither could she be said to
have any definite hope of inducing her future nephew-in-law
to bestow any of the performent of which he was patron,
upon any chosen vessel that she might recommend to him.
She gave her entire thoughts to the proper womanly business
of making the most of Lord Goldstable's visit, so as to render
it evident to himself, as well as to the wrong-headed Kate, that
a marriage between them was a matter so decidedly fixed upon,
as to render any notion of breaking the engagement too dishonourable, not to say disgraceful, for either party to fancy
the doing so any longer possible.

Lady Juliana certainly hated Walter Harrington most
hartily; nevertheless, she was too conscientious a person to
deny, that he had acted in this very delicate and difficult affair
with admirable acuteness and skill.

The reason of his being on a visit to Brandon Abbey,
appeared just as obvious, and as much beyond the reach of
doubt, to her, as it had done to her nephew James; and when
they found themselves *tête-à-tête* together—a gratification
which was easily obtained, by her Ladyship's telling the future
peeress that, as the morning was fine, she would do well to
take half-a-dozen turns up and down the gravel walk—they
mutually wished each other joy at being thus admirably assisted
by accident, in advancing the great object which had been
entrusted to them.

"Nothing, certainly, could have been more fortunate, my
dear James, than this Quixotic whim of your queer old uncle!
I dislike him exceedingly," she said, "I shall never deny that,
under any circumstances—and most criminal should I hold
myself to be, if I did so; for I have heard him utter sentiments
so greatly unbecoming a Christian and a gentleman, that anything short of deep dislike would be a crime on my part. But on
occasions of duty like the present, James, neither liking or dis-
liking ought to have anything to do. Can we have a stronger
proof of this than the trouble and inconvenience which the

dislike, forsooth, of your sister, Miss Kate, has occasioned us ? My sense of duty is imperative, James ; and greatly as I dislike this old man, you shall perceive that I will be perfectly civil to him. As to Lord Goldstable, I certainly do feel a very considerable degree of family regard and affection for him already. He has shown not only a tender heart, but very great good sense in this business. Though your father is not noble, James, your mother is ; and you may take my word for it, that this has had great influence with him, as most assuredly it ought to have."

"Yes, indeed! I think Lord Goldstable has behaved extremely well in this business," replied James, taking advantage of a momentary pause in his noble aunt's harangue; " and I shall certainly receive him," he added, " with all the attention in my power."

" Of course you will, my dear James," she replied. " Both as the master of the house, and as the brother of the young lady whom he is about to marry, you owe him every attention! And moreover, I think that upon this occasion, at least, both you and I are bound to treat Mr. Walter Harrington with rather more consideration than we can either of us think he deserves. But we both of us must approve the object which it is evident he has now in view, and our present object should be to stand on the best possible terms with him, for it is only by doing so, that we can be able to further his present laudable object."

"Fear nothing from me on that point, my dear aunt," replied James. " I fully agree with you in thinking that my uncle's present conduct towards Lord Goldstable, is not only everything that it ought to be, but also that it is such as ought to make us forget, for the present at least, all the many objectionable points which we are aware of in his character. Personally, indeed, I may consider myself as a stranger to him ; for it is ten years—very nearly the half of my life—since I last saw him. But I confess that I have gathered enough information respecting his peculiarities, from my mother's letters, to convince me that he is in no way a person entitled to my respect, except inasmuch as he is the brother of my father, and in actual possession of the family estate. But at the present moment, I am quite ready to allow that he is something more. As patron of the living, I have a strong claim upon his assistance for the repairs of the church ; and his present position, as the guest of Lord Goldstable, gives him an importance that decidedly

ought to make us forget, for the time, all points of difference
between us."

Lady Juliana's speculations and views respecting the
expected visit, were much more single and unmixed than
those of her nephew. She had no hopes of his patronage for
any favourite chapel or church, though she was perfectly
capable of feeling the value of such patronage, could it be
obtained in the right direction. But all she thought of on the
present occasion was, that his coming was a masterly move in
the great game which was to make herself the aunt of Lord
Goldstable.

Walter Harrington was most assuredly a very special object
of aversion and reprobation to her serious Ladyship, and the
having to play the part of hostess to him for the evening, was
to her feelings a very detestable task ; but although it never
entered into her contemplation to shrink from it on the present
important occasion, it occurred to her that the evil might be
alleviated by making a further addition to the family party.
No sooner had this idea suggested itself, than she said to her
nephew : "Do you not think, James, that it might be as well
to ask the Crosses for this evening ? It must be done some
time or other, you know, while we are with you ; and it might
help to lessen the horrid bore of talking to Mr. Harrington, off
our hands."

"But might there not be danger of—of dividing Lord Goldstable's attention ?" suggested James. "Might not Miss
Olivia—"

"My dear James, what *are* you thinking of ?" exclaimed
Lady Juliana, interrupting him with evident displeasure, as
well as impatience. "Danger that Olivia Cross should attract
any man's attention ? Surely you must be joking."

"Why I don't know, aunt. However, all that is much
more in your province than in mine, and of course I should
wish you to do exactly what you think best about it. Ask
the Crosses by all means, if you wish it. If the danger to
which I alluded is no objection, I certainly do not know of
any other."

"Trust me," returned the scornful lady, with a most expressive curl of her lip, "trust me, James, you may make yourself
perfectly easy upon that score ; Miss Olivia will never do mischief of that kind to anyone ! I will therefore write the note
immediately, if you please ; and I daresay your man will find
some village boy or other who will take it."

"Oh! there will be no difficulty about that, Lady Juliana. I will take care to send the note, if you will write it," returned the Rector, with very polite alacrity And the note was immediately written, and dispatched accordingly.

~~~~~~~~~~~

CHAPTER XXXVIII.

It was at about eight o'clock, of a fine, warm, summer evening, that little Mrs. Cross and her tall, well-grown daughter, set off from "The Widow's Rest," in obedience to the above-mentioned note, to walk up the village street to the Rectory. The dress of the little old lady, consisting of a black silk gown, with a snow-white kerchief pinned across her bosom, and a most becoming little cap upon her head, was the very perfection of neatness. The dress of Olivia was neither so simple, nor so easily described. The whole resources of her wardrobe had been put in requisition, to furnish forth her adornments upon this occasion. It was not, however, the expectation of meeting Walter Harrington, though he was her mother's old acquaintance, and the Squire of the parish to boot; nor yet the still more exciting and extraordinary event of making the acquaintance of a young nobleman, possessed of eighty thousand a year; it was neither of these remarkable events that constituted the principal interest of the invitation to poor Olivia. No! Alas! it was that servant of Anti-Christ, the Romanizing Rector himself, who caused all the vehement palpitations of that rebellious heart. Yes, it was indeed that glorious creature! that fallen angel! that precious brand, to be brought forth from the burning by the handsome Olivia herself, even as a drowning babe is brought out of the water by a faithful Newfoundland dog! It was, in short, that beautiful, though fearfully wicked Lucifer, in a stiffly-starched white neckcloth and silk cassock, for whose too dear sake all these floating ribbons, and bits of trinketry, had been put in requisition!

Alas! alas! poor, poor Olivia! The fatal truth will out. The Evangelical maiden loved the Puseyite parson. The perversities of Cupid will, probably never end. He was wont of old to amuse himself by making high-born dames lose their gentle hearts to squires of low degree, and Christian Caballeros captive to Moorish maidens. But what was that to the wilful, wicked *espièglerie* of filling the heart of a regenerate spinster with the cassock-clothed image of a Puseyite Rector? Surely not even Cupid himself can go beyond this in perversity.

As might naturally be expected under the circumstances, Mrs. Cross and her daughter were the first division of the expected party who arrived at the Rectory. They were received by Lady Juliana in a style compounded of aristocratic condescension, and that peculiar sort of cold quietism which the spiritual pride of "serious people" assumes in its efforts to ape humility. By Kate they were welcomed with simple and sincere cordiality. The Rector himself advanced one stately step towards them from the hearth-rug on which he had been standing. His slight gentleman-like figure was drawn up to its utmost height, apostolical dignity sat upon his brow, and he stretched out his white hand towards his visitors very much with the action and manner of a pontiff flinging forth his benediction on a kneeling multitude. He controlled himself, however, sufficiently to say: "How do you do?" instead of "Benedicte!"

The guests from Brandon Abbey arrived shortly afterwards, and while Walter was making acquaintance with his reverend nephew, Lord Goldstable, after a somewhat blushing and embarrassed recognition of Kate, was receiving the outpourings of Lady Juliana's delights and felicitations on his arrival at Brandon. As soon as this was over, his Lordship was presented to Mrs. Cross and her daughter, with a whispered intimation from the noble aunt of the Rector, that they were the widow and daughter of a clergyman who had for many years held a living in the neighbourhood, and that they were very good people.

Lord Goldstable looked at Olivia's handsome face, tall figure, and well-formed bust, and certainly thought, in his heart, that she deserved a more complimentary introduction; he bowed low in return for the young lady's low curtsey, and immediately entered into such very friendly conversation with her, that Lady Juliana positively coloured with vexation, as she remembered the tone in which she had rejected her nephew's hint upon the possibility that the young peer might find her attractive.

It was not long before the party were invited, in country fashion, to place themselves around the well-spread tea-table.

Walter seated himself between Lady Juliana and his old acquaintance Mrs. Cross. Kate would fain have sat next her uncle herself, but Lady Juliana so imperatively motioned her to a chair between Mrs. Cross and Lord Goldstable, that no alternative was left her. But her Ladyship failed in her attempt to place Olivia between herself and James; for the audacious young lordling, who was evidently emancipating himself at a very rapid rate from the control of all old ladies, however noble, called out as he seated himself, with a very comfortable appearance of being quite at his ease, and in a tone of the most frank good-humour: "Here is a seat, Miss Cross. Do come and take this chair between me and Mr. Harrington."

An arrangement to which, of course, the young lady could offer no objection, and she obeyed with a crimson blush and a sparkling eye, to the immense disgust of Lady Juliana.

"I must compliment you on the prettiness and good taste of your dining-room, James," said Walter, as soon as the party were seated. "Where did you get the carved oak of that chimney-piece? It assorts most admirably with your Elizabethan windows, and the style of your furniture. You did not get such carving as that at Stanton Parva, I presume? It is really admirable."

"Indeed it is a native production of Stanton Parva, my dear uncle," replied James, much pleased. "But not only the execution, but the design also is the production of a Stanton carpenter. He is, I do assure you, a genuine artist. His name is Brandling: he is a very worthy man, and, moreover, he is my churchwarden into the bargain."

"I shall be delighted to make Mr. Brandling's acquaintance," returned Walter; "but an introduction to Goldstable here would be more to the purpose just now. I think," continued the old man, addressing his new friend across the table, "I think, Lord Goldstable, that this Mr. Brandling would be just the man to intrust with the direction of the workmen who are to be employed in some of the alterations we were planning this morning at the Abbey."

"Yes, to be sure, just the man," replied his acquiescent Lordship. "I should like to have such chimney-pieces as that in all the rooms."

James was in raptures at hearing this. There was something in Lord Goldstable's wholesale style of approbation, that seemed to promise the most enthusiastic patronage, not only of his friend Brandling, but of all spiritual as well as temporal mediævalism, and he already saw his petted church refitted and beautified at the hopeful young peer's expense; maybe a pleasant hope suggested itself that, perhaps, all the pauperism and poor-rates of the parish might be got rid of by means of a daily distribution of alms at the Abbey gates.

"And yet," pursued his youthful Lordship, innocently, after nibbling for a minute or two the biscuit he held in his hand, "I think, perhaps, that they would look better if they were made of marble, and had large looking-glasses over them."

The Rector fell from the height of his hopes plump into the dismal slough of disappointment.

Walter smiled quietly, but said gravely enough, even to satisfy his solemn-looking nephew:

"But tell me more about this village carpenter, James. Is he really a self-instructed man? The design and finish of that carving seems to me to bear the stamp of a real artist."

"And he is a real artist, although a self-taught one, Uncle Walter," replied James, eagerly. "But the miracle is soon explained, my dear Sir. He has sought inspiration from the only genuine source of all that is truly beautiful—namely, the *Church*, Uncle Walter. He has found his teachers in the venerable remains which have come down to us from the ages which were ages of *faith*, and, consequently, were ages of heroism in virtue, and of beauty in art."

"You mean, I suppose," said Walter, after a little reflection, but looking, in spite of it, most completely mystified, "you mean that he copied that carving from some ancient work in the church?"

"I mean, my dear uncle," returned the Rector, with much solemn yet benevolent dignity in his manner, "that the sound Church feeling of a better day can alone elicit that artistic excellence which we all know was produced among us when it was in the ascendant; and this lost artistic excellence can only be recovered in proportion, as we retrace the path of heresy, which this unhappy nation has been following for the last three hundred years."

These last words were delivered with an unction and a tone which called the attention of every member of the little party to the speaker.

Lord Goldstable, with a vague idea that the clergyman was preaching, whispered to Kate:

"Is your brother very strict, Miss Harrington?"

Lady Juliana turned her head away, half closed her eyes, and muttered in a tone not, perhaps, intended to be audible, the word "Blasphemy!"

Little Mrs. Cross, in a voice equally subdued, exclaimed: "Heresy! Fiddlestick!"

Olivia gazed on the Rector with an expression in her large black eyes that was compounded of horror and admiration, the natural result of the painful, yet fascinating, contemplation of the good gifts of comely young bachelorhood, united with so great spiritual abandonment.

Poor Kate looked vexed, and heaved a quiet sigh; but Walter was the only person present who attempted any direct reply.

"Heretical, or not heretical, my dear fellow," said he, "the path which the world has been walking in, as you say, for three hundred years, it will continue to walk in still, even if by so doing it may have to relinquish all chance of carved chimney-pieces. But, perhaps, all this may be Puseyism, James; for they tell me you are a great Puseyite. Is it so? eh?"

"A nick-name, Sir, can never fitly describe a great principle," replied the Rector, still preserving the tone of mild, though dignified authority. "But if by your question you mean to inquire whether, as a priest of the Anglican branch of the Catholic Church, I am one of those who highly prize, and would jealously maintain, the privileges and authority of that Church, I answer most assuredly, Yes."

"You meant to say, I suppose, the Catholic branch of the Anglican Church," rejoined Walter, after a short interval, apparently given to meditation on the meaning of what his reverend nephew had spoken.

"My dear uncle," he replied, appearing to be as much taken aback by the fearful extent of Walter's ignorance, as Walter himself had been by the startling statement of his own retrogressive notions, "I fear that you have never paid sufficient attention to the great questions which are now, alas! dividing our Church. I fear that you may not have read enough on this momentous subject to enable you to understand it rightly."

"No, indeed," replied Walter, "I do not understand it at all; and I should be well pleased to receive instruction on the subject. But observe, James, I object in the very beginning to your *beau-idéal* of religion, as shadowed forth in your favourite model ages of some three centuries since."

"A little closer investigation of the present state of things, my dear uncle, might lead you to acknowledge the necessity of retracing the steps which have brought us to the position we now occupy," replied James. "Let me cite to you a case which occurred in this parish the other day, as a specimen of things as they are. I was called upon to perform the burial service over the body of a person who, I had every reason to believe, had never been baptized. The rubric directs that the burial service shall not be performed for such. And as a priest, I am bound in the most solemn manner that can regulate and bind the conscience of man, to obey the rubric. I, accordingly, refuse to bury the body. Whereupon the civil power steps in, with impious opposition to ecclesiastical ordinances, and without heed of, or reference to, the difficulties of the case, compels me, simply by superior force, to act in disobedience to the authority I am solemnly bound to obey. I put this case to your candour."

"And I," answered Walter, "have no hesitation in replying, that such intervention of the civil power is a monstrous and unrighteous oppression."

"I am delighted, my dear uncle—" began the Rector, eagerly.

"But stop," interrupted Walter; "there are one or two things to be observed. Of course I do not meddle with the reasonableness, or the righteousness, of the rubric; that is nothing to the purpose. Those who most object to it, must, nevertheless, see that you are bound to obey it. But it seems to me, James, that all the parties concerned are acting as unreasonably as the civil power of which you complain. The poor departed one, over whose body the civil and spiritual authorities are fighting their battle, why does he, or why do his friends for him, want you to bury him? If he received none of your ministration during life, why seek it after death? Then, as to the priest's side of the question, it strikes me that a truly believing and conscientious minister of the Church to which this rubric belongs, would not permit himself to be compelled by the civil power to disobey its ordinances. I admire your dining-room very much; but do you not think, James, that the endurance of a little martyrdom mildly administered according to the fashion of the times, would be proof still stronger of reverence for the by-gone ages of faith, than carved oak and Gothic ornaments? But the simple fact is, my dear nephew, that a Church cannot accept its food and lodging from the State, or from State protection, without becoming the servant of the State. It is just as monstrous that the State should interfere to coerce the consciences of the priesthood by compelling them to perform spiritual functions which their sworn faith forbids them to use, as that they should compel the laity to pay for spiritual ministrations which they do not value or desire to receive."

"The Church holds a position, and claims a prerogative, my dear Sir, which ought to prevent any confusion between the authority of the civil power when backing and supporting that of the Church and the using that power, which in fact emanates from the Church herself, for the purpose of thwarting her.

"It does certainly appear, my dear James, that the Church and the State, between them, have contrived to get themselves into a very awkward dilemma; the proof of which is, that a conscientious, well-disposed clergyman, like yourself, finds himself obliged either to refuse the performance of an office at the risk of being pointed at as a monster by the majority of his countrymen, or commit a positive disobedience to the authority he has most solemnly bound himself to obey, by performing it. There must be something wrong in the machinery, for it does not work well."

"I confess, Sir," replied the Rector, "that under the present painful circumstances of the Church, many of her wisest and best sons are anxious to see her severed from all alliance with an unfaithful and heretical State."

"And your wise men are quite in the right of it," returned his uncle. "No Church can be free that wears the livery of the State. And as to a State held in servitude by the Church, as the alternative to which your wishes seem to point, my young friend, I suspect that there is but small chance of your living to see them gratified. A State in subservience to the Church, is a tremendous spectacle, let it appear wherever it may; but in Great Britain, it would indeed be a terrible and monstrous calamity—so terrible, and so monstrous, that in these days of reading and thinking, there is no danger of its befalling us. We should be just as likely to extinguish gas, and prohibit the use of steam by Act of Parliament, as to permit the priesthood to take possession of the Government. No, James, you must not look for that, you must rest contented with the perfectly free use of the tongue, and the pen; these are decidedly the only *spiritual* arms proper for reasonable creatures to employ. But then, you know, you must allow an equally free use of them to all; and then with a free stage, and no favour from either privileges, endowments, or dignities, all parties may fight a faithful battle for the truth; and no honest partisan of her cause ever wished to employ any other weapons in her defence."

CHAPTER XXXIX.

The little country town of Doucham was about equally distant from Stanton Parva and from Brandon Abbey, not being above four miles distant from either. It was one of those quiet, unpretending, and apparently unmeaning congregations of houses which suggest to a passing stranger many puzzling speculations as to why they ever congregated there at all. Doucham possessed no commercial or manufacturing facilities whatever; neither had it a cathedral, or an important agricultural market, or a venerable fortress, nor even the slightest trace of a ruined castle. Yet there stood the whitewashed clean-looking little town, with its two thousand and odd inhabitants, all apparently finding the means of subsistence by selling bread, cheese, bobbins, beer, and calico, to each other.

Some few years ago, indeed, the little town of Doucham really possessed an important source of prosperity; but this had quite passed away from it, and left it stricken with a species of apathy, which it shared with many other townlets.

It was situated on one of the most frequented high roads in the kingdom, and at a very favourable distance from London for all the purposes of a great hotel; and accordingly it possessed a great hotel, which brought employment and profit to very many.

It was a great "coaching station," and nearly fifty well-appointed mails and stage-coaches had been wont to pass through Doucham every four-and-twenty hours, and the majority of them had stopped to breakfast, dine or sup at "The Castle;" for in the days when railroads were not, and the English public were contented to creep along, either for business or pleasure, at the rate of twelve miles an hour, "The Castle" at Doucham had been one of the most celebrated inns in England. Its ale, its trout, its rounds of beef, and its cheese, had all earned a reputation, known and admitted "all down the road."

The straggling High Street of the little town was accordingly very rarely to be found without a handsome team, and its attendant throng of ostlers and idlers, standing before "The Castle" door. In truth, the custom at the inn, and the busy movement in the town, were pretty nearly unceasing. No sooner had the 'Highflyer,' up, rattled off on its way to the capital, than the 'Wonder,' down, dashed into its place. Even the old 'Heavy Blue,' carrying its six insides, and travelling only at the lazy rate of nine miles an hour, and which was decidedly looked upon as an antediluvian specimen of a former era—even the 'Heavy Blue' managed to reach "The Castle" at Doucham on its way down, in time to get its early breakfast there after its night's journey.

But all this prosperity, and all this bustle, forsook both Doucham and its "Castle" when steam was made to do the work which horses had done in by-gone days. The wide-spreading, great inn, with all its huge appendages, looked as forlorn and as useless as a wrecked vessel left high and dry upon the shore.

As it had not business enough left to pay its window-tax, it was perforce closed, and was rapidly progressing towards decay, when the melancholy process was suddenly stopped, and a new period of existence opened to its renovated roof, stuccoed walls, and newly-sashed windows. It fortunately occurred to the active brain of the now celebrated Dr. Limpid, that the old "Castle" inn at Doucham would be admirably well suited for an hydropathic establishment.

He was a man of great energy, and very heartily in earnest, both in his faith in the curative effects of cold water, and in the power of courage and enterprize to convert the poor bankrupt, miserable-looking " Castle," into a flourishing and highly profitable place of resort for invalids. The country was beautiful ; and the streams by which it was watered were as clear and almost as cold as those of Gräffenberg itself.

The result proved him to have been well inspired when he boldly resolved to risk all he possessed in the world upon this speculation ; for, at the time that the closely united friends, Lady de Paddington and Mrs. Fitzjames, decided upon paying it a visit, the establishment enjoyed so high a reputation, both for the success of the system practised there, and for its many agreeable features as a place of fashionable resort, that none of its very numerous apartments were un-tenanted for many days together.

Our two ladies, however, and their one attendant waiting-maid, were fortunate enough to find a set of apartments un-occupied, which they both declared would suit them better than any other in the house; and they were both perfectly sincere in saying so, for they were the best and the dearest ; circumstances which were equally agreeable to them both. For Lady de Paddington never thought anything too good, or too dear for her use, provided she had nothing to do with the paying for it ; and Mrs. Fitzjames was in the humour to think that scarcely anything could be dear enough, and that for the especial reason that she was to pay for it ; for did she not know, that the more she paid, the more precious she should become to her valued, her most sincerely valued com-panion ; and that, moreover, the more highly she paid, the more certain she became of being *repaid* with very stupen-dously compound interest ?

The usual plan of life among such of the inmates as really came there in search of health, was for each of them to inhabit a somewhat miniature bed-room during the few spare half-hours which were allowed between the duties of ducking, packing, exercising, and eating.

The latter operation was performed by the majority of the patients in a very large dining-room, at a table presided over by the doctor in person. But Dr. Limpid was much too observing and too clever a man, not to have discovered that he should cut himself off from one very important source of profit, if he insisted upon it that all his visitors, or even all his patients, should conform to one mode and manner of life. It was, therefore, his invariable custom in the first inter-view between himself and all newly-arrived guests, to ascertain by the careful exertion of all the acuteness, and all the skill he possessed (and he was by no means deficient in either), what their condition of health really was. If they had any malady which in his heart he believed could be removed, or alleviated by the application of his special remedy, and the assisting discipline by which he knew it ought to be accompanied, no man could be more stedfast in the rigid rules he laid down for their observance. "Sancho's dread Doctor, and his wand," was nothing, in the way of tyranny, to be compared to him; and so genuine was his faith in his recipe, and so sincere his love of the science he professed, that he absolutely and constantly refused to receive any such patients, if they refused compliance with his regulations.

But far different was his system, when he discovered that the parties applying for accommodation at his establishment were seeking amusement, instead of health. To these he was as indulgent as he was the reverse to really suffering invalids; but they had to pay for this indulgence in current coin of the realm, and rather extravagantly, perhaps; whereas, his really most valued customers, if they were but obedient to command, had nothing to complain of on that score.

It was about six o'clock on a bright summer evening, that the neat travelling chariot, hired for the occasion by the spirited Mrs. Fitzjames, rattled along the High Street of Doucham, and drew up in high style at the ever-open door of the very gay and thriving-looking "Hydropathic Establishment."

The inquiry for "rooms" having been promptly and satisfactorily answered; and the sufficiently high price demanded for them having been agreed to by Mrs. Fitzjames, in an audible aside dialogue with the doctor's confidential factotum and manager, the travellers were immediately ushered into their comfortable-looking apartments; and requested to say, whether it was their purpose to take their meals at the doctor's table "with the patients," or in their own rooms.

"Mercy on me, Mrs. Fitzjames! what does the man mean?" ejaculated Lady de Paddington, almost in a scream. "Eat our meals at a public table kept on purpose for sick people? What could have made you bring me to such a place as this? Eat with the patients! For Heaven's sake do not let them take the horses off! Let us return instantly. I would not stay an hour in this house, if you would give me a thousand worlds!"

This was uttered with such passionate vehemence, that any
effort to stop her Ladyship before the burst was over must
have been in vain.   But the moment she paused to take
breath, the civil factotum on one side, and the affectionate
Mrs. Fitzjames on the other, united their efforts to tranquillize her agitated mind; and by degrees they brought her to
comprehend, that if she chose to order that a table should be
spread for her in private every hour of the day, she would be
obeyed.

This assurance had the effect of making her rather more
composed; but, nevertheless, there was something in the
wording of the factotum's assurances, which seemed to make
a painful impression on the nerves of Lady de Paddington.

"I order meals for every hour of the day?" she replied, in
a tone of fretful resentment.   And then turning round on her
companion, she added, in a half-whisper: "You know,
perfectly well, Mrs. Fitzjames, that I never agreed to order
anything."

"Good Heavens! no," exclaimed the beautiful widow, "of
course not.   Sit down, dearest Lady de Paddington, upon that
pleasant-looking sofa near the window, and let me settle everything.   That was our bargain, you know; and we can remain
together on no other terms."

"Yes, my dear, I will leave everything to you," said her
Ladyship, now looking round at the pretty little showy room
with very considerable satisfaction.   "I will not plague you,
my dear Mrs. Fitzjames, by saying anything more about anything: you shall manage it all yourself, my dear."

Perfectly well satisfied that so it should be, Mrs. Fitzjames
turned with a very business-like air to the factotum, and
said:

"Perhaps, Sir, it would be the best plan for me to see
Dr. Limpid himself?"

"Yes, to be sure, my lady," replied the man; "and of
course he will come to wait upon your Ladyship in no time,
without my going to call him; for he would never think of
neglecting his duty by staying away from such ladies as you
are.   But if you will be pleased to wait only for one minute,
I will let him know."

And so saying, the profoundly respective deputy placed an
arm-chair at the window, into which the widow threw herself,
saying, as she did so: "Make haste, if you please."

But no haste was just now necessary on the part of Mr.

Brown, the worthy factotum, for before he could reach the door, it was opened by Dr. Limpid himself.

Dr. Limpid, some fifteen years ago, had started in life as a "general practitioner," and, for a few years, got on in the neighbourhood of London very prosperously. But then, unfortunately, he fell in love with one of his patients; and, as her family would not consent to the marriage, he ran away with her. And, as they neither of them wished to return to the gossiping little town from whence they had made their escapade, he took it into his scheming head that he would set off with his bride for Gräffenberg, and make himself acquainted with the mystery which was in action there.

It is but justice to the honesty of Dr. Limpid, to say that there was no mixture of quackery in the determination at which he soon arrived—that thenceforth he would practise hydropathy in preference to any other medical system. But if there was no quackery in the manner in which he adopted the principle, it is impossible to deny that there was a little in the style in which he adopted the practice. In former days, when Dr. Limpid, then plain Mr. Limpid, had been a "general practitioner," he had always, with very scrupulous attention to propriety, assumed the garb of his profession, and attired himself in black; moreover, he had constantly presented himself to his patients with an aspect and carriage of very profound and philosophical-looking gravity. But with a change of scene came, as was perfectly proper and fitting it should do, a change of decoration. A blue silk handkerchief was now always loosely knotted round his throat, in place of the former spotless white neckcloth. His black hair was now worn rather long, and rather in disorder; and a loose grey shooting jacket, and still looser pair of trousers, completed an habiliment which, speaking of any branch of his profession, save the one he had adopted, was as little professional as it was well possible it could be.

Nor had the versatile philosopher neglected to adopt with equal skill his voice, his bearing, and the tone of his conversation to his present style of practice. In place of the subdued, grave, thoughtful aspect of his early life, he now spoke and moved like a man always in a state of the most gay and exuberant spirits. His voice was loud, and his laugh louder. True it is, that the doctor's patients almost invariably manifested a similar appearance of emancipation from all the cares and sorrows of life; and that after a short residence under his

19

roof, they almost all seemed animated by the same abundant
animal spirits, and youthful joyousness.

Whether all this was quite genuine, may perhaps be doubted;
but it was quite impossible to believe that it was all feigned.

"Welcome to Doucham, ladies," joyously exclaimed the
joyous-looking doctor, as he entered the room.

"There can be no hope I presume," he added, after contemplating the elder lady for a second, and the younger one
for rather more, "there can be no hope of your joining our
evening family meal to-night? Tired, I suspect, ladies?
Fatigue of journey, followed by a little lassitude? All quite
natural. Nothing to alarm. You will soon forget all that
sort of thing here. Nobody is ever languid here; no lassitude
at Doucham; debility absolutely prohibited. Ha! ha! ha!"

"Of course, all that is very desirable," replied the beautiful
widow, languidly. "But just at present, Sir, we really are
very much fatigued, and we were just going to order tea
when you came in."

"Tea at Doucham!" exclaimed the gay doctor, laughing,
and rubbing his hands with every appearance of being excessively amused. "Tea at Doucham! Poison in the temple of
Hygeia! Oh! fie! fie! fie! Why, the very act of boiling
water, my dear ladies, is turning the glorious element into the
means of destruction, whether administered inwardly or out-
wardly. However, my dear ladies, I, myself, am no fanatic;
I am only a philosopher. It is therein that my establishment
differs from all others of the kind. I most carefully guard
my mind from everything approaching fanaticism. What tea
do you take, my dear ladies—black or green?"

"Let us have both, if you please," replied Mrs. Fitzjames,
dismissing him with a somewhat haughty, but very graceful
bow, "it is possible that we may take it mixed."

"Both!" exclaimed the doctor, again laughing and gaily
rubbing his hands. "God grant that the black may prove an
antidote to the green, and the green an antidote to the black.
And now, ladies, I must wish you good-night, that I may
watch over the evening meal of those not blessed with
sufficient vigour of constitution to resist the tremendous
effects of tea."

And so saying, the merry doctor bowed himself out of the
room, and went to join the large party of patients who were
assembled round the great table in the public room, drinking
copious draughts of cold milk, and eating prodigious quantities
of innocent bread and butter.

CHAPTER XI.

THE two newly-arrived visitors at the Doueham establishment, sat down to their *tête-à-tête* tea-table with a queer and rather uncomfortable sort of feeling, of having transported themselves to a somewhat savage region.

"What a detestable old fool this doctor seems to be!" exclaimed Lady de Paddington, in a tone which left no doubt as to her being in that state of spirits which is commonly called cross.

"Thank Heaven, dear lady, we shall have nothing more to do with him," replied Mrs. Fitzjames; who, although not at all more disposed to sympathize with the doctor's hydropathic vivacity than her companion, was most deeply anxious to remain where they were, because it was so very particularly certain, that they were at the nearest possible point to the present abode of Lord Goldstable, that it was in their power to reach. "Do let me butter a bit of this toasted roll for you, dearest Lady de Paddington," she continued, in a tone of very affectionate coaxing; "it really is not badly toasted, and the butter looks very countrified and nice."

The only reply to this was the emission of a sound, which was very like a grunt; but Mrs. Fitzjames was engaged in too important a game to permit her skill in the playing it to be in any degree interfered with by her temper; and the toasted roll was prepared, and presented with a most beautiful smile, and such a coaxing request that her dear, dear Ladyship would try to eat, if only a little bit, after her fatiguing journey, that any heart less hard than that of her sour companion must have been melted by it.

"I wonder, Mrs. Fitzjames, whether it would be quite impossible to get anything in the way of sweetmeat in this out-of-the-way place that you have brought me to?" whined Lady de Paddington, as she looked down with ineffable scorn at the little plate so gracefully presented to her.

"At any rate we can but make the experiment," cried tho fair creature, springing up, and running to tho bell with the most fascinating good-humour; "and if we fail in getting sweetmeat, my dear lady, we will try to get something else.

19—2

Now you have so kindly and condescendingly consented to be
my guest, I shall break my heart if I cannot contrive to get
you anything you can eat."

The bell was very promptly answered, and sweetmeat
obtained.   But Lady de Paddington was one of those hard-to-
manage individuals of whom we have probably all seen specimens here and there, who, although particularly well disposed
to have all they want and wish for, provided at the cost of
another, have, nevertheless, a strong propensity to disparage
everything which they have not provided themselves; and the
sweetmeat, although very good sweetmeat, was voted by her
Ladyship to be very miserable stuff indeed.

Mrs. Fitzjames was at first very seriously alarmed by this
declaration, backed as it was by remarks equally unfavourable
upon the tea, cream, bread, butter, &c.; and her very heart
sunk within her as she contemplated the possibility of her
dainty Ladyship's declaring that she must go home again or
starve.   But this anxiety was speedily removed as the business
of the tea-table proceeded; and being ere long requested, with
very little ceremony, to ring the bell for more cream, more
bread, and more butter, the spirits of Mrs. Fitzjames rose to
such a degree, that she joyously clapped her little hands, and
rather danced than walked, in order to comply with the
welcome command.

And then it was that she recollected, with unmitigated
satisfaction, that she was at that moment actually within a
short mile or two of the game she was hunting! She had
great confidence in herself and in her own powers of fascination, feeling no doubt whatever of being able both to
strengthen and to rivet the chain which she had already so
very adroitly thrown over her intended prey, could she only
keep him sufficiently within reach, to enable her to use the
power she was so fully conscious of possessing over him.

Yes! there she was, within three short miles of him : and
there sat the only relative he had left in the world, who could
attempt to exercise either authority or influence over him.
There she sat, in such evident enjoyment of the gratis goods
provided for her, that the clever widow, despite all her acute
anxiety on the subject, felt most comfortably certain, that if
she could but contrive to go on with this venerable relative as
successfully as she had began, her most ambitious hopes
would be realized.

"What was to be done next?" was the question she asked

herself, while Lady de Paddington was sipping her third cup
of tea. Of course the first step for her to take would be to
convey the news of her near vicinity to her adorer. That, it
would be very easy to do, and so far all was well. She was
disagreeably conscious, however, that the strange accident,
whatever it might be, which had brought Walter Harrington
to Brandon Abbey, might put some difficulties in her way—
such difficulties, indeed, as might have proved fatal had she
not, *per contra*, been armed by the presence and protection of
so very important an ally as Lady de Paddington.

She never examined herself as to the reasons which made
her so confident that Walter Harrington was, and would be,
her enemy. This was quite a matter of instinct, and she had
no more doubt about it than she would have felt concerning
the danger of being drowned if she had been bound hands and
feet and thrown into the sea.

Having seen Lady de Paddington push her empty cup away
with the air of a person very decidedly determined to make
no further use of it at present, she took the said cup in her
hand, and deposited it on the tea-tray with a gentle but rather
melancholy sigh.

"You will take no more?" she said. "Ah, my dear lady,
I fear that you did not bargain for so arduous an undertaking
as our expedition is likely to prove. You did not expect to
find yourself so badly accommodated?"

"Miserable enough!" grunted her Ladyship, pushing herself and her chair away from the no-longer interesting tea-
table.

"I am afraid so; and it grieves me more than I can tell
you! But at all events, dearest Lady de Paddington, let us
lose no time in achieving our object, so that our stay at this
dismal place may be as short as possible. I should be so
delighted to take you with me, if you would do me the honour
to accompany me, to some gay watering-place, where you
would be more comfortable. But now that we are in this
disagreeable place, our great care must be to make our coming
here contribute to forwarding the object before us. Perhaps,
dear lady, the best way will be for you to write a little note
immediately to our dear Edward, apprising him of our near
neighbourhood. What think you? I really cannot bear
asking you to exert yourself to-night, when I well know that
you must be so completely tired. And yet, dearest Lady de
Paddington, it is impossible to deny that your doing so would

be the best way of our putting everything *en train*. If the note can be written to-night, I will take care that it shall be sent over to Brandon Abbey before you are up to-morrow morning.

And so saying, the active beauty immediately opened her little travelling writing-desk, and placed it, with all writing materials ready, before the yawning Lady de Paddington. Nor was this prompt activity in vain, for after a few grumbling expletives, the following letter was written :

"EGERIA HOUSE, DOUCHAM.

"I flatter myself, my dear nephew, that you are sufficiently aware of the very sincere affection I have for you, to feel some degree of pleasure at hearing that I am near you. I have come to this place because it has been so strongly recommended to me on account of my rheumatism ; and if it agrees with me as well as I hope and expect, I shall probably remain here for some time. You will not be displeased, I imagine, though it is probable you will be a little surprised, when I tell you that your new acquaintance, but nevertheless the old friend of your early youth, has very kindly accompanied me hither. Strange as it may seem to you, my dear Edward, it is really quite true, that Mrs. Fitzjames is with me. A happy chance has made us better acquainted with each other than we were before you left town, and I can truly say that the more I see of her, the more I am delighted at being able to class her among my intimate friends. She certainly is a very charming person, my dear Edward, and your having so immediately discovered this, does honour to your taste and your discernment. This is all I have time to say on the subject at present, excepting that I feel myself bound in honour to confess to you, that I no longer wonder at your sudden change of sentiment respecting that silly Miss Harrington ; she really was not decently civil to me when her mother brought her to call upon me after their ball ! And I must be stupid indeed, if I could not appreciate the difference between her manners and those of my present charming companion. But I must not run on scribbling about her any more now, for it is getting quite late, and I am very tired. In truth, my dear Edward, I am very far from strong, and it was quite necessary that I should come here, or somewhere, to recruit after the London season. It is all very well for young people to go on all through the summer, calling it spring all the time ; but it won't do for me.

"God bless you, my dear Edward! Do not let it be very long before we see you. I am quite impatient for you to show us your beautiful Abbey; I am told that it is really a very noble place. Believe me now and ever, your affectionate aunt,

"MARY DE PADDINGTON."

Nobody, I presume, will doubt that Mrs. Fitzjames took excellent good care that this important epistle should be forwarded to its address with as little delay as possible; and the result of her prompt measures was, that the letter reached his lazy Lordship's hands at least half an hour before his usual hour of rising.

CHAPTER XLI.

THE first effect of this most unexpected announcement, of the near vicinity of the *most* charming, and the *least* charming lady of his acquaintance, was to flush his young Lordship's cheeks to crimson. The only distinct impression that his great-aunt had left upon his memory was, that beyond all comparison she was the ugliest and the most disagreeable old lady he had ever seen in the whole course of his life. To hear, therefore, that she was within three miles of him, could not be very agreeable to his feelings.

It was not, however, because he any longer dreaded her interference and assumed authority, for he had already become very completely and very agreeably conscious of his perfect independence of all the old women in the world. But although he had, in a very great degree, got rid of the excessive shyness which had so tortured him when he first presented himself to his redoubtable great-aunt, he could not forget it; neither could he forget nor forgive the disagreeable tone of authority in which she had pointed out to him his own deficiencies; and still less could he either forget or forgive the terrible scrape she had got him into, by persuading him

that the only way in which he could feel himself comfortably
at ease, like other men of rank and fashion, was by immediately proposing himself to Miss Harrington.

The very undisguised offering of eye and lip worship, which
he received from pretty nearly everyone who approached him,
had already taught him very effectually to understand how
utterly false all the old lady's assurances had been, as to the
necessity of his being immediately married in order to be considered as a man of consequence ; and this, together with the
galling recollection of his having promised his dearly beloved
old Walter Harrington, that he would write to his solemn,
dignified, and awfully reverend brother, to announce the
withdrawal of his silly proposal, caused the sight of her name,
and the announcement of her vicinity, to produce nothing in
the first instance, but the very vehement pronunciation of the
single word "d—nation."

Could the beautiful Sophia have heard this, and could she
have been aware how very completely (for the moment at
least) her adored image, and her worshipped name, had been
merged and lost sight of in the detested image and the
execrated name of her costly and very troublesome companion,
she might have been tempted to suspect that this said companionship boded more mischief to her hopes than could easily
be counteracted by all the patronage which the noble dowager
could give, and which she had toiled for and obtained with so
much trouble and expense.

She would not, however, have thought her cause quite lost,
could she have seen the smile and heightened colour which
was produced by the memory of her fascinations, as soon
as his first emotions of anger and vexation at hearing of the
threatened visitation of his terrible great-aunt had subsided.

He decidedly felt a good deal touched, and a good deal flattered too, at her having so speedily arranged a journey which
had certainly not been in her contemplation when they parted,
and which he could account for only by believing that the
most earnest wish of this beautiful creature was to be again
near him.

And when this very agreeable idea had once got possession
of him, he speedily forgot all about the disagreeable old lady
who was her companion, and a multitude of pleasant thoughts
and pleasant projects succeeded to the fit of ill-humour, which
the sight of Lady de Paddington's name had produced.

He suddenly remembered that his bewitching Sophia had

never yet seen him with any of the appendages of rank
and station about him. He had walked from his own lodgings to hers, just as any ordinary person might have done;
but now the case would be widely different. He remembered, with very great satisfaction, how very big and
how very grand-looking his house was, and he was fully
determined that it should not be long before she saw it.
Neither did he forget that he had abundance of carriages and
horses, and servants, all of which should be speedily displayed
before those beautiful eyes of her's. And then he grew by
degrees to be quite sentimental, and began thinking how
delightful it would be to pass hour after hour with her under
the fine shady trees of his own park, where it would be so
easy for them to wander and wander away, like true lovers as
they certainly were, where nobody could see them!

It is true, that in the midst of these delightful thoughts the
puzzling question more than once recurred to him, as to how
in the world it could have happened that his old aunt and the
beautiful widow should so speedily have formed a friendship,
intimate enough to have brought them together as companions
to the Water Establishment at Doucham?

The arrangement was certainly a strange one, and might
have puzzled a much more acute personage than our friend
Lord Goldstable. He could scarcely be said to have suspected
any mischief in this sudden and improbable intimacy; still
less could he suspect that if there were mischief, he could be
intended as the victim of it; but he certainly would have felt
more comfortable, had his lovely widow presented herself in
his neighbourhood with a less disagreeable companion.

Either, however, upon the principle of taking the goods the
gods provide without grumbling, or else because he was really
too happy at the thought of so soon seeing his bewitching
enslaver again, to be disposed to quarrel with anything, he
prepared to meet his old new friend at the breakfast-table
with a gay aspect and a light heart.

Walter Harrington, meanwhile, had also received a letter,
not in his bed indeed, like his lazy young Lordship, but in the
open air. The active old man was pacing backwards and forwards on the noble terrace behind the house; but his step was
less alert than usual, for his thoughts were busy with rather
gloomy meditations on the subject of poor Kate's future
destiny; for not all the sanguine hopefulness of his temper
could prevent him from fearing that the chances were heavily

against his receiving any good news from Henry as the result of his promised inquiries concerning the character and habits of life of the young man who he had liked so cordially, and esteemed so sincerely

These meditations, which were not interrupted, though they were loudly accompanied by the far from unpleasing chorus of the thriving rookery which had held its domain in the great avenue much longer than the lords of the land who had planted it, was brought to a sudden conclusion by the arrival of a servant, who presented him with a letter, which had been brought by the same hand that had conveyed the dispatch of Lady de Paddington to Lord Goldstable.

Walter perceived at the first glance that it was from his nephew Henry. The consciousness that this letter brought the tidings which he was so painfully anxious to receive, sent the blood in a rush to his hale cheeks. He waited for a moment till the man who brought it was at some distance, and then he tore open the paper and read as follows :

"MY DEAR UNCLE,

"I have lost no time, and spared no diligence, in making such further inquiries respecting Caldwell as you suggested before you left town; and most sincerely do I grieve to say, that I have no good news to communicate."

The old man suffered the hand which held the letter to fall heavily at his side, while his active step suddenly ceased to advance ; and with his eyes fixed upon the ground, he stood for a moment or two with an aspect of such profound discouragement and grief, as proved that these words had quite overpowered his usual philosophical serenity.

"Poor child! poor child!" he groaned aloud. "How shall I find words in which to tell her this? And yet," he added mentally, "ought we not to rejoice, earnestly and thankfully to rejoice, that the information has reached us in time to prevent her becoming the wife of a gambler? It might so easily have chanced, had I had time before this terrible discovery, to remove all obstacles, as I so fully purposed to do. Thank God! that I have not this to answer for" Assuredly there was consolation in this, though it came mixed with so much present suffering ; and old Walter returned to the perusal of the letter, which went on thus :

"I have never seen the fellow since the memorable evening of our excursion to Aylesbury Street, but I have contrived to

hear much concerning him from three or four of his intimate
associates. It is but justice that I should repeat among the
rest, that the only vice that seems to be laid to his charge is
that of gambling. All these men speak of him as a careless,
good-tempered fellow, and as being a fool only in his infatuated
passion for play. They, every one of them, I think, used in
speaking of him, the phrase so constantly repeated in describing individuals who pass their lives in the active pursuit
of their own destruction. Every one of these dear friends of
Caldwell's would, I daresay, be ready to sign a certificate in
his favour, declaring that he was 'no one's enemy but his
own.' But even to this meagre praise *we* could not put our
hands. Alas, poor Kate! I greatly fear that he will have proved
himself an enemy to her, and that it will be long, very long,
before she recovers her peace of mind. She is not the sort of
girl to have attached herself lightly, and I know that it will
not be lightly that she will forget him. This idea is very,
very painful! Her temper is so sweet, and her gaiety so bright
and so innocent, that I cannot endure to think of the cloud
that is hanging over her, though as yet she sees it not. There
is comfort, however, and very solid comfort, in the fact that
our information came not too late to save her from becoming
Caldwell's wife. There is no doubt in the world that he is a
confirmed, habitual, and very desperate gambler. I comfort
myself with thinking that when the first burst of grief at this
terrible discovery is over, she will be as thankful as we are for
its having been made in time to save her from being the wife
of such a man. By the way, I will give you an odd bit of
information, which I picked up by mere chance in the course
of this painful investigation, and which may serve as a useful
hint to your young host, leaving it to your discretion to make
such use of it as you may see fit. You cannot, I am sure,
have forgotten the beautful vision which flashed upon us upon
the famous night of our grand ball, in the form of a very
lovely widow called Mrs. Fitzjames. She certainly was one
of the most beautiful women I ever saw. We owed the
doubtful honour of her appearance among us to the free and
easy patronage of my mother's old, but not very highly valued
acquaintance, Miss Puddingthwaite. This beautiful Mrs.
Fitzjames attracted and fixed more eyes upon herself on that
memorable occasion than any other person present. One reason
for this was unquestionably the extraordinary beauty of her
person. Another, scarcely less influential, was the marked

devotion paid to her during the greater part of the evening, by the great golden lion of the season, Lord Goldstable.

"Now it so happened that in the course of my perquisitions among the low play-world of the West End, I was thrown in the way of a certain Captain Fowler, who, as I have every reason to believe, is a most complete and thorough scamp, of the genuine black-leg breed.

"It is not very probable that you should have ever seen him, but if you have, you would not easily forget him. He is very tall, and strikingly handsome, though evidently on the wane in that respect, probably more from fast living, than from slow time.

"But my attention was specially attracted to him by the strange, and in some sort puzzling, discrepancy between the undeniable advantages of his striking person, and the strangely strong feeling of dislike, instead of admiration, which it inspired.

"'Who is that remarkably detestable-looking, handsome man?' said I to the friend who I had selected as my aide-de-camp in my search after gambling gossip.

"'Oh! that fellow! He is a certain Captain Fowler, and about as atrocious a *chevalier d'industrie* as London can boast at this moment,' was the answer. 'He is, they say,' continued my informant, 'the very particularly dear friend of that beautiful woman who somehow or other contrived to get to your mother's ball, and to whom the newly-risen star, Lord Goldstable, paid such marked attention.'

"Now, if that very fair lady contrives to introduce that very young gentleman to this very great rascal, you may depend upon it, Uncle Walter, that his acres will make themselves wings and be off. As such accidents as the melancholy one I have thus predicted are, unfortunately, not particularly rare, I doubt if I should have remembered the risk of it thus long, had it not been for the interest you seem to take in the golden calf, who in the present instance seems to be in such imminent danger of being melted.

"Believe me, my dear uncle, your very affectionate nephew,

"HENRY HARRINGTON."

It was some time before the gossiping hint contained in the latter part of young Harrington's letter received much attention from his uncle. The confirmation of all he had so earnestly tried to disbelieve respecting Caldwell, and the immediate necessity of making known to poor Kate the terrible discovery that had been made concerning one whom she had so perfectly esteemed, and so devotedly loved, occupied all his thoughts. He immediately decided upon no longer delaying to communicate the fatal news to her. The old man felt that there would be no mercy in adopting any half-and-half measures in doing this, and that there could, in truth, be nothing but cruelty in allowing her to cherish any sort of hope in her heart that there could be any exit but one from the affair. In short, however painful it might be to her, it must be put an end to by herself, and that peremptorily, definitely, and at once.

It was with an aching heart, good man, that he resolutely determined upon walking over to Stanton as soon as breakfast was over, in order to perform the painful duty that had fallen upon him.

CHAPTER XLII.

HAVING decided upon this, he turned his slow and melancholy steps towards the house, and as he walked he glanced his eye again over his painful letter; and then the latter part of Henry's communication awakened more attention than it had seemed to call for before. The first bitter thoughts which the letter had awakened about poor Kate, had made him feel as if everything else in it was only of the light nature of a jest; but now he became quite aware that the paragraph respecting Mrs. Fitzjames, deserved more serious thoughts. The extreme freshness and simplicity of Lord Goldstable, which would probably have excited nothing but ridicule in most people, had generated a feeling of kindly interest in old Walter; and he immediately determined to be a little on the look-out, in case the beautiful widow, whose appearance and manners he had observed, admired, and condemned on the night of Lady Augusta's ball, should venture to bring herself forward and take the field against the wealth and the wisdom of Lord Goldstable.

That the poor youth should be entrapped into marriage with such a woman as that, even without this episode of Captain Fowler, would be, in the estimation of the venerable philosopher, a very lamentable commencement of his young friend's adult existence; but the addition of this sporting accomplice in the attack rendered the idea of such a marriage too detestable, to permit anything approaching to a feeling of indifference on the subject, to remain upon his mind. "He is, however, perfectly safe for the present," thought Walter; "and it will be time enough for me to begin my look-out when he shall be again within reach of this fair mischief."

Meanwhile, Lord Goldstable having risen and agreeably amused himself during the process of dressing, by anticipating an early morning call at Doncham, prepared to descend and meet his venerable guest at breakfast. The ready, briskly-flowing young blood again mounted to the boyish lordling's cheeks, as he remembered that he must of course tell Mr. Harrington of the letter he had received, and announce to him that he was going to ride over to Doncham immediately after breakfast, in order to pay his compliments to his aunt, and the "lady who was with her;" and in order also to invite them both to come and pay a visit to the Abbey.

Had Lord Goldstable been required to state, in plain and intelligible words, why he disliked the idea of introducing Mrs. Fitzjames to Mr. Harrington, and receiving her as his guest while old Walter was his guest also, he would have been much puzzled how to set about it. Nevertheless, it is quite certain that he had such a feeling; and though it was equally so that he had conceived more love and respect for the old man than he had ever felt for any one living, he would not have been sorry if his venerable guest had greeted him with the intelligence that he had received news by that morning's post, which obliged him immediately to set off to London.

He got the better, however, of this feeling, sufficiently to meet Walter at the breakfast-table with a gay laugh, and to tell him in a very sprightly manner, that he had news for him.

Walter's head and heart were at that moment too full of his own affairs, and of those of the sweet girl, who had decidedly become dearer to him than anyone else in the

world, to have power to make any reply to this beyond a
vague smile, and the unmeaning words "Have you?"

"Yes, upon my life, I have," was the rejoinder. "My
old aunt, Lady de Paddington, and a particular friend of
hers, Mrs. Fitzjames, are come down together to the Water
Establishment, at Doucham. I did not think they were at all
likely to grow so intimate together when I left town. However, there they are, together; and, of course, I must ride over
to Doucham immediately after breakfast; and then, you know,
I must invite them. You won't dislike it, Mr. Harrington,
will you?"

Walter, notwithstanding the very slight degree of attention with which he was listening to the communication of
his young host, started on hearing the name of Mrs.
Fitzjames.

Lord Goldstable saw it, and felt half frightened, and half
angry "I thought, perhaps, that you would like to ride over
with me to Doucham," said the young man. "It is a very
celebrated place, you know"

He was vastly well pleased, however, when Walter replied,
though with a ceremonious manner that was not usual to him:
"No, my Lord, I cannot ride with you to Doucham, I am
going this morning to Stanton. But, before we either of us
start, there is a trifling matter of business that I could wish
to see done. It would not take you ten minutes, my Lord."

"I know, Mr. Harrington, I know," replied the young
man, exceedingly embarrassed. "You mean the letter I
promised to write to Dr. Harrington? I meant to have done
it before now, I did indeed. But I can't do it this morning
all in a hurry, you know I must have time to think what I
ought to say: don't you see? Give me a little more time,
Mr. Harrington; pray do!"

"Whenever your Lordship pleases," replied Walter, gravely.
"But you must remember, if you please, that our understanding upon that point was decisive, and that your shrinking
from the line of conduct upon which we then decided would
lead to very disagreeable consequences."

"Oh, Mr. Harrington, you can't think I want to be off—to
be off writing the letter, I mean. I give you my word of
honour that I will stick to the bargain we made about it.
Trust me: will you trust me, Mr. Harrington?"

"I am quite content to do so, my young friend," replied
Walter, touched by the earnestness of his manner, and kindly

giving him his hand; "only we should remember, you know, that the young lady all this time—"

"Oh no, Mr. Harrington!" exclaimed Lord Goldstable, eagerly; "oh no, Sir! not *that*. I am quite sure that Miss Harrington knows—that is, I swear, that she does not think—I mean that when I sat by her at tea the other evening, you know—indeed, I am quite sure, and you may quite entirely depend upon it, that she knows I don't mean to teaze her any more."

There was so much of honest, simple truth in this, that Walter, with all his sorrow, could not help laughing.

"Well, my Lord," he replied; "if you are sure that you understand each other better now than you did at your first interview, I daresay there will be no more blunders made between you. And now, my Lord, I must wish you good morning: we shall meet again at dinner."

"Good-bye! good-bye!" returned his young host, affectionately wringing his hand. "I almost wish you were going my way, instead of your own, for I always feel comfortable with you."

If Walter's first new walk across the old fields between Brandon and Stanton, had been saddened by thinking of Kate and her doubtful fortunes, his present walk over the same well-known ground, was sadder still; for now all doubt had given way to certainty, and it was no longer in his power to postpone the terrible duty of telling her that her bright dream of life was gone, and nothing but a dark reality left to take its place.

He now blamed himself severely for having so postponed it, and felt conscious that he had clung to a hope in which he had little faith, because it put off the dreaded moment of extinguishing—"it might be for long, or it might be for ever"—the joyous brightness of the innocent young face that was so dear to him. He looked at the very least a dozen years older now, than he had done at his last visit to her; and no old acquaintance, had they met him now, would have exclaimed upon the extraordinary vigour of his steps, or the youthful brightness of his unquenched eye. He was putting himself to the torture from motives of the very purest affection, and yet he felt as if he were preparing to do the duty of an executioner.

CHAPTER XLIII.

WALTER HARRINGTON succeeded in finding Kate as before, alone. James was again from home, and Lady Juliana had not yet left her room.

It needed but one glance at her uncle, as he entered the room, to assure Kate that some heavy evil was near. The genial, cordial smile, the fresh, open, hearty greeting were gone!

"My uncle!" she cried, "what is it?"

"Are you alone, my darling?" said he.

She nodded assent, but did not speak.

"Then shut the door," he said, "and come and sit by me, my Kate. I have something to tell you, which I know it will be very painful for you to hear. It will cause you a bitter pang, dearest! But I thank God, it reaches you in time to save you from future misery."

"Uncle!" gasped poor Kate. "What is it? Speak the worst at once."

"My child!" replied old Walter, his firm voice faltering with painful emotion, "my child! The man who has stolen your pure affection, by false seeming excellence, is—a villain!"

"Frank?—Frank Caldwell? Uncle Walter, there is some mistake in this. You have been deceived. It is impossible?"

"Long and pertinaciously, my sweet Kate, I too clung to the belief that it was impossible. But there is no room for error, my poor child! Your brother Henry and myself have, with our eyes, beheld the acts upon which the terrible report I have now made you is founded. We have discovered, beyond the possibility of any doubt, that the man we thought so high-minded, so pure in feeling and in taste, so honourable a gentleman, and, in one word, so every way excellent, as to deserve the happiness of being your husband, Kate—this man we have discovered to be a low gambler, a constant associate of scoundrels and swindlers, and a constant frequenter of places haunted only by the very dregs of society. This we

20

have ascertained by the evidence of our own eyes, my poor Kate! But again I say, and I call upon you, my child, to say it with me, thank God, that we did discover it before your fate was linked to his!"

Kate sat like one petrified, with her hand clasped in that of her uncle. She neither groaned, nor screamed, nor fainted, nor moved. She scarcely seemed to breathe for a minute or two; but at last she raised her eyes, and fixed them on the old man's working features, and then she said:

"Uncle, this cannot be. There has been some mistake, Uncle Walter. Where, how, and with whom, I know not; but there is some mistake in this. The thing is impossible, and therefore cannot be. The Frank Caldwell I have known cannot be the person you now describe: the two persons are different, and cannot be the same."

"Alas! alas! my poor love! my own, dear, pure-minded Kate! I wonder not at your incredulity!" returned the old man, with a sigh. "It was not easy to make even me believe that it was possible; and yet I have lived long enough to learn that a mask may be worn, and that feelings may be feigned. But that the facts in this unhappy case are as I have stated them to be, is as certain as that you now hear me speak to you. Do you think, Kate, that I would have come upon this hateful errand, had the very slightest gleam of hope remained that Henry and myself could have been mistaken?"

"Nevertheless, Uncle Walter," returned Kate, very solemnly, "I do not believe it. Do not blame me for this apparent obstinacy. It is not the act of my will, it is truly and completely involuntarily. I have no power to believe it. Forgive me, dear, dear uncle, I *cannot!*"

"What can I say to you, my poor child?" exclaimed the greatly distressed old man. "Shall Henry come down to state to you what he has seen, and what he has heard? It is quite certain, Kate, that the testimony of one so little used to the world and the world's ways as I am, should not be too implicitly received. Listen to Henry, my dear love! He may be a more trustworthy evidence than I am. It is likely enough, in such a case, that he might see more, and feel less. And yet I doubt if I am not doing him an injustice by saying so. For, on my life, Kate, he has felt this shock severely. Let me write to him, and tell him to join us here for a day or two."

"No, Uncle Walter. Nothing that Henry could tell me

could possibly make any difference. Bear with me, dear
uncle, and believe that I only speak the truth when I say
that my mind has not the power of receiving the statement
you have made, as true."

Walter got up from his chair, and for a minute or two paced
up and down the room. His head was sunk upon his breast,
and his hands clasped together behind his back.

"I love you for the earnestness of your faith, my sweet
Kate," he said at last. "Fear not that I should blame you
for it; for, if it were possible to believe with you, despite the
irresistible evidence of my senses, I should do it. But, alas!
my love, the long and sad experience, learned by the study of
mankind, teaches us but too plainly that it is not safe to trust
to such pure and beautiful enthusiasm. Or why should we
see so many lamentable instances of miserable marriages?
Were the winning a love so nobly confiding as yours a certain
test of worth in the winner, the rapid wearing out of love's
illusions would not be so old and oft told a tale. Alas! my
Kate, you seem to think that Love is lynx-eyed, whereas the
sad experience of mankind has found him blind!"

Poor Kate drooped her lovely head upon her bosom, and
remained silent, but the eloquent tears streamed fast from her
eyes the while. At length she looked up to meet the sympathizing, and not tearless, eyes of the old man, who was hanging
over her.

"It must needs be, uncle," she said, "that you know much
of which I am ignorant; and I must, and I ought to, listen to
your opinion, as to the voice of wisdom, while I consider my
own as nothing but ignorant and presumptuous folly. But I
have always thought that, in all those unfortunate cases where
worth is found mated with worthlessness, the love which led
to the union was not built on the foundation that it ought to
have been; but that it must have been the mere idle liking
which may be caught by an agreeable exterior, and brilliant,
though superficial talents. But, alas! alas!" cried the poor
girl, with a fresh burst of weeping, "if all I now hear be true,
am I not at this very moment persisting in my unbelief from a
hard and haughty confidence in my own judgment, and in my
power of distinguishing genuine from fictitious excellence?
And if it be so, may not the dreadful sorrow that has fallen
upon me be sent to correct me?"

"Hush, hush, my Kate!" exclaimed the old man,
earnestly; "fall not into the presumptuous folly which so

20—2

many well-meaning persons mistake for piety, of fancying
you can scan the intentions of Omniscience. Trust me, dear
child, the system of those who think they can bring the
government of the universe within the grasp of their dim
comprehension, by construing all the miniature events of their
daily life into a series of warnings, judgments, and vengeances,
is a miserable lowering of our conceptions of the Deity to our
own level, and not, as is pretended, a purifying elevation of
them. Your duty in the present case, my dear love, appears
to me to lie very plainly before you. It is absolutely necessary, that an end should be peremptorily and immediately put
to this ill-starred intercourse between your family and this
very worthless young man. He must be written to, Kate, and
it is you who, I believe, ought to do it."

"Oh, uncle! dearest Uncle Walter!" sobbed poor Kate,
almost convulsively, "do not let me write to him. I could
not, oh! I could not do it. Dearest uncle, write *you* whatever ought to be written. It was only a few short hours since
I wrote to him, and not more than half a one since I sent off
this letter, in which I bid him hope, as I did, that the opposition to our union was not likely to last!"

"And why did you so write, dear Kate? What led you to
entertain that hope?" said Walter, looking at her with some
surprise.

"Perhaps," she replied, colouring, "it may not be very
easy to make you exactly understand the reason. And yet I
am quite sure I am right, Uncle Walter. When Lord
Goldstable and you were here at tea, and Lord Goldstable was
sitting next to me at the table, there was something in his
manner that convinced me he had by some means or other
been cured of all his ridiculous notions, poor boy, about
marrying me. And still more than that, I think he intended
to make me understand this. If I am right in thinking this,
Uncle Walter, I was justified in believing that papa and
mamma would no longer have been so violently averse to—to
what I know that you so cordially approved. Was I wrong,
uncle, in writing so as to give him a share in the hope which
had made me so very happy?"

"No, dearest, no!" replied Walter, with a heavy sigh.

"Then you will not ask me to follow that letter by another
so very terrible? You will write yourself, Uncle Walter,
will you not?"

"There is only one objection to my doing so," replied

Walter, thoughtfully. "The authority of a dismissal, such as this, is often doubted, I believe, unless it comes from the lady herself."

"There will be no such difficulty in this case," returned Kate, with a slight tinge of bitterness in her accent, "if *you* tell Mr. Caldwell, uncle, that I do not wish to see him any more."

And here a fresh burst of tears interrupted her words, but she added immediately :

"If you write this, he will not believe that my wishes are other than you represent them to be. Nevertheless," she continued, grasping his hand, and speaking with very solemn earnestness, "write to him the exact truth. Say that those—that *all* those—who have the best right to guide my judgment, think that I ought not to marry him; and that I, on my part, feel and know that it is my duty to yield myself to their guidance, and that it is my purpose so to do. But do *not* tell him that I believe him to be unworthy, for I do not. Forgive me for this, Uncle Walter. I will not deceive you as to the real state of my mind. I do not believe Frank Caldwell to be unworthy."

"I will not seek further to convince your unwilling judgment now, my dear child," replied Walter, gently. "In permitting me to write to him as I think I ought to write, you have granted all that I can reasonably require of you at this moment ; and in writing this necessary but most painful letter, I will be careful to base your rejection of his addresses on the reasons you wish me to assign, and we cannot doubt that this will be sufficient."

Kate bent over the arm of the sofa on which she was sitting, and buried her flushed face and throbbing temples in her hands, while Walter, determined that the whole of the painful duty which he had undertaken should be got through at once, sat down before a writing-table, and produced the following letter :

"SIR,

"Had you been all which I once believed that I knew you to be, you would be better able to appreciate the pain with which I now address you, than I at present think it possible you can do. Miss Harrington's parents, as you know, have, from the first knowledge of your addresses to their daughter, expressed their disapprobation of them. While I, on the contrary, fancying that I discerned in you the qualities which I conceived calculated to ensure my niece's happiness, encouraged your hopes of obtaining her hand, trusting that, with time and a fuller knowledge of you, their opposition would be withdrawn. On me, therefore, devolves most fitly the very painful duty of announcing to you, that circumstances which have recently come to my knowledge, and to the knowledge of other members of Miss Harrington's family, respecting your manner of life, and ordinary pursuits, have rendered the family of Miss Harrington unanimous in their wishes on this subject, and we are all equally desirous that no further intercourse should take place between that young lady and yourself. I have only to add, that it is her determination to be guided in this matter entirely by the judgment of her friends, and to yield herself without opposition to their decision.

"I am, &c., &c.,
"WALTER HARRINGTON."

The old man's hand was somewhat less steady than usual, perhaps, as he wrote this letter; but he immediately folded it up, for it was his first impulse to seal and dispatch it to the post, without torturing poor Kate with any farther discussion on the subject; but his next thought told him that it was due to her that she should be made aware of the compliance he had shown to her wishes, and that she should know that her request had been strictly complied with as to the reason assigned for her rejection. He therefore read the letter to her.

She meekly listened to it, meekly bowed her head when he had concluded, but made no reply or observation whatever.

"God bless and comfort thee, my poor child!" said the old man, bending down and impressing a kiss upon her forehead. "It is a hard task for one who had built all his schemes of happiness on the notion of making one loved being happy, to take the labouring oar for the purpose of making him miserable. I will go now, my poor Kate! I do not want to encounter your aunt. Farewell, dearest! you shall see me again ere long."

And so saying, he put the fatal letter in his pocket, and left the Rectory with a step that seemed to have lost all its long-preserved elasticity.

Nevertheless, he felt more inclined for a solitary walk than for any other occupation during the hours that must pass before it would be dinner-time; and accordingly he took the road towards Doucham, intending to post the letter there, and so return to Brandon.

~~~~~~~~~~~~~~~~~~~~~~~~~~

CHAPTER XLIV.

We must now adjourn to one of those strongly-marked old world oases in the midst of modern London, called the "Inns of Court." It is strange how long and obstinately some localities will retain traces of the character originally stamped upon them, while others start forward and pride themselves in taking the van in everything tending to change and innovation. Nowhere, perhaps, in the whole of our vast metropolis is there to be found so strong a perfume of the past (to borrow a French phrase), as in our Inns of Court, and beyond all others, in the Temple.

It would be difficult, perhaps, to describe with any very satisfactory degree of accuracy, in what this peculiarly characteristic savour consists. The present occupants of these courts and squares are undeniably modern nineteenth century men, engaged in pursuits intimately connected with the busy modern life going on outside their precincts; yet, certain it is, that scarcely the least reflective individual can pass the venerable gateway, which separates the tumult of Fleet Street from the quiet courts and gardens of the Temple, without feeling as if they had suddenly stepped back into a former age.

To those a little more observant and imaginative, it really seems as if some living traces of the old knightly monks remained there still. None such can have walked up and down that noble terrace—that one green spot on the grimy bank of poor old dirty Father Thames, without being, in some little degree, conscious of an influence still spread around them by those mysterious mailed and cross-legged figures, lying in stony state beneath the venerable edifice, before which they have just passed.

It was on the third-floor of the tall pile of buildings, which forms the western boundary of this garden terrace, that two young men sat *tête-à-tête* at breakfast on the morning at which our narrative has arrived. Their table was placed at an open window, for the day was a fine summer day, even in London, and this window commanded a view of the garden, the river, and the dim smoky bank beyond it.

The inhabitant of many a low-roofed cottage in merry England, and of many a sunny garret in Paris, would have difficulty in believing that this small dingy room, reached by hard climbing up three flights of dark, steep, dirty stairs, with its window commanding in addition to the preciously quiet, but very dingy garden, a countless collection of mud-embedded colliers, was a possession so coveted, and so valuable, that its annual rent was double the entire income of many an independent well-to-do *rentier* who *flânés* away his elegant leisure hours amid the gay alleys of the Tuileries.

It is really, however, a very sober truth, that the inhabitant of chambers overlooking the Temple garden, pays a sum for his dwelling, which lazier and poorer nations deem a comfortable competency for the support of a gentlemanlike sort of existence.

The fortunate master of the three small rooms, with coal and clerk holes complete, situated as we have described, was our unlucky friend, Frank Caldwell. And the gentleman breakfasting with him was his brother—his twin-brother; and in truth it would have been well-nigh impossible for the eye alone to have known them apart, or to have guessed which was the hard-working young barrister, and which "the man of pleasure about town."

It seems consistent with all we know of philosophy, and with all we can guess of the proximate causes of character, to suppose that two beings so alike in all of which the eye can take cognizance, should be equally alike, or very nearly so, in intellectual and moral qualities. And probably such was, in a great degree, originally the case between these two brothers. Although in saying this, we reason greatly in the dark, for the causes of intellectual and moral varieties of character are much too subtle for us, as yet, to follow them with any very satisfactory degree of accuracy. But at the beginning of life, and before education, professional habits, and other accidents moulded and shaped the education, it is highly probable that Richard Caldwell, and Frank, his brother, born half an hour after him, were greatly more alike in all respects than after they had both undergone the shaping process by which the accidents of life make us individually what we are at the end of it.

In the case of the brothers Richard and Francis Caldwell, many circumstances existed calculated to produce a greater difference between them than nature appeared originally to have intended; and among these the inheritance by the first-born of a considerable fortune from an uncle, was, perhaps, one of the most influential in making them both what they now were.

The spur to talent and to industry, which necessity had applied to the younger, had given activity to his faculties, if it had not created them; while the total absence of such a stimulant in the case of the elder, had naturally produced the contrary effect, and many good gifts bestowed upon him by nature, had been either suffered to rust in idleness, or to display themselves by an activity of ill, instead of well-doing.

Widely dissimilar as they were in character, however, they now sat brother-like together at their breakfast, while the following conversation passed between them:

"Well, Frank," said the more sprightly-mannered, but somewhat older-looking of the two brothers, "it is a very charming thing, I know, to fall in love, and doubtless more charming still to discover, that the loved one loves again. And more charming than either, must, I daresay, be the prospect of entering into the holy state of matrimony. But 'for a' that, and a' that, and twice as much as a' that,' I could not, if I were in your place, purpose to leave the old rooms for ever without a disagreeable twinge at the heart."

"The years I have passed here have certainly been very peaceful and very happy years," replied the other, more gravely; "but nevertheless, Dick, to a reading and somewhat home-keeping man, the life in chambers is a lonely one."

"That is as one may choose to make it!" replied the other. "It is the true life of liberty. Who is it that says: 'That only free man, the man of chambers?' Whoever said it, he spoke truly, and perfect freedom is a glorious thing, put what you will in the balance against it."

"Yes. There certainly is a charm in perfect independence," replied Frank, "and I do not deny that I have felt a great charm in that perfect absence of all restraint, which enables a man to set off upon an excursion to the Himalaya mountains with no greater preparation than the turning a latch-key. But happy as my Temple life has been, I tell you, Dick, that the felicity to which I am now looking forward, is as much superior to all that I have enjoyed in these dim, snug, quiet, and comfortable rooms, as is the inspiring joy created by looking at the cupola of St. Peter's, bathed in the glowing light of Italy, to the gratification of gazing upon that black mass of St. Paul's there, seen through the smoke of London."

"Very eloquent, and very sublime! which is all very natural upon the present occasion, because you are in love with the pretty thing that is enticing you away from your dear old chambers," replied his brother; "but if you are sentimental in one way, I may be sentimental in another, and I declare to you, I do feel a great deal of tender regret at the idea that this snug retreat is closed against me for ever. I have passed many a pleasant evening here, Frank!"

"And those evenings, which I am afraid have been the most respectable portion of your existence, have decidedly been the least respectable portion of mine. Therefore, it is but natural, you know, that I should regret the loss of them less than you do," replied Frank.

"Now come, my good fellow! Don't let us have any preaching now. I expect an awful amount of lecturing as soon as you shall be fairly seated in the magisterial chair of a father of a family. But you are not there yet, you know, so pray do not begin beforehand," returned the other.

"You know, very well, that I am not given to preaching, Dick; especially to you, who are my elder brother by several minutes," returned the junior. "But it is exactly because it is beforehand, as you say, that I want to talk to you about your way of life for the future. Little as we have lived together, Dick, these rooms have always been, as you know, a sort of second home to you, and many an evening has been spent here in such moderate carousals as you could seduce me into, and which would otherwise, I am afraid, have been passed by you in much less harmless places. Should my hopes for my future destiny be realized, my dear Dick, you will no longer have this harbour of refuge; and unless you will break through your mischievous resolution of remaining a stranger to my sober friends, we must, for the future, see less of each other than ever, and this would be a cause of very sincere sorrow to me."

"Thirdly and lastly," interrupted Dick. "On with you, most solemn brother! Do get to the end of it as soon as you can; and draw it mild, will you?"

"Well, then, thirdly and lastly," returned Frank, "I want you to consent to my introducing you to a little respectable society. If you would only agree not to cut utterly and altogether, all the decent-living portion of the world, it would be gaining something—nay, I should think that it would be gaining a great deal, for in that case I should be sure of not being altogether separated from you. If you would only occasionally consent to pass your evenings in good society, it would at least be some hours saved from the dangers of the gaming-table; nor do I at all despair, my dear Dick, but that after making the experiment, you may feel disposed to confess that, upon the whole, it is as pleasant to consort with decent, honest folks, who want nothing from you, as with scoundrels who are on the *qui vive* to rob you every time you come within their reach."

"Rob me! By Jove you are not far wrong. But your sage proposal, my dear brother, has in it a good deal of that species of wisdom which suggested the closing of the stable-door after the steed was stolen. I am very nearly safe from any farther robbery, brother Frank, I can tell you that," said the gambler, gloomily. "But never mind; you may think it is all for the best, for I am quite in the humour now to do whatever you like. And as I feel greatly inclined to believe that my own particular friends, the blacklegs, will have no more to say to me as soon as they find I have no more to lose, I shall, you see, be reduced to the necessity of becoming respectable, *bon gré, mal gré*. There, Frank," he continued, drawing from his pocket some few pieces of silver money, and tossing them in his hand; "that is the amount of all my present possessions in current coin of the realm, so you perceive that your homily could not have been pronounced at a more auspicious moment. Now, then, for the adventures of Richard Caldwell, Esq., in pursuit of respectability. Where is your first cover, Frank, eh? Where are we to throw off to-night?"

"There's a good fellow!" returned his brother, greatly pleased by his ready compliance with a request which, heretofore, he had often made in vain. "You shall go with me to-night to—"

"Now don't come it too strong just at first, Frank!" returned the other. "If you plunge me neck and heels into pure virtue at once, I shall never be able to stand it. Don't you think it should be respectability with the chill off to begin with? A draught of propriety swallowed neat would be sure to take my breath away. If you could take me now, for example, to the chambers of some hard-drinking judge, or to the *soirée* of some five-guinea-point dowager, it would be very judicious! The first steps to virtue made easy, you know. Let us begin gently!"

"I doubt if my visiting-list contains anything so convenient," replied his brother; "but I was going to propose taking you to-night to a house celebrated for the miscellaneous variety of its guests. I think you know the Miss Wigginsvilles?"

"Now, Frank, that's too bad!" cried the other. "By way of accustoming me gradually to the highly-rarefied atmosphere of decorous drawing-rooms, you dash me at once into the midst of three old maids! You have no mercy! You catch a naked savage, and by way of gently coaxing him into civilization, you begin by cramming him into the boots and leathers of a Lifeguardsman! You should do things by degrees, I tell you. Fancy me tossed, battledore and shuttlecock fashion, from political economy to physical science, and from evangelical piety back again to political economy. Everybody playing the old schoolboy game of 'no child of mine' with me."

"Come, come! be reasonable, Dick," returned his brother, coaxingly. "I might turn one of your own metaphors against you, and tell you that it is far easier to plunge into the water at once, than to stand dipping your toes and shivering on the edge of it. But metaphors apart, I really think you might pass an evening in the Wigginsville drawing-room pleasantly enough. You are sure to see a great variety of characters there; some among them decidedly worth contemplating. Besides, it is a house almost always open some part of the evening: and if you seriously intend to give up your pernicious old haunts, you might often find it an amusing lounge when you have nothing else to do with yourself."

"I can conceive nothing more seducingly delightful," replied the gay rake. "But don't you think, Frank," he added, "that such a society, indulged in habitually, might be too exciting for one unused to anything so brilliant? Might not my nervous system suffer, think you, from the too great tension produced by enjoying the society of three old maids at once?"

"The sharp arrows of your wit, my dear Dick, are sad random shots, and fly very wide of the mark, I do assure you. I believe I can obtain for you the *entrée* to the Wigginsville house; but I by no means undertake to ensure you any portion of their individual attention, beyond that of a kind welcome. Their rooms are always full, and all and each of the sisters are sure to be too much occupied with their own particular set, to have any troublesome attention to bestow upon a new-comer like you."

"Well, Frank, you shall have it all your own way this time. I am yours for to-night, to be disposed of altogether according to your sovereign will and pleasure. And our rallying cry is to be 'Wigginsville and Virtue!'" was the good-humoured reply; and then the strongly-contrasted, yet strongly attached twin-brothers nodded a mutual adieu; the elder wandering away, probably without any fixed purpose at all, and the younger placing himself at a table covered with papers and books, and assiduously setting himself to the perusal of a brief.

CHAPTER XLV.

THAT evening was a great evening at the Casa Wigginsville, as Frank Caldwell was wont to call the hospitable mansion of the sisters. It was known to be the last of the Wigginsville *réunions* for the season, and each of the three sisters had done her utmost to muster her special following in full force; the general gathering was, accordingly, as heterogeneous and brilliant as the contents of the kaleidoscope, although the scientific management of the prismatic arrangement was perhaps wanting; for it occasionally happened, that although the materials were brilliant, their symmetry of position was a good deal left to chance, and, was, therefore, occasionally rather grotesque than graceful.

On the present occasion, Miss Hannah's forces mustered particularly strong, as was often the case at that season of the year. The flock of the gentle Mary Jane was ever most numerous in that once merry month of May, to which Exeter Hall has done so much to impart a sombre hue. Her gathering, however, was a very respectable one also, and she smiled upon them all, with a serenity that was quite seraphic.

Nor had the scientific Miss Jemima any cause to be dissatisfied, for F.R.S.'s and F.L.S.'s, and the F's of all other S's, are always in season when partridges and grouse are not.

The rooms were already crowded when Frank Caldwell and his brother arrived : and before they had succeeding in winning their way to the place in which the elder sister was stationed, the laughter-loving Dick was well disposed to confess that Frank was quite right in declaring that much amusement might be found there.

The crowd, in fact. was thickly studded with notabilities, and whenever this is the case, an intelligent looker-on is sure to find amusement of one sort or other. One of the first figures which caught the attention of Dick Caldwell was that of Mr. Muggridge, the great statistian, whose mania is to reduce everything to tables : and there was no mistaking the vocation to which he had devoted himself for a moment, after getting within hearing of his voice.

A little further on they came upon Sir Benjamin Scales, whose whole time, intellect and energy, are devoted to increasing the activity and productiveness of our fisheries. According to him, all the social misery arising from short commons would vanish at once and for ever, if mankind would only be persuaded to catch more cod-fish and herrings.

Immediately behind him stood Triptolimus Delve, Esq., the philanthropic patron of spade husbandry ; and before you had listened to him for two minutes, you would be sure to hear that "burn the plough" must take place of the old agricultural toast before England can hope to see any more merry days.

Various other incarnations of the various abstract ideas which are moving the surface of our social philosophy were to be found right and left as they moved onward through the crowd. Amongst these was the active Mr. Suttaby, whose ceaseless cry is, "Consume your coal smoke!" and the energetic Mr.

Balquerma, whose equally constant refrain is, "Consume your dead bodies!"

At no great distance stood the reverend and amiable Mr. Seeker, whose whole life may be described as a contest with Juggernath and his car. Standing with his back to this excellent and painstaking individual, was the equally reverend and amiable Mr. Hoaxum, who cares for nothing but circulating the Scriptures among the inmates of the Sultan's seraglio; while a little further on stood the gentle Mr. Milduc, whose days are devoted solely to the task of converting to the doctrines of the Reformed Church, the little Italian boys who come to this country to grind hurdygurdies and sell images.

Then they came upon Mr. Pinion who was discoursing eloquently on the certain application to ordinary travelling (and at no very distant date) of the flying machine, of which he had the honour to be the inventor; while near him stood, studying the effects of light and shadow upon the different groups around him, Mr. Closate, the patentee of a new daguerreotype process.

It is quite true that all these, with many others, might be very fairly classed as monomaniacs, yet most of them were very useful men in their generation; for much of the rapid progress which the world is now making may be traced to the strenuous exertions of some enthusiastic labourer, whose devoted fanaticism confines his efforts to one point.

The age of treatises on universal knowledge is past. We have no admirable Crichtons now, who know everything; but we have specialities who, each in their own way, do more work in the "go-ahead" line in one day, than crowns the live-long labours of many an universal genius. This is the happy result of the division of labour carried into the sphere of intellectual exertion.

The Wigginsville rooms were now full to overflowing, and the roar of talk produced by this high-tide of human tongues was incessant. But in the midst of this most desirable and flourishing condition of drawing-room affairs, Miss Jemima happened to perceive that our neophyte friend, Dick Caldwell, was standing silent. Now Miss Jemima had an especial dislike to seeing any of her guests unengaged or unamused, and she instantly accosted him, saying rather abruptly: "My dear Mr. Caldwell!—oh, you are so like your brother!—do let me introduce you to my friend, Mr. Battiscomb, who has invented a sounding board for pulpits! I know you

would be delighted if he would have the kindness to explain
it to you. It will, beyond all doubt, turn out to be the most
important improvement in church architecture that has been
made for many years. Mr. Battiscomb—Mr. Caldwell. Mr.
Caldwell—Mr. Battiscomb. Mr. Caldwell is excessively
anxious to hear all about your new sounding-board, Mr.
Battiscomb ; will you have the kindness to explain it to
him ?"

So Dick was handed over to listen to a lecture on acoustics,
while Miss Jemima tripped on, perfectly satisfied by having
so well performed her duty in one place, and anxious to be
equally successful elsewhere.

But ere she had made many steps in advance, her scientific
propensities caused her to stop suddenly, and stand profoundly
still ; for it was impossible that she could abstain from listening to a celebrated surgeon, who was detailing in a very animated manner, some of his recent experiments with chloroform.
Neither could she altogether refuse at the same time, to give a
little attention to a most interesting account of some recent
mesmeric experiences, which a well-known enthusiast in that
line was relating, rather *sotto voce*, to two or three ladies who
were eagerly listening to him. From the mingled statements of these two gentlemen, the delighted Miss Jemima
carried away the conviction, that a patient under the influence
of chloroform had conversed fluently in French, though previously quite ignorant of the language.

After about an hour of these varieties, which the new-comer
really enjoyed much more than he expected to do, the two
brothers met in the third drawing-room.

" I say, Frank," whispered the other, " I thought that you
were to bring me among people warranted to rob be of nothing
—by way of contrast, you know, to my worthy friends in
Aylesbury Street—but before I had been here an hour, by
Jove, a fellow had done me out of my own body !"

" What do you mean, Dick ? What jest have you got hold
of now ?" said his brother.

" It's no joke at all," replied Dick. " I tell you that it is
all up with me, as far as Christian burial is concerned ; for
there is a fellow in the next room who has coaxed me to give
him a *post-obit* on my own carcass, that he may burn it down
into ivory-black, I believe, or something of that sort."

" Oh, I see ! You have fallen into the hands of Mr.
Balquerma. I'll engage for it that he told you *cremation* was

the only mode by which a civilized people ought to dispose of their dead. Have you really enrolled yourself under his banner?" said Frank.

"I believe so," he replied. "The fellow set at me with his deadly-lively talk about graveyards containing countless millions of dead bodies; the disagreeable effects of which he dwelt upon so eloquently, that I really felt quite ashamed at the idea of adding to the nuisance; so I told him at last that he should be welcome to my body as soon as I had done with it; and he appeared perfectly delighted by my generosity. But it is about time to go, isn't it, Frank?"

But before this question could be answered, a small man approached the brothers, and laying a finger on the sleeve of the younger, said:

"Mr. Frank Caldwell! I beg pardon for interrupting you, Sir, but may I ask your attention for two minutes? It is a little matter of business, not quite in my usual line, but tolerably important, nevertheless. May I say a word to you?"

"Certainly, Mr. Garbel," replied Frank, turning towards him. "What is it?"

And then having looked at him for a moment, he added:

"I think I can guess. It is something about the marriage-settlements. Am I right?"

"No, Mr. Caldwell; that's not at all settled as yet. But, nevertheless, we are to be married the day after to-morrow, Mr. Caldwell; and Mary Jane begged me to say that it would give her great pleasure if you would join our little party at breakfast on the happy morning, Mr. Caldwell."

"I shall be most happy to do so, my dear Sir," replied Frank, with a friendly smile; "and I wish you joy with all my heart. The day after to-morrow, is it? What is your hour?"

"Breakfast, eleven o'clock; ten o'clock to go to church; twelve o'clock, off we go, carriage and four, and no mistake!"

"Well, Mr. Garbel, as I said before, I heartily wish you joy. I think you will have a very good wife, and I hope you will be a very happy man."

"Not a shadow of doubt of it, Mr. Caldwell, I certainly shall be a very happy man, and a very fortunate man, Sir. 'A virtuous wife is a crown to her husband!' That's in Solomon's reports, you know, Sir. And *I* assure *you*, Sir,"

21

said the little man, lowering his voice to a confidential tone,
"*I* assure *you*, that Miss Mary Jane is out-and-out the most
virtuous young woman that ever *I* knew. Why, bless you,
Sir, she would not fix the day without consulting the Lord.
However, *I* consulted Miss Hannah, and we soon settled it!"

"And what did Miss Hannah say to the match?" asked
Frank, not a little amused by the outpourings of the young
attorney's happiness.

"Why, you know, Mr. Caldwell," replied Garbel, "that
Miss Hannah has not the affable ways and pleasant lady-like
manners that Miss Mary Jane—Mrs. Garbel that is to be—is
so greatly admired for; and we must allow for that you know.
Between ourselves, and as speaking to a friend of the family,
I don't mind telling you that Miss Hannah did not take
altogether kindly to it at first. Though she is only an elder
sister, everybody may see that she is as much the mistress of
the family as if she were the mother; and that is where the
shoe pinches. Her first words about it were certainly anything but civil.

"'Mary Jane's a fool,' she said, 'and you would never
think of her if it were not for the sake of buttering your
bread.'

"Very rude that, wasn't it, Mr. Caldwell? However, I
told her I was above any such low considerations; but at the
same time I told her that I considered it as my duty, to look
to the means of maintaining a family before I put myself in
the way of having one. And then she answered very short:

"'I'll tell you how matters stand Mr. Garbel,' said she,
'and then you may do as you like. My half-sister, Miss Mary
Jane, is not worth one shilling in the world, beyond a few
hundred pounds. All my father's property, worth mentioning,
was settled on the children by his first wife, of whom I am the
only survivor; and my two half-sisters,' says she, 'are altogether
dependent upon me.'

"Anybody might have seen, Mr. Caldwell, how truly I was
in love with Mary Jane by the way I took this. I declare I
was all over in a cold sweat. And then, after a minute, Miss
Hannah went on again, by saying:

"'And now Mr. Garbel, you had best listen to what I am
going to say next. My half-sister, Miss Mary Jane, is a very
good sort of a body in her way, but she is a fool. I have
always foreseen that some day or other she would be wanting
to marry somebody, and I have made up my mind,' says she,

'upon what I intend to do. I don't mean to say but what she might have done worse,' said Miss Hannah, very civilly.

"And then, of course, I said that I was very much flattered by her good opinion. And then she said :

"'Well, now, Mr. Garbel, I don't intend to let my father's daughter starve, while I have a comfortable fortune of my father's earning; and if you choose to marry her, now that you know she has got nothing, and if you make her a good husband, it may be, perhaps, as wise a thing as you can do. I don't say so for certain, observe. I give you no encouragement, no promise. You must know your own affairs best. I only say what *may* be. But don't fancy that you are going to get possession of Miss Mary Jane's fortune, for she has got none.'

"Well, Sir," continued the little attorney, still in a low whisper, and still keeping possession of Frank by keeping his finger on his sleeve—"well, Sir, I tried hard to get her to say what her intentions really were ; but devil a bit.

"'If you marry my sister, and make her a good husband, I don't think you'll want for bread, or for a little butter either, perhaps.'

"But not one inch beyond that would she go, and I don't think Sir Badgerly Browbeat himself could have got a word more out of her."

"I should think you might very safely trust to Miss Hannah's kindness," replied Caldwell.

"Well, I suppose so," replied the somewhat disappointed, but not despairing, lover. "I have talked the matter over with Mary Jane, and she says she is sure her sister means to do something handsome. She says that Miss Hannah always is very generous, but very fond too of being mistress. So, in short, Mr. Caldwell, we have decided upon making a match of it. My own sentiments, I am sure, are very honourable, and I am willing to flatter myself that Miss Hannah, on her side, means to come forward as she ought to do. But what I was coming to, Mr. Caldwell, is just to ask, as Miss Hannah has so very high an opinion of you, whether you would have the great kindness to speak to her on the subject. You see it would be a great satisfaction to me if I knew something for certain. Would you just speak to her about it, Sir ?"

"Impossible, Mr. Garbel," replied Frank. "I have no such intimacy with the family as could justify my doing so."

"Very well, Sir," said the little man, backing at once;

21—2

"just as you please about that.   But I hope you will have no objection to tell Miss Hannah that you have promised to come to the breakfast?"

"Certainly not, Mr. Garbel.   There is Miss Hannah.   I will go to her immediately and tell her of your obliging invitation."

The full-dressed, and very magnificent-looking spinster was seated at a table at no great distance, in her favourite attitude, with one knee crossed over the other, and armed with a huge ivory paper-knife, with which she was triumphantly pointing out to Sir Benjamin Scales a passage in a newly arrived review.

"Just read these two or three pages, Sir Benjamin, that's all," said she, with a tremendous wave of her cimeter-like paper-knife.   "You will find my old argument admirably well put.   Depend upon it, my good Sir, you cannot substitute herring and cod for beef and mutton, without lowering the type of the race so fed."

Sir Benjamin obediently took the volume in hand to do as he was bid, and Frank took possession of a vacant chair close to the old lady.   Her attitude, and her dress too, was magisterial; she really looked glorious in a mighty turban of crimson and gold, with a pair of heavy spectacles across her high nose, and a flowing robe of richly embroidered silk to match the turban.

"So the wedding is to be on Thursday, I hear?" said Frank, "and I have an invitation to the breakfast, though it did not come from you, Miss Wigginsville."

"No, indeed," she replied, "I have invited nobody.   I have meddled very little in the matter, Mr. Caldwell.   Fools will act according to their folly.   There's no help for it.   So I make up my mind to it as a *fait accompli*."

"Then I can hardly hope that I may congratulate you upon the event?" said Frank.

"Well! I don't know why it should not be as much a matter of congratulation as many an event of the same nature which people agree to consider so," said she.   "I told Mr. Garbel that I thought Mary Jane might do worse, and he seemed greatly flattered by my saying so—which certainly told well for his humility.   And if he makes the poor little silly body a good husband, which I don't think at all improbable under the circumstances, it will be a very good match for him, and it will do well for her.   For Mary Jane, you see, though

a very good sort of little woman in her way, has not the gifts
of mind and character which might justify her in determining
to be an old maid."

" It is certainly a condition of life, my dear Miss Wigginsville, which offers many opportunities, not always taken
advantage of, for the manifestation of superior qualities,"
replied Frank; "but it would be unreasonable to look for
these qualities in all. At what hour on Thursday shall I be
with you? At ten for the ceremony? or eleven for the
breakfast?"

" I advise the latter, Mr. Caldwell," replied Miss Hannah.
" There is no great satisfaction, according to my notions," she
continued, "in seeing a couple of people solemnly pledging
themselves to do that which they themselves, and everybody
else, know perfectly well it is wholly out of their power to
promise honestly, because it is wholly out of their power to
tell whether they will have the power of doing it or not. And
this statement, you know, is descriptive of the best cases, for,
in very many, both parties are vowing what they know to be
false. I really do think, Mr. Frank Caldwell, that some
alteration ought to be made in the wording of that ceremony.
It is quite shocking to think how many people feel themselves
legally constrained, as it were, to march boldly up to the altar
for the express purpose of formally pledging themselves to a
lie."

" Come, come, Miss Hannah," replied the happy and hopeful young man, laughing, "you are too hard upon love and its
believing votaries. If you are so very fiercely indignant
against all the lads and lasses, I must run! Good-night.
Au revoir. On Thursday."

As to the rest of the heterogeneous assemblage, those who
had talked more than they had been called upon to listen,
went to their homes, declaring that the party had been a most
delightful one, and that they did not know how the Miss
Wigginsvilles contrived to make their receptions so particularly pleasant; while those who had been obliged to listen,
more than they talked, retired yawning to their beds, and
wondered how people could contrive to be so very stupid.

CHAPTER XLVI.

On the morning following the party at Casa Wigginsville, Frank Caldwell and his brother were again seated at the same window, enjoying the same dingy landscape, and discussing the party of the previous evening, over their breakfast.

"It was not so very bad now, after all—was it Dick? Confess the truth, honestly, Have you not passed duller evenings in more dangerous places, than you passed last night at the spinsters' menagerie?" said Frank.

"Yes upon my soul, have I," replied his brother, very cordially. "I was exceedingly well amused. They ought to keep some of their animals muzzled though! But, upon the whole, and all joking apart, it really was a very pleasant evening. But one would not like to live in the zoological gardens, you know!"

"That is the affair of the ladies themselves," replied Frank.

"Clearly so; and they have evidently selected their vocation as a matter of choice," returned his brother. "But I should think the trade of a paviour a perfect sinecure in comparison! As it is, and despite the good-will which they evidently, one and all, bring to the business, I think that pale one, that you call Miss Jemima, is sinking under it. It was evident to me that the attacks of that man with the flying machine shook her poor nerves very considerably. I suspect that her brain reels, as it were, under the vibration occasioned by the inevitable concussion of the various ologies she receives into it. I should think that another very clever invention would finish her. It is the last ounce that breaks the horse's back, you know."

"Poor dear Miss Jemima!" returned Frank, with a pitying smile. "She certainly does look a little overpowered sometimes. But you can have no anxiety of the same kind on the part of Miss Hannah. She has, I promise you, stability of brain enough to stand the wear and tear of all the conflicting theories, mechanical or metaphysical, that may be let loose upon her."

"You mean the old lady with the hook nose, gold spec-

tacles, and grand turban, I presume?" said the other.
"Yes," he added, after meditating for a moment, "I am
inclined to think that nose, turban, and spectacles, would stem
anything; like the figure-head of some gallant ship! But I
was afraid of her, and cautiously steered out of her way. She
is a terrible old lady, I suspect!"

"No; she is not a terrible old lady at all!" replied
Frank, in a tone of very cordial liking. "Despite the nose,
spectacles, turban, and other kindred infirmities of humanity,
Miss Hannah is a very fine sort of creature. She has a hard
head and a soft heart; and her eccentricities have all a smat-
tering of fun, I might almost say of wit, in them, which
creates a much stronger inclination to laugh with her, than
at her."

"At any rate, it would take some time to get used to her,"
returned Dick. "And then there is the little one—the dainty,
gentle, flaxen, middle-aged little one! What have you got
to tell me about her?"

"Why, that you must take care not to fall in love with her,
young man! I have not told you that I have been invited to
a wedding on Thursday next. The bride being no other than
this same flaxen little one," said Frank.

At this moment the sharp, peculiar, and unmistakable rat-
tat of a London postman was heard at the outer door of the
chambers, and in the next moment the youth, who officiated
as Frank's clerk, and who, as a matter of course, performed
all the various functions incidental to the clerkship of juvenile
barristers, entered the room, and approaching the cheerful
breakfast-table, met the extended hand of his smiling master
with that dread epistle, at the writing of which by Walter
Harrington, at Stanton Rectory, we were present. Frank
knew the firm, bold handwriting of the old man right well,
and tore open the letter with eager impatience.

The letter which he had received the day before from Kate,
had inspired in him the same sanguine hope which had inspired
the writer; and he felt now with an equally sanguine conviction, that seemed almost to approach to certainty, that this
letter from Walter would confirm all his hopes and banish
all his fears.

For he knew that the old man was most warmly his friend.
He knew also the influential position he held in the Harrington
family; and this, with the assurance of Kate, that Lord Goldstable had withdrawn from the field, was sufficient to persuade

Caldwell that his venerable friend's dispatch could bode him
nothing but good.

Dreadful indeed was the transition from this state of mind
to that which followed upon the perusal of Walter's terrible
letter. Had such a letter reached him from any other man,
it is probable that the consciousness of his own worth would
not only have sustained his spirits, but have suggested, also,
the probability of some mistake.   But greatly as Frank
Caldwell admired and venerated the old philosopher, he was
quite aware that some of his opinions not only ran counter to
the ordinary opinions of mankind, but that, in some cases, they
produced a feeling of hostility to usages, not only authorized,
but entirely approved of by society.

Yet even with this broad field for conjecture as to the
possible ground of the censure expressed in this mysterious
letter, the unfortunate young man was totally at a loss to
guess what it was he could have done to produce so sudden a
change in the old man's judgment of him.   In all honesty of
heart, he felt it was impossible for him to accuse himself of
anything to justify, or even to explain the manner in which
Mr. Harrington now addressed him ; yet he could not in this
case, as he might in any other, have turned upon his accuser
and defied him to prove that he was not worthy of Miss Harrington, for with all the diffidence of real love, he felt it
impossible that he could be worthy of her.

In reply to his brother's naturally anxious and naturally
eager demand of " What on earth is the matter with you,
Frank ? " he put the letter into his hands.

" My dear fellow," he exclaimed, after reading it, and with
a voice and manner that testified as much sympathy as it was
possible he could feel for a disappointment in love, " my dear
fellow ! for God's sake exert yourself, and snap your fingers at
them all.   The case, Frank, is as clear as daylight.   Probably
some pique of some sort caused the old fellow, in the first
instance, to oppose the rest of the family, and to support you
in opposition to this lordly Crœsus.   But it is clear that they
have now managed, somehow or other, to change his mind.
She told you in her letter, you know, that her uncle was staying in the house of your rival as his guest ; and though she
might not have found it out at that time, you may rely upon
it, that the old fellow would not have been there, if he had
not changed his mind about his offer.   Now can you believe,
Frank, that any man in the wide world, whether old or young,

can find himself in close intimacy with a lordling possessed of eighty thousand a-year, without feeling a little more tenderly disposed towards him by way of a nephew, than he possibly could towards another young fellow with about eight hundred? The whole thing is as plain as a pike-staff! He says that you are not what he thought you. No doubt, Frank, that may be very true, for anything we know to the contrary. He may have thought, and if the old gentleman says so, I dare say he did think that you were possessed of a very comfortable competency. But depend upon it, his notions on that subject have undergone a very material change by the near contemplation of eighty thousand a-year."

"I tell you, Dick," replied his brother, sadly, shaking his head, "that if you had the very slightest acquaintance with that sublime old man, you would know that all you are saying is utter nonsense. Walter Harrington is not at all more likely to approve Lord Goldstable as the husband of his niece because he has rejected me; and I am quite sure, moreover, that he would never have become the young man's guest if he had not been well convinced that every thought of such a marriage had been given up. You will never see Miss Harrington the wife of Lord Goldstable. She may be induced to give *me* up, and I am sure she would do so without resistance, the moment she was made to believe that I was unworthy. Nay, this cruel letter seems to say that she has not waited for that, but that she has consented to obey the wishes of her family—of *all* her family, by which Walter Harrington evidently means to include himself. But nevertheless, Dick, Miss Harrington will not marry Lord Goldstable. That is not it; I am not sacrificed to any rival. It is not that I fear; but what I do fear is, that Mr. Harrington has, by some means or other, been induced to think less highly of me than he did."

"Less highly than he did!" exclaimed his brother indignantly "Less highly than he did! And is that any reason, or any excuse, for writing to a man as he has now written to you? Less highly, indeed! Nothing but thinking devilishly lowly of a fellow could justify such a tone as this insolent old man adopts."

"That is true," returned the miserable young man, suddenly changing colour, and evidently awakened to a keener perception of the severity of his old friend's language than he had been at first. "You are right, Dick—too, too right!" he added with a groan. "But what can he have heard of me? I am not conscious of being at enmity with any human being. Who is there who could have maligned me to him? Is it possible that I have an enemy?"

"Of course you have, my dear fellow; plenty and plenty. Who has not?" returned his brother, promptly. "But the more pressing question is, what do you mean to do? What will be your next step?"

"The worst of the misery is, that I can give no answer to that question," he replied. "I cannot at this moment perceive any possible line of conduct for me to pursue, to which there would not be heavy objections: and this uncertainty as to what my conduct ought to be, is dreadful!"

"I should have no doubt about the matter if it were my own case," returned Dick, starting up, and pacing the room with rather a menacing aspect. "If the case were mine, I would not lose an hour before I made an attempt to see the girl herself. And there would be nothing so very difficult in the enterprise."

"If I had less perfect faith in the truth and honour of old Walter Harrington, I should do so," replied Frank; "and the proposal is a very tempting one." And then he, too, began pacing up and down the room; and for a minute or two seemed deeply absorbed in meditation. "But, no!" he said at length, suddenly standing still, and facing his brother; "I will not do it! I will not put her to the agony of repeating to me, face to face, the rejection which she has commissioned her uncle to pronounce for her. You do not know this noble old man as I do, Dick, or you would understand the perfect, though most miserable certainty which I feel in his statement, that Miss Harrington acquiesces in the rejection which he has transmitted to me. If this were not the fact, Walter Harrington would not have stated it to be so. He states unequivocally that it is her determination to be guided in this matter by her family; and as he has stated this simply and exactly, be very sure that it is simply and exactly true."

"But are a young lady's purposes immutable, my good fellow?" returned Dick. "Lord bless me, Frank! you talk as if a girl's promise to her pa and ma, to be good, and mind what they say to her, were as immutable as the laws of the Medes and Persians! See her, my dear fellow—see her; and take my word for it, if you are right in believing she ever cared for you at all, you will find no great difficulty in making her change her purposes. Can't you see something like hope in the scheme I propose?"

There was a tone of kindly interest in the manner in which this was said by the usually careless and thoughtless elder brother, that touched the younger one sensibly. He wrung his hand affectionately, and said: "If I don't follow your advice, Dick, it will not be because I doubt the affection which prompts it. But if you knew this old man, or his niece either, as I know them, you would understand better than I can now make you, why it is that I do not follow counsel which seems so reasonable."

"Well, then, I can only wish that I did know them," replied the other; "as I might then have a better chance of saying something that should be really reasonable, instead of only seeming so."

"That is true—perfectly true. And your saying it, has suggested a new idea to me. There is at least one person who knows them, and knows them well, and who is, moreover, a truly kind friend of mine. I really must tell Miss Mary Jane that I cannot be at her wedding-breakfast; and when I do this, I will contrive, if possible, to get a *tête-à-tête* with my friend Miss Hannah, and confide the whole matter to her. *She* can have heard no harm of me, as yet, that is quite certain, for she never received me more cordially than she did last night. She knows perfectly well the terms which I have been on with Walter Harrington. I will show her this letter, and hear her opinion of it;" and so saying, Frank seized upon his hat and prepared to leave the room, adding as he did so: "Well, Dick, I will leave you here; there are plenty of books lying about, but I don't think you will read very steadily. I am sure you feel for me."

"Upon my soul I do, with all my heart!" was the reply, and uttered in an accent that conveyed more than the words. "And I'll tell you what, Frank, while you go to your Miss Hannah, I'll go—let me see—no, I've nothing particular to suggest; only, Frank, as you walk along, just think over the large chapter of accidents, chances, mistakes, blunders, and all the rest of it, that may have led your peerless old gentleman with all his goodness, and all his wisdom, to get the wrong side of the post; and if that's all, you know, he'll be sure, with all his goodness and wisdom, to get right again, and then everything may go well at last."

Frank nodded, and smiled as gaily as he could, and so the brothers parted : Frank taking his melancholy meditative way to his friend Miss Hannah, and Dick setting off in a contrary direction, deeply intent upon a scheme he had conceived for, at least, getting at the truth concerning old Walter Harrington's mysterious change towards his brother.

CHAPTER XLVII.

DICK CALDWELL's project was a very simple one, yet nevertheless it was one, the execution of which, presented some difficulties which he did not very well know how to get over.

"Since Frank, for some fine feeling or other, won't make any effort to find out where the loose screw is, I must do it for him," thought he. "I'll go "—it was thus his meditations proceeded—"I'll go and ask the old boy himself what crotchet he has got in his head? It can do no harm, and may do some good. He can't eat me, though I am such a graceless scamp. I know that it is a delicate sort of a thing having to do with a virtuous old gentleman of fourscore, with lots of silver hair always ready to be brought down with sorrow to the grave, if any young scapegrace takes a disrespectful sort of liberty with him. I know they are ticklish customers to deal with ; and all the world come out so strong in the expression of their virtuous indignation against anybody and everybody who is rude to them. But I can sport virtuous indignation too, on poor Frank's behalf, for I don't believe that he ever did anything wrong in his life ; nay, for that matter, I am perfectly sure he never did. Confound the old fellow ! what business has he to turn round upon him in this bullying style, and tell him that he is not the man he thought him? I can't call out an old boy of eighty, that's quite certain ; but I can tell him he ought to be ashamed of himself, and bid him beware, old sinner, of evil

speaking, lying, and slandering; and that's what I will do.
I'll be off at once! Frank must know nothing about it, or
he'll be sure to stop me."

Such were the meditations of the reckless, but kindhearted,
twin-brother of the unfortunate Caldwell, when left in
solitary possession of his chambers. But when he had
arrived at this conclusive and very satisfactory determination,
he suddenly recollected the extremely unsatisfactory condition
of his purse.

"Confound it!" he muttered, bitterly. "It is easy to say,
I'll be off at once, but how the devil am I to get off without
cash?" And then he pulled forth the identical silver coins,
which he had recently exhibited to his brother as the sum
total of his ready money possessions. "How far will this
carry me?" he murmured very dejectedly. "The old fellow
is a hundred miles off, or thereabouts. A five-pound note is
the very least that would do for me. But where to put my
hand upon a five-pound note between this and to-morrow
morning, who shall tell me? A little bit of luck, now, and I
might easily turn these shillings into pounds. I can but try, and
try I will," said he, as he put on his hat. "I must get to
the little go in thingamy street, I shall be sure to find that
open; they're always at it, and there I'll try to make my
crown a pound. Now we shall see if fortune has any respect
for virtue. I am going to the silver hell with the very purest
of motives. And certainly there is something very delightful
in the consciousness of virtue!"

And thus cogitating, Dick Caldwell left his brother's
chambers with an eager step, telling the young clerk that his
master was not to expect him till he saw him. An arrangement which was unfortunately too common with him to
require any particular explanation.

Frank, meanwhile, wandered disconsolately onwards, alter-
nately proposing and rejecting a dozen different solutions of
the mystery which so painfully hung upon the conduct of his
equally loved and honoured old friend; but he had arrived at
the door of the Casa Wigginsville, without having hit upon
one that appeared to have the slightest mixture of probability
in it. To few others, even of the intimates of the family,
would the doors have been opened on that morning, for all the
three sisters were in some way or other very busily occupied
by preparing for the important event which was to take place
on the morrow.

The gentle Mary Jane herself was earnestly occupied in the back drawing-room, penning about a score of hot-pressed, and touchingly affectionate little farewell notes to the best beloved of the fair company of spinsters she was about to quit. They differed very slightly from each other; they were all crossed of course, but being written in that peculiarly running hand, which carries the pen with the least delay over the largest space, the time allotted to each was not very long. Most of them were illustrated by a tear drop, which by a happy chance always fell on the passages to which such a commentary was most appropriate, so that, notwithstanding the haste in which they were necessarily written, they were all, as the heart of Mary Jane told her, exactly what they ought to be!

Miss Jemima had the entire possession of the front drawing-room, where she was arranging an immense amount of white satin ribbon into little bows, and tying together a countless quantity of name cards in hymeneal bonds of silver cord. Miss Hannah herself was in the dining-room, engaged in the graver cares incident to preparing for the splendid breakfast of the morrow.

But in spite of all this, the servant who opened the door to Frank Caldwell, though he hesitated for half a moment, did not deem it his duty absolutely to refuse him admittance; but upon being desired to tell Miss Hannah that Mr. Frank Caldwell particularly desired to speak a few words to her, he undertook to deliver the message, civilly apologizing for leaving him to wait in the passage while he delivered it. And this judicious Cerberus received immediate proof that the bold measure of announcing a visitor on such a day was not an unpardonable offence, for it was in an accent of very cordial welcome that the busy lady replied:

"Tell Mr. Frank Caldwell that I shall be very glad to see him if he will have the kindness to come to me here."

Many, nay, most ladies would certainly have been discomposed, if not absolutely offended, by being interrupted at so very busy a moment; but Miss Hannah was not one of them. Knowing, however, how her sisters were respectively engaged in the drawing-rooms, and that they would have been by no means pleased to see a visitor, particularly of the male sex, walk in to interrupt their labours, she never dreamed of ordering Frank to enter any presence but her own; but as far as she herself was concerned, she was glad to see him now, as she always was; for he was an especial favourite, and valued at his worth by the critical and discerning old lady.

With her own hands she placed two chairs at a convenient distance from the prodigious table, and seating herself in one, with the air of a person by no means unwilling to take a little rest, she motioned to him to take the other, not, however, till she had first cordially shaken hands with him.

"Can you pardon me, my dear Miss Hannah," said he, "for breaking in upon you at a time when it was so more than likely that I should find you very busy? But I really had great need of seeing you for a few moments; for the fact is, I want your advice, my good friend."

"I am never too busy to see friends whom I value as sincerely as I value you, Mr. Frank Caldwell," she replied. "But I don't quite like your looks, Mr. Frank," resumed the old lady, looking at him with friendly interest. "In the first place, I don't thing you are well, for you look paler than usual; and in the next place, you look anxious and uneasy. You have had no painful news, I hope, of any kind?"

"I have received the very worst news, my dear Miss Hannah, that it was possible I could receive," replied the unhappy young man, with a forced composure of manner, which plainly enough betrayed much inward suffering. "It is quite impossible, Miss Hannah, that I should come to you to-morrow morning, and I preferred coming to tell you this myself to the sending a mere formal note of excuse."

"My dear Mr. Caldwell, you frighten me!" returned the old lady, looking at him with affectionate concern. "For goodness sake tell me what has happened! I do indeed see that you are suffering. Something painful, I am sure, has happened to you! I would to God that 1 had the power of doing you any good. But, at any rate, my dear Mr. Frank, let me know what has happened to you."

"I am quite sure that you would help me had you the power to do so," he replied; "but I fear, I fear that you have no such power. I have this morning received a letter from Mr. Walter Harrington, who was at Stanton when he wrote it, telling me, with much apparent sorrow, but very decidedly, that I must no longer think of his niece."

"Good Heaven, Mr. Caldwell! Not think of her? Not think of dear, beautiful Kate? From Mr. Harrington? —Mr. Walter?—Impossible! It cannot be, Sir. I am quite sure that there is some mistake among you. I certainly cannot call Mr. Harrington an *old* acquaintance, for, as you well know, he has not been amongst us very long; but, nevertheless, I feel as if I knew him thoroughly, and it would be a difficult thing to make me believe he could behave ill to anyone."

"Neither do I accuse him of doing so, my dear Miss Hannah," replied Frank. "On the contrary, I am quite as much disposed as you can be, to believe that he is acting in this matter as he believes it to be his duty to do. But *why* he thinks so, or what can possibly have happened to make him so suddenly change his opinion concerning me, I am totally at a loss to conjecture."

"He has told you that you must no longer think of his niece?" said Miss Hannah, knitting her brows, and looking at him almost sternly. "And Miss Harrington, Mr. Frank—my dear, sweet, pretty Kate? What does she say about it?"

"Her uncle only says that Miss Harrington is determined to be guided by the judgment of her family. Here is the letter, Miss Hannah. Perhaps you will understand my position more completely by reading it."

The ready spectacles were on her nose in a moment, and she set herself very earnestly to the perusal of the document which had produced so sad an effect upon her miserable-looking visitor. Nor did one perusal of Walter's epistle satisfy her; having read it once, very attentively, she deliberately turned back again to the beginning, and read it a second time; and having done so, she rose from her chair, placed herself immediately before him, and having returned the letter into his hand, she said:

"When you make any one your confidant, Mr. Caldwell, even if that confidant be an old woman, it is a very foolish thing to trust her only by halves. Tell me, therefore, openly and sincerely, whether you are conscious of having done anything, in any part of your past life, which could lead Walter Harrington, upon becoming acquainted with it, so completely to change his opinion of you?"

"Since reading this terrible letter, Miss Hannah," he replied, "I have asked myself the same question a dozen times, and I will now answer you as truly, my good friend, as I have answered my own heart, and that must be by assuring you that I am wholly and most completely at a loss to guess the motive for this change, or to recal any circumstance of my past life that might account for it.

There are none of us, I believe, who can look back upon all the years they have lived, and find in their memory no recollection of any folly which they may rationally wish they had never committed. But I most sincerely assure you that I cannot accuse myself of anything that in my conscience I think would, could, or ought, to have produced this change."

"Then depend upon it, my dear young friend," returned Miss Hannah, cheerily, "depend upon it, there is some mistake in the matter; and if so, you may also depend upon it, that time will clear it up. I most sincerely and heartily sympathize with you for the pain that this unaccountable letter must have given you, but I cannot consider the business in so serious a light as you do. We know that you have clear heads and honourable spirits to deal with in this matter; and when that is the case, error can never last very long."

"But where is the conceivable source of any error, my dear lady? I have no enemies, I feel sure that I have none; and if so, no one is likely to have spoken of me as being worse than I am," returned Frank, dolefully shaking his head.

"And where is the conceivable source of *any* error?" replied Miss Hannah. "The moment it is discovered, it is always declared to be inconceivable that it should ever have existed; and yet we all know that not a day passes without errors of all sorts arising, respecting all the subjects that people talk about. Inaccuracy in speaking, inaccuracy in hearing, inaccuracy in comprehending, may one and all occasion it; all which you know, my dear Mr. Caldwell, a great deal better than I can tell you—and you would not need to be reminded of it if the case concerned anybody else. Be very sure that there is some blunder of some sort, and in all probability nothing but a little time and a little patience will be required for its rectification. At any rate, it is impossible that the matter can rest as it now stands."

"But what would you have me do to change it, my kind friend?" replied the young man, looking considerably less miserable at the bare suggestion of such a change being possible.

"If you have no friend in the world who could do it for yourself, I would have you at once address yourself to Mr. Walter Harrington, and ask him to state to you explicitly the grounds on which he had changed his opinion of you."

"Yes! I feel that this would not be asking too much, and

22

that it ought to be done," replied Frank. "But yet," he
added, in a tone of deep feeling, "I could not bear to stand
before that old man, and dare him, as it were, to refuse answering me whatever questions I choose to ask."

"If you would have no objection to such a measure,"
said the old lady, indulging herself with a pinch of snuff
from her very capacious snuff-box, "I would, myself, very
willingly undertake the task of questioning the dear old
gentleman upon the subject. It is evident that the task
would be a painful one to you; but I declare that it would not
be in the least degree painful to me. If he should think fit to
open his mind to me on the matter, well and good, and of
course I should listen to him with great interest and attention;
but I should ask for no confidences on the subject. My communication with him, as far as I am concerned, would consist
of the simple statement of your ignorance of anything that
could justify his letter to you, appealing at the same time to
his sense of justice, as to the necessity of explaining himself
more fully on the subject. Should you have any objection to
my doing this, Mr. Caldwell?"

"My dear, kind friend!" he eagerly exclaimed in reply,
"if you would really undertake this office for me, you would
lay me under an obligation that I can never forget, yet never
be sufficiently thankful for. But, Mr. Harrington is at this
moment at a considerable distance from London, and I have
no idea as to the probable time of his return. Who knows
when you may be likely to see him?"

"As soon as all this foolery here is over to-morrow," she
replied, pointing rather contemptuously to the elegantly prepared table, "the married pair will, of course, move off to
hide themselves in honeymoon twilight, and then I shall be
at liberty to go to the land's end, if the fancy takes me.
Where is Mr. Walter Harrington at present?"

"He is at Brandon Abbey, near Doucham, on a visit to Lord
Goldstable," replied Caldwell.

"Then as soon as our turtles have taken wing, I will go
down to Doucham," said Miss Hannah, stoutly, "and somehow or other I will contrive to get at him. I should have
liked it better if the dear old man had been in his own Manor
House, which is also at no great distance from Doucham. But
it does not much signify. The young lord won't murder me
if I do storm his castle. It was not my fault, you know, if
Kate liked you better than she liked him. D.V., Mr. Frank

Caldwell, I will sleep at Doucham to-morrow night, and it shall not be very long before you hear from me."

" I will not attempt to thank you, Miss Hannah," said the greatly comforted young man, affectionately taking her hand. " You must feel yourself that no words can adequately express my sense of the kindness you are showing me. I could not half an hour ago have believed it possible for anything to have revived a feeling in my heart so nearly resembling hope as that which your words have inspired. I no longer feel as if there was nothing in this world worth living for."

"And I don't feel it either, Mr. Frank. I intend to enjoy my odd little journey exceedingly. And now, methinks, you are looking almost sprightly enough to be a wedding guest. What say you? Can you not take heart enough to join our fooleries to-morrow?"

"No, Miss Hannah; I had better not attempt it. You could not be reasoning with me all the time, you know, upon the wisdom of hope, and the folly of despair. I should in spite of all my efforts, be feeling and looking more doleful than would suit the occasion."

"Nay, as to that, Mr. Caldwell, I am quite sure that the silly little bride will be dissolved in tears the whole morning. However, I know the whole thing would be a bore to you, as well as to me, and I will not press your attendance. So good-bye—we shall meet again soon, I hope; and we may both of us then be in a gayer mood, perhaps."

And so they parted. Miss Hannah being left to resume her cares respecting gelatines, trifles and champagne; while poor Frank, almost dreading to find himself alone again, wandered back to his quiet chambers in Paper Buildings.

CHAPTER XLVIII.

MEANWHILE, the time had now arrived at which it was the annual custom of Dr. Harriugton to lead his family from the overpowering and overshadowing dissipations of London, to the calm dignity that nestled round his prebeuded residence at Glastonbury. The exemplary divine performed his yearly orbit from London to Glastonbury, from Glastonbury to Oxford, and from Oxford again to London, in the early spring, with a regularity that had something almost solemu iu it.

Judging of the importance of his presence to his London parish, as estimated by himself, aud the right-minded portiou of his parishioners, deep must have been the ecclesiastical night which settled down upon the west eud of London, when the rector, canon, warden, set iu the metropolis, in order to rise again and dawn upon his cathedral town of Glastonbury.

But, upon the present occasion, the long established regularity of this important transit was interrupted by the desire of Lady Augusta ; and instead of passing from his house in Vale Street to his extremely well-appointed residence iu the prebended "Close" at Glastonbury, the Doctor and his noble spouse, the Lady Augusta, determined upon taking a rather circuitous route, for the purpose of paying a visit to their son James, at Stanton. It was a long time since the reverend Doctor had been there ; for it was no light matter which could take him out of his accustomed circuit. And even their usual well-arranged and comfortably prepared-for journey was uot submitted to and endured by the Doctor, without many a painful complaint of roads, and Spring, and sunshine, and wind, and many other disagreeable accompaniments to the moving from one place to another. His consolatiou for all this was evidently found where so good a man ought to seek it, uamely, in his own conscience ; for not seldom was he heard to mutter, *sotto voce*, and accompanied by a deep sigh, some allusion to his peculiar position and duties, in which the words "in journeyings oft," might be distinctly heard.

It evidently did not occur to him that all this locomotive fatigue might be avoided, if he would consent to devote all his

energies, corporal and spiritual, only to one scene of exertion.
But it is more than probable, that after a deliberate consideration of the subject, he had arrived at the conclusion that the
monopoly of a dignitary, as pre-eminent in ecclesiastical learning and every other sort of ecclesiastical excellence as himself,
might weigh heavily upon the conscience of any one congregation to which he might be induced to devote himself. There
can, indeed, be no reasonable doubt whatever that he would
have accused himself severely of short-coming in his professional duties, if he had, upon any occasion, refused ecclesiastical
preferment; nor can it be doubted that he considered the
frequent journeyings of St. Paul as an indisputable testimony
in favour of pluralities.

It was but a few days previous to the usual time for this
annual flitting, that the Doctor and his admirable wife, the
Lady Augusta, found themselves *tête-à-tête* at their breakfast-
table in Vale Street.

"I am not at all sorry, Doctor," the lady but then said to
him, "that our time for leaving London has arrived. Kate's
absurd conduct about Lord Goldstable has spoilt the season
for me entirely. I hope you feel as inclined to be off as
I do?"

"I am ready, as you have always known me to be, my
dear, at the call of duty," replied the martyr Doctor. "But
I will not deny that this frequent necessity of abandoning one
home, to encounter all the risks and hardships of the wayfar-
ing which must of necessity precede my arrival at another, is
becoming at my time of life a grievous and painful burden to
me! But I suppose," added the excellent man, with his
usual gentle sigh of pious resignation, when contemplating
the inevitable evils consequent upon our present mortal condition, "I suppose I shall die in the harness, as many another
labourer in the vineyard has done before me!" And as he
spoke, he gently helped himself to a second slice from a
magnificent collar of Oxford brawn, which flanked his plate.

"At least we shall have the consolation of knowing that
your labour in the vineyard has not been so severe as to
prevent your helping yourself to a few of the grapes, my dear
Doctor," said his lady wife, who now and then yielded to the
temptation of quizzing him a little when there was nobody
by.

"Helping my family to them, my dear, you should say,"
replied the courtly Doctor, with much suavity. "The doing

so is at once a duty and a pleasure. And were it not for this very sacred duty, I should, Heaven knows! be only too happy to throw off the burthen of my cathedral preferment. May I trouble you, my dear, for another cup of tea? that Pekoe has a very particularly fine flavour. Not quite so much cream, my dear, as in the last cup, if you please."

"Yes, certainly," replied Lady Augusta, after a short pause, during which she gave, as in duty bound, her undivided attention to the duties of the tea-tray. "Yes, certainly; we all of us are fully aware how much we owe you. But for goodness sake, do not talk of dying in harness yet! I am sure your last year's journeys did you no harm; on the contrary, I thought you seemed all the better for the exercise."

"An ardent spirit, Lady Augusta, and a determined will, may carry the body through much. But it is a hard life, my dear wife! a very hard life; and that *will* tell upon the health and strength in the long run. Few persons can tell what it is, after many months of anxious and unremitting toil among the harassing duties and responsibilities of an important London parish, to be obliged, instead of taking that repose which body and mind alike require, to be obliged to hurry off to fresh labours in distant provinces, separated by hundreds of miles of rugged roads, or else by frightfully dangerous railroads, and bad inns."

There was, perhaps, a little consciousness of the bathos of this winding-up which caused the Doctor to have recourse to one of his sadly-suffering sighs to assist him in this statement. But he roused himself again to add, though still with a very anxious expression of countenance: "This reminds me that I must beg you, my dear love, to take care that the travelling chariot be sent to Jobson's, that the springs and axles may be properly looked to. And do not forget, my dear, to write in time to the man at the White Hart, at Brompton, that he may be perfectly ready to receive us at about five o'clock, as usual. He could not do better than give us a haunch of that small South Down mutton they have there. Nothing can be too simple for travelling fare. And let Barnes put up a pot of her own currant jelly. That is one of the things that one is often apt to find bad."

"But I was going to propose a plan, my dear Doctor, which would make that odious night at an inn unnecessary," replied his lady. "Suppose we were to pay James a visit? We should be able to get to Stanton in one day, if we start early, even if you will not consent to go by the railroad; and there will be no difficulty in getting across from Stanton to Glastonbury."

"Humph!" pronounced the Doctor, doubtingly. "One might get across; certainly, my dear, one might get across. But I don't know what to say about those cross-roads, Lady Augusta. We never have gone that way yet," said he, with a Conservative churchman's conviction of the strength of this argument against trying the experiment.

"That is quite true, my dear Doctor," returned the lady: "but, on the other hand, we never before had such strong reasons for trying this route. I do think, my dear Doctor, that it is highly proper and highly necessary that we should see Kate. It strikes me that we shall be greatly to blame if we do not endeavour to improve the intimacy which your brother has so very judiciously formed with Lord Goldstable. And now we have an excellent opportunity for doing this. Remember that Stanton is but three miles from Brandon Abbey."

"Yes, I know it; and I feel the truth of what you say, my dear," replied the Doctor, thoughtfully. "Walter and James, I have no doubt, are both of them doing everything in their power to bring our foolish girl to a sense of her duty; but, nevertheless, I feel quite as strongly as you can do, that your presence might be of the very greatest importance, and might most effectually assist them in bringing matters to the conclusion which we all desire, and hope for. Besides, my dear, I confess that I think it would be very desirable that I should myself make a little further acquaintance with the young man. If old Dr. Barringham should drop, his deanery, you know, must be given to some one; and I happen to know that—well, well! write to James at once, my dear. I am quite sure that he will try to make us as comfortable as he can. But I remember, the old Rectory used to be full of draughts. However, if you think Lady Augusta, that it will be for the benefit of my family that I should go there, you may depend upon it that I shall brave every danger and inconvenience. The additional fatigue may certainly be considerable. But never mind! Let it be arranged, Lady Augusta."

"I have no doubt, Dr. Harrington, that Lord Goldstable will make a point of paying a visit at the Rectory as soon as he knows you are there," said Lady Augusta. "And nothing would be so likely to bring matters to a pleasant conclusion at

once. It cannot be denied that your brother, notwithstanding all his eccentricities, has shown a great deal of tact and
cleverness in his management of this affair, and I have no
doubt that he will continue to do so. His contriving to
become the guest of Lord Goldstable has raised him excessively
in my opinion. He certainly does say strangely foolish things
sometimes; but I cannot help thinking *now*, that he certainly
must be a man of ability, though he is not an agreeable
person."

"When we were at school," replied the Doctor, meekly,
"I cannot deny that my poor dear brother was considered as
a very dull boy in comparison to me. But even then, I
remember perfectly well that my poor mother used to say, that
Walter was no fool. And I never felt so strongly as I do at
present that she was right."

"Well then," said Lady Augusta, "I will write to James
at once, and tell him our plans; and just give him a hint or
two about being ready to receive us."

"I trust my dear," said the Doctor, with a very anxious
expression of countenance; "I trust that James won't
think of putting us into the east room over the hall? I
remember that room of old, Lady Augusta! I think that you
might give a useful hint or two on several points, my dear,
respecting his manner of receiving us. A young bachelor's
housekeeping arrangements are not always of the most comfortable kind, you know."

"Perhaps I had better give my sister Juliana a line," said
Lady Augusta. "She knows our ways better than James
does, and is quite aware of what will be necessary in the way
of making you comfortable, after a fatiguing journey."

"That is a very good idea, Lady Augusta; it may be useful
in many respects. I do trust that James will not be playing any
foolery about fast-keeping, or any Puseyite trash of that sort.
Neither my religious principles, nor my bodily health could
stand it Lady Augusta. God knows what might be the consequence to me at my time of life! And a pretty story it
would make at Glastonbury and Oxford. I do trust that
James will not attempt anything of the kind."

"Oh, dear no! there is not the least danger of it, my dear
Doctor. James is too well aware of your principles," she
added, with a slight smile, "to expose you to so painful a
trial. He will be guilty of no such absurdity, while we are
with him, you may depend upon it."

"I trust you are right, my dear," replied the Doctor, with dignity. "But, my dear Lady Augusta," he continued, "there is one other point which I must mention. We shall pass next Sunday with him, and I think it highly probable that James may wish—naturally enough, perhaps—that I should preach from his pulpit. Now this I cannot do, Lady Augusta. I shall by no means have recovered from the fatigue of the long day's journey to Stanton Parva; and with the prospect of another day of equal fatigue before me when I leave it, I could not safely venture upon making any such exertion. It would be quite too much for me, nor must it be expected. I know the effect that preaching has upon me. Others may not feel it in the same degree, but I should be very wrong to attempt it, and therefore I will not attempt it. Everything tells heavily at my time of life. But perhaps James had better make it known in the parish at once, that my doing this may not be expected, and that disappointment may not ensue. It may be as well for James to make it known in the parish, that I think it right to confine my ministry to those flocks which it has pleased Providence to intrust to me, and that I make it a point never to interfere in another pulpit. Pray let this be thoroughly understood before my arrival."

Lady Augusta promised to make this very important point clearly comprehended by her son James, and then the dignified divine retired, a little out of breath, to his study, to repose himself after the exertion he had made to make his views and wishes clearly understood, while her more active Ladyship proceeded to take the labouring oar in the needful preparations for the scheme which she had so satisfactorily arranged.

CHAPTER XLIX.

THE result of this very satisfactory conversation was the
immediate production of two letters by the ready pen of the
Lady Augusta, and the dismissal of them to the post without
a moment of unnecessary delay ; for her Ladyship was too well
pleased at having conquered all the difficulties, whether real
or imaginary, which she had found might impede her visit to
Stanton, to run the risk of any second discussion on the
subject.

In truth, she was extremely sanguine as to the result of this
visit. No shadow of doubt rested on her mind respecting the
motive which had induced old Walter Harrington to become
the visitor of young Lord Goldstable. She looked upon her
brother-in-law as a capricious humourist, whose pleasure it
was to manage matters in his own way ; a privilege which he
doubtless considered to be the right of every rich old bachelor.
But she no longer looked upon him as the sort of imbecile
idiot that she had considered him to be, when she believed
that he positively wished to impede the marriage of his niece
with the best *parti* of the season. On the contrary, she now
truly believed, not only that he wished for this splendid
marriage, but that with all his eccentricities he had, probably,
by keeping the young man completely under his own eye, hit
upon the best possible means of ensuring it.

Such being her view of the present state of affairs, it was
natural enough that she should wish to be using her influence
on the mind of her daughter as actively as the worthy Walter
was employing his on that of Lord Goldstable ; and great
indeed would have been her disappointment if she had failed
in pesuading the Doctor that their best way of going to Glastonbury would be by passing through Stanton.

Her letter to her son James was as follows :

"You will, I am sure, be very sorry to hear, my dear
James, that your good father has not of late been so well as
usual, and I do not feel quite easy about him. Heaven knows,
my dear James, that I have enough upon my mind just now,
without this addition ! You will easily imagine all the

anxiety I must feel that the splendid proposal that has been made for your sister Kate should not fall to the ground in consequence of any childish folly on her part.

"We had at first great reason to fear that your Uncle Walter was at the bottom of this opposition of hers; but it is now evident that we wronged the dear old man, and that he had only determined upon bringing about the desired result in his own way   That he could have done nothing better under the circumstances than constitute himself the guest of Lord Goldstable, while Kate was staying with you in his immediate neighbourhood, is quite certain; but I cannot but think that my presence also at this moment might be very important.   I have, naturally, more influence than anyone, with the foolish, frightened girl, who really seems terrified at the idea of so suddenly becoming a peeress.

"You will, I well know, my dear James, agree with me in thinking that no stone should be left unturned when seeking the means of securing a connection so desirable for us all, and that you will approve of my having used all my influence with your good father to induce him to brave the fatigue of the lengthened journey, in order to give me the opportunity of seeing your sister.

"We only propose remaining with you for a day or two.   I shall be sorry to occasion you trouble in your housekeeping, my dear James, but your poor father's state of health requires much case.   And you must be aware that his life is very important to us all.   I feel confident, therefore, that you will endeavour to make him as comfortable as possible.   There are, I believe, some differences of opinion between you and your father on Church matters, but I have much too high an opinion of your good sense, to fear that you should vex your father by any display of the innovations which he so greatly disapproves.   If I mistake not, you, like many other young clergymen of the present day, make a point of dining on fish every Friday.   Your father objects to this on principle; and though I never meddle in such matters, as you well know, thinking it exceedingly unfeminine and unladylike to do so, I must say that I should be very sorry indeed to see your father attempt to dine upon fish, being very sure that it would be seriously injurious to his health.

"We shall get to you on Thursday: this hint, therefore, may be useful.   I do not, however, wish to make you think that your father would object so far to accommodate himself to your views as to eat fish with you on the Friday, provided that it were of good quality (he is rather particular on that point), and that a proper dinner followed after it, which would not only prevent any danger of suffering in health, but guard against a danger which would be at least equally painful to him—namely, that of appearing to give his sanction to what he considers as a superstition at variance with the doctrine of the Established Church.

"There is one other point to be observed, my dear James. You must not on any account ask your father to do any part of the service on the Sunday that we shall pass with you. His life, as he says, poor man, is so very laborious a one, that it is but fair that he should enjoy a holiday when it comes in his way.

"I shall write a few lines by to-day's post, to your Aunt Juliana. Tell Kate that her mother sends her, by you, her most fervent blessing, and that she trusts she shall find her in a better frame of mind than when they parted.

"Adieu, my dear James,
"Always your affectionate mother,
"AUGUSTA HARRINGTON.

"P.S.—We fully hope to reach you in time for six o'clock dinner on Thursday. But at all events we shall not be later than seven, or at most, half-past."

We will now give Lady Augusta's epistle to her sister. It run thus:

"MY DEAR JULIANA,

"We have determined upon paying a visit at Stanton on our way to Glastonbury. The Doctor does not half like it, and it certainly is a great undertaking for him. He has misgivings about James's housekeeping, which, *entre nous*, I fully share. You know what our habits are, and do just try to see that things are as decent and as comfortable as may be. You will be at no loss to guess the reasons which have induced us to take this step. Of course you will take care to let it be known at Brandon Abbey, that we are expected at the Rectory. In haste.

"Yours affectionately,
"A. H."

It so chanced that these two letters on their way from London to the post-town of Doucham, passed another letter on the road addressed to Lady Augusta Harrington, from her sister, the Lady Juliana, and it is fitting that this letter also should be communicated to the reader. The pious and right honourable lady wrote as follows:

"MY DEAR SISTER,

"As the whole of the task which my sense of duty led me to undertake when I came hither was, in all respects, a very painful one, I can only consider the business of my present letter a natural part of it. You no doubt remember a most particularly bold and in my judgment) very revolting-looking young woman whom that most odious person, Miss Puddingthwaite most audaciously brought to your house on the night of your ball. I feel it due to my own principles, Lady Augusta, to point out to you that such misfortunes are among the minor judgments which such ungodly compliances with the world for ever expose us to. The creature's name, as you probably remember, was Fitzjames. The very particularly disgusting manner in which, upon that occasion, she contrived to force herself upon the notice of Lord Goldstable, was quite enough to prevent your forgetting her. I perfectly well remember your indignation at the time, nor have I forgotten the equally strong indignation of Lady de Paddington—a feeling on her part most perfectly natural and proper, from her near relationship to the young nobleman. I leave you, then, to imagine my astonishment and indignation upon hearing that your friend, Lady de Paddington, was arrived at the Doucham water establishment, accompanied by this identical Mrs. Fitzjames!

"I never, I think, was so astonished or so disgusted in my whole life as when I heard of it, and I am still perfectly at a loss to comprehend what it means, so on that point you must look for no explanation from me. I have not seen Lady de Paddington, and you will readily believe that I have no inclination to expose myself to the risk of meeting the creature whom she has chosen to make her companion.

"Perhaps, Lady Augusta, you may understand all this mystery better than I do; for my part, I cannot pretend in any way to comprehend what it means. I have not, as I have said, seen Lady de Paddington, nor do I mean to take any steps towards doing so; I will not expose myself to the risk of

seeing the very decidedly doubtful creature she has thought
proper to bring into her nephew's neighbourhood.   I have not
heard anything as yet respecting Lord Goldstable's movements
since their arrival; but I should not be in the least degree
surprised if I were told that he was immediately going to be
married to this horrid woman.   I begin to think very badly
indeed of Lady de Paddington.   A pretty piece of work Miss
Kate has made of it!

"You must not imagine, as you are so very apt to do,
Augusta, that there is the least possibility of my having made
any blunder in this matter, for incredible as my statement
may appear, it is nevertheless most correctly true.   A most
respectable lady whose pew I have agreed to share in the
chapel of a very faithful minister at Doucham (for my sitting
under my nephew James is of course impossible), this lady who
is very intimate with Mr. Limpid, the doctor at the water-
cure establishment, told me yesterday of the arrival of these
two ladies.

"They not only, she says, came together from London,
but they have taken between them the best and most expensive set of apartments in the house, which, as you well know,
is not at all in Lady de Paddington's style of doing things.
But doubtless her nephew can assist her *now*, if she should
chance, as I suspect has happened before now, that she should
want assistance!

"I hope, my dear sister, that you will not take it amiss
that, after deep consideration, I should have decided upon not
sitting under my nephew James, but I really think that the
Doctor himself would approve my determination if he could
see how James goes on   Such impious mummeries! such
candles! such keeping of days! such fasting!   It was really
quite impossible for me to overlook the safety of my immortal
soul for the sake of pleasing James.   I could not peril my
hopes for all eternity by giving my countenance to such rank
and undisguised Popery!   And now, my dear sister, hoping
soon to obtain your opinion as to what I ought to do under
such very extraordinary circumstances, I remain your affectionate sister,

                              "JULIANA WITHERBY.

"P.S.—I open my letter, my dear Augusta, to tell you
that I have had a visit from Mrs. Slater (the lady I sit with
at church).   She has just been calling on Mrs. Limpid, who

told her that Lord G—— paid a visit last evening to Lady de P——, and remained there nearly two hours. That creature, Mrs. Fitzj——, was with them the whole time; and Mrs. Limpid is pretty sure that Lady de P—— left them together part of the time, for she is quite certain that she heard the bed-room door open and shut. This is almost too bad to believe, and perhaps Christian charity should lead me to say that it is *possible* it may not be true. Yet I own it is very difficult to doubt it.

"J. W"

The effect which this letter produced both on the venerable Doctor and his devoted wife, may be in some degree imagined. It was with a crimson cheek and a flashing eye that Lady Augusta repaired to the *sanctum* of her dozing spouse, and totally unmindful of the hallowed tranquillity which for ever ought to reign there, she threw wide open the confidingly unbolted door, without even the ordinary ceremony of a preparatory tap, and rushing into the room, threw the open letter upon the table which flanked the Doctor's easy-chair.

"I will trouble you to read *that*, Dr. Harrington, if you please!" she said, with a vehemence of tone which, if he *was* asleep, was certainly sufficient to wake him, adding rather sarcastically, "that is to say, if you can so far attend to the most important affairs concerning your family, as to keep yourself awake for half an hour."

"Lady Augusta!" he gasped, in very genuine alarm. "This vehemence greatly confounds me! Such things are too much for me, Lady Augusta—I don't understand—I protest that—I really must beg that your Ladyship——"

"Will you read that letter, Dr. Harrington?" reiterated his wife, now speaking, however, with the calm superiority of perfect composure.

"I must beg that you will have the goodness to shut the door," replied the angry Doctor. "And may I trouble you for that flask of Eau de Cologne from the chimney-piece? This sort of thing is a great deal too much for me. I do assure you that I am not able to bear it."

"I am sorry I waked you so suddenly," said Lady Augusta, with something a little approaching to a quizzing smile.

"I slept not, Lady Augusta!" he replied, with great solemnity. "Heaven knows that I have but little leisure for repose. They who are placed as watchmen on the tower—"

Lady Augusta took up the letter again, and putting it into his hand, said, in a rather reproachful, matter-of-fact sort of tone:

"Will you be so good, Dr. Harrington, as to occupy yourself with the affairs of your family for half an hour? Here is the very strangest letter from my silly sister, Lady Juliana. And whether we fully believe her statements or not, I think you will agree with me in feeling that we ought to pay some attention to them."

Thus urged, the Doctor (though not without a slight groan) proceeded to arrange his spectacles on his nose, and set himself to the far from easy or agreeable task of deciphering his noble sister-in-law's cross-bars.

But it soon became evident that the alarming contents of the letter more effectually roused him, and more thoroughly chased all inclination to slumber or sleep than all her Lady-ship's vehemence had done.

"God bless my soul, Lady Augusta!" he exclaimed, when he reached the bottom of the first page. "This is a most extraordinary communication indeed! Yes, I certainly do perfectly well remember the very particularly handsome young woman by whom our incautious acquaintance, Miss Pudding-thwaite, was accompanied on the occasion in question. But such toys, as you must well know, my dear Lady Augusta, are the last things in the world at all likely to rivet my atten-tion. I saw her, and just looked at her, nothing more. I have no recollection of anything further about her."

"But this same toy," returned her ladyship, with a sneer, "seems likely enough to carry off the son-in-law you hope for; and what is to become of the Deanery then?"

"Lady Augusta!" replied her husband, restored by this inroad into his own peculiar territory, to all his ordinary pomposity; "Lady Augusta! The position which I have held in the Church for half-a-century has, I flatter myself, been such as not unfittingly to point me out to those who, under Providence, have the conferring its higher dignities without the aid or interference of any *lay* influence whatever. More especially, Lady Augusta, I am bound to point out to you that these are subjects on which it does not become your sex to enter."

"Very possibly, Dr. Harrington," she replied, with rather more indifference of manner than he thought quite becoming after so solemn a rebuke. "If, however, you wish on any

other grounds," she added, "for the alliance of Lord Goldstable, it will be desirable for us to examine into the circumstances related by my sister."

"Assuredly, assuredly!" replied the vexed and puzzled
divine. "The conduct of Lady de Paddington," he continued,
"is altogether incomprehensible; and I quite agree with the
Lady Juliana, that it is wholly impossible to understand it."

"And I, on the contrary, do not agree with her at all,"
rejoined Lady Augusta, tartly. "Juliana is a simpleton in
this, as in most other things. To me, Dr. Harrington, the
motives of Lady de Paddington are as visible as the sun at
noon-day. Nor is she, perhaps, altogether mistaken in the
conclusion at which she has arrived. Lady de Paddington is
poor, Dr. Harrington, very poor for her rank, we all know
that; and she has decided in her speculative meditations, that
it will be more profitable for her to league with this audacious
Fitzjames woman, for the purpose of making Lord Goldstable
marry her, than to suffer him to marry into an honourable
family, such as ours. *I* understand Lady de Paddington perfectly, whatever Juliana may do. She fancies that it will be
easier to manage a Lady Goldstable, made out of nobody, than
to manage a daughter of mine! I see through it all, Dr.
Harrington!"

"The motives which you attribute to Lady de Paddington,
my dear Lady Augusta," replied the Doctor, looking greatly
shocked, "are alike treacherous as a friend, indelicate as a
woman, iniquitous as a Christian, and derogatory as a member
of the aristocracy!"

There was something so soothing to the feelings of the Doctor
in the delivery of this striking climax, that, when his wife
modestly remarked in reply, that it was very fortunate they
had already settled everything for going to Stanton, for that,
after all, was the only rational thing for them to do, he replied with an amiable smile, and a voice of the most bland
courtesy:

"It is indeed fortunate that you will be on the spot, Lady
Augusta, for it is an affair which evidently requires all your
delicate tact and admirable management!"

"Why, yes, Doctor; I confess I think that it is quite as
well I should be there. Lady de Paddington seems to forget,"
she added, with two or three little mysterious nods of the
head, that there are certain circumstances which ought to
make her a little cautious how she offends me. Yes! it is

23

quite right that we should be on the spot at once.   Juliana is really too silly, protesting that she cannot guess this abominable old woman's motives!"

"You are right, my dear! But we must not expect to find in every one, your powers of mind.   For instance, I must confess that in respect to James also, I think she seems to show great want of judgment.   What she says of his peculiarities may probably be all very much deserved, and I grieve to say it; yet surely it would have been more becoming in one of the laity, and a lady too, if she had attended the parish church, without meddling with the doctrinal opinions of the pastor. She speaks too in her letter, I see, of 'sitting under a *minister*,'" added the orthodox divine, with infinite disgust. "I do hope, Lady Augusta, that she has not suffered herself to be led into the indecency of attending any dissenting place of worship ?   There is no knowing what she may mean by the ambiguous term she uses—what *does* she mean by a *minister* ? I do trust that the deep humiliation of seeing a member of my family join the ranks of dissent has not been reserved for my old age! "

"These are subjects, my dear Doctor," returned Lady Augusta, very meekly, " on which, as you observed just now, it does not become one of my sex to enter."

And with these words, and with a particularly submissive air, she left the room to its accustomed stillness, and the Doctor to meditate himself to sleep again ; while she returned with renewed energy to superintend all the arrangements which necessarily preceded her departure from town.

CHAPTER L.

It so happened, that the day on which Lady Augusta's letters to her son and her sister reached Stanton had been fixed upon by the gay and particularly happy Lord Goldstable for a social pic-nic gathering, at a spot which old Walter Harrington had mentioned to him as one of exceeding beauty, at the distance of a mile or two from the Abbey.

The invitations to this pic-nic, as his Lordship chose to call the banquet, which he had ordered to be spread at the spot pointed out to him by his old friend, included, as a matter of course, his aunt, Lady de Paddington, and her friend and companion, Mrs. Fitzjames, as well as the Rector of Stanton, and his sister, and the Lady Juliana Witherby, their aunt.

When all this was settled, and the day fixed, Lord Goldstable, from a movement of constitutional good-nature, asked Walter if he did not think that old Mrs. Cross and her handsome daughter might like to join the party?

The reply to this question was uttered precisely in the same spirit in which it was asked; and the consequence was, that old Walter volunteered to walk over to Stanton, in order to present the invitation himself to his old and much respected acquaintance, Mrs. Cross.

The evident delight with which this honour, glory and pleasure, was accepted by both mother and daughter, was quite sufficiently evident to repay the trouble the old gentleman had taken, ten times over; and yet, this evident satisfaction was at an immeasurable distance, in point of intensity, from the real feelings of delight which caused the bosom of the fair Olivia to palpitate, as she dwelt on the delightful idea of passing almost an entire day, and it might be, some portion of the dear twilight hour also, in the presence of that glorious and too fascinating, though fearfully backsliding creature, the Rector of Stanton.

There were, indeed, moments in which the rapture with which this idea inspired her, positively alarmed herself; for she had hitherto succeeded tolerably well in persuading herself, that her feelings respecting him had their foundation and origin solely in her ardent desire to turn the steps of one

23—2

so excellent and admirable into the way of life, instead of permitting to go on, as he had unhappily began, groping darkly through the valley of death.

And it was under the influence of this pious persuasion, that she permitted herself to think of him by night and by day, constantly comforting herself with the delightful idea, that if she gave all her thoughts, and all her energies, to the godly work, she should finally succeed by "snatching this precious brand from the burning."

This was her favourite phrase, and she murmured it without ceasing to her own heart; for it was equally soothing to her tender passion and her fervent piety. But when it happened, the night after receiving this enchanting invitation, that she caught herself whispering to her pillow, the unweighed words: "Oh, that dear darling brand!" she began for the first time to be a little alarmed at her own condition; and secretly determined, that if he offered her his arm in walking, she would decline it, unless it happened that the road was really very rough. Nor while thus deliciously musing, was it with any trifling degree of satisfaction that she remembered how well she knew, poor girl, how to make herself look very nice in a morning dress, without laying out one single farthing.

Nor was her good little mother at all insensible to the pleasure offered by this good-natured invitation; for she well remembered having eaten syllabub in Bickley meadow thirty years or more ago, when her dear Nathaniel Cross was Curate of Bickley Parish, and when they were waiting to be married, till he should get a college living.

The Reverend James Harrington was also exceedingly well pleased at receiving the invitation. He liked the idea of any opportunity of cultivating the acquaintance of Lord Goldstable. So near a neighbour, and so wealthy a peer, could hardly refuse, if he became sufficiently intimate to ask it of him, to distribute a "daily dole" in the good old mediæval fashion—a dole, which should include his own parish, as well as that of the noble Lord; and not more than five minutes had elapsed after the arrival of the invitation, before his imagination suggested to him the great probability of his seeing his church filled at "matins," in consequence of this anticipated "dole."

That Lady de Paddington and her fair friend were well pleased, cannot be doubted, because they both immediately perceived that such an excursion, if properly managed, could not fail in giving excellent opportunities for pushing forward the business of the drama in which they were engaged. Had it not been for this important consideration, indeed, they both felt that the scheme would have been detestable enough; for the old lady hated nothing so much as being put out of her usual snug routine in any way, and the idea of fatigue of any kind was positively hateful to her.

But she had what she and her companion both called "the great object," so much at heart, that no sacrifice appeared too great which had the promotion of it for its motive. Mrs. Fitzjames, too, though exceedingly anxious that so favourable an opportunity for love-making should not be lost, actually looked forward to it with a shudder; for had she not for hours to be fascinating, amusing, and tender, while enduring the direful bore of a country scramble, with an odious blockhead making love to her all the time.

As for poor Kate, she was much too miserable to care greatly what she did, or where she went; her only possible source of satisfaction from the scheme, being that it might enable her to keep more out of the way of her aunt than she found it possible to do at the parsonage; while that troublesome old lady, on her side, consoled herself for the fatigue which threatened her, by remembering that the expedition would give her the best possible means of forming a correct idea of what was going on between "that creature" and Lord Goldstable, a species of information which she was particularly anxious to acquire before the arrival of Lady Augusta.

As to Walter Harrington, he was always ready, despite his age, for the enjoyment of any scheme which had for its object a country expedition and the exploring some spot particularly worthy of notice.

And such, most assuredly, was the pretty nook known by the name of Bickley Cell. But on this occasion, he looked forward to the additional pleasure of visiting a scene which he well remembered had been a favourite with him during the rambling days of his boyhood.

This Bickley Cell had been, in old times, a small priory belonging to the Benedictine Abbey of Brandon, and in later days had attained no small celebrity, among the picturesque scenery-hunters and pic-nic fanciers, from the interesting and graceful ruins of the little gothic chapel, and the wild beauty of the scenery around it. A holy well, also, of great repute in days of yore for its curative sanctity, and still renowned for

its limpid purity, added to the interest of the spot, and contributed not a little towards the satisfaction of those who
wished to dine with comfort and coffee.

When people are, like Gilpin's spouse, "on pleasure bent,"
we all know that a very slight attraction is sufficient to draw
them afield; but the beauties of Bickley Cell were really
sufficient to redeem its visitors from the charge of being drawn
thither solely by the hope of meeting Strasburg pie, champagne, and flirtation.

A small stream which took its rise among some hills a mile
or two to the northward, flowed towards Bickley, through a
deep ravine. Immediately above the site of the old priory,
the general level of the soil fell suddenly, and changed its
geological character, and the stream having lost its hitherto
tranquil bed, took courage, and reached the lower country at
one bold leap.

When the Benedictines of Brandon inhabited Bickley
Priory, the waterfall must probably have been some few feet
higher, and some few feet nearer their cell, so as to have
mingled its music with the notes of the Bickley sacristan;
and even now, though the perpendicular little cliff may have
receded some feet, by the wear and tear of the fall during the
last three centuries, or thereabouts, the never-failing cascade
is still near enough to furnish a very harmonious *running*
accompaniment to the chatter and laughter of the frequent
pic-nic parties who are in the habit of spreading their gay
banquets among the picturesque relics of the old building.

The spot on which those relics stood had been chosen by
those admirably good judges, the monks, in a lovely meadow
at the foot of the cliff, which formed the boundary line
between the higher and lower district. Above this boundary,
the country was bare and bleak; but below, the whole expanse, which sloped gently towards the south, was very richly
wooded.

The situation of the holy well, and the little lady-like
difficulties which stood in the way of a near approach to it,
were not, perhaps, among the least attractive features of this
favourite excursion.

Close beside the waterfall was a huge natural grotto, or
cave, which reached under the cliff to the distance of a
hundred yards or more; and at the further extremity of this
cave welled forth, from its rocky termination, a bright stream,
which was received into a stone reservoir of very ancient

workmanship, and it was this old cistern which was honoured by the appellation of the " holy well."

The entrance to this grotto was the spot at which arose the difficulty of the excursion. It was about half way up the cliff, and the path which led up to it was kept in tolerably good condition; but the running stream, which, after filling the cistern, had worn for itself a channel, that brought its waters to a point where they were merged in the neigbouring cascade, had so meandered in its course through the grotto, that it had to be crossed by a plank before the holy reservoir could be reached.

Now this plank was not very wide, and was generally rather wet, and rather slippery. The distance, however, between the two sides of the little water-course, was only a few feet, and though a tumble into the stream would decidedly have been attended with considerable danger, from the brisk rate at which it ran to join the larger one, no fatal accident was on the record as having happened there; and the pic-nic party must have been badly arranged, at which there would not have been a more certain assurance of help than there was of danger in passing to and from the Holy Well.

The pic-nic, which is at present to be recorded, was most assuredly Lord Goldstable's pic-nic, on more than one ground of ownership. But it may be doubted whether it would have ever entered into his young Lordship's unassisted brain to con- ceive a project of such bold originality.

In all probability, the first birth of the idea might be traced to that interesting hour which, if the acute ears of the highly intelligent Mrs. Limpid might be trusted, was passed *téte-à-téte* by the young nobleman and the lovely. widow, in the apart- ment usually occupied by the said lovely widow and her faith- ful friend, Lady de Paddington.

To a person as highly intelligent, and as thoroughly ex- perienced as, notwithstanding her youth, Mrs. Fitzjames certainly was, in all the mysteries of love-making, the importance of a romantic country excursion was perfectly well understood. Had it been required of her, indeed, she would have been perfectly well able, also, to set down, in numerical proportion, the respective value, in this line, of every occurrence likely to be produced by the accidents of human life.

For example: supposing the sum total of one thousand to be the amount required for the achievement of any given conquest, she would systematically have set down the relative value of every separate manœuvre somewhat in this wise:

First sight, under all advantages of dress, one hundred.

Under disadvantage of ditto, but not presumed to be actually disfigured, fifty. Morning occupation, with hands ungloved, and hair hanging in disorder (nicely arranged), fifty.

Caught reading a newly-arrived review (if the chase be literary), twenty-five. Transcribing music, if he be musical, one hundred and fifty.

A ball well lighted, with a good reposing room, seventy. Fancy-dress ditto, one hundred and sixty.

Caught singing an Italian bravura, or a French ballad, if you have a voice, and he has ears, one hundred and seventy-five.

To be seen at early church, if he be a Puseyite, seventy-seven.

At an evening lecture, if he be an Evangelical, seventy-seven.

To be seen darning stockings if he be a rich miser, one hundred.

To be seen embroidering in gold and seed-pearls, if he be a poor elegant, one hundred.

A pic-nic, everything being *couleur de rose*, fifty.

Ditto with a storm, seventy-five.

Ditto, with a moon, and a little dancing after, one hundred and fifty.

Ditto when matters are tolerably far advanced beforehand, two hundred.

And so on, with an infinity of items, every one of which would have shown an admirable knowledge of the human heart.

It was, of course, this last and longest recompense that Mrs. Fitzjames anticipated from proposing this pic-nic to the spot that Mrs. Limpid had, as usual, boasted of as one of the most attractive features of the neighbourhood; and the eagerness with which Lord Goldstable caught at the proposal, proved that he enjoyed the idea of being enchanted as much as she did that of enchanting.

But while thus dilating upon the talents of this beautiful Mrs. Fitzjames, I seem to be forgetting all my other *dramatis personæ*, as well as the identical pic-nic itself, which was to bring many of them together, and prove worth two hundred out of one thousand towards winning the game at which the **lovely widow** was playing.

CHAPTER LI.

It happened on the occasion of the Bickley Priory pic-nic, as I believe it generally does happen upon all similar occasions, that a good deal of skill and manœuvring was put in practice in order to arrange the various parties in the different vehicles which were to convey them, so as, if possible, to content everybody. In no case is it very probable that this benevolent object can be completely obtained. Nor could any such perfect success be boasted of in the present instance. All that can be said in its defence is, that it would have been difficult to make it better.

Lord Goldstable had a very elegant little double-bodied phaeton which he intended to drive himself; he had also in his coach-house a somewhat lumberous old family coach, which the young owner would not have chosen to drive himself; it was, however, in perfectly good condition, and would, as his man Simpson very sensibly observed, be able, with four good posters before it, to convey all the provender with perfect convenience, and any four of the company beside.

The Rector's gig, also driven by its owner, would take two, and thus the whole party, amounting to ten (for Lady de Paddington had asked, and obtained Lord Goldstable's permission to invite their agreeable host, Dr. Limpid), found themselves perfectly well accommodated. This arithmetical process of first reckoning noses, and then seats, was easily and speedily performed; the subsequent one of deciding who and who were to be together was rather more difficult, but this also was achieved at last.

It had been fixed that the *point de départ* should be the Rectory, and at the Rectory all the party were duly assembled at twelve o'clock on the appointed morning.

The Rector had, after a good deal of consideration, made up his mind so to arrange matters as that he should drive his Uncle Walter in his gig. He felt that this would give an excellent opportunity of pressing him home on the subject of lending a helping hand to the great work of re-seating the church. He also very conscientiously intended to take

advantage of the same opportunity for the purpose of setting
him right upon some very important items in his theological
opinions, a subject upon which he thought he had detected a
very lamentable degree of ignorance in this aged, but far from
well-instructed relative.

Of course it had been the intention of Lady Juliana that her
niece Kate should occupy the somewhat perilous elevation of
the driving-seat of the phaeton beside Lord Goldstable; while
she intended herself to occupy one of the luxurious seats
behind it.

Walter felt very strongly tempted to walk the distance, and
meet them at the dinner-table; but all these aspirations
were doomed to vanish into thin air by the will of one who
was wont, when she wished for anything, not to balk her
wishes from any scruples about doing anything and everything within the compass of her power for their gratification.

It is but waste of time to mention to the reader that Mrs.
Fitzjames had decided in her own mind that she herself, and
no other, should occupy the post of honour and of danger
beside Lord Goldstable on the driving-seat; and most assuredly
his Lordship was perfectly well inclined to vote that so it
should be; but the wily widow rightly judged that it might
not be safe to leave this very important point solely to his
discretion and management. She, therefore, with that pretty,
playful air of being determined upon having her own way,
which some beautiful women know so well how to assume,
carried her point by the aid of her own cleverness, as she was
fully determined to do.

This was not achieved, however, without a little sharp, as
well as resolute, manœuvring.

The Rectory was, as we have said, the place of rendezvous
before starting; and Lady de Paddington, Mrs. Fitzjames, and
the joyous-looking Dr. Limpid reached it in the old coach,
which had been sent from the Abbey to Doucham for their
accommodation. Lord Goldstable and Walter arrived there
also a few minutes later in the phaeton.

The meeting of the ladies from Doucham, and the ladies at
the Rectory, could not be expected to prove a very cordial one
on either side. The only external symptom of stiffness, however, was on the part of Lady Juliana, whose reception of the
two Doucham ladies was about as heartily glacial as decorum
could permit it to be in the house of her nephew, of which,

for the time being, she considered herself to be in some sort the mistress.

Lady de Paddington's manner, in return, was what is not unfrequently found among the scheming dowagers of *haut ton*, whose long hardening in the annealing furnace of fashionable life, has imparted to them a sort of brazen courage, which effectually protects them from betraying anything like the embarrassment of shame, let their real position be such as to produce it in the most vehement degree in persons of less audacious effrontery.

The style of Mrs. Fitzjames's entrance, however, into the Rectory parlour would, to any one uninitiated into the secrets of such charmers and their winning ways, have appeared to be the arrival of one fondly looked for among dear friends, whose well-known affection she most cordially returned.

Nothing could, in its way, be more clever than the graceful skill with which she eluded the risk of having her proffered hand refused by Lady Juliana; and this was effected by the seeming haste of the eager cordiality with which she greeted Kate. A smiling, low, and very elegant curtsey being in the same moment almost performed to Lady Juliana, while she simultaneously uttered, with the same sort of zealous *empressement*:

"I must ask you to present your brother to me, my dear Miss Harrington. I quite long to know him; for I have heard of nothing else since I came to Doucham but of his astonishing eloquence in the pulpit, and all the good he is doing here among the people. And I can tell you, from what I have already heard and seen myself, that the state of things at Doucham is such as greatly to require a little real proper religion somewhere.

It was impossible to have administered a more judicious morsel of ecclesiastical *soft solder* than this, the materials for which had been picked up from the local gossip of Mrs. Limpid. Doucham was, in fact, a nest of low churchmen and dissenters; and the Rev. James Harrington was not a man to listen to such a statement with indifference. He was, in fact, so completely won by the evidently orthodox words of the fair stranger, that his evangelical aunt would have found it extremely difficult to make him believe any evil report against so lovely and so right-thinking a daughter of the Church.

At that moment he would assuredly have been well con-

tented to give up the immediate chance of leading both Walter
and his purse in the right way, for the satisfaction of driving
to the pic-nic a lady, whose opinions he felt sure were in such
perfect accordance with his own.

He would, in fact, have liked nothing better than groaning
over the theological delinquencies of Doucham to so charming
and highly intelligent a listener. But this would not have
suited the widow at all; so she did not hear a word of the
pretty little speech he began about flattering himself that he
was a very safe driver. And how should she, when she was
so eagerly listening to something that Kate was saying to her
aunt about cloaks and shawls for the evening drive home?

But if she did not hear the pretty little speech, it nevertheless sufficed to put her on the alert; and no sooner had Walter
and Lord Goldstable made their appearance, than the lively
lady exclaimed, turning to Walter:

"Oh, Mr. Harrington! do tell me quite honestly now, do
you think I may venture? Lord Goldstable has made me
promise to sit by him on the driving-seat of the phaeton.
But I am such a sad nervous creature."

"In that case, Madam, you would certainly find it more
agreeable to go in the coach," replied Walter, secretly con-
gratulating himself upon having thus separated his foolish
young friend from the dangerous widow during the drive.

"Alas! alas!" returned the pretty lady, with a melancholy
shake of the head, "you are prescribing what would be infinitely more dangerous to me, my dear Sir, than all the bold
driving in the world. I dare not sit in a close carriage this
morning, for I have a headache that would make it perfectly
intolerable to me. Dr. Limpid tells me I must be as much in
the open air as possible. What do you say, dear doctor?
Which would be worst for me; the danger of being driven by
Lord Goldstable, or that of being shut up for hours in a close
carriage? Come, now, you shall decide for me."

Dr. Limpid was by no means a dull man; and he answered
not only promptly, but with considerable earnestness:

"I very strongly advise you to give up the party altogether,
dear lady, rather than go in a close carriage. The road is a
very safe one; you have nothing to fear; and a drive in an
open carriage will do you more good than anything."

"Well then, so be it," said she, turning her eyes with a
sunny smile on the delighted Lord Goldstable; "and if you do
overturn poor me into a ditch, it would be quite as well, or

rather better than turning anybody else there, for I know that I am but a useless sort of a person."

What Lord Goldstable said to her in reply nobody could tell, because he stood very close to her, and spoke in a very low whisper.

Meanwhile, Miss Cross had contrived to place herself at no very great distance from the Rector, and was pouring forth with great energy, and not without some eloquence, the delight she felt at the idea of revisiting the beautiful spot which, having seen once, she had never forgotten.

"But I had no one near me then," she said, with great *naïveté*, "who could give me the slightest information respecting either the date or the original extent of the picturesque ruins."

Now this was coming quite as near to an expression of admiration for an idolatrous superstition, as the safety of her soul would permit; nay, perhaps it was going rather further than her conscience perfectly approved; but the temptation which beset her was too strong to resist, for was it not possible, nay even probable, that this profession of ignorance on her part might lead to the wish of imparting a little information on his? And so perhaps it might have done, had time been given him to think about it; but Lord Goldstable spared the doubting young man the trouble of deciding between the pleasure of enlightening the mind of handsome Miss Cross, and the profit of coaxing his uncle out of money enough to re-seat his church; for his Lordship having just recollected that James was the only young man in the party besides himself, and that he could not flirt with his own sister, the good-natured youth determined that the tall beauty should be driven by the handsome young person into whose face she was looking up so kindly; and he therefore stepped gaily across the room, and said :

"Mr. Harrington, you will give Miss Cross a seat in your gig, won't you? You hear what Dr. Limpid says about the open air for young ladies. You are not afraid, are you?"

The two questions were answered at the same moment, by the gentleman and the lady. The former saying, "Certainly, if Miss Cross will permit it," and the latter declaring with a bright blush, that she "Should like it very much, because she was not at all afraid."

Having settled this point much to his good-natured heart's content, the young Amphitryon of the day remembered that he had by no means as yet done all that his hospitable duties demanded, but that, on the contrary, the majority of the party he had brought together, still remained in a state of uncertainty as to what was to become of them. But the moment he recollected this, he set manfully to work.

"Perhaps," said he, "Lady Juliana will accept—"

But before he could add another word, Walter, who saw, or fancied he saw, a glance of his Lordship's eye from the Lady Juliana to himself, and who was seized with a strong fear that he was about to be doomed to a *tête-à-tête* with his fine sister-in-law's fine sister, suddenly exclaimed: "I want to persuade my old friend, Mrs. Cross, to get into the phaeton with me and Lord Goldstable, that we may have a chat together about old times, old people, and old places."

Mrs. Cross looked delighted, and ardently exclaimed: "Oh, yes!" Whereupon, Lord Goldstable clapped his hands and cried: "Bravo!" And then added: "Let us move off then," very rationally considering that the difficult business of dividing the company among the different equipages was concluded as Kate, her aunt, Lady de Paddington, and Dr. Limpid, must *perforce* go in the coach, as both the other vehicles were disposed of, and there was, in fact, no other conveyance for them.

From the arrangements thus proposed and ratified, there was, in truth, no appeal; but there were at least two individuals of the party who, far from being contented, had the greatest possible inclination to declare that they were suddenly taken ill, and had rather not go. The one of these, as the reader will readily divine, was Lady de Paddington, and the other her quondam friend, the Lady Juliana Witherby.

But they both felt that it was too late to recede, and the two noble ladies stepped into the carriage with feelings as little befitting a friendly party of pleasure as it is well possible to imagine.

As to poor Kate, she cared not one single sou where she sat, or who were her companions; and as to Dr. Limpid, he would have been well pleased anywhere, for he was certain of enjoying a very good dinner, without having any patients to watch his manner of dealing with it; and certain too, of "increasing his connection," by the opportunity thus offered of making himself useful and agreeable as a cicerone.

To the majority of the party, the drive proved a very pleasant one. Mrs. Fitzjames was a little fatigued by the

exertions she felt it her duty to make, in order to be rather
more fascinating than ever; but she was repaid for it all by
Lord Goldstable's whispering in her ear, as he lifted her in his
arms from the last step of the lofty carriage : "If I did not
think we should be married before the end of the month, I
should blow my brains out."

CHAPTER LII.

AND now they were all seated round the well-spread table,
pretty nearly in the same manner, as to juxta-position, as
during the drive. The first vehement clatter of plates, knives,
and glasses had subsided, the ladies had all taken a glass of
champagne, and some of them two, and the party in general
began to eat less, and talk more.

"I have not yet told you the news that reached us this
morning," said the Rector, turning to his Uncle Walter. "My
father and mother are coming down to pay me a visit on their
way to Glastonbury."

"Really!" cried Walter. "I assure you I am very glad
to hear it. When do you expect them?"

"On Thursday, to a late dinner," replied James.

"And your good father and I shall stand side by side again
beneath the roof under which we were born! I like to think
of it, James!" said Walter. "But I wish," he added, "that
the old manor-house had been in a condition to receive them.
I should like to have had my brother there for a few days at
least."

"I am sure I heartily wish you were living there, Uncle
Walter," returned James, with great sincerity; for his imagination carried him at once to the re-opened gates of the old
manor-house, and daily doles and well-attended matins again
occurred to him as blessings by no means beyond the reach of
hope. "But I am afraid," he added, "that it would be
impossible for you to get into it immediately."

"Perhaps before they go, my dear James," said the kind
old man, touched by the evident sincerity with which his
nephew had spoken, "perhaps we may be able, if we set all
the tidy old women in the parish to work upon it, to get the
dust swept away. I don't believe there would be much
more required to make it habitable. We must see about it,
James, and I must consult old Margery."

This news was far from being as agreeable to all the party as
it had been to the venerable Squire. Mrs. Fitzjames started
at hearing it. She was annoyed and disquieted, she hardly
knew why. She certainly felt that she had no longer anything to fear from the rivalry of Kate. She looked with her
bright, keen eye at the melancholy girl as she sat opposite to
her at the table, and to say truth, felt no more dread of any
rivalry in that quarter than was inspired by the venerable
Mrs. Cross who sat next to her. But such ladies as Mrs.
Fitzjames are always painfully afraid of having any very
intelligent eyes fixed upon them while they have any interesting affair going on, and the eyes of Lady Augusta Harrington
were very intelligent. She knew, too, what peril there was
in every newly turned leaf in the chapter of accidents; and
things were going so particularly well with her just at present,
that it was perfectly natural she should not wish for any
arrivals that might by possibility derange their course.

Lady de Paddington, too, was exceedingly annoyed by the
intelligence. She would have given her Brussels lace lappets,
dearly as she valued them, could she thereby have avoided
coming in contact with her dear friend, Lady Augusta Harrington, till after the marriage of Lord Goldstable and Mrs.
Fitzjames had taken place. She felt more and more convinced
that if she faithfully continued to bestow her important
patronage on the widow, she should not only ensure that fair
"creature's" marriage with her silly, but very ductile young
relative, but achieve beforehand such an arrangement with
the future peeress, as would very effectively improve her own
exchequer for the remainder of her venerable existence. And
being convinced of this, it would have shown a degree of weakness unworthy the character she had sustained through life,
had she shrunk from this unexpected encounter with her
quondam ally, greatly as she disliked the idea of it.

Her decision upon the subject was as rapid as it was valiant.
She looked across the table at her beautiful *protégée*, and
at once perceived that this unexpected news annoyed her;

for the eye which had instantly sought hers, glanced from beneath a contracted brow, and all the bright hilarity of the fair face had vanished. But it was restored again as if by magic by the slight grimace and meaning smile by which her glance was returned.

There was, moreover, one other individual at table, whose gay laugh was converted into a look of dismay by the intelligence, and this was poor, dear, silly, good-natured Lord Goldstable. It was not that he in the least degree feared any impediment from the family of Kate, which would interfere with his present ardent love-fit. This was certainly no moment for any such fear on his part, for it was impossible that any love-affair could be going on more prosperously than he was conscious his own was doing. His annoyance arose solely from his regret for having permitted his cowardice and his idleness together to prevent him from keeping the promise he had so solemnly given to his venerable friend Walter, that he would rescind his hasty and very imprudent offer of marriage to his niece, by a letter to her father.

The sudden thought that this disagreeable ceremony of formal renunciation must now be performed either by writing or speaking, caused the poor young man's face to become scarlet, and such a melancholy change from mirth to misery took place in the expression of his features, that old Walter's kind heart could not stand it; and though he felt that the naughty boy certainly deserved to be punished, rather than pitied, he could not resist the impulse which led him to raise the empty glass beside his plate, and to cheer his repentant host by the gay challenge: "A glass of champagne, my Lord?"

This effort to restore the mirth of the meeting, which certainly for a moment had seemed on the wane, succeeded completely. The greatly comforted Lord Goldstable insisted upon it that Walter's challenge should be considered as general, and it was so received and duly honoured, save by little Mrs. Cross and quiet Kate. But the declining shake of the head by which the circulating flask was dismissed, was so quietly performed by both, that the livelier part of the company did not perceive it, which of course spared both the old and the young lady a world of remonstrance on their social deficiencies.

A third glass of champagne, however, can rarely be taken by the more easily inspired sex without its effects becoming

24

audible, if not exactly visible. Mrs. Fitzjames, equally charmed perhaps by the eloquent glance of Lady de Paddington and the sparkling draught which followed it, felt an irresistible inclination to propitiate the handsome Rector.

She had perceived with that ready quickness of perception with which *enchanting women* of her sort are always endowed, that the bit of ecclesiastical flummery which she had uttered during her short visit at the Rectory, had told well. It was evident to her, that it had been eagerly seized, and greedily swallowed, and she now felt herself in the humour to follow up the favourable effect she had then produced.

" What a lovely spot this is ! " she exclaimed, with enthusiasm, and suffering her sparkling eyes to fix themselves, after sending their upturned glances round the enclosure, upon those of the young Rector. " How gloriously, how touchingly lovely ! Yet nature has worked only half the charm, the other half, as we must all confess, is due to art. And what an art it then was ! What a nobly-inspired ambition must it have been which could have raised those mighty pillars, and turned those bold arches, that seem to defy the power of gravity, as if conscious of some magic power to resist it ! "

Mrs. Fitzjames had been once taken by a very youthful lover to a lecture, in which Sir Isaac's apple-theory had been pithily brought forward, and she had a happy knack of never forgetting anything that she thought might be brought into use hereafter with advantage. She used the collection thus made, much as a patchwork proficient does the miscellaneous treasures of her work-basket, taking out a scrap, and making the most of it whenever she found a place where she thinks it would fit. Her present air of knowing well what she was talking about, answered admirably, at least as far as the Rector was concerned, for he looked both delighted and surprised.

" Those arches, my dear lady," he replied. " were indeed reared in the most palmy days of all that is sublime and beautiful ; and the creative power then at work had *more* than magic in it. But let us ask ourselves," he continued, with an amiable and becoming smile, but with an aspect which had withal a mixture of sublimity in it, " let us ask ourselves, my dear Madam, *why* those were the palmy days of the true sublime and beautiful ? Let us ask ourselves why all that was then produced was so truly noble, and so truly tending to elevate the mind ? "

The eyes of the Rector of Stanton were of course fixed upon the eyes of Mrs. Fitzjames, and the eyes of Mrs. Fitzjames were of course fixed on those of the Rector of Stanton in return; and the eyes of all the rest of the company were fixed either upon the one or upon the other of them; but there was only one pair, and those were in the head of old Walter Harrington, which thoroughly enjoyed, and thoroughly understood what they looked at. Like a wise man as he was, he chose the eyes of the beautiful lady for his study, and keenly did the old man enjoy the threefold expression that he found in them. Expression number one, was altogether belonging to the business of making the Rector fully aware of the excelling beauty of the said eyes; expression number two was intended to express an intense degree of interest in what the Rector might be about to say; and expression number three, spoke plainly enough, according to the interpretation of old Walter, though certainly not intending it at all, that she knew little and cared less about the glorious subject they were so sublimely discussing.

"If we seriously ask ourselves this question," resumed the Rector, by no means unpleasantly conscious that the whole of the party were listening to him, "if we seriously and solemnly ask ourselves this question, the answer, perforce, must be, that it is not because the physical appliances possessed by the workers of those days were greater or better than those which we have at our command in these latter days; nevertheless, they were indeed glorious."

"Oh yes! they were indeed glorious," she replied, turning all the lustre of her beaming eyes upon the greatly delighted parson. "Would that it had been my lot to live in those days!" she added, in a tone of deep sensibility.

"Oh, dear me! Don't say that," cried Lord Goldstable, reproachfully and looking as if he did not quite understand the lovely widow's style of conversation with his reverend, and decidedly very handsome neighbour. "You forget, Mrs. Fitzjames," he added with a melancholy accent, "that in that case the old monks would be the masters of Brandon Abbey instead of me."

There was a *naïveté* about this tender remonstrance which tickled old Walter exceedingly, and he could not help laughing heartily.

Mrs. Fitzjames who was considerably less slow of comprehension than her adorer, blushed the colour of a bright carna-

tion, and the look she darted at Walter might be described as
a scowl, rather than a glance; but he saw it not, and said,
with a good-humoured nod to Lord Goldstable:

"It must be admitted, my Lord, that in this case, as in
many others, there would be considerable inconvenience in
pushing the world backwards for three hundred years; and I
would decidedly not barter your Lordship as a neighbour,
against a society of monks. Nevertheless, it must be confessed,
I think that the architecture of our reformed days does not
equal in beauty the works which were achieved in that line
by the unreformed. We call those ages dark, and dark
enough they were in many respects, but certain it is that our
lights have not enabled us to raise such noble fabrics as they
did."

"That is, I believe, acknowledged on all hands," replied
his nephew; "and as all our material resources are undeniably more ample," he continued, in a very decidedly triumph-
ant tone, "and as all our facilities for producing such works
are incomparably greater than their's were, what other
explanation for so remarkable a fact can be assigned, save
that which I was pointing out?"

The widow, who had no sort of intention or inclination to
be set aside or condemned to silence by the saucy laughter of
so antiquated and quizzable an individual as old Walter, again
fixed her eyes with a pretty, pensive, meditative air on the
face of the Rector, and replied:

"Oh, yes, it is so indeed. You are so right, Mr. James
Harrington! Assuredly those arches could never have been
built," she added with an uplifted eye, and an exquisitely
beautiful hand directed towards them, "without faith; oh!
not without a deal of faith in—the Scriptures."

The Rector looked a little annoyed, but Miss Cross looked
absolutely disgusted. She had previously felt not a little
indignant at the obvious encroachment which this beautiful
unknown was making on what she wished to make a strict
preserve, and she could not refrain from saying, with a bitterness at once feminine and theological:

"You forget, Ma'am, that the people were deprived of the
use of the Holy Scriptures in those days, so it can't be *there*
that we must look for the spirit which inspired the building
of these beautiful, but often Pagan-like edifices."

Mrs. Fitzjames, in return, bestowed upon the rustic damsel
a thoroughly fashionable stare; and then, with a little smile

expressive of a sort of playful compassion at the poor girl's ignorance, but with a tone which was intended effectually to put her aside, she said with a look of beautiful intelligence fixed upon the Rector:

"These pretty ruins are very old, no doubt; it is quite certain they could not be so beautiful if they were not so. But they are not quite so old as the Bible, I believe."

"Do you allude to the Old or the New Testament, Mrs. Fitzjames?" said wicked Walter, with a treacherous smile.

It was by no means in his usual way thus to supply the rope with which an entangled ignoramus might accomplish suicide. But he thought, very conscientiously, that Mrs. Fitzjames was not only fair game, but that he might do more good than harm by leading her to show herself off a little.

The acute widow instantly felt conscious that somehow or other she had been quizzed by the odious old man; but she had no intention to be browbeat by a half-crazy old grey-beard, and she replied with a little scorn, and a great deal of sparkling vivacity:

"Oh! The Old Testament of course."

Miss Cross opened her large black eyes to their widest extent, and fixed them on the face of Walter. Kate stole at the same moment a half-glance at the old man, and ventured a slight shake of the head as a reproof for his wickedness. It was only to the look of the former lady, however, that he thought proper to reply:

"My dear Miss Cross," he said, "you look as if you had never before heard anybody talk of matters of which they were ignorant. If this be the case, you have had better luck than I have. Though to be sure the present is rather remarkable."

Walter would never have said this, or anything else approaching it in severity, had it not been that he was fully aware of the decidedly nefarious attack which the beautiful lady was making upon his very guileless and very helpless protégé.

Seeing her as he saw her, and understanding her object as he understood it, he felt it to be a positive duty to give her a check whenever he found an opportunity of doing so.

The widow, however, appeared to be wholly unconscious that what he said had any application to her, and she turned as smilingly as ever to the real business of the hour, which, notwithstanding her admiration of the Rector's good looks, she remembered, with very perfect constancy, was the exerting all her fascinations, in order to have and to hold the luckless boy at her side, and everything that belonged to him.

Nor had she, on returning to this her vowed duty, the least reason to suspect that her recent blunder, if she had made one, had produced any mischievous effect on him, for he greeted the renewed glances of her eyes, and the soft dimples of her smiles with unmitigated delight.

But the Rector was not to be unhorsed from his favourite hobby by the discomfiture of an ally, whom it was certainly not his intention to accept as an authorised advocate of his cause. He therefore resumed the conversation, by addressing his uncle.

" But to return to what I was saying, my dear Sir," he resumed, " I really wish you would tell me what cause you can hit upon to assign for the confessed superiority of the mediæval church architecture over that of modern times, if you do not find it in the purity and intensity of the genuine Church spirit by which society was then animated, and, as I may say, inspired. Most emphatically, and most truly might those ages be designated as ages of faith, and, in lamentable contradistinction to the rank materialism amidst which we live, as spiritual ages."

" Your question, my dear James," replied his uncle, " is one which has often occurred to my own mind ; but my medita-tions on it have led me to a conclusion which I fear may startle you, for it is in direct contradiction to your own. It is my conviction, James, that if the question were philoso-phically analyzed, it would be found that it is precisely because we are more spiritual-minded than our forefathers that we no longer rear such magnificent fabrics, and not because we are less so."

The astonished Rector was silent for a moment, being too completely dismayed by so monstrous a proposition to find ready words to answer it ; but then he said :

" I must confess, Sir, that your paradox is not only startling, but so wholly incomprehensible to me, that I have no concep-tion of your meaning."

" Well, my dear James," replied the old man, with a good-humoured smile, " I have no particular wish to dogmatize on so grave a subject at so gay a moment ; but I can tell you, in a very few words, how the matter strikes me. I have little, or rather no doubt, but that structures equal or superior to any of those which we so much admire, might be raised at the present day, provided only that the requisite funds were forthcoming."

"Well, Sir!" cried James, triumphantly, "you surely have mistaken your brief, as a celebrated barrister is once said to have done, and are advancing directly to my conclusion, instead of to your own. I perfectly agree with you as to the possibility of raising such edifices. But *why* are not the funds forthcoming?"

"Why are not the funds forthcoming?" returned the old man. "Ay, James, that is, indeed, the question. During your favourite ages of faith, people of all sorts, old men and maidens, young men and children—ay, and old women, too, who by no means ought to be left out—all eagerly contributed their substance, and their power, and energy, in various ways to the great work of rearing magnificent churches, and filling them with costly decorations, in order to demonstrate their piety as a claim to eternal reward. But the reformed worshippers of latter days take a different view of the investment. People of all classes would still willingly contribute their substance and their energy to the achievement of vast and sublime works, only they wish first to know what percentage of interest they would receive in return. You may depend upon it, that Gothic cathedrals would be springing up in all directions, if it could only be ascertained that there would be a return of five per cent. for the money expended on them."

"Once again, my dear uncle," returned James, "I cannot help saying that if I were arguing in support of my own opinion, I could not do it so ably as you are now doing it for me."

"Have a moment of further patience with me, my dear fellow. We shall soon reach the point at which our roads diverge; and after that, I believe you will find that they proceed diametrically right and left," returned Walter.

"We appear to agree in thinking that the reason why people do not build many cathedrals now-a-days is, because they do not perceive that they will get a good remuneration for money so invested. That they did during the ages of faith believe that they should receive a rich return for money so invested, you do not doubt nor I either. Nor can we either of us reasonably deny that no degree of worldly wisdom could suggest a more profitable investment for superfluous wealth, than the purchasing an eternal annuity of heavenly beatitude. Let a prudent capitalist be made *practically to believe* that he can make his money available to such a purpose by expending it in building churches, and the work would begin forthwith. But the present age refuses, for the most part, to believe that man can enter into any such compact with his Maker; and I must confess that I think his refusal indicates a much higher degree of spirituality, and a much more sublime appreciation of things unseen, than can possibly be shown by accordance with the contrary principle."

"You are now entering upon ground, Sir, where it is impossible I should follow you," replied James, hastily, and with a visible augmentation of colour. "I dare not listen to you, Sir. Your arguments evidently tend to an abyss of heresy that I dread to contemplate, and would embrace consequences which I am able dimly to perceive through the mists of your sophisms, but which I would really rather not approach more nearly.

"And I, my dear nephew," replied the old man, mildly, "cannot see that good can arise from discussion with one who dreads to follow wherever a conscientious wish to discover truth may lead him. Moreover, I readily admit," he added, in a lighter tone, "that this is not exactly the fitting time and place for such a discussion. Will you take a glass of champagne with such an unorthodox old fellow as your uncle?"

"With all my heart, my dear Sir," replied James, almost as cordially as if he had been so challenged by the most Puseyistic bishop on the bench; "and I am quite sure," he added, doubtless for the purpose of reconciling his pious spirit to so very tolerant an act, "I am quite sure, that if you would only listen to the teaching of the Church—"

"At Stanton, or at Doucham, my dear boy, shall it be?" returned the old man, with a merry eye. "And now," he added, "as I think we have all done dinner, I propose an expedition for the purpose of exploring the perilous passage to the holy well. But you must not mistake what I have been saying to you, James," said Walter, drawing near his nephew, and laying his hand affectionately on his shoulder. "You are not to suppose that I am second to any in my veneration of the holy feeling, which has often caused such temples as this has been, to rear their bold columns towards the sky, or that

I am insensible to the value of their spiritual use. I hope and believe that the age is becoming more and more sensible of this, and will continue to do, as intellectual and truly spiritual culture increases."

No sooner had old Walter risen, than Lord Goldstable was on his feet also.

"Now then for our beautiful romantic walk," he cried; "I am longing for the delightful grotto that the Doctor talks about."

When Lord Goldstable rose, of course everybody else rose also; and scarfs were resumed, and parasols sought for, with every appearance of eager interest in the proposed expedition.

CHAPTER LIII.

But notwithstanding all this apparent zeal, the proposition of visiting the holy well was not accepted unanimously. They all rose indeed, and all the ladies appeared to prepare themselves for walking, but Lady de Paddington said something about damp, and about catching one's death from cold in those wild, strange underground sort of places.

Little Mrs. Cross had visited the holy well a great many long years ago, but she remembered it just as well as if it were but yesterday; and she thought, and said, that the air of the grotto would certainly do no good to her rheumatism.

Lady Juliana candidly confessed that, for her part, she had no pleasure in contemplating the memorials of idolatry and superstition; and that, in her opinion, it would be a great deal better to let them sink into oblivion and be forgotten, instead of making them a show.

Dr. Limpid, although assuring these three ladies that they had no reason to fear either damp or draught, provided they would only be faithful to cold water, nevertheless very politely volunteered to remain with them during the absence of the rest of the party on this exploring expedition. This offer was accepted as civilly as it was made; and the separation of the two squadrons immediately took place.

Old Walter, who never missed any opportunity of seeing anything, and who on the present occasion was especially anxious to examine the changes the action of the well-remembered stream had made in the spot since he had last seen it, was the first to step forward in the right direction; and Kate who was ever well pleased to look at anything when her uncle was showman, looked at him with almost one of her usual smiles, as she took his arm. The Rector, who had, of course much too sincere a veneration for Saint Bridget to fail in visiting her holy well whenever a favourable occasion for doing so offered, was more than usually so on the present occasion, and felt eager to recount the legend to anyone whose ear he felt conscious he could command so completely as that of the fair Olivia; and the fair Olivia was too much delighted by the offer of his escort and his arm during the expedition, to listen to any scruples of conscience concerning the probably superstitious turn of his conversation, and continued to satisfy the inward menitor by the ever-present consideration, that her only chance of ultimately saving him, was by first making him her own for ever and at all hazards.

As to Mrs. Fitzjames, she really manifested a high sense of duty, and of that first of duties—namely, the duty which she owed to herself, by the alacrity with which she obeyed the signal to move; for she had made a very good dinner, and really felt exceedingly comfortable where she was; whereas the exertion she was now called upon to make, was in every way distasteful to her. She hated a country walk beyond all things; and the having to listen and respond to all the wearisome ardours of Lord Goldstable's tender passion, was a bore of the most ponderous quality. But no price was too great to pay for the glory of becoming a wealthy peeress; and radiant was the smile with which she started up to encounter all the promised perils by land and water, which were to throw her upon the masculine protection of the silly boy who was of course to be her escort. She detested the idea of going into the nasty, damp, dirty hole that had been described to her; but the nicest observer would have failed to detect any trace of such a feeling in the tone with which she exclaimed:

"Oh! I shall so like it!"

Lord Goldstable's delight was quite as genuine as hers was false; and the gentle pressure with which she returned the ardent grasp with which he took possession of her arm, would have convinced him that he was fondly beloved, even if he had not been tolerably sure of it before. So while the oddly composed group of the three elder ladies, and Dr. Limpid, remained sitting, and perhaps dozing, under the shade and shelter of the old Priory wall, the three pair, composed of Walter and Kate, Lord Goldstable and the widow, and the Rector and Miss Cross, sallied forth on their romantic expedition.

"Was it not awful, Mr. Harrington," said the handsome Olivia, as they energetically stepped forward in the van of the party, "was it not really awful to listen to the soul-destroying ignorance displayed by that presumptuous lady from Doucham? I really did not think it possible that in these latter days, any Christian could be so profoundly ignorant."

"Ignorant certainly," replied the Rector; "yet, nevertheless," he added, in a tone of gentle toleration, "she seemed inclined to listen to the teaching of the Church," replied James, who belonged to that class of teachers who have far more indulgence for ignorance linked with submission, than for information if allied to independence. "But, as I was telling you," he resumed, "she received the veil from the nephew of St. Patrick."

"What did she receive?" asked Miss Cross, opening her fine eyes, as she looked up to him with an expression of extreme astonishment.

"She received the veil," replied the Rector, gravely. "You know the meaning of that phrase, I suppose?"

"Oh yes! certainly I do. But of whom were you speaking," returned the lady.

"Of the holy Saint Bridget," he replied, a little stiffly. "I thought you would like to hear some of the particulars of her singularly interesting history."

"Oh yes! indeed I should. For I am very fond of history," returned poor Olivia, colouring vehemently from the struggle that was going on within her between her religion and her love.

"Saint Bridget's story is a highly suggestive one," replied James, a good deal mollified by the evident eagerness of her wish to listen to him. "Saint Bridget, Miss Olivia, became superior of a little knot of holy women who wished to devote themselves to religion under her guidance; and she constructed

a small cell under the shelter of a majestic oak, which grew
at no great distance from the place where she was born. The
spot was thence called *kill dara*, or the cell of the oak, a name
retained to the present day by the town of Kildare, which, in
process of time, arose round the sight of the nunnery "

"And is it known what connection there was between this
Irish Saint and the well here, which is called by her name?"
said Olivia.

"I am not aware that any legend has been preserved," he
replied; "but, in all probability, some relic—it may even
have been one of her holy bones—must have found its way
hither; and being deposited where the well rises, may have
been found to perform miracles. Saint Bridget is known to
have been very powerful in working miracles," he added,
with a simple matter-of-fact air, as if he had been speaking of
a well-known event which had occurred the day before.

"Oh, Mr. Harrington!" cried the sorely-tried Olivia, with
a heavy sigh.

"Of course they were duly examined into, and satisfactorily
proved at the time of her canonization," rejoined the Rector,
exactly in the tone he might have used, if speaking of one
who had been tried and found guilty, or innocent, at the Old
Bailey.

Meanwhile, Walter and Kate, who followed next in the line
of march, were engaged on a little lecture on geology, which
the old man probably thought was a safer theme, notwithstanding all the dangers of infidelity which have been attributed to it, than anything connected with the said subject,
which, in truth, occupied the thoughts of both.

Taking his text from the illustrations furnished by the
action of the Bickley stream within the period of his own
memory, old Walter pointed out to his attentive listener the
great part which the incessant labourer, water, played in the
arrangement and fashioning of our globe.

"It is curious to reflect, is it not, my Kate, that all the
myriad tons of soil composing the rich plain that stretches
away yonder with such glorious fertility, have been carried
atom by atom, from the hills in front of us?" said the meditative old man.

"There are very few things which excite so agreeable a
state of mind," replied Kate, "as the being able to trace the
great and universal operations of nature with the certainty
afforded by common sense. When we are so occupied, we feel

that we ourselves assuredly do hold an exalted place among created things. But these waters, I presume, uncle, are not the only agents in this vast operation?"

"It is rarely, if ever the case," replied Walter, "that any of the operations of nature, whether sublime from their stupendous immensity, or astonishing from their marvellously delicate minuteness, are effected by one operating agent. In such geological changes as that before us, not a frost or thaw occurs, not a grass or lichen germinates on those hills, without preparing and helping forward the work of their disintegration. The beautiful harmony, which a little observation will enable us to trace through the infinitely diversified operations of nature, is to my mind one of the most irresistible sources of adoration of the Divine Creator."

And so they talked, till they almost forgot the companions of their walk, and the object of it.

The conversation of the third couple offered another variety. It is certain, however, that in this case also, the gentleman talked of *adoration* to his companion; but it was of a kind quite different from that discussed either by the philosophical Walter, or his ecclesiastical nephew. The discourse of Lord Goldstable and Mrs. Fitzjames was, indeed, a good deal interrupted by a multitude of little adventures occasioned by the heedless stepping of the lady, and the impassioned eagerness of the gentleman in assisting her; but notwithstanding these dangerous litttle accidents, the delighted youth declared again and again, and with the most perfect sincerity, that he had never enjoyed a walk so much in his whole life—"No, never!"

His fair companion also had formed an opinion equally decided upon the pleasures of the expedition. She felt convinced at the very bottom of her heart, that no woman had ever made so detestable an excursion, or been made love to by such a booby and bore as her companion. But, nevertheless, her resolute purpose was not changed, nor did her courage—her noble courage—give way. She could still "smile and smile;" and so she did, till the poor, guileless boy felt persuaded that she was quite as much delighted, and quite as much in love as himself.

And in this manner the tripartite company passed under the dripping ledge of rock, which formed the roof of the grotto. Walter talked geology, James talked legendary lore, and Lord Goldstable whispered soft things, till at length Mrs. Fitzjames, thinking she had fully accomplished the task she had set herself, began to express some very serious fears, that the damp of the grotto might cause her death.

The agitation of poor Lord Goldstable at hearing these terrible words, uttered in a tone of sweetly resigned gentleness, was very vehement indeed ; and hastily declaring that he wished the holy well, which, though it was at the farthest extremity of the cavern they had safely reached, at the devil, he said they must instantly turn back, and get away as fast as possible.

Now, it so happened that a pair of idle urchins, who had been stationed to frighten away the crows from a neighbouring corn-field, had been attracted by the arrival of the gentlefolks at the Priory, and had quitted their post, in order to follow them at a respectful distance, in the hope of receiving a splendid sixpence, as a reward for their services as ciceroni at the legendary precincts of the holy well.

Opportunities of this sort were, by no means, of very rare occurrence; and the experience of the young chroniclers had taught them that their services were, for the most part welcomely received, when offered in the dim recesses of the grotto ; but that they were pretty regularly pooh-pooh'd away, if they bothered the gay folks as they walked towards it.

On the present occasion, they had hung back, and in fact, kept out of sight till they had seen the whole party cross the plank, which served as a bridge over the little rapid stream, which, having overflowed the holy cistern, had worn for itself a channel, which led it to join the waterfall, as before described. The two unseen attendants of the party had permitted the three gentlemen to hand the three ladies over the plank before they themselves entered the grotto; but this passage being accomplished, the two boys rushed eagerly forward, each of them eager to be the nearest to the party, and foremost in proffering the services for which they hoped to be paid. But while thus jostling each other, the foremost of the two managed to strike his clouted shoon against the plank with such violence, that he dislodged it from its narrow holding on the bank, and caused it to fall with rather an appalling splash into the stream. The boys, who were lucky in escaping the same fate themselves, instantly took to their heels, and ran back to their forsaken post in the corn-field, stedfastly deter-termined to ignore the whole business, should any inquiry into the matter be made.

It was with no small dismay that the party heard the sound
of the falling plank at the very moment that, in compliance
with Mrs. Fitzjames's wish, they had turned away from the
well, in order to leave the grotto with as little delay as might
be; and upon reaching the stream and perceiving that their
retreat was thus suddenly cut off, the wish that they were all
safely beyond the precincts of the said grotto certainly became
general, though varying in degree. The width of the little
stream did not exceed four feet, perhaps it was not so much;
but the banks were on both sides wet and slippery, and the
light by no means sufficient to permit a very satisfactory
examination of the ground. Had it not been for this obscurity,
there would have been little difficulty in the matter, a firm
foot, and a sure eye, being all that was necessary to ensure a
safe arrival on the further side. Olivia Cross and the Rector
were the first of the party who reached the spot.

"There has been an awkward accident here, Miss Cross,"
said the gentleman, looking with rather a blank air at the
unbridged stream before them. "I could cross easily enough
myself, I daresay; but really I do not see how the ladies
are to manage."

"Oh, it is nothing, Mr. Harrington!" cried the eager Olivia,
gaily. "I am not the least afraid. Let me go first, shall I?
When I am across, I'll stretch out my hand to you. Let me,
will you? I am quite sure of myself at this sort of work."

"Oh, Heaven! what is to become of us?" screamed Mrs.
Fitzjames, in the most vehement agitation. "Oh, Edward,"
she softly murmured in the ear of Lord Goldstable, "all escape
is cut off, and we shall perish by famine in this dreadful spot.
At all events, my own Edward, we shall perish together!" she
added, in a manner which seemed to indicate that *together*, in
her affectionate interpretation of the word, signified *as one*, so
closely did she cling to him as she uttered it.

"Well, but, Sophia dearest, I can jump," replied the brave
young nobleman. "I am a monstrous good jumper—I am
upon my word and honour—and I would jump over anything
in the world to save you, my dear, beautiful Sophia! And
so here goes!"

And as he spoke, he gently shook her off, and put himself in
act to spring. But his Sophia had no notion of being treated
in that matter-of-fact sort of style, and clutched him tightly
in her arms, uttering at the same moment a shriek, that made
the vault of the cavern ring again.

"What a fine echo!" said Walter, drily, while approaching with Kate to the point where they had left the plank, and reaching it just as the magnificent scream of the beautiful lady had ceased to vibrate. "I wonder who has been so mischievous as to break down our bridge behind us?" he added, laughing. "Some wicked wag, I trow. Do you think you can skip across it, Kate?"

"Oh yes, very easily," she replied. "But I should like you to skip across first, Uncle Walter, that you may stretch out a hand to steady me on my arrival, for the bank on the other side looks wet and slippery."

Walter nodded his head, and, placing his stout stick firmly on the edge, and with a movement, that was half a jump and half a stride, was in an instant on the other side; and then, rendering his position firm, despite the mud, by means of grasping with his left hand the corner of a rock very conveniently within reach, he stretched his right out to meet that of Kate, who with that assistance made her transit to the other side with a movement as fearless as his own.

"Well done, Kate!" cried the old man, gaily. "And now, ladies, what can I do for you? Shall we send men with ropes and planks from the village? Or do you think you can play at 'follow the leader?' Come, Miss Olivia! I suspect that if you had been alone, you would have found your way across long since."

"If Miss Cross is really not afraid," said the Rector, "I have no doubt that I could pass her across as safely as you did my sister."

"Oh, I am not the least afraid, if Mr. James Harrington will give me his hand," said poor Olivia, with a blush.

"Certainly I will, Miss Olivia," replied the Rector, leaping across as he spoke; and then following his uncle's example, by grasping the jutting crag, he stretched across his other hand to meet that of his long-legged companion. But Olivia, animated by the energy which characterised all her movements, immediately made so vigorous a spring towards the gentleman, that the momentum imparted to her person not only sufficed to carry it to the opposite side of the little stream, but completely to overpower the resistance opposed to it by the person of the well-grown, but not very stoutly built young clergyman; and the bank being very slippery, they both lost their footing, and measured their nearly equal length upon the ground.

Olivia was the first to recover her feet, and then eagerly

offered her hand to assist the prostrate Rector to rise. He declined this assistance by uttering, as he rose without it, "Thank you," in rather a ceremonious accent, the coldness of which was greatly more chilling than the wet mud to the feelings of the unfortunate Olivia. However, upon the whole, the young man behaved very well, for he, too, was exceedingly mortified; his dignity, as a priest, having been as painfully wounded by his tumble, as her vanity, as a woman, by his cold reception of her proffered aid; so that there was some merit in the effort which enabled him to say, in about a minute after he had recovered his feet:

"I hope you have not hurt yourself, Miss Cross?"

"Vaulting ambition hath o'erleaped, not only itself, but you into the bargain, James," said Walter, laughing. "But never mind, you will neither of you be the worse for the adventure half an hour hence. A little of this pleasant sunshine that we have got back to, and a touch of a clothes-brush, will soon set all to rights again."

• And so it fell out that Lord Goldstable and Mrs. Fitzjames were left alone on the wrong side of the gap.

"Do you think, dearest," whispered the enamoured young man, in the very tenderest of tones, "that you could manage it as they have done? I don't mean like Miss Cross," he added, "but like Miss Harrington. I think I could receive you on the other side better than the parson did Miss Cross."

"Oh, Edward! how can you propose to me so frightful an attempt? Am I formed to scramble about like that horrible giantess of a girl? As to Miss Harrington. it is evident she is a romping school-girl, and I daresay she would climb a tree if her uncle told her to do it. Your affianced wife, my Edward, has been reared with more refinement."

"But what are we to do, my beautiful angel? If we are ever to get home again as long as we live, we *must* cross that ditch. Come now, Sophia, let's have a try, and jump together, hand in hand."

"Nothing on earth could induce me to attempt it!" replied the lovely widow, solemnly. "Oh, Edward! how could you dream that it was possible for such a creature as I am to clear that hideous chasm at a leap? Alas! I am not formed for such exploits. No, Edward, let us remain here together, and be forgotten. It is a sad fate for creatures so young, but at least we shall be together. Not that I would refuse to be saved, if you yourself would be my preserver. If you thought

25

that you could clear the yawning abyss with your poor Sophia in your arms, I would venture, so encircled, to brave the attempt. If we escape, I shall owe my life to you; and if we perish, we shall perish together'"

"Dear, lovely Sophia!" replied the soft-hearted boy, with something very like a sob, "I am sure it is enough to melt a heart of stone to listen to you. At all events, I'll do my very best; so let me try, dearest." And so saying, he took the very pretty lady in his arms, much as an indulgent nurse might take up a tall, naughty child, who prefers being carried to walking.

"Oh, you are no weight at all! I am quite sure that I can jump across as easily with you as without you. So here goes!" And so saying, he retreated for a step or two to take a little run at it, and then, with a youthful, active spring, he alighted with his fair burden in perfect safety on the other side.

"Bravo, Goldstable! well jumped," cried Walter, who had been looking on with great amusement, though he had not heard the tender whisperings which had preceded the feat; "but it was a silly thing to attempt," added the old man, "you might both of you have very easily got a ducking." And having said this, he gave his arm to Kate, and prepared to walk back to the ruins.

But the widow, who had been perfectly well aware that she had run some risk by being carried across the gap, and who had very deliberately determined upon running it for the sake of what she intended should follow, was not to be easily foiled in her object. So heaving a very profound sigh, she sank gracefully upon the ground, and with one melting glance up into the face of Lord Goldstable, fainted away!

Walter looked at her for half a moment, and then quietly drew forth his watch, remarking that it was getting late, and quite time that they should be looking for the carriages.

Lord Goldstable looked very uncomfortable, but kept his eyes fixed upon his Sophia, calling upon her in a very piteous voice, yet not seeming to think, nevertheless, that she was positively dying; and by degrees, in consequence of taking off her bonnet, letting her hair fall about her face, taking off her gloves, and bathing her forehead with eau-de-Cologne, he succeeded at last in persuading her to open her eyes.

"My deliverer! my preserver!" she cried passionately, clasping her hands, and looking wildly up into the sky.

"Oh, Edward!" she softly murmured, "I shall never forget this hour as long as Heaven gives me life and recollection. Never, no never, shall I cease to remember the heroic courage and devotion with which you risked your precious life to save that of your poor trembling Sophia. May I live to reward you for it, by a whole existence of love and gratitude!" And here she covered her face with her hands, and appeared to weep.

It was evident that these tears relieved her; for perceiving, upon looking up, that the rest of the party was so far in advance as to be very nearly out of sight, though a good half mile of the road was visible, she "sat herself to rights," and declared that she was quite ready to return to their friends.

"And oh, my Edward!" she cried, "with what delight shall I recount this day's noble deed to Lady de Paddington! She is already well enough inclined to be proud of you; but, ah! what will she say to me for suffering you to risk your precious life to preserve mine?"

And with such honey-sweet talk the way was easily beguiled, till they reached the spot where the elder ladies, and the still smiling Dr. Limpid, awaited the return of the party. The perils they had encountered furnished a most interesting narrative, which lasted till the carriages were ready; and the various commentaries upon it, furnished ample matter for conversation during the drive home; and on the whole, Mrs. Fitzjames, who was by no means a bad judge, considered that the pic-nic had been very successful.

CHAPTER LIV.

A few days after the pic-nic at Bickley Priory, Walter
Harrington and Lord Goldstable were sitting over their
breakfast-table at Brandon, when the unfortunate young host
had again to be reminded that he had not yet redeemed his
promise of releasing Kate from the embarrassment he had
brought upon her, by informing her father that he resigned
all claim to her hand. As far as his niece herself was concerned, old Walter very frankly confessed that no such avowal
on the part of his Lordship was necessary; but the case was
different with respect to the rest of the family. It had been
quite in vain that, in the first instance, Kate had explicitly
declared that she neither had, nor ever would, accept Lord
Goldstable; her refusal was treated by her father, mother,
aunt, and younger brother, as the petulant coquetry of a silly
girl, who thought she had not been sufficiently made love to
as yet.

Had she not received the fatal blow which had so cruelly
destroyed all her hopes of a union with Caldwell, she would
have attached more importance to this silly delay on the part
of Lord Goldstable, and so would her uncle also; and it
was this which had led him to permit above a week to
pass without again insisting on the foolish boy's redeeming his pledge. But Kate had reminded her uncle that
she should now be in danger of a much more active and
authoritative persecution on the part of her mother, than
she had as yet endured on the part of her aunt; and, moreover, that her father would be likely to treat the subject,
notwithstanding all the absurdity mixed up with it, in a style
of solemnity, that would effectually overwhelm all her efforts
to make that absurdity visible to him. " In short, dear uncle,"
she said, during their homeward drive from the pic-nic;
"in short, there is nothing that can save me from a persecution, which I do not feel very able to bear, but Lord Goldstable's keeping the promise which he made you. Do you not
think," she added, with a touch of her former playfulness,
"that if you were to tell him that I had quite made up my

mind to accept him, if he delayed the performance of his promise any longer, it might act as a spur?"

"Perhaps it would, Kate," replied Walter, with a laugh which would have been more genuine had poor Kate been less perfectly at liberty to perform the threat, as well as to utter it. The same thought probably occurred to both; for both became silent, and remained so for a minute or two.

When their drive was over, however, and Kate set down at the Rectory, Walter returned to Brandon, very fully determined to attend immediately to her remonstrance; but accident had prevented his doing so. In the first place, the late hour at which his young host breakfasted, made it very inconvenient that they should take the meal together; and after Walter had breakfasted, he was sure to be off to superintend the labours of old Margery and her assistants; and when he got back to the Abbey, he found he had but barely time to prepare for dinner, at which ceremony Lady de Paddington and her fair friend invariably assisted. It was absolutely necessary, however, that this long delayed business should be achieved, and Walter had accordingly waited for his breakfast till Lord Goldstable came down and joined him.

After a little idle chit-chat respecting the preparations that were going on at the Hall, Walter said: "I wish, my Lord, that you had followed my advice, and written to my brother when you first came down here. I told you then, if you remember, that the business would not become less disagreeable by being delayed."

"But I am sure, Mr. Harrington, I never thought there was any danger of the Doctor's coming down here," replied Lord Goldstable, looking very red. "If I had I would not have lost a day in writing."

"I assure you, my young friend, that I had no more idea of it than you had," replied Walter. "As it is, however, there is now no possibility of avoiding the saying, what is absolutely necessary you should say, by word of mouth."

"Why don't you think, Sir, that I might still be able to write it in a note, and send it over by my groom to Stanton? There would be nothing disrespectful in that, would there, Sir?" said the young man, looking dreadfully terrified at the idea of what he had before him.

"Yes, certainly, Goldstable, you could send a note over to Stanton, and there would be nothing disrespectful in your doing so. But it would be nearly impossible that you should avoid seeing my brother afterwards," returned Walter, gravely. "Indeed, you could not avoid calling upon him without great rudeness, and your embarrassment would only be increased by attempting to avoid it. No, no, my good fellow! you had better take the bull by the horns at once."

"Yes, certainly, Sir; I am sure you know best; and I would not, on any account, attempt to differ from you in opinion. Only don't you think yourself, Mr. Harrington, that the thing might be much better done if you were to have the great kindness to see Dr. Harrington for me yourself?" replied the frightened boy.

"No, Lord Goldstable! that would not do at all," answered Walter, firmly, and almost with sternness. "You must yourself do that, which you will forgive me for reminding you that you promised you would do; and without that promise, I should never have been here. It is absolutely necessary that the withdrawal of the rash and hasty offer which you made to my niece should come from yourself; for it is so only that she will be considered as exonerated from all blame by her parents. My brother will be here to-morrow night, and on the following morning you had better go over to Stanton, and speak to him."

"So I will, Mr. Harrington, I will indeed," replied the penitent peer; "and I do assure you, that I never intended to shirk off doing it: I only thought that perhaps some little word from you might help me."

"Thus far I will help you," said Walter, good-naturedly interrupting him; "I will go over to Stanton with you, and will be present at your interview with my brother, if you think that my doing so will be any support to you."

"Oh dear me, yes, Sir!" replied his greatly-comforted Lordship. "I should be so grateful—it would be everything! And then, you know, you could perhaps find an opportunity of expressing that you think I am not acting wrong. That would be a great help; at least, Sir, if you do not object to letting Dr. Harrington know that you think so."

"I seldom conceal my opinions on any subject," said the old man, with a smile; "and you may depend upon it, my Lord Goldstable, that the interview will not come to an end without my letting my brother know that you are, in my opinion, acting very uprightly."

"Oh then, my dear Mr. Walter Harrington, you are very,

very kind to me! That is exactly what I should like to think about myself, and what I should like to make everybody else think about me. The day after to-morrow, then, we will go over and call upon Dr. Harrington; and in less than half an hour, you know, it will be all over, and I shall feel all right again."

The silence of a minute or two which followed, seemed to indicate that Lord Goldstable was in a deeper reverie than was at all usual with him; but it was at length broken by his saying: "But tell me now, Mr. Harrington, will you? Do you think that, in speaking to the Doctor, it would be better or not to say anything about Mrs. Fitzjames?"

This was the first time that the poor young man had made any approach towards speaking to his venerable friend in a confidential manner on the subject of the widow, and Walter was not at all prepared for it. He remained silent and thoughtful, therefore, for a moment before he replied, and then he said:

"I should think not, Lord Goldstable. I should think it better, when speaking to my brother about his daughter, that you should confine yourself to that special subject; and I do not see how the lady whose name you have now mentioned can have anything to do with it."

"Why I thought," said his Lordship, colouring, "that perhaps Dr. Harrington, you know, would expect—that is, that he would be more satisfied—I mean that it would seem more proper, you know, to give some good reason."

"Good reason for what?" said Walter, very greatly disposed to laugh.

"Why for my no longer wanting to marry Miss Harrington, you know. Won't he be apt to ask me why I have changed my mind?"

"I do not think that it is very likely; but even if he did ask such a question, I don't see why that should lead you to say anything about Mrs. Fitzjames."

"Why, good gracious, Mr. Harrington!" cried Lord Goldstable, "it seems to me that the most natural reason in the world for me to give for not marrying the one, is that I am immediately going to be married to the other."

"Your Lordship forgets," replied Walter, smiling, "that this is the first intimation I have received of any such purpose on the part of your Lordship. It certainly makes your change of purpose respecting Miss Harrington perfectly intelligible;

nevertheless, if you will take my advice, you will not mention
it to my brother."

"I shall certainly take your advice," replied the puzzled-
looking boy, "because I should always like to take your
advice about everything. There is something in your face, in
the look of your face, you know, when you speak to me, that
makes me sure that you mean just what you say and nothing
else. And I don't know anybody in the world that I feel just
the same about. But Doctor Harrington will be sure to ask
me my reasons, won't he? And if he does, what shall I say,
my dear friend?"

"Why, in that case," replied Walter, "I should tell him
the simple truth. I should tell him that you had made this
very improperly hasty proposal in obedience to the wishes of
an aged relative, who ought to have known better, but that a
little reflection had convinced you that it would be more for the
happiness of both parties, that this hasty offer should be withdrawn, and that you must trust to his kind consideration for
your youth and inexperience for excuse and forgiveness for your
rashness."

"Will you have the very great kindness to say all that over
again, Mr. Harrington?" cried the delighted young nobleman,
who had been greedily swallowing every syllable that Walter
uttered. "It is so exactly what I should like to say if I could
only remember it!"

The old man slowly and deliberately repeated the words,
and the young man slowly and deliberately repeated them
after him; and when this was accomplished, Lord Goldstable
rubbed his hands, nodded his head, and looked greatly comforted.

But now it was old Walter's turn to feel nervous and
uncomfortable. He was conscious that, in order to induce the
silly boy to undo the mischief he had done, he had led him on
to a degree of intimacy which had produced a feeling of unlimited confidence on the part of the poor youth, whose
abounding wealth and defective wisdom combined, were sure
to make him the victim of the first wicked woman who got
hold of him; and the ice being thus broken between them by
the mention of Mrs. Fitzjames as his affianced wife, the old
man felt that it was a positive duty to use the influence he
was conscious of having obtained over him, by putting him
on his guard.

"Make yourself easy, my dear Goldstable," he said, "about

your interview with my brother; it will be soon over, and you will never have any further trouble about that foolish blunder afterwards. But before I set off to look after my old housekeeper's proceedings at the Hall, I must say a friendly word or two about the announcement you have just made to me. I must say, that I am very sorry to hear that you are going to be married to Mrs. Fitzjames."

"Oh, dear me, Mr. Harrington, don't say that! I am quite positively sure that you would be very fond of her indeed, if you did but know her a little better."

Walter shook his head, but said nothing.

"I am quite sure that I know what you are thinking of—I am quite certain of it," said Lord Goldstable, looking earnestly in the face of the old man, which certainly wore a much graver expression than usual. "It is quite sure, and no mistake, that you are thinking that she is not rich enough for me. That's it, Mr. Harrington! I am as sure of it as that I stand here, because you look so grave. But my dear—dear Mr. Harrington, have I not got plenty of money already? I declare to you, upon my word and honour, that I think I love her the better because she has not got much money, pretty, sweet, beautiful creature! Isn't she a beautiful creature, Mr. Harrington?"

"Yes, my dear young friend, she is a very pretty woman," replied Walter, who felt a good deal at a loss as to the best line of argument by which he could meet this incontrovertible fact.

"Well now, I am glad we agree upon that point!" returned the lover, triumphantly; "and about everything else you know, Mr. Harrington. I must be better able to judge of her than you are, for you do not know her at all, and I know her so very, very well! I do assure you that she is by far the most affectionate being that I ever knew in the whole course of my life, she is indeed, Mr. Harrington! I really think I should be in love with her for that, if it was for nothing else. Of course it could not be expected that I should love her quite so much if she was ugly, instead of handsome; but I am quite sure that I should love her a great deal, let her be as ugly as she would, if she only was as fond of me as she is now. Dear, darling, affectionate creature!"

"Tell me, my Lord, will you, has this lady any written promise of marriage from your Lordship, under your own hand?" said Walter.

"Oh dear me, yes, I believe so. Everything of that sort was settled between us long ago. And the settlements are all ordered to be written out by the lawyers, all regular; and I am to let her have five thousand pounds next week for her to go up to London to buy her wedding-clothes. Shan't I like to draw that dear cheque, I wonder?"

Walter remained profoundly silent for a minute or two. The business seemed to be rather worse, or at least to be further advanced, than he had supposed; but he had not forgotten his nephew's hint on the subject of the fair lady's friend, the tall Captain, who had been encountered when the whereabouts of poor Frank Caldwell had been considered a subject of sufficient importance to lead Henry Harrington to explore them in the places where the most industrious specimens of tall captains are to be found. He remembered this at the present moment with feelings of very friendly satisfaction, for the sake of the ardent young lover, who was evidently intending to make him a convert to his own faith respecting the inestimable qualities of the lady whom it was the first wish of his heart to convert into Lady Goldstable, for without waiting for any answer from Walter, he burst out afresh with increased energy.

"But I say now, Mr. Harrington, just see how unfair you are about my angelic Sophia? Why should you say that you are sorry I am going to be married to her, when you can't possibly know anything about her, good or bad, excepting that she is so divinely beautiful, and the most affectionate creature on God's earth? Why then should you say, Mr. Harrington, that you are sorry I am going to marry her?"

Walter was not quite as well prepared to answer this question as he expected to be hereafter, and he felt puzzled how to evade it; but he was fortunately relieved from his embarrassment by the entrance of a servant with a note addressed to him, and which the man said had just been brought by a messenger from Doucham.

"More arrivals, my Lord!" exclaimed the old man, gaily, as soon as he had read the four lines which the note contained. "I have not a great many English friends, but all the people I know seem to have given themselves rendezvous in this neighbourhood. This note is from an old lady who is a great favourite of mine, who begs to see me immediately at 'The George Inn,' at Doucham. I believe our breakfast is over, my Lord, so with your good leave I will set off at once."

"Who is it, Mr. Harrington? Do I know the lady? If

she is a friend of yours, do pray invite her to come and dine at the Abbey to-day."

"Many thanks, my Lord," replied Walter; "but I do not think you know the lady The note is from my friend Miss Hannah Wigginsville; and though she is neither more nor less than an old woman, and an old maid, I consider her as a very charming personage, and on this occasion she will, undoubtedly, entice me away from my duties at the old manor-house."

"I wish you would let me walk with you to Doucham," said Lord Goldstable, coaxingly. "I must call upon the ladies, you know, and I should so like to walk with you, and talk a little more about my beautiful Sophia!"

Old Walter felt that the time had not yet arrived when any such talk could be turned to profit; he made up his mind, however, to become a patient listener upon a not very interesting theme, and they set off together for Doucham.

CHAPTER LV.

AT the entrance to the little town they separated; Lord Goldstable quickening his steps in one direction, in order to reach his love with as little delay as possible, and old Walter somewhat relaxing his pace in another, in order to give himself a minute or two to meditate upon what could have been likely to bring his friend Miss Hannah to Doucham, and what the particular business could be which had caused her to summon him to her presence.

His inquiry, on arriving at "The George," for a lady newly arrived from London, procured him immediate admission to Miss Wigginsville, and he found her installed in solitary state in the best parlour of the little hotel, engaged in looking through the columns of the same newspaper which she had used the day before in London.

"Miss Hannah!" he exclaimed, cordially extending his

hand to her as he entered; "I am delighted to see you! But what in the world has brought you into the country so suddenly? I cannot flatter myself that you have undertaken the journey solely because you knew that I should be glad to see you; and yet, as I learn by your note, you have sent for me as early as possible after your arrival. Can I be in any way useful to you? Few things could give me greater pleasure."

"The object of my journey, my dear Mr. Harrington, was to procure you, as I trust, a much greater pleasure than that of being merely useful to me. So now sit down, and you shall hear my story."

"I am all impatience, I promise you," said the old gentleman, drawing a chair close to her.

"I am a great respecter of proverbs, Mr. Walter. They have been very well called the wisdom of nations. But there is one, pithy enough, which inculcates the minding business that concerns ourselves, in preference to all other, in the very teeth of which I have been acting, and am about to act. But I must trust to your good-nature to excuse me if it should turn out that I am only blundering, and really doing no good to anybody."

"I am quite sure that I may promise you my gratitude beforehand, if the business in question be business of mine," replied Walter. "I know your clever head, Miss Hannah; and that you are not likely to blunder."

"Well then, to come to the point at once," said she, "I must tell you that it has come to my knowledge that the high esteem in which you lately held Mr. Frank Caldwell has been much impaired."

Walter looked at her earnestly for a moment, and then said:

"Should you have the means, my dear Miss Wigginsville, of convincing me that I have been wrong in thus changing my opinion of him, you will render me a greater service than you have perhaps any idea of."

Miss Hannah nodded her head rather mysteriously in reply; but there was an air of self-satisfaction in her countenance and manner, which seemed to indicate that she knew a good deal.

"May I, as a mutual friend," said she, "ask the grounds of your altered opinion of Mr. Frank Caldwell?"

"As a mutual friend, and especially with the object you have in view, Miss Hannah, I will not scruple to tell you all that has come to my knowledge respecting him," returned Walter, with a heavy sigh. And he then recounted to her shortly, but distinctly, the result of his visit to Aylesbury Street, and of all Henry's subsequent inquiries.

Miss Hannah listened to the painful statement very eagerly, and her evident cheerfulness and contentment rose higher and higher as he went on.

"It is all right!" she triumphantly exclaimed, as soon as Walter had finished his statement.

"All right, Miss Wigginsville!" exclaimed Walter; "what can you mean, Madam?"

"I mean that I was right," she replied, rubbing her hands with an unmistakable air of satisfaction.

"Then I have been very wrong!" returned Walter, looking deeply hurt. "I have most strangely misunderstood you, Miss Wigginsville; but I daresay the blunder was mine, and not yours. I was so anxious to hear what I wished, that I seemed to have been incapable of comprehending the contrary."

"How can you comprehend, if you won't listen to me?" retorted the almost angry Miss Hannah. "What I meant by saying I was right was this: at a party at our house, the other evening—"

But here Miss Hannah's narrative was cut short, by the sound of a loud voice from a person who had just sprung from a railroad omnibus.

"I say, you fellow," said the voice, "can any of you tell me where an old chap called Walter Harrington can be found?"

"If it is Squire Harrington, Stanton Hall, that you are asking for in that queer way," replied another voice, which sounded very like that of a landlady, not particularly well pleased by the manner of a newly-arrived guest, "you have not far to seek, for Squire Harrington, of the Hall, is in that parlour?"

All this had been very distinctly heard by the Squire and Miss Hannah; and they were looking at each other with no little surprise, when the door of the parlour was thrown open, and in rushed our acquaintance, Dick Caldwell.

"Miss Wigginsville, by all that's fortunate!" cried the young man, bowing low to the lady. "Everything will be right now, I am quite sure!"

Walter stood with eyes wide opened, staring at him, and

apparently struck dumb with astonishment. The whole style, air, manner, and address of the young man who stood before him were so totally unlike—not to say contrasted with—those of his young friend Frank, that he could not believe it to be him ; yet so completely identical did they seem in feature and form, and even in voice, that it was not in his power to believe that it could be any other. In short, old Walter stood utterly confounded and amazed.

"You have arrived exactly at the right moment, Mr. Caldwell," said Miss Hannah. "If you had been a moment later you would have lost hearing the extremely bad character I am going to bestow upon you.

"No! Are you really? Then I suspect, Miss Wigginsville, that we are both arrived here on the self-same errand? and if that is the case I am most exceedingly obliged to you, Miss Wigginsville ; I am, upon my soul! And since I have been so, beyond all expectation, lucky as to meet a friend here, perhaps you will have the kindness to present me to Mr. Walter Harrington?"

Walter's astonishment and mystification seemed to go on increasing with every word he heard. Miss Hannah, however, who, on the contrary, appeared to comprehend everything that was going on, immediately complied with the request made to her, and without a moment's delay, said very distinctly : "Mr. Harrington, permit me to introduce to you Mr. Richard Caldwell, the twin-brother of your friend, Mr. Frank Caldwell."

"The brother! The twin-brother!" ejaculated Walter, with vehement agitation. "Heaven and earth! Was there ever such a likeness! My darling child! My poor dear Kate! You must excuse me, if you please : I suppose I can get a post-chaise here? I understand it all!—everything. And you, my dear, good Miss Wigginsville, have taken this journey on purpose to make me understand the desperate blunder into which I had fallen. God bless you for it, Miss Hannah!"

"Yet, what is Miss Wigginsville's self-sacrifice compared to mine?" said Dick Caldwell, with an aspect half saucy, half sad. "She has made the journey to prove her friendship to a valued friend ; and I have made the self-same, to prove satisfactorily to everyone that I am a scamp!"

"At any rate, Sir, you have proved that you have a brother's heart for one to whom it is an honour to be kin.

And for myself, I shall ever feel grateful to you for delivering me from an error, that was a most heavy grief to me.

"Then I have the satisfaction of understanding that all the fault you had to find with poor Frank, when you wrote him that thunderbolt of a letter, was that you mistook him for your humble servant?"

"Indeed, I very sincerely hope and believe that such is the case," replied Walter, with a comic little bow. "Frank never was a gambler then, Mr. Caldwell?" added the old man cheerfully.

"Never rattled a dice-box, or turned up a trump in his life," replied Dick.

"And he has never under any circumstances, been in the habit of frequenting a hell in Aylesbury Street?"

"Never! And, upon my conscience, I do not believe that my brother Frank knows of the existence of any such place."

"Nor has any intimate acquaintance, then, with the set that assemble there?"

"Only with one, Mr. Harrington!—only with one. Frank is very intimate with me; and truth obliges me to say that he has always been very kind to me. But I hope you will forgive him for that, Mr. Harrington, on account of our being twins. And then, luckily for him, I have been very little in London, but almost always with my regiment; so that altogether I do not think he can be much the worse for me."

"Then the person I saw on that memorable evening, in Aylesbury Street, was—"

"Myself, and no other!" interrupted Dick, eagerly. "And if I want to know your opinion of me, Mr. Harrington, I have only to turn to your letter to Frank."

"Nay, my dear Sir!" replied Walter, "had it not been for the position in which your brother was placed with respect to me and mine, I should not have expressed any opinion at all upon what I saw and heard there, however little it might be in accordance with my ideas of what is desirable."

"And for that matter, Mr. Harrington," replied the young man, dolorously shaking his head, "I believe my own ideas as to what is desirable, are not so very much different from yours—that is to say, as long as I am out of the way of temptation. But I am in a hurry to be off again by the next train, that I may have the pleasure of telling poor Frank that everything's right again. I suppose, Sir, I have your permission to say so?"

"My dear Mr. Caldwell!" said Walter, kindly, "you have done me a great service, and I would willingly requite it if I could. Let this comedy of errors turn out a happy performance for all the parties concerned in it. I shall, of course, write to your brother Frank directly; and depend upon it, my letter will bring him here in a few hours. Stay with us, then, till he comes! And if we can keep you out of temptation thus long, who knows, but that among us, we may muster influence enough to keep you longer still? My old house will be ready in a day or two, to receive more friends than I shall be able, I fear, to collect together on so short a notice, and I shall greatly like to have you among them. But during this short interval, I am staying with a friend, who, I am quite sure, will gladly extend his hospitality to you. I cannot invite you, Miss Hannah, to any bachelor's house but my own," continued the old man, gaily turning to the delighted Miss Wigginsville; "but you must positively wait here till my house is ready for you, and then we will have *a gathering*. The Rectory, at Stanton, you know, is full of your friends, and you will be sure of having Kate here before long."

Nothing could be more cordial than the acceptance of this proposal by the old lady, and the young gentleman. Lord Goldstable was summoned from "the Establishment," to ratify the promise of hospitality which had been made in his name; and though this summons withdrew him from a very tender love-scene, he behaved admirably well; and the radiant good-humour with which he welcomed his unexpected guest, and tried to make Miss Hannah promise to meet the very charming ladies who were coming to dine with him at the Abbey that day, confirmed his old friend Walter that he was well worth saving from the clutches of such a harpy as the beautiful Sophia; and even Miss Hannah herself, though she had registered more than one oath in Heaven, against holding communion with fools whenever it was in her power to avoid it, now caught herself promising, that though she could not come to dine with his Lordship on that particular day, yet that she should not forget his kind invitation, and should be very glad to accept it, if repeated upon any future occasion.

CHAPTER LVI.

WHEN Walter Harrington came down stairs on the following morning, to take his usual walk upon the fine terrace, which stretched along the whole extremity of the garden-front of the so-called Abbey, who should he find already parading there but Miss Hannah Wigginsville. She was walking backwards and forwards with a brisk step, and great appearance of enjoyment.

"How now, Miss Hannah!" exclaimed Walter, gaily. "Have you taken possession of my quarter-deck before me? I thought I was a tolerably early riser; but if you have walked over from Doucham this morning, you beat me hollow!"

"I thought I might have a chance of meeting you, if I walked towards the Abbey, Mr. Harrington; but as to lying late at Doucham, it is quite out of the question; for 'the Establishment' turns itself inside-out at five o'clock in the morning; and as it was impossible to sleep, I thought my best plan was to walk. What a fine rookery your young host has got here!"

"Glorious, Miss Hannah! And if he loves their well-tuned croaking as well as I do, he was lucky to find them here; for a rookery, Miss Hannah, is one of the things that neither king nor kaiser can command. The music of my busy collegiate old friends there would be vastly more difficult to bespeak than a new commemoration of a thousand performers at that other abbey, bright Westminster. It would be almost as easy to command a new comet as a new rookery."

"True, and most curious are the ways and habits of that queer society of antiquaries!" she replied.

"I suspect that there are some of our modern ways of going on that they do not altogether approve, for they certainly do not colonize among us so freely as they used to do. But shame upon me, Miss Hannah, for thinking about an old colony of rooks, instead of a new colony of Christians. I have never once thought of wishing you joy, or asking how the wedding went off."

"There was no great novelty about it, Mr. Harrington.

26

It went off just as such things always do go off; and the bride and bridegroom went off after it. I have allowed them three weeks to get through their billing and cooing; and I hope that will suffice them, and that we shall live in peace afterwards."

"Then, I presume, the plan is for the newly-married couple to live with you and Miss Jemima afterwards?"

"Why, where else could they live, Mr. Harrington?" returned Miss Hannah. "Mary Jane has nothing; and I fancy, there is but little chance of Mr. Garbel's finding her such a home as she has been used to, poor silly child."

"Then, I fear the marriage is rather an imprudent one," said the old gentleman, shaking his head.

"Of course it was," replied the old lady, briskly. "But what was I to do with Mary Jane? If I had kept her from marrying Mr. Garbel, she would have been sure to fall in love again directly with somebody else, whom I might have found more troublesome perhaps. We shall make him useful in the house, somehow or other; and I daresay it will all do very well."

"I am sure I hope so heartily! And now, my dear Miss Hannah, let me tell you once again, how deeply grateful I feel to you for what you did for us yesterday," said Walter, stopping short in his walk, and affectionately taking her hand. "Perhaps I have more happiness to thank you for than you are aware of."

"Not a bit of it, Mr. Harrington; I know all about it, I promise you. I know that there is a very dear creature, still more deeply interested in it than you are yourself," returned Miss Hannah.

"You were in Kate's confidence, then? I am not much surprised to hear it. But I wish you could have seen the sort of magical change which took place in her, upon listening to the news I carried her after I left you yesterday It really was the most touching thing I ever saw in my life."

"Dear, pretty, gentle Kate, I can fancy it!" said the stout-hearted Miss Hannah, quickly getting rid of a tear by means of blowing her nose, as if seized with a violent cold. "But here comes your young host, Mr. Harrington. What a good-natured looking boy he is. If I were you, I really would take a little trouble to keep him out of mischief. He might do so much good, you know."

"I think I shall keep him out of a little mischief, if I have tolerable luck," replied Walter.

The noble young host seemed perfectly delighted at seeing
Miss Hannah, and listening to her commendations of his
beautiful park; though he looked a good deal puzzled by a
few cursory remarks which she made upon the change of
church lands to lay, and the disadvantages of the mortmain
tenure.

"I shouldn't wonder!" replied his Lordship. "I daresay
you are right, very. But, I say, Mr. Harrington, I got a bit
of news this morning, and I want your advice about it.
Since we eat our pleasant dinner at Bickley, the clergyman,
poor old man, has died. He died that very night, I believe,
or else the night after, poor old man! The living, you know,
Mr. Harrington, is in my gift. They tell me it is worth above
seven hundred a-year; and that beautiful house belongs to it
—that sweet pretty place, commanding a view of the fall, and
the ruins, you know, and all that pretty part that everybody
admired so much. And Mrs. Fitzjames said, that it was just
the spot that she should like to live in, with one dear companion that she could love, and be forgotten by all the rest of
the world, because she was so fond of the roses that grew all
over the house. She is such a dear, sweet, affectionate
creature! But, nevertheless, I can't live there myself, you
know; though I am sure I should like it excessively with
her! But I can't, you know, Mr. Harrington, because I am
not a clergyman. But I may have the pleasure of giving
it to anybody who is. Who shall I give it to, Mr.
Harrington?"

"Bickley always used to be reckoned the most desirable
piece of preferment in the whole neighbourhood," said Walter;
"but the disposal of it ought to involve many serious considerations."

"What considerations?" demanded the church patron,
with great simplicity.

"Considerations, as to how the appointment may be made
most conducive to the welfare of the parish," replied Walter.

"And that I am sure I don't know; and I don't know
how I am to find out," said Lord Goldstable, shaking his
head.

"It is one of the instances so perpetually recurring,
demonstrative of the evils of lame impropriations," said Miss
Hannah, with more truth than politeness.

"Very true, Ma'am!" returned the impropriator, with a
very hazy notion of what she meant, "I am quite sure it's

26—2

true; but I did not appropriate it myself, you know, by my own act. And as it is mine to give away, the question is, who shall I give it to? And that is what I want you to tell me, Mr. Harrington."

"Look about you for a good, kind-hearted, active man," said Walter; "and if you make these qualities your *sine quâ non*, you cannot go far wrong."

"Good, kind, active!" repeated Lord Goldstable, meditatively. "Good, kind, active!" he reiterated slowly. "I wish, with all my heart and soul, that I could give the living to Miss Cross!"

Not to laugh at this sally, was pretty nearly impossible; for the earnest sincerity of the accent in which it was uttered, rendered the drollery of it irresistible; but Walter speedily recovered his gravity, and said, with great sobriety: "I am afraid, my Lord, that livings have been often given upon less notable demonstrations of praiseworthy qualities than were demonstrated in Miss Olivia's courageous jump in Bickley cavern. But that is all you know of her, is it not?"

"No, Mr. Harrington, it is not," replied Lord Goldstable, stoutly. "When I was talking to her the pic-nic day, and offering her some *bon-bons*, and asking her if she would like another pic-nic, and all that sort of thing, she stopped me short in all my nonsense, to ask if I knew of a very, *very* poor family, that live almost close to the park-gates on the further side, you know, which is a good deal out of the way; and she told me that there was a wife and six children almost starving, because the father cannot work on account of being ill; and then she said, blushing like a full-blown rose all the time, that a little help in the way of food might save their lives. And she did not say a word that was not true; for I found that out the next day. Now I take it, Mr. Harrington, that Miss Cross is the sort of person that you would like me to put in the living?"

"I certainly think, that in many respects, the parish could not be in better hands," replied Walter. "But you know, my Lord, that although ladies certainly do preach sometimes, we never make parsons of them. We may have heard of a a lady's being a priestess; but never of her being a clergywoman. I do not remember that they have ever aspired to any ecclesiastical preferment since the days of Pope Joan. Though more than one amongst them has contrived to draw captains and colonels pay in the other great militant profession.

"I declare, that in these days," said Miss Hannah, "the spiritual seems the more militant of the two. Truly, it might be supposed, from the present state of things in England, that religion was the most pregnant apple of discord that had ever been thrown among mankind."

"Indeed we seem to make it so," returned Walter. "For instance, there is the young lady we have been talking of. She is really an excellent creature; but like the Lady Juliana Witherby, she is constantly ready to run a tilt against everybody who thinks differently in religious matters from herself."

"And on the same side as her Ladyship, is it not?" said Miss Hannah.

"Oh yes!" replied Walter, "she belongs to the Evangelicals, as they call themselves, and as they are also called curiously enough, by their opponents, although I presume the latter would not consent to denominate themselves 'anti-evangelists!'"

"I don't very well understand how Lady Juliana and James contrive to live in peace together," added Walter, after the silent meditation of a minute or two. "He, you know, is quite as violent in the opposite direction, as she is in her way."

"Perhaps they don't live in peace," suggested Miss Hannah. "I know, by my own experience with Mary Jane, that it is no very easy matter to live at peace with a low-church professor. I should like," she added, "to see something more of the other sect; I have never had any good opportunity of talking to a Puseyite."

"I can recommend my nephew James to you, Miss Hannah, as a fine specimen," returned Walter, laughing. "You may study the habits and peculiarities of the creature very advantageously in him."

"Dear me!" cried Lord Goldstable, who had for some minutes been seeking very earnestly in his thoughts for some proper and fitting candidate for his vacant living. "Dear me, Mr. Harrington! I wonder I should have never thought of it before! Why should I not give Bickley to your nephew, Mr. James? I daresay he would like it, because it is so pretty, you know; and it would be such a very great pleasure to me to offer anything agreeable to a relation of yours."

"You are very kind, my dear Lord," replied Walter, "and as to James's liking it, I fancy there would be no doubt about that. But it is evident that you have no prejudices in your theology; for James, as we have been saying, is the exact antipodes of Miss Cross on all theological questions, and I confess that if I had a living to give away, I should prefer somebody of more moderate opinions than either."

"Dear me! It certainly seems to be a very difficult thing to do properly!" said the perplexed patron, with a deep sigh.

"May I presume to offer a suggestion on the subject?" said Miss Hannah, suddenly standing still, and preparing to indulge herself with a generous pinch of snuff.

"Pray do, Ma'am! I should really be so very much obliged to you, for I don't know anybody in the world that I can think of."

"Then give the living to both the lady and the gentleman you have mentioned. From your park-gate anecdote of the lady, and from the general character of Mr. James Harrington, I am quite sure it would be very easy for your Lordship to do worse."

"I don't understand, I am afraid," said Lord Goldstable, with a puzzled air. "Livings can't be divided, I believe, can they, Sir?"

"Livings cannot be divided, my Lord Goldstable," returned Miss Hannah, with grave solemnity, "but gentlemen and ladies may be joined, you know."

"Bravo, Miss Hannah!" ejaculated Walter. "Why, what an admirable match-maker you are!"

"Capital, by Jove!" shouted the delighted young patron. "Thank you a thousand times over for your clever thought, Ma'am! You can't think how pleased I am about it, because of its being Mr. Harrington's nephew, and because, too, of my thinking her such a handsome girl, and so inclined to pity poor people. And then you know, Mr. Harrington, that they kept close together all the pic-nic day, and take my word for it that's a sign that they like one another. I understand something about that, don't I, Mr. Harrington? But now you must tell me," he continued, almost out of breath with his eagerness, "now you must tell me how I can explain to them what I want. What shall I say? I don't know the least in the world how to set about it!"

"Oh, there would be no difficulty about that, I should think," said Miss Hannah. "You have only just to mention to Mr. James Harrington that you greatly wish to make some provision for Miss Cross, as the daughter of a highly respected clergyman in your neighbourhood, who you understand is left but slenderly provided for; and that as you think you have perceived some symptoms of a mutual liking between him and the young lady, you would be happy to give the living of Bickley to him if you were right in your conjecture, and that a marriage were to take place between them."

"Capital, capital!" cried the delighted Lord Goldstable, clapping hands in a perfect ecstasy. "I am sure it will do! How very clever you must be, Miss Wigginsville, to think of all that off-hand, in a moment! Don't you think it will do, Mr. Harrington?"

"Yes, really, I think it may," replied Walter, "if James's Romanising tenets about the celibacy of the clergy do not stand in the way of it."

"I don't think you will find it so," said Miss Hannah, indulging in another pinch of snuff. "Circumstances, Mr. Walter, have often, I believe, great influence in *modifying* principles."

"I certainly should not be greatly surprised if it proved so in the present instance," replied the old man, with a grave and decorous smile, "and if so, I trust our morning cogitations will turn to a happy issue."

"And that must begin by our all breakfasting together," said the young peer, offering his arm with a very good grace to the old lady. "I don't think I ever felt so happy about anything, but I owe it all to you, Miss Wigginsville!"

Miss Hannah very frankly declared that she was extremely hungry, and the well-pleased though oddly assorted, trio turned gaily through an open window from the terrace into the breakfast-room.

CHAPTER LVII.

At precisely half-past six o'clock in the evening of the appointed day, a somewhat heavy, but very handsome travelling chariot, drawn by four post horses, drove up to the door of the Rectory at Stanton Parva. An old man-servant carefully wrapped up, and a somewhat younger, and equally comfortable-looking abigail, occupied the rumble; two huge imperials formed the roof, but every inch of available space about the vehicle was occupied by well contrived, and neatly fitted cases and boxes of all sorts, sizes, and shapes. In the interior were the persons of the Rev. Dr. Harrington, and his high-born wife, the Lady Augusta.

A beautiful little silver sandwich-box, and a small flask for sherry (both empty), occupied the carriage pocket on the Doctor's side, and a recently published volume of controversial theology (uncut), the pocket in front. A smelling-bottle and the paper of the morning flanked her Ladyship.

Great was the interest occasioned by the appearance of this equipage in the village street of Stanton. It drew a whole posse of idle boys in its train, who formed a gaping semi-circle but at a respectful distance, as the dignified divine alighted. The first object which gratified the curiosity of this eager group was a foot incased in a very large cloth shoe, and a stout leg to match, buttoned up in a soft looking gaiter. This foot and leg as they were slowly and cautiously protruded from the carriage, were gazed at with great reverence. And next appeared a fat grey-gloved hand, grasping the uncut volume, and as the arm to which it belonged was immediately taken possession of, and supported by the ready arm of the old servant from the rumble, the remainder of the Doctor's person soon appeared, and by gentle degrees lowered itself, and was lowered till it finally reached the level of the solid earth. The much-enduring divine made one or two faint signs of salutation to the awe-struck young crowd, and then stepped on towards the house with very much the air of a martyr walking to an *auto-da-fè*.

"Show me to my chamber, and let my son come to me!" he said, in a deep, hollow voice, as he entered the house.

The stairs were surmounted at length, with infinite apparent effort, and having reached the very comfortable-looking room that had been prepared for him, the Doctor sunk into a deep arm-chair, to all appearance very alarmingly overcome by the exertion he had made to reach it.

The Lady Augusta and her maid followed, accompanied by the Lady Juliana; and James immediately appeared, and having ushered them into the room, approached his father's chair.

"I fear, my dear Sir," said he, with very dutiful gentleness, "that the fatigue of the journey has been too much for you!"

The Doctor gave a slight, feeble wave of his cambric handkerchief across his temples, and muttered, "In journeyings oft!" but he presently added, in a trembling but impressive tone, "James, if it will be more than twenty minutes before your dinner is served, I should be thankful for a glass of sherry! Nature is well-nigh exhausted!" Poor little Kate, who had not yet received a word from either parent, ran out of the room, and returned in a moment with the desired cordial, which she presented to her father.

The old gentleman swallowed it with the air of being exceedingly comforted thereby, and then returning the glass to her, laid his hand upon her head as she stooped to receive it, and said with great unction, "Thank you my child."

"Dinner will be ready directly, dearest papa! and I am sure you must want it," said Kate.

A feeble and rather melancholy shake of the head was the only reply.

"Your father is a good deal tired, James," said Lady Augusta, "and to confess the truth, so am I. We have had a broiling sun the whole way. I should greatly prefer having some tea here to going down to dinner, and if Juliana will kindly keep me company, we might have a snug chat together."

The dependant sister was far too well trained to make any objection to this proposition, though she certainly did feel, poor lady, that though she had been very busy she was not too tired to eat her dinner. She did not, however, allude to this difference in their respective sensations, but replied in a most amiable manner, that she should like it of all things.

In a very few minutes the dinner was announced, and the Doctor and his two children placed themselves at table.

James stood up stiffly in his place, and paused a moment in
doubt whether he should venture to give the long, half-
chaunted Latin grace with which he usually indulged himself;
but the Doctor took the matter into his own hands, and
settled it very shortly, by seizing upon the soup-ladle
and mumbling out the words, "Thank God for all good
gifts."

The son and daughter had the satisfaction of seeing their
father recover rapidly under the genial influence of the repast;
and after the cloth was removed, and that Kate had ran up
stairs to join her mother and aunt, the Doctor was sufficiently
recruited to enable him to question James as to the present
aspect of affairs between Lord Goldstable and Kate.

In reply to these enquiries, the Rector assured his father
that, to the best of his knowledge and belief, everything was
going on prosperously   "The great proof of this my dear Sir,
is, that my Uncle Walter is not only living in Lord Goldstable's house when he might easily have been accommodated
either in his own or mine, but, moreover, they really appear
to be more on the terms of a father and son than anything
else.   And as to Kate, so far from treating his Lordship with
anything like coldness or repulsive formality, she seems as
much at her ease with him as if they had been engaged for
months."

"Enough, my dear James, enough!" replied the well-
pleased father.   "Your Uncle Walter has managed the whole
affair most admirably!   And now you shall let me sleep for a
few minutes, James, my exhausted strength has need of it,"
and with these words he settled himself into his well-
cushioned chair, and sunk into profound repose.

Kate, meanwhile, had found it rather a difficult task to
keep the promise she had given her uncle, to leave to him the
task of explaining her present situation, and yet not to answer
her mother's questionings without more disingenuousness than
she chose to be guilty of.   Her mother had been prepared,
however, to be very easily contented by the statement of Lady
Juliana, which was, in fact, essentially the same as that given
by James to his father, and led her to the same satisfactory
conclusion; so that when at length Kate said, by way of
putting an end to the discussion, that she believed it was
Lord Goldstable's intention to come over to Stanton on the
morrow, with her Uncle Walter, in order to speak to her
father, Lady Augusta very graciously replied, "That is quite

as it ought to be, my dear, and you will therefore say no more on the subject till after this interview is over."

Meanwhile, old Walter, after returning from the happy interview with Kate, which had left her too much comforted for any trifling amount of annoyance to be of much importance, retired to his own room at Brandon Abbey, and was anything but an idle man for the next hour or two. In fact he had a great deal upon his hands, and he was quite aware of it. Though he had hitherto lived with a marvellously strong feeling of indifference concerning the superabundant wealth of which he was in possession, he began to think of it now with great complacency, and, moreover, he thanked the gods that all men were not as indifferent upon the subject as he had hitherto been himself; for if they were, he would not now be the influential personage that he felt himself to be.

He was far from being indifferent to the disappointment which he knew would fall upon his brother upon hearing Lord Goldstable's intended communication, of softening the blow as much as possible. But he knew it would be a difficult thing to convince his brother and his brother's wife, that it would be better for their daughter to marry a young lawyer with a few hundreds a-year, than a peer of the realm with many thousands. Yet this was the task before him.

He happened to know perfectly well, for Kate herself had told him so, that the only painful pecuniary anxiety which troubled his brother, arose from the position of his eldest son. This by no means very bad, but decidedly greatly spoiled young man, had constantly resisted every attempt to make him adopt a profession; his chief argument for this being, that he might go into the army at any time. There can be no doubt that this would have been listened to very differently, both by his father and mother, had he *not* been the eldest nephew of a rich batchelor uncle. But old Walter had been but a very short time an inmate of his brother's house, before very grave doubts suggested themselves both to the Doctor and his wife, as to the certainty that their eldest son was to be his uncle's heir.

It was indeed quite evident that the old man was on an excellent friendly footing with the young one, but it was at least equally so that it was not Henry, but Kate, who was Uncle Walter's darling.

Many were the consultations which took place between the parents upon the probable good, or evil, that might arise from

speaking upon the subject to Walter, but they both agreed
that the experiment might endanger the pleasant and profitable way in which they were living together, and, therefore,
that at any rate it had better be postponed.

But greatly as they approved and admired the skill with
which the venerable Squire of Stanton had contrived to in-
gratiate himself with Lord Goldstable, so as to ensure this
splendid marriage for his darling niece, they both agreed that
his conduct on this occasion gave the death-blow to their hopes
for Henry; for there was no other way of accounting for the
strangely close union that evidently existed between old Walter
and the young nobleman, but by supposing that he considered
Kate as his adopted daughter, and that she was to be portioned
and dowered as such.

So completely, indeed, had they made up their minds to
believe this, that the Doctor determined, with as little delay
as possible, to consult with his brother upon the best means
of at once persuading Henry to decide upon entering the army,
thinking it not unlikely that he might do something liberal to
help them in the way of purchase-money.

But in all these cogitations upon the feelings, the wishes,
and the intentions of old Walter. The deeply-reasoning pair
had never hit upon one particle of truth, excepting the pretty
tolerably evident fact that Kate was the old gentleman's
darling. Not for any single moment had the idea of making
her his heiress entered his head. He would as soon have
thought of crowning her Queen of May or Empress of
Germany. His common sense had pointed out his nephew
Henry to him as his natural and proper heir; he had never
dreamed of any other, and it was because he considered this
as too obviously a matter of course to be doubted, that he
had never thought it worth while to discuss the subject with
anybody. If any additional reason for this silence had been
wanted, he would have found it in his own averseness to the
idea of being thanked for doing what he would have deemed
it very wrong not to have done.

But the present state of affairs had produced a complete
revolution in the mind of the old man respecting the arrangement of his large property, not, indeed, as respected the
succession of Henry to the family acres, for it appeared to
him that nature had made that arrangement for him, but
concerning the rarely thought of, and never calculated amount
of the large sum which had been accumulating during the

many years that he had been in possession of an income which he had never half spent, but which he knew his trusty agent, Mr. Tapley, had regularly invested in the English funds. The existence of this sum was now become a matter of great importance to him. Of the amount, or even of the existence of it at all, he knew that his brother was perfectly ignorant, and he flattered himself, not without good cause, that it might enable him to sooth, his feelings under that disappointment which awaited him.

The exact result of the busy hour or two during which he was shut up with his writing desk in his own room at Brandon Abbey, will be made manifest hereafter; but though an old, he was by no means a slow man, and he contrived to dismiss two important letters to the post before their late dinner-hour. The following morning he held a short conversation with his young host upon the subject of his Bickley living, and contrived to learn from him, with very satisfactory certainty, that he was very seriously determined upon disposing of it in the manner proposed by Miss Hannah, provided he could only find out that the proposal would be agreeable both to the gentleman and lady.

"As to the lady, indeed," said Lord Goldstable, looking very intelligent, "I would bet ten to one I could answer for her. I am quite sure that she would not have jumped over to him in the way she did in the cavern, you know, Mr. Harrington, if she had not liked him. It would not have been natural, would it? But how shall we find out about the gentleman? I wish you would ask him. You would do it so much better than I could."

"Well then, I will ask him, if you commission me to do so," replied Walter, laughing. "It will make him stare a little I suppose, but it will not be the first time that I have produced that effect upon my nephew James."

"But when will you do it?" returned Lord Goldstable, earnestly. "How I do wish it could be done before I go over there, to call on Dr. Harrington."

"Well then, it shall be done first," said Walter, who perfectly understood the good feeling which suggested the wish. "I agree with you," he added, "that it will be better to settle this matter before than after you have explained yourself to my brother."

"But when will you find time to do it?" persisted Lord Goldstable.

Walter meditated for a moment, and then replied:

"I will tell you, my Lord, how we will manage it. My brother and Lady Augusta are to arrive at the Rectory to-morrow evening; they are expected to dinner, and by Kate's account, her father will be too much tired to receive a visit from me that night; but you know my early ways, and that it will be easy for me to walk over in good time for their breakfast the next morning. This I will do, and will take care before the hour arrives at which your Lordship will make your promised visit, that your kind proposal shall be properly explained to James."

"Thank you a thousand times for all your kindness to me," returned the young peer, as cordially as if he had been returning thanks for the reception of a charming house and comfortable income, instead of being assisted in offering these good gifts to another; and after the interval of a moment he added, with equal earnestness, though with less hilarity, "and don't fear, Mr. Harrington, that I should not keep my promise of calling upon the Doctor. I'll do it, you may depend upon it, if it should be the death of me."

CHAPTER LVIII.

It had rarely happened during the course of Walter Harrington's long life that he had ever broken any promise, little or great, nor did he do so now.

He had no wish, however, to disturb the party at the Rectory, though it was his purpose to breakfast with them, and he therefore set off upon his pleasant walk across the fields, at, what was to him, rather a late hour, than an early one. But he had calculated his time very accurately, and reached the Parsonage, as he intended to do, exactly as the family were seating themselves round the breakfast-table. He found his brother happily recovered from the fatigues of the previous day, one proof of which was, that he had already agreed at the very earnest request of his son James, to go with him into the church as soon as the breakfast was over.

"I am very glad Uncle Walter," said the young Rector, "that you are here too, that you may go into the church with us. As the Squire of the parish, my dear Sir, and as patron of the living, you know, you ought to know something more about our proceedings than you do at present. Don't you think so, Sir?"

"I should like to know a great many things more than I do at present," replied Walter, "but I don't find the days long enough. At this particular moment," he added, "I have something very particular that I want to say to you, James. Can you not spare me a few minutes before we go into the church?"

"Impossible, my dear Sir," replied the unconscious James. "Do you not see that my father is already drawing on his gloves? If we do not go now we shall never get him into the church at all, and I am in great hopes he may do something to help us about the repairs."

"Very well then, James, I must speak to you afterwards; only remember, will you, that I really have something important to say, and that I wish you to hear it before Lord Goldstable comes here to call on your father, and he will start to come here immediately after his breakfast, I believe."

James replied with an intelligent sort of look and nod, signifying that he already understood all about it, and that he knew as well as if he had been told a dozen times over, that this visit from Lord Goldstable was for the purpose of settling the preliminaries of Kate's approaching marriage with his Lordship.

But there was no time now for Walter to convey any intimation that the communication which he wished to make to James was of a more personal nature, for the Doctor was already advancing towards the house-door, and James, who considered the business he was upon as a very important one, was at his side in a moment.

A few slow and panting, but very dignified steps, brought the Doctor, and those who had the honour of attending upon him, to the porch of the parish church. Having arrived there, he stopped a moment to recover his breath, and then turning to his brother, he said:

"You see how it is, Walter; James thinking, it seems, that I have not enough of duties and responsibilities on my shoulders already, insists upon my undertaking the office of amateur rural Dean in his parish."

"No, no, my dear Sir, I would not give you a moment of unnecessary trouble for the world. But I cannot help hoping that you will feel interested in my little embellishments. And it is such a lucky chance, having you and my uncle here together," said James.

The puffing and almost groaning dignitary perceiving that it was impossible to escape, struggled no further, and the party entered the venerable little church, where they found the Rector's favourite churchwarden and carpenter, Mr. Brandling, waiting to receive them. This estimable personage had probably been desired by the Rector to explain to the Doctor what were the particular objects which they had in view for the repair and embellishment of the sacred building, for it was to him, Mr. Brandling especially addressed himself.

"Our great object, Sir," said he, "has been to impart a mediæval air to our new work. This quatrefoil ornamentation is, I think I may venture to say, Sir, in the style of the best period."

"We have done the very little that our limited means permitted," joined in James, addressing himself chiefly to his uncle, "in as good taste as we could afford. But if you, my dear uncle, as Squire of the parish, and patron of the living, would help us, we might, perhaps, improve the religious feeling among us by removing these hideous penfolds of pews and re-seating the church with open benches in a becoming manner."

"Any good that I could do to the parish, I should be happy to perform," replied Walter. "But why do the parishioners want new seats, my good fellow? These seem to be in very good repair."

"Alas! my dear uncle, you do not appreciate the matter justly," replied James. "There is a spiritual meaning, a symbolism, in all these things, Sir, that is very important."

"Why, begging your honest pardon," said Mr. Brandling, following his superior on the same side, "what is a parcel of shabby Memel deals good for in a church? A fair range of low-backed oak benches, now, has a church spirit about them that is of the right sort, Sir."

"There is a church spirit in oak, is there?" said Walter, "and no spiritual meaning in Memel deals?"

"These things are more important than you think for,"

pleaded James; "and so I am sure my father will tell you," he added, turning to the Doctor, who had seated himself on a bench in the nave, and was wiping his brow with his handker-chief.

"Your father looks too much heated and exhausted to speak upon the subject, just yet," said Walter, passing his arm under that of his nephew as he spoke; "and you shall come with me, James, just for two minutes, while he is resting himself: "and he then added, in a whisper, "I have some-thing for your private ear." These words, as they were intended to do, excited the curiosity of the Rector, and he therefore obeyed the impulse of the arm that had taken posses-sion of him; but it was not without reluctance, for he had hoped much from this lucky encounter of his uncle and father in the church. The north side of the little building afforded a shady and a perfectly retired spot, and thither the mysterious old uncle led the somewhat impatient nephew. "James," he began, with a little more solemnity of manner than was usual with him, "James, you have, I believe, known Miss Cross for many years. I want you honestly and frankly, to tell me your opinion of her."

"My opinion of Miss Cross, Sir?" returned the young man, colouring. "She is certainly a very fine young woman; and, as far as I know, she is a very good girl too—that is to say, that she is an excellent daughter, and though she is far from rich, she does a great deal of good among the poor people in all directions. But her religious opinions are so absurdly erroneous, that we are not always on such good terms as we should be if we thought alike. However, my dear Sir, I am the last man in the world, you know, to pass judgment on a young lady; for my principles lead me very strongly to think that men of my profession would do well never to think of ladies at all."

"Really! are you so nearly a Romanist as that?" said Walter. "Then there can be no good done by my going on with what I was about to say. However, if I have awakened your curiosity, it will be hardly fair to leave it unsatisfied. The case is this, James: my good-hearted young friend, Lord Gold-stable, has, you know, the living of Bickley to dispose of. He has been telling me that he has heard Miss Cross spoken of as an excellent young woman, but not so well provided for as he thinks the daughter of so very respectable a clergyman as her father was, ought to be; and he has taken it into his

head that he should like to give the living of Bickley to a
young clergyman, about her own age, who might happen to
like her, and whom she might happen to like. And to tell
you the whole truth, James, it occurred to us both, that as you
had been long neighbours and friends, it was not impossible
that seven hundred a-year, and a good house, might make a
marriage desirable between you now, though it might have
been very imprudent to have thought of such a thing before."

"And it is within distance, too," were the first words that
James uttered.

To these words, however, his Uncle Walter, made no reply,
but continued to walk on beside him in silence. This silence
was broken, after the interval of a few minutes, by James, who
said, in a very grave and rather reproachful accent:

"You are mistaken, Uncle Walter, in supposing that I am
a Romanist. I am not. If I were, I should neither retain
my present preferment, nor accept any other that could be
offered me."

"Your explanation is perfectly satisfactory, James," replied
the old man; "and it now only remains for you to tell me
whether, in all other respects, the proposal of Lord Goldstable
is agreeable to you."

"It would be very ungracious of me to say it was not,"
said the young man colouring; "and it would be even more
than ungracious, for it would be untrue. But it will not do,
Uncle Walter, for me to accept this conditional offer without
consulting the young lady as to her feelings concerning it."

"Very properly thought of," replied Walter, with an intelligent smile. "But somehow or other, James, I have a
notion that the young lady will prove herself to be as tolerant
and as reasonable as yourself."

"I am willing to hope so, Sir," said the Rector, very
modestly; "and if you think you could excuse my absence to
my father, I would wait upon Miss Cross immediately. Do
you not think that it would be desirable that I should do
so before I see Lord Goldstable? for it would be equally
awkward, you know, either to thank him or not to thank
him."

"I agree with you perfectly, James," replied the old man,
looking as grave as a judge. "Go at once, my dear nephew,
and if your father inquires for you, I can very truly say that
I have sent you on an errand."

"That you certainly may," returned the lover with a hopeful smile; and gaily kissing his hand, without adding another word, he jumped over the churchyard-stile, and was out of sight in a moment.

On re-entering the church, Walter found his brother looking exceedingly cross, and expressing a very strong persuasion that James was out of his senses, to have dragged him into that cold vault of a church, and then to have left him.

"Let us walk home again in the sun," said Walter, "and that will effectually warm us. At any rate, you must not be angry with James, for it is I who have sent him off. I am the patron of his living, you know, and therefore he could not well refuse to do a little errand for me."

The pompous Doctor thought there was some joke a-foot, and he was not fond of jokes; but he felt upon this occasion, as he had done upon many others, that his brother had lived too long in wild and savage regions, to be at all aware of the respect which was due to a man who was a rector, a canon, and the head of a college, to say nothing as to his being the brother-in-law of an earl.

He condescended, however, to take the arm of his daughter who had dutifully stood beside him during the whole of Walter's important colloquy with James, and without deigning to take the slightest notice of the disappointed churchwarden, walked majestically out of the church.

CHAPTER LIX.

OLD Walter was too good-natured to follow him without first saying a few civil words to the discomfited Mr. Brandling, and the rustic artist was too much elated by this consolatory notice to let him escape, without first coaxing him into the examination of one or two morsels of his own very clever handiwork. This delay lasted so long, that Kate and her father had already entered the Parsonage when Walter left the church. He quickened his steps to follow them; but before

he had advanced many yards beyond the churchyard, he was
stopped by one of the men employed in the gardens at the
Manor House, and informed him that two gentlemen had
arrived there, both of whom seemed very anxious to see him
immediately.

"Already!" was the first word uttered by Walter, on
receiving this intelligence; and "two?" was the second.

The more satisfactorily reply of "go back, and say I am
coming directly," followed; and having thus dismissed the
messenger, the old man drew out his watch, and pondered
over it for a moment before he set off to follow him.

"Poor Frank!" soliloquised Walter, still hesitating, as it
seemed, as to what was first to be done. "He has come by
the first train, instead of the second, as I calculated; and very
natural that he should do so, though I did not guess it. Who
the other is, Heaven knows!" And here, instead of following his gardener, he took a rapid stride or two in the contrary
direction. "I have promised this terrified boy that I would
be at his side when he made the speech which was to release my Kate, and I must not disappoint him. And yet to
keep Frank Caldwell waiting at such a moment is terrible!"

The dilemma was in truth not an easy one to escape from;
and the very rare occurrence of an impatient look on the noble
brow of the old man seemed approaching, when the sight of
Lord Goldstable, advancing with a tolerably quick step
towards him, caused a sudden change both in his physiognomy and his plans.

"I am quite ready, Mr. Harrington," said the young peer
a little out of breath, and a good deal flushed. "I hope I am
not behind my time. Just say it over to me once more, will
you? I will do my very best, Mr. Harrington, not to mistake
a word of it."

"I shall always consider your coming here to perform your
promise notwithstanding its being so disagreeable to you, as a
proof both of your courage and your honour," returned Walter,
shaking him very cordially by the hand. "But accident has
befriended you, my dear Goldstable, and I must now consent
to do what I refused before."

"Do you mean that you will say it for me, instead of my
having to say it myself?" demanded Lord Goldstable, looking
inexpressibly delighted.

"Yes, I do!" replied Walter. "The thing must be done
directly for many reasons; and yet it is impossible for me to

go with you now to my brother, as I promised to do; and the best apology I can make for this breach of faith, is to undertake the task myself."

"Oh, thank you! thank you a thousand times!" returned the happy boy. "Then I suppose I may turn back again, mayn't I! and walk to Dougham if I like it? Because, you know, it would not do for me to call upon the Doctor, if I have nothing to say."

"Oh no! certainly; it would not do for you to call upon him just now, said Walter. "I think I shall be able to manage better for you than that. One word more, my Lord, and then I must leave you, for I have a friend waiting for me at the Manor House: I think your Lordship will find no difficulty in arranging the partnership presentation to Bickley. James is with the lady at this moment, and I cannot say I have any doubt as to the result of their interview."

"That's capital!" cried the young patron, joyously clapping his hands. "Good-by, then—good-by! I shall see you at dinner."

"No, my dear Lord, I rather think not," replied Walter; "for I have a good deal of business to do to-day. But there is a full moon, or something near it, and it is very likely that I shall walk over and take my coffee with you. But I must sleep to-night under my own roof, for I have invited company."

Lord Goldstable was about to utter a hospitable remonstrance, but Walter gaily waved his hand, and turned rapidly away, saying: "I must go now, but I shall see you again by-and-by."

And, in truth, it was but right that he should so hurry away; for there was one waiting for him, who, as he well knew, could be in no very tranquil frame of mind; and to whom, moreover, he certainly owed the debt of a tranquil spirit, as most unquestionably he had been the means of depriving him of it. On entering his now comfortable-looking drawing-room, at the Manor House, he found as the gardener had announced, two gentlemen waiting for him. The one was indeed Frank Caldwell, whom we had certainly expected to find there; the other was his old friend and agent, Mr. Tapley, whom he certainly did not expect to find there. Had this first meeting between Frank Caldwell, and his penitent friend, Walter, been *tête-à-tête*, the atonement and the acceptance of it might have been more explicit—but it

could not have been better understood; and the grasp of the
old man's hand, and the cordial pressure with which both of
Frank's received it, sufficed to satisfy them both that no
misunderstanding of any kind any longer existed between
them.

And then Walter turned to the lawyer, and paid him a
compliment but rarely offered to gentlemen of his profession,
for his first words were: "My dear Tapley, I am delighted
to see you; but I had no notion that you could have been
ready so soon.   Have you really brought the papers with
you?"

"Yes, really, Mr. Harrington," replied the lawyer.   "The
business was very simple, Sir.   But I will not pretend to say
that it would have been quite so rapidly accomplished, had it
not happened, by an odd chance, that we have another piece of
business to execute in this neighbourhood, and it was as well,
you know, to kill two birds with one stone.   Are you in the
commission, Mr. Harrington?"

"Not I, Tapley!   I have been too much an absentee to
have meddled with anything of the sort," replied Walter.
"But what is the matter in hand?"

The lawyer drew the old gentleman into the recess of a
window before he answered him, and then he said: "This it
is, Mr. Harrington.   There is a certain fellow called Captain
Fowler, who is rather an illustrious member of the company
of scamps, and we have an unfortunate client who has already
been victimised by him, and who is in danger of being more
victimised by him still.   But though we know all this, we
have great difficulty in getting him within the grasp of
the law.   At last, however, our sharp scamp has so far
forgotten what he was about, as to allow the said victim
to supply the stamp on a promissory note, which he has been
done out of, and we shall trounce him, if we can catch him,
on the charge of stealing a stamp.   We have learnt that he is
lying snug at Doucham.   I have a warrant against him all in
order, and I want to find a local magistrate by whom it can
be backed."

Had no such name as Captain Fowler occurred in this
statement, it is probable that Walter would not, at that
moment, have listened to it with quite so much interest; but
he immediately recollected the passage in his nephew Henry's
letter, respecting the reputed connection between a Captain
Fowler, of rather worse than doubtful respectability, and the

very dangerous enslaver of his really well-beloved *protégé*, Lord Goldstable.

It immediately struck him that this coincidence might be turned to good account. Having satisfied the lawyer as to the facility of finding a magistrate, he begged him to do nothing in the business for the next half-hour, the reason for which he would explain to him, as soon as he had exchanged a few words with the friend who had arrived by the same train with him.

"I have considerably more than half an hour's work to do, Mr. Harrington, before I can profit by the information, so do not hurry yourself. I have a clerk, who, I suppose, is waiting for orders in your servants' hall. In truth, more than one of our young men were up all night, working upon your papers, in order to enable me to set off from London this morning; and you will do me a favour if you can admit us into a room where we can put the finishing stroke to what we have been about."

This request was immediately complied with, and then, at length, Walter and his young friend Caldwell found themselves at leisure, and at liberty to talk over all that had passed during the eventful period which had elapsed since they last parted.

On the subject of the terrible mistake which had been made by Walter and his nephew in Aylesbury Street, Frank would not hear a word of apology, declaring, and with all sincerity, that they had in this acted exactly as they ought to have done.

"Nor, fearfully as I have suffered," he continued, "can I find room in my heart for anything but rejoicing at the speedy termination of an error, which, if it had lasted much longer, would, I believe, have made me fly my country."

"I am quite willing to take your view of the case, my dear fellow," replied the old man. "There can be no wisdom in mourning over sorrows that are past, and I flatter myself I shall be able to atone for what my blunder made you suffer by smoothing some of the difficulties which were in your way before I committed it."

"And when may I—" said Frank, beginning a speech in rather a plaintive tone of voice.

"You need not go on, Frank, I perfectly well know what you are going to say, and the only answer I can give must be summed up in the one word *patience*. I cannot possibly arrange any scheme for your seeing Kate, till I have seen what my influence can achieve with my brother and his wife towards obtaining their sanction for the interview. And during this not very agreeable interval, I really have nothing better to propose to you than that you should first take some luncheon, and then set out upon a ramble for an hour or so under those fine trees yonder in the park."

"Yes, I will wander in your park till you summon me to your presence again; but I can dispense with your hospitable offer of luncheon," replied Frank, in an accent that was by no means particularly gay. And then drawing out his watch, he said, "It now wants ten minutes to one, Mr. Harrington, may I return to the house at two?"

" No, Frank," replied Walter, laughing, "for if my house-keeper should happen to see you looking as you do now, I should not be the least surprised if she sent off an express for the apothecary. No, it will be better for me to come to you, my good fellow. I will look for you under that avenue yonder, and trust me I will waste no time in the interval."

And so they parted.

Considering that old Walter had all his life been more of a wanderer than a housekeeper, he had really managed matters very cleverly; for not only was his own room ready for him, but sundry other things, and sundry other rooms were ready beside. About five of his very precious minutes were all that he now found necessary to bestow upon the principal and prime minister of all his domestic manœuverings.

" Well, Margery, everything goes right, I hope? Cook arrived? Rooms ready? And all things prepared according to order?"

"Everything, Sir," replied the old woman, in a tone of very satisfactory confidence.

"And if I shall have a dozen people to breakfast with me the day after to-morrow, you really think you could manage to find cups and saucers, and something to eat?"

"I wish, Sir, you could find time to look into the china closet," she replied; "and with Doucham so near, there is no great danger of wanting anything to eat."

"That's well, Margery. I can't look at the china closet now, because I am in a hurry, but I will bring Miss Kate with me to look at it to-morrow may be."

And so saying, Walter set off on his rather important visit to the Rectory.

CHAPTER LX.

ON entering the little drawing-room at the Rectory, Walter found his brother slowly recovering from the immense fatigue of having walked to the church and back again, and the three ladies seated at a work-table at no great distance from his arm-chair. The presence of the Lady Augusta he considered as very decidedly desirable, but not so that of her sister; and as to Kate's being present at a discussion so deeply interesting to her, he considered it as being more objectionable still. While pondering on the best way of dismissing these superfluous auditors, James entered the room through the open window. Walter perceived at the first glance that the now gay-looking young Puseyite was speedily to become the Rector of Bickley, and the husband of Miss Olivia Cross. There was no doubt about the matter; Walter read the whole thing as distinctly as if it had been placarded on a board before him, in letters of a foot long.

Nothing but his indulgent pity for the impatience of poor Frank Caldwell, had prevented Walter from delaying his interview with his brother till the result of James's visit to Miss Cross had been made known to him, and he hailed his timely arrival as a good omen.

"Let me speak to you for a moment, James," said he, suddenly rising and leading his nephew back again through the window by which he had entered. "I think I may safely wish you joy, James, both of the living and the lady," said he. "Is it not so?"

"You may, my dear uncle; I flatter myself that it will not be long before I possess both."

"Your interest with the lady was decidedly your own," said Walter, "but I think my interest with Lord Goldstable may have been useful to you; and all I ask in return, my dear James, is that you should give me your vote and interest upon a matter which touches me very nearly, and in which both your father and mother have great influence. The first thing, however, that I want you to do for me, is to get Lady Juliana and your sister Kate out of the room. When you have achieved this, I shall wish you to return to it. You will have no objection, I presume, that among other matters, I should inform your father and mother of Lord Goldstable's intentions in your favour?"

"On the contrary, my dear Sir, I should wish them to know it immediately—and of my intended marriage also."

"Very well, James, I will announce both," replied his uncle.

"And I will get my aunt and sister out of the way. Which I shall do by taking them into the dining-room, and telling them that they must not return to the drawing-room till I summon them," said James. "No measure less peremptory," he added, "would suffice to secure you from the intrusion of my aunt."

This decisive manoeuvre, however, was successful, and old Walter found himself at liberty to begin his very delicate negotiation with the assurance that the banished ladies should not break in upon him. He was not an adept at long speeches, nor was it his intention to say more than was necessary on the present occasion. It was to his brother that he addressed himself.

"I am come to you brother," said he, "with a message from Lord Goldstable."

"I thought that Lord Goldstable would have been here himself this morning," said Lady Augusta.

"It is my fault if he has not done so, Lady Augusta," replied Walter. "He certainly was coming here, not merely to make an idle call of ceremony, but to enter upon an important explanation."

"It was something of that kind that we were certainly expecting," returned her ladyship with a very gracious smile; "but his being so evidently a favourite, and a friend of yours, Mr. Harrington, has sufficed to convince us that the delay of this explanation has arisen from accident, and not from anything dishonourable on his part."

"The boy appears to me to be a very well disposed good-hearted boy, and I see nothing dishonourable about him, poor fellow. Unfortunately for him, however, his only near relation, I mean Lady de Paddington, is not a person who can be spoken of so favourably; on the contrary, I believe her to have acted towards this poor young man in a manner highly dishonourable. For personal reasons of her own, which you may perhaps understand better than I do, she took it into her scheming head that it would be advantageous for her to arrange a marriage between him and your daughter, and he was simple enough to comply with her wishes, and to propose to your daughter, in the abrupt and unauthorized manner that he did. Nothing but his profound ignorance, and singular simplicity of character could have rendered this possible; and I am now come to offer every possible apology on his part for having addressed himself to Kate in a manner so offensively presumptuous."

There might be seen on the countenances of both the Doctor and his lady, as they listened to this speech, a mixture of anger and uncertainty, of hope and of fear, that very nearly approached the comic. But Walter Harrington never quizzed anybody; he was too single-minded, and too kindly tempered for it. He knew perfectly well upon the present occasion he was giving pain, and he only wished to make the necessary endurance of it as short as possible; he therefore waited for no reply, but hastened to say with a very pleasant smile:

"I flatter myself, however, that you will soon look upon this foolish affair in the same light that I do. It is like most things of a mixed nature. It is, beyond doubt, disagreeable to us all that our dear Kate should have been addressed in so idle and offensive a manner; but, on the other hand, the kindness of Lord Goldstable to James—"

The Doctor had up to this point been silent, partly from dismay, and partly from wanting breath to express the indignation he felt, both at the conduct of Lord Goldstable, and at his brother's manner of treating it; but now, in a voice of ill-restrained anger, he said:

"Whatever may be the nature of the intelligence which you have to communicate, brother Walter, it must be desirable that you should make it intelligible. I only look for this. I look not for any sympathy on your part. It is only too clear that I should look in vain. Do you mean to tell us that Lord Goldstable withdraws his proposal of marriage to Miss Harrington?"

"Yes, certainly, I mean to tell you so, my dear Henry," replied Walter. "What else?"

"It is impossible! absolutely and totally impossible!" ejaculated Lady Augusta, with great warmth. "I do not and cannot believe that you would permit yourself to be made the deliverer of such a message, and still less that you should deliver it as if it were praiseworthy instead of infamous!"

For half a moment Walter looked a little angry, and he

might have felt and looked so a little longer still, had it not
been for the consciousness that he came there to confer very
important benefits upon his brother's family ; the remembrance
of this soothed him in a moment.

"We certainly do not look upon this affair exactly in the
same light, Lady Augusta," said he. "The offensive part of
this young Lord's behaviour was, according to my judgment,
the presuming to address my niece in the sudden and unauthorized manner he was so ill-advised as to do. His sorrow
for this, and his apology so frankly and honourably expressed,
does him, in my opinion, great honour ; and I sincerely hope
that some ten or a dozen years hence, his education may be
sufficiently advanced, and his character sufficiently formed, to
justify his offering his hand and coronet to an estimable woman,
though no additional number of years can ever make him a
suitable match for such a being as your admirable daughter.
But though truth obliges me to confess that I do not contemplate the possibility of his ever becoming a suitable companion for such a person as Kate, I am very far from thinking
lowly of Lord Goldstable's character. There is much, very
much, that is estimable and amiable in it, and I will tell you
one anecdote that tends to prove this. He has heard, from
more quarters than one, that Miss Cross, the daughter of our
old acquaintance, formerly curate of Bickley, is but very
slenderly provided for, and also that she has the reputation of
being, notwithstanding her poverty, very actively kind and
useful to the poor people round her. These two facts together,
put it into his good-natured head that he should very much
like to see Miss Cross in the character of the Rector's wife at
Bickley ; and having seen, or fancied, that James and the
young lady appeared to like each other, he has determined
upon giving the living of Bickley to my nephew, provided only
that he will marry Miss Cross."

"He will give the living of Bickley to James ?" said the
Doctor, in a tone of great solemnity. "It is a noble piece of
preferment, brother Walter, and the house might be coveted
as the residence of a man of two or three thousand a-year.
Moreover, it is within distance of Stanton Parva. It would
be a most desirable thing for him indeed !"

"Desirable ! It would make him richer than his elder
brother is ever likely to be !" exclaimed Lady Augusta, with
considerable agitation. "But Juliana assured me that James
will never marry. She has told me more than once, since we

have been here, that he holds celibacy to be the duty of a priest, as he chooses to call himself. It really," she added, with her hands clasped, and her eyes raised to Heaven, "it really will be too hard to bear if he too, as well as Kate, chooses to consider himself as too much above the world to be fit to live in it."

"I do not believe that James will make any objection to the condition annexed to this offered preferment," said Walter, with very encouraging confidence.

"Thank God!" exclaimed Lady Augusta, who evidently listened to this opinion with very perfect faith in its being well-founded. "I confess that such a provision for my son will be a great consolation to me," she added. "I own I have suffered dreadfully from seeing a child of mine living with two maids and a man, all looking, too, as if they come out of the hay-field, and a one-horse dog-cart as his only equipage! His income, with the house and garden fairly valued, will be equal to fifteen hundred a-year. This is a great comfort, certainly!"

"It is a pleasure to me to hear you say so," said Walter, kindly; "and by way of making you feel reconciled to his marrying a young lady who brings nothing that can be settled upon herself and her children, I will myself settle five thousand pounds on Miss Cross, the income to become hers immediately; at least I will do so upon one condition—namely, that your Ladyship will yourself have the kindness to make her a visit, and will announce this my intention to her and her mother."

Lady Augusta was silent for a moment, but then she said: "Very well, Sir, I accept the condition. I flatter myself I am too good a mother to stand upon trifles. I am very glad, I must say, that I shall never again see James living in the style he does now. It is really heart-breaking! There is only one drawback to the pleasure of knowing that it is over, and that is poor Henry! Poor dear fellow! I am sure I heartily wish that he had been brought up to the church!"

The Doctor here shook his head and groaned.

"There is no good, Dr. Harrington, in making ourselves miserable about it. We must trust to Providence!" said Lady Augusta, in a tone of the deepest melancholy.

"And Providence certainly seems to have provided for him," said Walter, laughing. "for my being a bachelor, you know, is clearly providential."

On hearing these words, the Doctor looked at Lady

Augusta, and Lady Augusta looked at the Doctor. It was
the first time that Walter had ever alluded either to his being
a bachelor or to the future prospects of his eldest nephew,
for it was only of late that he had become aware that Henry's
succeeding him in the Stanton property was not in their estimation as much a matter of course as it certainly was in his own.
It is probable that had there been no difficulties in the way of
his dear Kate's marrying the man she loved, this uncertainty
respecting Henry's future would have been removed as soon as
it was discovered. But the old naturalist had not studied the
propensities of all animals so very perseveringly as he had done,
without giving some little attention to the *genus homo* among
the rest; and this had given him a sufficiently comprehensive
view of the varieties to be found therein, to suggest the idea
that they, too, as well as all other creatures, might be managed
by attention to their peculiar propensities; and it was for
this reason that he had proceeded very differently from what
he would have done had no difficulties stood in the way of
Kate's union with Frank Caldwell. As it was, however, he
felt no scruple in profiting for her sake, from the power that
was vested to him. And with this view, he harangued his
dignified brother and his noble sister-in-law, as follows:

"It is a great pleasure to me, dear Henry, to see how
cordially both you and Lady Augusta seem to approve the
arrangements I have been so fortunate as to assist in respecting
James; and this encourages me to go on in my plottings
and plannings about your other children. Rich old bachelor
uncles are likely, I should think, to be busybodies; and if
they do not dispose of their wealth in any very outrageous
wicked way, I suppose they are generally forgiven for being
so. We all seem very well satisfied about your son James,
and I hope and trust that my projects concerning Henry and
Kate will be equally successful. But I must tell you fairly,
that what I propose to do for Henry, will not be done unless
I have your consent and approbation as what I intend to do
for Kate. I believe that you all know that I am fond of
Kate. I suppose I am what is generally called partial to her,
and this being the case, it is but natural that I should wish to
make her happy—that is, according to her own notions of
happiness. Now I happen to know that she has no idea and
no hope that she ever can be happy unless she marries my
young friend Frank Caldwell."

On hearing these words, the Doctor started so vehemently

that he almost jumped out of his chair, and Lady Augusta clasped her hands, closed her eyes, and looked very much as if she were going to burst into tears.

"I am sorry to see you both so painfully affected by what I have said; but pray bear with me while I explain to you what I wish to do in the way of providing for your children, and also the conditions upon which it will be done. I am quite aware that my ideas of what may be best for Kate may differ very widely from yours, and this perhaps may be accounted for by the very different manner in which we have passed our lives, and this difference may very naturally appear to you to be a great misfortune; but then, on the other hand, you should remember that if my past life had not been thus different, I should not now be the rich man I am, nor would your children be my most obvious heirs. I dare say I shall surprise you both when I tell you the amount of the property that has accumulated in the funds. I certainly was surprised at hearing it myself. Tapley tells me that I am worth above eighty thousand pounds! independent of the Stanton estate."

"Eighty thousand pounds!" exclaimed both his auditors at once.

"Yes, even so; and you may depend upon it that his statement is correct. I certainly was not aware how rapidly the money was rolling up, for I never refused to indulge myself with any reasonable acquisition. But I rather suspect that the living without any establishment makes a great difference in the expenditure of money. But whatever the cause, you may safely receive the fact to be as I state it. Besides the estate in this parish, I have above eighty thousand pounds at my disposal. Now, in my judgment, your daughter Kate has already a very sufficient fortune, and if she had happened to fall in love with a rich young man instead of a poor one, I should probably have left my eighty thousand pounds to some scientific institution. As it is, however, I propose to settle the whole sum upon her and Frank Caldwell, jointly, and upon their heirs after them. But I know Kate well enough to be quite certain that my doing this would not suffice to render her marriage with Frank Caldwell possible. She never will marry him as long as you live, unless you both sanction the marriage by your consent. And this brings me to the question about Henry. If you both of you freely and graciously consent to the immediate marriage of Kate to

Frank Caldwell, I *immediately* make over the Manor House,
and all that is in it, together with the whole property appertaining thereto, to my well-beloved nephew Henry. Now,
then, brother and sister, I await your answer."

It was quite impossible to doubt for a moment as to what
that answer would be. Both the Doctor and his lady looked
very much as if they felt disposed to fall at his feet; but as the
expression of this abounding delight and gratitude in any way
would have been very decidedly the reverse of pleasant to the
old man, he suddenly started up, exclaiming, in a tone which
showed his satisfaction to be fully equal to their own:
" Now, then, everything is right between us, and as a proof
of this you must promise to breakfast with me—that is to say,
you must all promise to breakfast at the old Manor House, at
ten o'clock the day after to-morrow."

This promise was promptly given by the startled, astonished,
but certainly much delighted parents; and when old Walter
added, as he left the room:

"Now then, I shall go into the dining-room where I
deposited Kate, while I settled all this business with you,
and tell her to prepare herself for a visit from Frank
Caldwell."

When he added these very decisive words, the only answer
he received was a gracious smile, and a still more gracious
nod of approbation, from both the dignified father and the
noble mother of Frank Caldwell's affianced, but still unconscious bride.

It was but a short whisper, however, that he bestowed upon
her, ere he started off with the activity of five-and-twenty to
release Frank from his miserably-anxious, tread-mill sort of
exercise in the avenue. But short as the whisper was, it
sufficed; and having told the Lady Juliana that her sister
wished to see her in the drawing-room, Walter had the satisfaction of leaving his darling in no very painful frame of mind,
though he ordered her to remain a prisoner where she was till
he returned to her.

How she bore this sudden change in the aspect of her affairs,
the old man had no means of judging, for he only escorted his
friend Frank to the door of the Rectory dining-room, which
he opened for him to pass through, without even looking in to
see if she were dead or alive.

CHAPTER LXI.

Mr. Tapley was not the only individual among our *dramatis persona* who had good and sufficient reason to know that Captain Fowler was, as the attorney had expressed it, "lying snug" within the limits of the town of Doucham. It was only the day before the arrival of Mr. Tapley at the Manor House, that a note had been mysteriously conveyed to the unfortunate Mrs. Fitzjames, informing her of this most unwelcome fact, and very peremptorily requiring her immediate presence at an obscure waggoner's inn, situated in the outskirts of the little town. Mrs. Fitzjames, notwithstanding her beauty, is not a person likely to excite much sympathy, either with her sorrows or her joys, but the excess of her dismay and horror at receiving this terrible summons was pitiable.

Her first wild thought was, that she would take no notice of it, leaving him to suppose that it had failed to find her. But a very few moments of meditation upon this scheme sufficed to convince her that it could not avail to prevent their meeting, and would only tend to exasperate his brutal temper. No, go she must, and go she did.

The style of the interview between them, as well as its aim, may be easily imagined. His immediate object, or at least his immediate demand was a personal introduction to Lord Goldstable.

"Let me once be enabled to claim acquaintance with him," said the ruffian, with a tremendous oath, "and I'll soon get all I want out of him. If I don't squeeze him as you squeeze an orange, I'll never ask you to help me more."

"Fear not, Fowler, that you shall not become acquainted with him. You know as well as I do, that there is no danger of that," replied the terrified beauty; "but for Heaven's sake," she very reasonably continued, "do not be so mad as to attempt this, before I am actually his wife!"

"And what is to become of me, Madam, in the interval? Your hundreds are gone to the devil, and if I don't intend to go after them, I must have more. What have you done with the other half of that money? Let me have it, and I'll let you wait a little longer before I make acquaintance with him.

28

Why don't you answer me?   What have you done with that money?"

"What have I done with it she exclaimed vehemently. "I have spent it, Sir.   I was over head and ears in debt when I got it from him, and I knew that I should be stopped as I left the house if I did not pay!"

"Then at this moment you have positively no money to give me?" said Fowler, with a threatening scowl.

"Not a shilling!" was her reply.

"And you refuse to introduce me to him?"

"Only till the important knot is tied," she replied.   "He is quite as much in a hurry for it as I can be, and when I am once his wife, you know perfectly well that whatever I have, you will share."

He looked at her in silence for a moment, and then replied:

"That may be, or it may not be, Madam Sophy.   But I know a fact which is considerably more free from doubt.   I must have money, woman! and that immediately.   Now I think I know a way by which I can get money out of him, without your becoming his wife: namely, my dear Mrs. Fowler, by saving him from ever becoming your husband. This would be a service worth paying for, and I will contrive to make him aware of this.   This scheme will suit me better than the other, for this plain reason: the marriage may take many days to accomplish—my scheme can be accomplished in one!"

The beautiful complexion of Mrs. Fitzjames suffered materially as she listened to this, for she turned as pale as death.   Again he looked at her for a little while in silence, and then he said:

"There is one way, and but one, by which you can prevent me from immediately putting this scheme in practice."

"Speak it!" said the trembling Sophia, in rather a hoarse whisper.

"You are still, by your own account," he said, "on the very tenderest terms with him.   If this be so, there can be little or no difficulty in coaxing him out of a little more money.   You can call it a loan, if you will.   Tell him some cock-and-a-bull story about your income having being accidentally delayed.   Do it how you will—but do it successfully, or prepare yourself to abide the result!"

"How much time, how many days will you allow me?" said she

"One day is as good as a thousand for such a business," he replied.

"No, no, you are mistaken," said she eagerly, and with very evident sincerity "I must have longer. I must pretend to receive a letter, and then to be very miserable; and then, at last, when he is begging and praying that I will tell him what is the matter, I must let him know, with a great deal of reluctance and delicacy, what is the cause of my distress."

"Bravo, Sophy! That's your sort, my dear. And as a reward for your clever scheme, I will grant you the delay of three days—but not an hour longer, remember!"

And so they parted, the gentleman promising to keep out of sight for these stipulated three days, and then to take himself off till the hoped for marriage was accomplished, on condition that she contrived to obtain, at the least two hundred pounds to pay his travelling expenses.

Walter, meanwhile, had transacted a great deal of very interesting domestic business; for not only had he arranged with Kate and old Margery, that a very handsome breakfast was to be procured *coûte qui coûte*, at the Manor House, but he had also obtained the promise of all the guests whom he wished to be present at it, that they would all favour him with their company on the appointed morning, precisely at ten o'clock. The party was to consist of the present family circle assembled at the Rectory—of Mrs. Cross and her daughter Olivia, of Lord Goldstable and Dick Caldwell, who was still staying with him; together with Lady de Paddington and Mrs. Fitzjames and Miss Hannah Wigginsville. Moreover, in addition to these, old Walter had no less than three gentlemen staying in his house, not to mention an old friend and neighbour of his, a county magistrate, who happened to have made him a visit that morning upon particular business, so that the party altogether amounted to no less than fifteen persons; but, nevertheless, and greatly to the honour of Kate and old Margery must it be said, everything was in the highest order, and the table was handsomely spread as if the old Squire had been giving *fêtes* there unceasingly for the last forty years, instead of having passed that interval in wandering over the earth for his amusement.

The reader, being perfectly well acquainted with the

28—2

motives and feelings which were likely to influence the
arrangements that took place among the company when the
gentlemen were requested by old Walter to hand the ladies
from the drawing-room to the dining-room, need scarcely be
told that Lord Goldstable gave his arm to the radiant and
triumphant-looking Mrs. Fitzjames, or that Frank took care
of Kate, and James of Olivia. Neither can it be necessary to
mention that Lady de Paddington kept as far from Lady
Augusta as she conveniently could. But somehow or other,
they all contrived to take their seats in very proper order,
save and except old Walter himself, who, instead of taking
the chair at the top of the table, contrived to establish himself
on one side of Kate, after perceiving that Frank had established himself on the other.

"But, how is this, brother?" said the Doctor, in a magnificent tone, that might have filled St. Paul's. "Do you not
mean to favour your guests by presiding at your own table?"

"It is the master of the house who must preside at the
table," replied the old man; "and here he comes!"

And as he spoke, Henry Harrington the younger entered
the room, upon which Walter left his place for a moment, and
passing his arm under that of his nephew, led him to the
vacant chair at the top of the table; and when with a little
gentle violence he had placed him in it, he addressed the party,
as he stood behind him, as follows:

"My good friends, I have this day made over Stanton
Manor House, and the estate belonging to it, to my nephew
Henry, who, I flatter myself, will do his duty by the premises,
better than I have done; for, instead of looking after my fields,
I have been ploughing the ocean; and instead of looking after
my own pheasants and partridges, I have been amusing myself in taming eagles, and playing with crocodiles. In short,
ladies and gentlemen, I think my nephew Henry will make a
better English Squire than his uncle; for which reason I
now instal him in his post, begging your indulgence for him
in his new capacity. Now then," added the old man, re-
treating to the vacant chair beside Kate, "begin your duties,
Squire Harry, by commanding that coffee and tea shall be
served forthwith."

Never, perhaps, did the grand pulpit-toned voice of the
Doctor make itself heard with better effect than at this
moment, when, after waiting till his brother had resumed his
place beside Kate, he said:

"My son has been placed by his noble-minded uncle in a position of great responsibility; for, not only has he been suddenly converted from an idle youth, to a rich-landed proprietor; but with all his youthful imperfections on his head, he has to take the place of one in whose praise every voice is eloquent, and who never forgot the interest of any human being, save his own."

This harangue was listened to with something more than a mere murmur of applause, and the "Hear! hear! hear!" of old Sir John Richardson, the county magistrate, was very cordially responded to by all the gentlemen, and most of the ladies present.

And then the business of the breakfast went on very prosperously; and appeared to be drawing to a conclusion when Mr. Tapley's clerk very noiselessly entered the room, and whispered a few words to his employer. Mr. Tapley looked at old Walter, who gave him what was very evidently an intelligent nod in return, for no other answer seemed required. The clerk retreated with the air of a man who had done his errand, and the result of it was made manifest before the door was again closed; for the said clerk re-entered, followed by no less a personage than Captain Fowler, his usual air of dauntless assurance but little mitigated by his being flanked on each side by a constable. A piercing, and on this occasion a perfectly unaffected, shriek burst from the lovely widow; and before Lord Goldstable could do more than throw his arm round her, and whisper "What is the matter?" the fair creature was addressed by the prisoner in a voice as far removed from a whisper as possible.

"Mrs. Fowler, by all that's lucky!" exclaimed the ruffian, kissing his hand to her! "I am truly delighted at meeting you at such a critical moment."

"Mr. Harrington," cried the unfortunate lady, addressing herself to Walter, "I place myself under your protection. You are too much a gentleman to permit my being insulted in your house! I have no knowledge whatever of this infamous person, or of the name by which he dares to call me. And I beg, Sir, that he may be taken away before he insults me any further."

"Fair and softly, my pretty lady!" ejaculated the prisoner. "I am not going to be taken away before we have had a word or two. This lady, who, at present, ladies and gentlemen, chooses, I believe, to call herself Mrs. Fitzjames, has known the time when she was only too happy at being permitted to call herself Mrs. Fowler; and to say the truth, she had, with the exception, perhaps, of the parson's licence, every right to the name. And do you really fancy woman!" he continued, with almost savage ferocity, "do you really flatter yourself that you are to share a man's fate and fortune as his wife, when your own poverty makes it suit you; and that you are to pass by on the sunny side of the way, when fortune has turned, and he is laid by the leg in the shade? No, my fine madam, we will fall together! You refusing to bring me to the acquaintance of your noble spark, when I might have had my share in plucking so fine a pigeon: I was to wait forsooth till you were married to him. I am now in custody for a peccadillo that will not hold me long. But how much will you now give me, my dear, for your chance of becoming Lady Goldstable?"

It will easily be understood that every eye was fixed on the prisoner as he uttered this harangue. The first that at its conclusion took another direction, were those of poor, kind-hearted Lord Goldstable; and it was with a gentle and pitying glance that he turned them towards the beautiful Sophia. But this pitying glance came too late; for she was gone! It was some minutes before either he, or anyone else thought of following her; but when they did, they found that, with her usual cleverness, she had replaced herself in Lord Goldstable's carriage, which had brought her from Doucham, and ordered herself to be driven back thither with all speed.

"Do you forgive me, my dear Lord," said Walter, "for my little plot? But how else could I so readily have convinced you, that this light lady was not worthy of being the wife of so good a man as I believe you to be?"

The blushing young peer only replied by cordially grasping the hand of the old man, of whose friendship he was considerably more proud than of his coronet; but it was not long before he fully expressed to him all the gratitude he felt for his escape. There was only one of the company remaining who did not feel satisfied by the events of the morning; and that one was Lady de Paddington. She felt that she had failed most egregiously in her attempts to turn her wealthy young nephew to good account; and this conviction was very far from being agreeable. But there was another idea which occurred to her, that was, if possible, more painful still. What if she should find on returning to Doucham, that Mrs. Fitzjames had departed, leaving their heavy bill unpaid? Unhappy lady! Her prophetic spirit did not deceive her. On returning to Doucham, she found that Mrs. Fitzjames had departed, by the express train for London leaving word that her friend, Lady de Paddington, would be driven to Doucham by her nephew, Lord Goldstable; and that she would settle their joint account on the following day, when she, too, would probably set off for London.

THE END.

W. H. SMITH & SON, PRINTERS, 186, STRAND, LONDON.

www.ingramcontent.com/pod-product-compliance
Lightning Source LLC
Chambersburg PA
CBHW031056110726
47900CB00003B/946